ARISTEIA

Book Three

TREE OF LIBERTY

BY WAYNE BASTA

Published by Grey Gecko Press, Katy, Texas.

www.greygeckopress.com

Printed in the United States of America

Design by Grey Gecko Press

Illustration / cover art by Oliver Wetter / Fantasio Fine Arts — http://fantasio.info

Library of Congress Cataloging-in-Publication Data
Basta, Wayne
Aristeia: tree of liberty / Wayne Basta
Library of Congress Control Number: 2013935823
ISBN 978-1-9388214-5-5
10 9 8 7 6 5 4 3 2 1
First Edition

To Eric, Beth, Chad and Liesl.

Great friends in any universe.

"The tree of liberty must be refreshed from time to time with the blood of patriots and tyrants."

--Thomas Jefferson

PROLOGUE

Pain. That was the first thought that came to Maarkean Ocaitchi's mind. His entire body ached. Welts and bruises covered every part of him. If he could have seen himself in a mirror, he felt sure his purple clan screfa would have been indistinguishable from the bruising on his face.

With difficulty, Maarkean forced himself to sit up. He had no idea how long ago he had been brought back to his cell. It could have been minutes or days. But he did know the longer he lay still, the more he would hurt later. That just meant he had to hurt a lot right now.

Forcing himself to resist the urge to collapse back onto the cell's cot, Maarkean slowly started to ease into the Ni'jar stretching techniques he usually started his morning with. After all the abuse his body had been put through at the hands of the Alliance interrogators, even simple stretches were agonizing. It was only the combination of his Braz tradition for meditation along with the advanced Ni'jar techniques that Gu'od had taught him that allowed him to push through the pain.

After completing his usual routine, Maarkean felt some semblance of personhood returning. He had lost track of the number of times he had woken up like this—the number of interrogation sessions he had been through. Even if he had managed to count them, he had no way of knowing how often they occurred. He'd lost all sense of time in this world of interrogation, torture, and pain.

The meditation and stretching allowed him to push the constant throbbing into the background of his mind. This allowed his sense of hunger to emerge. Looking around the small cell, he saw a bowl near the barred door. Picking up the bowl, he started slurping the foul-tasting goo. Alliance nutrition mix—standard fare for prisoners.

The goo tasted horrible, but it did serve to calm his stomach. Feeling better than he had in a while, Maarkean surveyed his surroundings again. His cell looked like a standard Alliance brig cell, like those found on any Alliance warship or station. The accommodations were sparse: a simple, double-bunk cot built into the wall, along with a retractable toilet and wash station, and three walls. The ceiling and floor were smooth metal with no visible seams. The other wall was a set of metal bars too close together for anyone to slip through, but wide enough to allow people outside to observe him.

It was only now that Maarkean noticed the other figure resting on the upper cot. Looking up, he recognized the green carapace as belonging to Lohcja Cargon. Ronids didn't bruise the same way most other species did, so any injuries he had sustained weren't as evident. Except for the antennae bent at an unnatural angle, his friend looked like he was just sleeping.

He considered allowing Lohcja to continue resting. The Alliance tended any of their life-threatening wounds, but sleep would be their best treatment for the rest. However, he had only seen Lohcja in the cell with him on a few occasions, and those hadn't lasted long. It wouldn't be long before the Alliance came and took one or both of them to another interrogation session.

"Lohcja," Maarkean said quietly, gently touching the Ronid's arm.

A rasping hiss escaped Lohcja's lips, and then he clicked his mandibles together a few times before going quiet again. With no eyelids covering his multifaceted eyes, it was not easy to tell if Lohcja had woken up. Maarkean gently shook his friend a few more times.

Finally, with a longer groaning rasp, Lohcja stirred. "Maark?" He groaned.

"Yeah, it's me. How you holding up?"

"By the looks of you, better than you," Lohcja quipped.

That was good, Maarkean thought. His friend's sense of humor hadn't completely vanished. He tried to smile, realizing for the first time that even that hurt. "I don't have a tough carapace to absorb all the blows," Maarkean said.

"If only they would hit my carapace, I'd be fine," Lohcja said, struggling to sit up. He looked around the small cell. "How long have we been here? I've lost count of the number of times they've taken me."

"So have I," Maarkean replied. "But it must have been a lot. They've stopped asking me any questions. They're just torturing me now."

Lohcja let out an angry-sounding noise with his mandibles. "Why would they need to ask us any questions? Kaars will tell them everything."

Maarkean shook his head. "I don't know Kaars all that well, but he's a trained intelligence officer. He'll hold up against the interrogation better than we will."

A thud sounded through the cell as Lohcja slammed his fist into the wall. Maarkean turned to look at the Ronid, surprised to see anger overtake the previous expression of pain—and a Ronid from the warrior caste was not something you wanted to see angry.

"They don't need to interrogate him!" Lohcja fumed. "He's a traitor. I trusted him and called him my friend. And he betrayed us."

Maarkean frowned. Having a traitor in their midst would explain how the Alliance had ambushed them over Sulas. They had jumped out of hyperspace at the perfect time to trap the Union fleet as they had headed toward the planet.

But the Alliance fleet was commanded by Admiral Katerina Sartori. Her reputation for cunning and tactical savvy was unmatched. Even the Dotran Confederacy respected her. Maarkean would not put it past Sartori pulling off that trick without the help of a traitor.

"We can't jump to any conclusions. Especially in here," Maarkean cautioned.

"Yes, we can," Lohcja fumed. "While the *Defiant Glory* was being boarded, we were pinned down, but holding our own. And then Kaars quite literally shot you in the back. He took out you, Davidus, and me. After that, I assume the Alliance marines were able to gain control of the ship."

Maarkean considered that chilling bit of news. The information that Kaars had provided the Union military had been invaluable. But it had also been their main source of intelligence.

"Well, even if you're right, he can't do any more damage now," Maarkean said, leaning against the cell wall. "He's back with the Alliance, but there isn't much he can tell them. Our fleet's destroyed and our army likely wiped out or stranded on Sulas. Nothing he can tell them will likely make that worse. He shouldn't have known the location of Irod."

"Maybe," Lohcja said grumpily. "But I don't see anyone else in those other cells. Where's Commander Brieni? Tadashio? La'ari? Any of the crew? Why keep us separate? Unless they're all dead."

"No," Maarkean said defiantly. "They can't all be dead. We're senior commanders. They're probably keeping the rest in a different facility."

Lohcja just shrugged. "It doesn't matter anyway. We lost."

Forcefully, Maarkean whirled toward Lohcja. "We haven't lost. Don't ever think that. Things are bad, yes. But we're alive. Congress is still safe. The Union will live on."

Those multifaceted eyes of Lohcja's stared up at him. Maarkean wished he could find some sense of what the Ronid was thinking there. But he got nothing from them, and Lohcja said nothing in reply.

The sounds of a door opening drew Maarkean's attention away. He turned back toward the cell door to see several Alliance guards outside. They held stun weapons and binders and didn't look friendly.

A junior lieutenant pointed toward Maarkean. "He looks to have recovered nicely. Take him."

The guards opened the cell door and came for him again.

"We have our orders from General Ocaitchi," Major Solyss Novastar stated, his voice rising above his normally quiet tone. "I intend to take the *Gallant* to Trepon Sector and get us the *Black Market*."

"That's crazy!" Major Fracsid Relis yelled back. "We need to hit the Alliance here. Raid their supply lines. Cut off communication. Keep them unbalanced."

Saracasi Ocaitchi remained quiet while the other two majors argued. They had had this debate more than once. She was tired of it. Fortunately, this time it was not just the three of them.

Sitting beside them in the small conference room in the UDF Inc. Headquarters building on Kol were Intelligence Officer Kaars Aerinstar and Delegates Lahkaba, Valinther, Zoeko Lide, and Lionell Mandrake. She had sent a report to the Union congress as soon as *Defiant Glory* had arrived in the orbit of Sulas under command of the suspected traitor Davidus Brieni. They had finally sent a response after several weeks, in the form of the delegates. They hadn't yet given an answer as to who would take over command of the military.

"We need to figure out who's in command," Solyss said, looking pointedly toward Lahkaba. "Then we can avoid these pointless arguments."

"First," Saracasi said, speaking for the first time, "we need to have a trial for Commander Brieni and find out if he's guilty of betraying us. If he isn't, then he's in charge."

Valinther said, "That will not be a quick process. Congress has convened a committee to investigate any possible traitors. Unfortunately, the membership is still being chosen."

Saracasi looked at the Kowwok, confused. "I thought that was what you four were here for."

Lahkaba shook his head, sand sprinkling out from his white fur. "No, we're just here to relay that Congress is looking into Brieni and will decide on a new commander in due time. We have a different mission. One we're going to need a ship for."

Lahkaba shared an embarrassed look with his fellow Kowwok, Valinther. Both looked ashamed of something, and Saracasi didn't think it was Congress being slow. She waited for Lahkaba to expand on his statement, but he said nothing more. Zoeko gave the two Kowwoks an aggravated hiss but also said nothing.

Finally, Solyss asked, "What kind of ship?"

"The best we have," Lahkaba answered. "I don't wish to take the *Gallant* away from her mission, though. I think you should carry on with your attempt to gain support in that sector and to get us the use of the *Black Market*."

Solyss smiled, but Saracasi interjected, "We can't divide our forces! We're seriously outnumbered. We need every ship we have to try to relieve our forces on Sulas and to rescue General Ocaitchi."

Regret was evident on Lahkaba's face when he looked at her. She decided to press forward on that. "When I was imprisoned, my brother risked everything to get me out. Now I have to do the same. With your help, he succeeded. Will you give me yours now to get him out?"

The white fur covering Lahkaba flattened and his shoulders drooped. Saracasi could tell she was getting through to him. She needed all the support she could get if she was going to take on the Alliance.

"I want to free Maarkean, Casi. Believe me, I do. Lohcja is still a prisoner as well, and he's like a brother to me. I know what you're feeling," Lahkaba said.

Before Lahkaba could relent, Zoeko spoke, her Dotran voice a hiss. "We cannot engage the Alliance yet. General Numba made that mistake already. We need more support. Our mission to the Confederacy must go forward."

Saracasi felt her eyes widen as the golden Dotran spoke. A mission to seek aid from the Dotran Confederacy? Maarkean had told her that the Dotrans had offered to take the worlds of the Kreogh sector under their protection. The recent vote for independence had been partially aimed at stopping that endeavor.

"You can't be serious," Fracsid stammered.

"I agree," Solyss said. "We cannot trade one master for another."

The regretful expression on Lahkaba's face shifted to determination. "We won't! That's why I have to go. We're seeking aid and an alliance. Not submission. We'll remain independent." Less forcefully, he continued, "But the fact remains, we need ships, troops, and equipment. The Dotran have those. Our goal is a trade and defense treaty, not to join them. A similar effort has been dispatched to the Camari Republic."

Saracasi let this news sink in. An alliance with the Dotran? What would her brother say? He would hate it, she felt sure. But if Lahkaba, whose Kowwokian people were subjugated by the Dotran, could go along with it, surely she could, too?

"In order to make a strong impression, we want to take our strongest ship. I believe that's this FX-21, that you're now calling the *Audacious*," Zoeko continued.

Before Saracasi could say anything in response, Kaars Aerinstar spoke up. "That would be foolish. The regenerative shield technology on that ship is years ahead of anything the Confederacy has. We can't risk it falling into their hands."

Saracasi nodded. "I agree. And besides that, her hyperdrive still isn't working 100%. She'll never make a journey of that distance."

"How about *Defiant Glory*?" Lahkaba asked, cutting off a comment from Zoeko.

"Repairs are underway," Saracasi said. "She was pretty banged up in the battle. We had to completely rebuild the main reactor. But she'll fly now. We're just about done with the exterior repairs, though there's quite a bit of internal work to be done."

"Good, she'll do," Lahkaba stated decisively. "It's almost a three-month journey to Confederate space. Repairs can be completed en route."

Saracasi wanted to stage a counter-attack on Sulas. But if *Defiant Glory* and *Gallant* went across the galaxy on missions to seek aid, any hope of a major assault was gone. She'd need every ship to pull that off.

"I'm not authorizing *Defiant Glory* to leave the repair yards," Saracasi said, trying to work as much authority into her voice as possible.

Lahkaba looked at her, an expression of regret on his face. "Casi, I'm sorry, but I'm going to have to overrule you."

She shook her head vehemently. "You can't. Congress can decide who's in charge of the navy. But I'm the chief engineer, and certifying ships for deployment is my responsibility. Not even Maarkean could override my decision on that. He could only replace me. And until the navy has a new commander, there's no one who can do that."

The expression of regret on Lahkaba's face changed to betrayal. Saracasi regretted having to come down against him so forcefully, but she couldn't let him take *Defiant Glory* away for almost six months.

"I'm going to have to agree with her, Delegate," Solyss said. "She has that authority."

"Very well," Lahkaba said slowly. "We'll have to find civilian transport. That will be all, Majors."

Formally, Lahkaba stood, followed by the other three delegates, and left the room. Feeling like she had betrayed a friend, Saracasi leaned back in her chair with a slight frown on her face. After a moment, the room was emptied of everyone but the three remaining navy majors.

"Thank you, Solyss," Saracasi said. "I didn't like having to do that. I'm glad you had my back."

Solyss nodded. "Of course. I hope that means you'll have my back for my trip to Trepon. *Gallant*'s not in the repair yards, so you can't stop me, but I'd prefer going with your support."

With a reluctant sigh, Saracasi nodded. "Let me know what you'll need. I hate to lose the ship when we need everything we have. But it looks like it's just you and me, Fracsid."

"That will be enough," Fracsid said with a confident smile. "The Lis and Ocait clans can take on the entire Alliance."

Saracasi whispered, "We may have to."

Chapter One

The explosion shattered the window above Zeric's head. *Oops*, he thought. *That wasn't intentional.* In the distance, he could just make out the light from the fire started by the explosion.

"Looks like Gu'od made his delivery," Zeric commented to the Terran boy beside him.

Kumus Stryker smiled. "You said he wouldn't disappoint, General."

The reverence with which Kumus said his title still made Zeric uncomfortable. Despite having been a general for more than two months, most of that time in command of the stranded Union Army on Sulas, he still hated it. To be fair, Kumus had acted the same way when the boy had been his aide back on Enro.

Several more minutes went by, and Zeric's initial pleasure faded. By all rights, Gu'od Dos'redna, their designated bomb planter for the evening, should have made it back to them before the thing went off, taking an Alliance troop carrier with it. That the fires had already started to dwindle and there was no sign of Gu'od meant something had delayed him.

Glancing around, Zeric frowned and then nodded, making his decision. "Something's happened. We need to go look for Gu'od."

Before he could stand up, the reddish-pink Camari in their group put a hand on his arm. Speaking quietly, to avoid Kumus hearing, she said, "Sir, I don't mean to be crass, but Gu'od knew the risks. We can't risk your capture—or anyone else's—just because he's your friend. The mission was a success. We should pull back."

"You know the motto, Major, 'leave no one behind,'" Zeric replied, just as quietly. Then, louder, he spoke to the small band that was hidden in the alley with him. "Fan out in pairs, try to find Gu'od, but stay out of sight. The Alliance will be sending out patrols. We have five minutes to find him, and then we need to pull back. Let's be sure we don't do it without him."

The small squad of six mixed marines and army, including Kumus, quietly acknowledged the order and spread out from the alley entrance. Zeric led Ymp down the dark street, heading toward a cross street that would give them access to the main avenue leading out of town. That road would give them a clear line of sight to the Alliance blockade that Gu'od had just bombed.

Zeric and Ymp walked the streets briskly, trying to remain unseen but also inconspicuous. While there was an Alliance-enforced curfew in effect, few citizens would report on others just walking the streets at night. But two people creeping through the shadows with guns drawn would elicit comments.

While they walked, Zeric kept expecting Ymp to comment on his decision. To her credit, she remained silent. Ymp had no hesitation about challenging every decision he made, but when the mission was on, she had his back. That was an assessment he never would have imagined making a year ago, when he still thought she wanted him dead.

They reached the intersection, and Zeric moved in against the edge of the nearest building. Peeking around the corner, he spotted the floodlights from the Alliance checkpoint. A burned-out hulk that had once been an Alliance SPC still smoldered about twenty meters away from the checkpoint where the Alliance forces had parked it.

The shockwave from their crude homemade bomb had been enough to topple the temporary hut and one of the floodlight stands. Alliance troops were buzzing around the area, a few of them tending wounded on the ground. Zeric was too far away to make out any details, so he had no idea if any of the injured was Gu'od.

As he watched, a group of figures emerged from between two buildings further down the street. Four figures guided another one between them, heading toward the checkpoint. With them in the shadows, he still couldn't make out any details, but Zeric felt confident that the middle figure was Gu'od, as he appeared to be holding his hands above his head.

Zeric drew his carbine out from under his coat and started to step around the corner.

Ymp once again reached out a hand and restrained him. Camari fingers were typically fairly limp and tentacle-like, but she made them go rigid, exerting enough force to stop him.

He once again cast a dark look at the Camari. "We've already been over this, Ymp," Zeric grumbled.

"Looking for Gu'od is one thing. The two of us charging an Alliance checkpoint that was just bombed is another," Ymp said matter-of-factly.

Zeric started to argue but stopped himself. Ymp was right. With the entire squad, they'd have a good chance at taking out the checkpoint. But reinforcements were undoubtedly on their way. Having another SPC full of troops roll up while they were in the middle of a firefight would not get them anywhere.

Another pair of figures appeared across the main avenue from them, crouching against the building just as they were. In the dim light from a nearby streetlamp, Zeric was able to make out Sergeant Obod Ocif and Kumus. The sight of the other two made him smile. He leaned in and whispered to Ymp, "Now it's not just the two of us."

To his surprise, she gave him a wicked grin. "I was thinking the same thing."

Gesturing to Obod across the street, Zeric signaled for them to target the Alliance troopers on their side. He then held up his hand, with all five fingers displayed. Ticking them off in a rhythmic pattern, he dropped his hand when he had two remaining, allowing himself and the others to finish the count in their heads. Lining up the sight on his carbine, Zeric aimed at the trooper on the right.

Two, one . . . Zeric counted and then pulled the trigger, unleashing three quick shots. Ymp did the same, and all six blasts hit the troopers they targeted. One of the other troopers dropped at the same time, leaving only one Alliance trooper guarding the figure.

Not wasting any time, the figure immediately lashed out, stripping away the gun and dropping the trooper to the ground. He then dashed toward the safety of the surrounding buildings. Zeric still couldn't tell if it was definitely Gu'od, but he felt sure he recognized the man's fluid fighting style. Either way, if the Alliance hadn't captured Gu'od, then they had surely grabbed an unlucky civilian and would have placed the blame for the explosion on his shoulders.

Shouts came from the damaged Alliance checkpoint and the floodlamps were redirected down the street. Zeric became momentarily blinded as one beam of light flashed in his face. He ducked back around the corner of the building. As he and Ymp took off down the street at a dead run, the sounds of blaster fire could be heard behind them.

Despite the sounds of gunfire, Zeric smiled. For the first time in a long while, he felt alive.

"I still don't understand why you have to go."

"Because we need Congress to name a commander for the naval forces so we can finally start fighting back against the Alliance," Saracasi snapped. The question from Asirzi grated at Saracasi's nerves. They had discussed her need to go to Irod several times, but now she had to make a decision. She had a duty to perform.

They pair of them were in Saracasi's quarters in the barracks of the UDF shipyards. Saracasi was in the midst of packing all of her belongings into a duffle bag. No matter what the results of this meeting on Irod, she had nearly made up her mind not to return here at all.

"But why *you*?" Asirzi demanded. "You're an engineer. You should be here working on more ships. Let Fracsid command."

"I can't. It has to be me. Fracsid is a good smuggler and a good gunship commander, but he's no admiral," Saracasi said.

"And you are?" Asirzi said, her tone disbelieving.

"I'm the closest thing we've got. Aside from Dav, but, unfortunately, we can't trust him. But I've been trained by him and Maarkean. I'm the best we've got."

"That's rather conceited, don't you think?" Asirzi said, bitter truth in her tone.

Throwing her last spare uniform into the duffle bag, Saracasi zipped it up and then turned her back to Asirzi. Things had been cold between them since the battle against the Alliance task force more than two months before. During that battle, Saracasi had decided she had to become what she feared, and what Asirzi didn't want her to become: a warrior.

She had destroyed an entire Alliance escort carrier with several hundred people onboard. She had killed unknown numbers of others when she had almost destroyed a corvette. There was no going back now. She had fought, she had killed, and she had to do so again. Asirzi couldn't seem to understand that.

The fight was helping her to make up her mind. It would be best for Saracasi to make her new home aboard *Defiant Glory*, leaving Asirzi behind. She had flirted with the idea of taking her aboard, but she had dismissed it almost as quickly. Asirzi was good at her job with Chavatwor, but she had nothing useful to do aboard a warship. Saracasi couldn't justify taking her lover aboard when no one else could.

"Maybe it is conceited," Saracasi said. "But it doesn't change the facts. And the facts are that I have to go and that my duty may not allow me to return anytime soon."

A tense silence filled the air between them. Neither woman looked directly at the other. After it seemed Asirzi wouldn't say any more, Saracasi picked up her bag and started for the door.

Before she reached it, she felt a hand on her shoulder. Not sure if she wanted to turn to face her, Saracasi allowed herself to be stopped. She reached up and covered Asirzi's hand with her own.

To her back, Asirzi said, "You said before that you were worried what fighting would do to you—that it would change you. I'm just worried that if you walk out that door, even if you survive, you'll never really come back."

Saracasi felt tears start to well up in her eyes. A part of her knew that what Asirzi said might be true. She felt no regret for the people she had been forced to kill so far in the war. Before the war, she would never have thought herself capable of that. And until recently, she had actively tried to avoid finding out.

The urge to turn around, to embrace and kiss Asirzi, almost overwhelmed her. More than anything, she wanted to allow herself that one indulgence. But it wouldn't be fair for Asirzi to sit around waiting for her. The odds were high she would be killed in combat anyway. It would be better for both of them if they accepted that.

"Then we'll just have to say that I'm dead, and that this is goodbye. Any me you see in the future will be a different person," Saracasi forced herself to say.

The sound of a sob forced back came from behind her and the hand on her shoulder slipped away. Not sure what she would do if she had to look Asirzi in the eyes, Saracasi strode through the door, not looking back.

Once in the corridor, tears started to stream down her face. She stopped in the building's stairwell, letting herself feel the sadness for a moment. For a short time, she had let herself believe the fantasy that she might live happily ever after with Asirzi. In a different time and place, they could have been together. But now, she had to be married to winning this war above all else.

The sound of a door opening on the stairwell above her brought Saracasi back to the present. She was the senior officer on this base. It wouldn't be good for anyone to see her crying in a stairwell. Wiping away the tears, she continued down to the ground floor and out into the Kol sun.

She soon joined a stream of people headed toward the landing field where shuttles waited to take them up to *Defiant Glory* in orbit. At her designated shuttle, Saracasi found Chavatwor and Lieutenant Arzesaeth Ernebee waiting for her. The Kowwok shipwright and her Ronid XO looked almost as nervous as she thought she should feel. Instead, she found she felt nothing but determination. She had shed all her other emotions with her tears over Asirzi.

"Casi," Chavatwor said by of greeting. "I've loaded the DeeGee's old reactor as well as the extra hull plating you requested. But they're going to take up a lot of room aboard. Why do you want them?"

"I've got a little surprise waiting for the Alliance," Saracasi said, giving her friend a small smile. As much as she trusted Chavatwor, she couldn't risk revealing those details to anyone just yet. She turned to Arzesaeth. "Lieutenant, the base is yours, as is *Audacious*. Take her on patrol just as we discussed. Show the Alliance we're not to be pushed around."

"Aye, Major," Arzesaeth said, saluting. He was one of a handful of people who knew Saracasi's plan, and he would have to play his part for it to work. "We'll give the Alliance a good fight."

Saracasi returned the salute and then turned to Chavatwor. She dropped her duffle bag and relaxed her body, anticipating the Kowwok's fervent hug. Despite her suggestions that it wasn't proper, Chavatwor continued to insist that letting a friend go into danger without a hug of friendship would anger the Great One. She knew he wasn't a big follower of his people's belief system, but she didn't want to offend the few traditions he did follow. Chavatwor had done too much for the Union.

When Chavatwor released her, Saracasi straightened her uniform and picked up the duffle bag. She glanced one last time at the shipyard, only a small part of her hoping to see Asirzi one last time, before boarding the shuttle.

The sounds of the celebration still drifted through the cavernous tunnels beneath the Ba'aar city hockey arena. After the previous night's successful raid, Zeric thought his people deserved the chance to relax, as they finally had something to celebrate. Everyone had made it home alive. Fortunately, the sounds from an ongoing hockey game being played above them covered the sounds of the Union soldiers. The massive crowds that came to the arena provided the perfect cover for the rebels.

"Now's the time to act," Zeric declared, a note of excitement in his voice. "We've been quiet for the last few months, and the Alliance thinks they've got us contained. But last night's raid shows they're just as over-confident as ever."

Standing around the table were Gu'od and Ymp. On screens along the walls were video feeds from the senior military commanders, including Pasha Alon and Jairyd Kil'dare. Spread out across the planet, they were using the stadium's live coverage of the game as a smoke-screen for their transmissions.

"I like it," Jairyd said. "If we hit them on multiple fronts, we can begin to weaken their resolve."

"Something like that." Zeric activated a tactical hologram of the planet and started pointing. "If we stage a series of strikes in these cities, we can draw off Alliance troops. Once they're distracted, we make a major push and take the military bases in Chuthor, Ba'aar, and Lashan.

"Then, we'll have strongholds to begin pushing out from to take the rest of the planet. With the planetary defense guns and base shields, we'll be able to avoid orbital bombardment."

A few of the faces on the screens nodded approvingly. None of them had been happy about abandoning their control over the guns captured during the failed invasion. Going into hiding had been a necessity they had all disliked.

"Didn't we abandon the batteries we already controlled because they made us easy targets for Alliance forces?" Jairyd asked.

Zeric nodded. "We did. But those guns were out in the middle of nowhere. We would have had no supplies and no support. They were chosen specifically because they were easy to take, which would have made them easy for the Alliance to take back. We only needed them to clear a corridor to get planet-side.

"Now, the batteries in the cities—those are a different ball game. It won't be an easy operation, but once we take them, we'll have a whole city to support us. Plus, the shields are several magnitudes stronger, since they're intended to defend a civilian population from orbital bombardment."

"This is all ridiculous!" Jairyd exclaimed, surprising Zeric.

Jairyd had been the most vocal advocate that further action be taken. Zeric had been sure the man would support the plan. That he didn't was problematic. Technically, Zeric and Jairyd were the same rank. Zeric was in command through a minor legal trick—he had been promoted first, giving him seniority. But this was Jairyd's home planet. He was respected here and seen as a war hero.

"We'll never be able to hold the cities against an Alliance assault, assuming we can even take them in the first place," Jairyd argued. "No, what we need to do is stop these pointless and dangerous discussions and become independent resistance cells. Right now, it would be a simple matter for the Alliance to track all of us down and win the war right there.

"Once we're operating on our own, each cell can begin performing surgical strikes against Alliance facilities and personnel. Hit and run attacks. Place bombs on Alliance vehicles. Take out officers. Make them run from this planet scared for their lives."

The intensity with which Jairyd spoke about his proposal gave Zeric a shiver down his spine. Clearly, the man had been thinking about this for a while. The passion with which he spoke also appeared to have an effect on some of the others, who voiced support.

"But to what end?" Zeric asked. "Hit and run attacks like you describe are fine as tactics to use against superior forces, or to throw an enemy off balance. But as an entire strategy, it doesn't work. There needs to be a goal."

"The goal is the same as it has been for every insurgency before us. To convince the Alliance that staying is more trouble than it's worth," Jairyd said, his tone like that of a bored teacher.

"I must agree with General Kil'dare," a new voice said.

The comm system automatically brought the speaker to the main screen, revealing to Zeric an elderly Terran man. He didn't recognize the face, and while he didn't know most of the unit commanders very well, he thought he could recognize each of them. That a new person was in on the conversation without his knowing it reinforced Jairyd's point about security.

"Who the hell are you?" Zeric asked. Beside him, Ymp and Gu'od both cringed.

"Hans Kantor, Prime Minister of Sulas," the man answered, annoyance clear in his tone. "General Kil'dare invited me into the meeting. I must agree, your plan for taking some cities sounds bold, but it's too risky. It will put many civilian lives at risk. Better to stick with his plan of small raids against the Alliance military."

"We're not an insurgency," Zeric said, getting angry.

"No," Kantor conceded, "which is why we won't be taking any actions that will endanger civilians. Such as full-scale battles for control of cities."

The statement hung in the air for a moment, and Zeric was reminded of his days in school. It felt like the teacher had just explained to him how his idea was stupid in the most belittling terms. He hadn't had very good teachers.

"However, General Dustlighter is correct about one thing. It's too soon to completely end these discussions. So for now, we'll give unit commanders operational autonomy and continue to discuss broad goals periodically," Kantor said, his demeanor making it clear the matter was settled. "Now, next on the agenda, I would like to discuss some minor supply issues."

As Kantor and Jairyd quickly took over the rest of the meeting, Zeric's initial anger faded, replaced with a sense of relief. This was Jairyd and Kantor's world, after all. Let them run things. That would give him the opportunity to do what he was good at—shooting people and blowing stuff up.

By the end of the meeting, Zeric felt pretty good about the turn of events. Based on the look Ymp bore into him, however, she didn't agree. His Camari companion had her eyestalks lowered and her hands were constantly shifting from ridged to floppy, almost like a Terran flexing their fingers.

"You have to deal with that," Ymp said as soon as the video links ended.

"Deal with what?" Zeric replied, trying to sound innocent.

"You completely let them take control. You're in command, you can't let that happen," Ymp growled.

"Kantor's the prime minister," Zeric shot back, but he knew his tone was too defensive.

"Of Sulas, yes," Ymp argued. "But this is a *Union* army. Your army."

"An army I never wanted to command. Stupid Maarkean," Zeric cursed, regretting it immediately. He still had no idea what had happened to his friend.

Beside them, Gu'od made a small noise, reminding everyone that he was there. Zeric sighed, bracing himself for one of his friend's lectures. They weren't a common occurrence—normally Gamaly did the lecturing—but he felt sure it was coming.

"I think Zeric's right," Gu'od said.

Zeric's counter argument was left dangling on the tip of his tongue. Ymp looked equally shocked, going so far as to raise her eyestalks from their combat position, as if she had to get a really good look at Gu'od. They both remained silent for a moment.

When no one spoke, Gu'od continued, "Fighting is clearly Zeric's Focus. Not being a general. He must do what he's good at."

"Thank you, Gu," Zeric said, seizing the support. He turned a smug smile to Ymp. "See, wiser people than either of us agree with me. Now, let's get to causing some mayhem."

Ymp fumed for a moment but then relented and activated the map of Ba'aar and surrounding areas. As they began discussing possible targets, a small hint of guilt started whispering in the back of Zeric's head. But just like he did every time that voice bothered him about how he was acting while trying to woo some girl, he ignored it.

Chapter Two

Solyss Novastar felt sure he had seen seedier bars than this one. He just couldn't recall one. Darkness pervaded the room, broken only by sputtering fixtures around the walls. The smells—a mixture of body odors and smoky chemicals—left him with a nauseous and dizzy feeling.

Fighting back the urge to release his stomach contents onto the floor, Solyss straightened and walked further into the bar, head held high. Vomiting on the floor would not befit the dignity of a Novastar. Being in a place like this didn't befit the dignity of a Novastar, either, but that was unavoidable.

For nearly three months, they had traveled through hyperspace to the Trepon sector. The night before, they had arrived in orbit of the gas giant Hollis. The coordinates for his meeting with the crime lord Josserand Renard had led him to a small colony on an orbiting moon.

Solyss had considered simply entering orbit of the moon with his corvette, *Gallant*, and demanding to speak to Josserand, but one of his companions, Gamaly Dos'redna, had convinced him a covert meeting would be the better approach. That was how he had ended up in this bar, accompanied by Gamaly and Asheerah, out of uniform and wearing his most threadbare clothes.

As they made their way through the bar, all eyes in the room shifted to follow them. Two beautiful Liw'kel women had that effect on a room. One, Gamaly, had light blue skin and wore a standard ship jumpsuit. She had only a simple pistol at her side. By comparison, his other companion, Asheerah Aru, wore an arsenal of weapons over an armored chest piece. Not much of her light red skin showed, but Solyss still felt unsure why she had elected not to wear her entire armored suit.

Stumbling up to them, an obviously drunk blue-skinned Liw'kel male gave Solyss an unfocused look and said with a slur, "You lost, fancy man?"

Solyss frowned at the drunkard. He had worn his most common-looking clothing, but knew he was still better dressed than anyone else in the establishment. Still, he took offense at the man's comment. He thought of himself as civilized and cultured, not fancy. "No, I'm not lost," Solyss answered, as politely as he could manage.

"I think you are," the man said. "For a few minutes alone with one of your pretty lady friends, I can show you back to your ship." The man leered at the two Liw'kel. His gaze drifted to Gamaly's rounded midsection for an extended moment, and his smile widened. "How about that one? No danger of getting her pregnant."

Gamaly just shook her head, ignoring the man. Solyss tried to step past him, but the Liw'kel moved with him. Frustrated, Solyss said, "Would you kindly move out of the way, friend?"

Now ignoring him, the man continued to leer at Gamaly. "I don't see a husband around. Did he succumb to the affections of another? So many of us do. But don't worry, I can fill his place."

Without warning, Gamaly lashed out, striking the man in the nose with her fist. At the same moment, Asheerah reached over and grabbed his antennae. With a wrenching twist, she bent the organ at an unnatural angle. The man made a blood-curdling scream of pain.

A few months ago, the two women had almost been at each other's throats. But ever since Gu'od—Gamaly's husband—had become stranded behind enemy lines on Sulas, they had grown closer. Together, they now grabbed the whimpering man and threw him back toward the bar's entrance.

Around them, the room had grown quiet. If everyone's attention hadn't been on them before, it certainly was now. Solyss tried to straighten his jacket and make himself look confident. As they had demonstrated, Asheerah and Gamaly could handle themselves in a fight. But that wasn't why they were here.

Much to his relief, a Terran male with dark brown skin and grey-streaked hair stepped up to him. The man matched the description of Kueth Kahl-Amar that Maarkean had given him. This would be one of Josserand Renard's minions. "Major Novastar, I was not expecting you. But please, come with me," Kueth said, gesturing to a booth over in one corner of the room.

Not surprised that Kueth knew him, since Josserand's primary trade dealt in information, Solyss nodded and followed him back to the booth. A very tall Kowwok stood beside the booth, muscles evident through his brown fur.

Sliding into the booth with Gamaly—Asheerah couldn't sit comfortably with her weapons and armor—Solyss looked across the table at Kueth. The man wore modest clothing, which for this establishment counted as being dressed up. He had no weapon visible on him, though the towering Kowwok standing beside him did. Solyss doubted that was the only guard nearby.

"Where's General Ocaitchi? This meeting was for him," Kueth said without preamble.

"Where's Renard? We're here to meet with him," Gamaly said before Solyss could respond. He suppressed a frown about her taking the lead. As the commander of this mission, it would be his responsibility to negotiate, but he had asked Gamaly to come because she knew and had worked with Josserand Renard before. He couldn't get mad at her for doing her part now.

"A fair point," Kueth conceded. He leaned back and looked toward the bar's entrance. "You have a way of making your presence known. Fortunately, now that they know you're with me, none of that drunk's friends will be foolish enough to retaliate." A dangerous glint came to his eye as he turned his gaze back to Solyss and Gamaly. "But don't make me rescind that friendship. I'll ask again, where's Ocaitchi?"

"The general's a busy man," Solyss said.

"We're here in his stead. You want to negotiate with him, you do so through us," Gamaly added.

Kueth held their gaze for a moment before breaking it with a nod. "Very well. I assume you've a ship in orbit? Something more powerful than a transport ship, I hope?"

"Maybe," Solyss answered noncommittally.

Gamaly said nothing. Despite Kueth's initial confident manner, he appeared more nervous than Solyss would have expected. He started to understand why Maarkean had decided to trust this man enough to meet with him. He appeared to lack the murderous vibe most minions excreted.

"Take me aboard and I'll explain the deal my employer has to offer," Kueth said.

Solyss glanced at the Kowwok beside the table and back to Kueth. "OK, but just you. Your friend has to stay behind."

Without missing a beat, Kueth nodded. "Agreed."

The shuttle jostled from a wave of air turbulence that the inertial dampeners failed to compensate for. Lahkaba ignored the discomfort to continue to look out the shuttle's window. They were descending from the orbiting *Desert Sun*, the civilian transport that one of Kol's mining corporations had loaned them, toward the Dotran Confederate capital of Motinor.

Despite having once served the Confederate army, he had never actually been to Confederate space. He would have preferred to visit his species homeworld of Kowwa. He was curious, yet terrified, about visiting Dotra. Aside from the irrational, instinctual fear his species held for large lizard creatures, the Dotran had oppressed his people for hundreds of years.

Beside him, his fellow Kowwok Valinther didn't appear to show any excitement about their destination. The closer they had gotten to Confederate space during the journey, the more distant and nervous Valinther had become. Lahkaba knew that his fellow delegate had once lived in Confederate space, but nothing about his time there.

Glancing up from where he had been staring at the shuttle's floor, Valinther said to him, "You shouldn't be so calm."

Lahkaba raised a furry white eyebrow. "Oh? We're arriving as invited foreign dignitaries. What should I be nervous about?"

"You never lived here or you'd know," Valinther whispered.

Lahkaba pondered the statement. The only things he knew about the treatment his people received at the hands of the Dotran were from stories told by others. Part of him felt bad that he had no first-hand experience to understand what they faced, but he also felt glad to have had the chance to grow up on Sulas, away from that kind of subjugation.

From the other side of the shuttle, a hiss emerged from the large golden form of Zoeko Lide, the only Dotran delegate from the Union congress. She cast a sneer at the pair of them. "It was a mistake to bring Kowwoks with us. We should have made up the delegation from Camari and Ronids. We must show my people that we're strong."

"And what exactly is that supposed to mean?" Valinther growled, anger showing through his distant demeanor for the first time in a while. Zoeko had a way of bringing out that emotion in him.

"It means exactly as it sounds. We're here to seek help from the Confederacy, not make a political statement about Kowwok rights. You two will remind my people just how different the people of the Kreogh sector are from them. We will seem similar to the Alliance, whose Terrans clearly should have subjugated the weak Braz when they first met," Zoeko hissed.

"While I appreciate your confidence in my people," Lionell Mandrake, the Terran delegate from Ailleroc said, "I don't view the Kowwok presence on this mission as a weakness. The Confederation came to us in the first place. It's up to them to prove that they're worth working with."

Valinther gave a grateful nod to Lionell for his comment. Lahkaba picked up on some deeper undercurrent of respect between the two that he had never noticed before. He hadn't known them to get along particularly well. Kol and Ailleroc rarely saw eye to eye.

"A noble sentiment, and one I might agree with if circumstances were different," Zoeko said, though her tone made it difficult to judge the truth of her words. "But the fact remains: we need the help of the Confederate military to defeat the Alliance. Agitating them over Kowwok rights will not make that task easier."

Reluctantly, Lahkaba nodded. "I'm forced to agree with Zoeko. We're here to negotiate a treaty. We cannot allow our species to affect that goal. The Union must come first."

Lionell nodded his agreement. After a moment, Valinther also bowed his head to the point. Lahkaba didn't want to ignore his people's plight, but they had been living under Dotran rule for more than two hundred years already. Things couldn't be that bad.

They passed the rest of the journey to the surface in silence. When they stood up to exit the shuttle, Zoeko made a point of positioning herself in the front, with Lionell behind her. Valinther started to protest, but backed off after Lahkaba shook his head at him. If the Dotrans found importance in the order that they emerged from the shuttle, it was a small thing to concede.

Following the golden Dotran down the shuttle's ramp, Lahkaba stepped out onto a wide tarmac. Beyond the field of concrete, he could see a towering city in the near distance. The city basked in the light from the dual suns above. In return, the buildings, seemingly designed to reflect and enhance the sunlight, cast the entire city in a radiant glow. The visage hurt his eyes to look at, but it was beautiful.

On the tarmac, a collection of figures waited. At the front, dressed in elegant robes, stood a golden female Dotran and a bronze male. Their scales were polished smooth and reflected the sunlight almost as much as the city behind them.

Lahkaba picked out the figure of a blue male Dotran in a Confederate naval uniform standing near them. Lieutenant Commander Bryel Prytoker, the officer who had first brought them the offer of a treaty, looked uncomfortable surrounded by all the well-dressed politicians, most of whom were golden or bronze. Only a few were from the second rung of Dotran society—reds and oranges. Bryel appeared to be the only blue.

"Welcome to Dotra. I'm Foreign Minister Sceglis Amib." The bronze male spoke, his voice a rasping hiss that was almost incomprehensible. Sceglis then clapped his clawed hands together, and two Kowwoks rushed forward.

The two members of Lahkaba's species kept their heads lowered as they approached and lifted a tray bearing several sets of eyewear. They offered it to Lionell, Valinther, and himself.

Sceglis made a sweeping gesture toward them. "Our fine city is bright to most non-Dotrans. I offer you this eyewear to protect your eyes from the sun."

Lahkaba took the offered eyewear, pulling them over his head. The spectacles padded his fur down, and he had to adjust them to be able see without obstruction. Once he did so, the glare from the city receded.

"Please follow me. We'll give you a brief tour of our city before we show you to your residence," Sceglis said politely, turning toward a group of waiting vehicles.

As they started to follow, Lahkaba caught a glance from Valinther. Following his fellow delegate's eyes, he turned toward the two Kowwoks who had offered them the eyewear. Neither of the servants wore any protective eyewear themselves, instead keeping their heads bowed toward the ground. Neither so much as looked up at them, remaining behind, quietly serving their masters.

Chapter Three

One of the main advantages to serving aboard a battle carrier was the ability to look out a window. Engineers avoided building windows, which were structural weak points, into warships, but on a ship as large as a carrier, with over a thousand confined crewmembers, they could afford a few weak points.

Fleet Admiral Katerina Sartori could have had the observation lounge to herself. As the supreme commander of all Alliance forces in three sectors, she had enough authority to clear a room. But she preferred the presence of others. As one of the few truly off-duty locations aboard the carrier *Dominance*, here she could at least pretend she was just another officer enjoying the view of Sulas out the window.

After the successful ambush of the rebel forces, she had kept the bulk of her forces over Sulas, in order to contain the fairly substantial army that had made it to the surface. She had dispatched the Marine Expeditionary Force to Enro to reoccupy the rebellious world. Aside from that, she had been reluctant to deploy her forces.

In truth, the rebels' string of victories worried her. She controlled Ailleroc and was now bringing Enro and Sulas to heel, but the rest of the sector had essentially thrown off Alliance control. And they'd done it far too easily.

The rebels never had more than a handful of warships, and their army consisted of washouts and mercenaries. Yet she still hadn't regained full control of Sulas. The rebels had disappeared like mice into the woodwork. She had a fleet ready to wipe them out, but the war on Sulas had become a guerilla campaign.

Meanwhile, the rest of the sector went largely untouched. She would need to commit a large portion of her forces to breach Cardine's planetary defenses. And the FX-21 protecting Kol had become something of a bogeyman for her forces, with one ship fighting off an entire taskforce.

It was only here, pretending to be just another officer, that she allowed herself to feel a tinge of that fear herself. It was a ridiculous notion, she knew. The rebels had been lucky. They had only actually destroyed one ship and they had even had fighter support from the planet. But the story went beyond that.

Having indulged herself enough, Katerina stood up and left the dark room behind. She now had to return to the business of putting down this rebellion. Making her way through the corridors, she strode purposefully into her command center. Unlike in the observation room, the crew here immediately snapped to attention when she entered.

"Commander Dolan," Katerina said, "coordinate with General Schuma about what troops he can spare from the remaining Marines. I'm sending TF-413 and what's left of 412 to Dantyne. Also, contact the commander of TF-422. I want to make a show of force at Mirthod."

"Any marines to accompany 422?" Dolan asked, his usual no-nonsense tone showing no sign of what he thought of the orders.

"No. The ones aboard the ships already will do. They just need to show the flag and conduct some inspections. Nothing elaborate. They just need to remind the rebels who's in charge," Katerina said.

"Admiral, Rear Admiral Garmoravi has contracted a strand of Sulasian flu that's been running through the fleet. Would you like Commander Martin to command TF-412 and 413?" Dolan asked, throwing a wrench into her plans.

Garmoravi had commanded 413 for many years and he had made a favorable impression on her when she'd met him. To have their senior commander taken out by a flu would seriously undermine the effectiveness of his task force. While Commander Martin, the other option, had experience fighting the rebels, he had previously seen most of his task force destroyed, including his commander. That potentially made him unpredictable.

A solution occurred to Katerina, and she smiled. "Actually, you'll be taking command."

"Admiral?" Dolan asked, surprised.

"I'm activating your promotion to commodore. You'll take command of Taffy-413 while Admiral Garmoravi recovers," Katerina said, keeping her tone serious, though she felt joy at being able to see her protégé advance. He had put aside his promotion to join her on this mission, but he was more than qualified to handle command of a task force.

"Aye, Admiral," Dolan finally said, realizing she had made her decision.

Major Samantha Anderson, Dolan's deputy, offered her congratulations, as did others in the operations room. Dolan looked uncomfortable with the attention but handled it with good grace. Now she would see if he really would handle the burdens of command as well as she hoped.

Saracasi started to feel sympathy for her brother. She had always known that he hated speaking in public. Every time he had had to go to Congress or address the troops, she had quietly laughed at his discomfort, even though she had always been impressed with how he had handled himself.

Now, the shoe was on the other foot, and she found herself addressing Congress. She had once considered herself a good public speaker. During her school years, she had always done well. She held this opinion of herself no more.

"Members of Congress, we need a new naval commander named until such time as General Ocaitchi can be rescued from Alliance detention or Commander Brieni cleared of charges. Our forces are scattered and without leadership. We cannot hope to make an effective counter-attack against the Alliance. I'm prepared to assume command at this time."

The statement was obvious and not very compelling, she thought immediately. Before she could expand on her point, Wilchu Num, one of the delegates from Cardine, said, "So you've abandoned all hope of finding General Numba?"

Caught off guard by the unexpected question, Saracasi said, "Not all hope, no. But we do have confirmed reports of the destruction of *Rogue Spirit*, apparently with all hands."

"With the loss of General Numba and General Ocaitchi, command should fall to General Dustlighter or General Kil'dare," Lei-mey, from Sulas, said.

"Neither of which we've had any contact with since the failed invasion," Saracasi replied. "The Alliance has Sulas under heavy blockade. Unless I can take full control of our remaining ships, we don't stand a chance of breaking the blockade."

She didn't add that they wouldn't stand a chance of breaking the blockade even then. And even if Solyss returned from Trepon with *Gallant* intact and the *Black Market* on their side, they still wouldn't really have much of a chance.

"And what of Commander Brieni?" Wilchu asked. "Are you sure of his guilt?"

Saracasi shook her head. "No. We only have our final report from General Dustlighter expressing his belief that Commander Brieni was a traitor. But he provided no evidence before we lost contact."

"Convenient for you," Inecki Ago'saw from Mirthod said.

The accusatory tone coming from the Liw'kel hit Saracasi hard, firing up her emotions. The rational part of her brain knew that the statement was intended to throw her off and that it was only effective because of the guilt she felt for jailing Davidus. But that part of her lost control of her mouth. "Convenient for me? We need someone with Davidus's experience right now. I had to choose between locking up a potentially innocent man that I've known almost my entire life or letting a potential traitor run our navy. That was not convenient. This body is supposed to be investigating that but has done nothing for the last two months," Saracasi said, her tone angry and slightly childish.

"With all of our generals dead, captured, or cut off, we should be selecting a new permanent military commander, not just a naval leader," Inecki Ago'saw said, ignoring Saracasi's statement. "Clearly, Major Ocaitchi is not up to the job."

"To command what?" Zhet from Enro demanded. "My planet has been invaded as well, and we don't have any troops to send to aid. We sent troops to join the Union with the understanding that this army and navy would be there to protect our world. But now we're on our own. We should abandon this farce of a congress and see to our own planets!"

The whole ordeal was suddenly spinning out of control. Somehow, the discussion had veered into the territory of disbanding the entire Union. What had she done to screw things up so badly? *Damn Lahkaba for not being here*, she thought.

Fortunately, she had at least one ally in Congress. Faide Darkthorne, still acting as chairman of the congress, stood up. "Ladies, gentlemen, please. We're here to discuss Major Ocaitchi's request for temporary command of all naval forces until such time as General Ocaitchi or General Dustlighter can return. Now, Major, what exactly do you propose to do if placed in command?"

Saracasi took a breath, saying a mental "thank you" to Faide. He had finally asked a substantive question about tactics and the war, instead of throwing accusations and engaging in political infighting.

Steadying herself, she tried to keep her tone calm, reasoned, and professional. "Our forces are currently limited, so a direct assault against Sulas or Ailleroc is out of the question. But we do still have army forces here on Irod, along with home-based units on every world, plus almost a company of marine trainees still on Kol.

"Using our remaining carrier, our gunships, and the cutters that are currently orbiting Irod and Cardine, we should be able to retake Dantyne, Mirthod, and possibly Enro."

Zhet, who moments before had been advocating dissolving Congress, suddenly looked contemplative. The idea of a naval force coming to Enro's aid clearly held some interest for him. Without Owrik on the Dantyne team, she wasn't sure how they would respond, but she doubted that the prospect of aid would go remiss.

She had chosen those planets not for their delegates' support, however. All had been reoccupied by the Alliance since the Battle of Sulas. Mirthod's and Dantyne's naval forces in orbit were relatively light. Each planet also had valuable resources.

"You mean to strip the defenses of Irod and Cardine away?" Wilchu said, outraged.

"Irod is safe as long as the Alliance doesn't know where it is. And Cardine is protected more by the ground batteries than by those ships. The Alliance will come despite them, but it won't be until Sulas and Ailleroc are completely pacified. For now, those cutters will do more good with the naval forces than as deterrents," Saracasi answered.

She held back from mentioning that the cutters weren't much in the way of warships and would be useless against the Alliance navy. That wouldn't be a good point to bring up while she was attempting to make the argument that she needed those very ships to fight the Alliance.

"Clearly Major Ocaitchi's inexperience and desire to go on the offensive is blinding her. Cardine will not hand over our only defense ships to this child," Wilchu said derisively.

The insult was clear, though for some reason, Saracasi found herself not bothered by it. Compared to everyone in this room, she was almost a child. They had a least a decade on her, some as many as five. But she also knew it was an irrelevant argument.

"This *child* fought off an entire Alliance task force and saved Kol from reoccupation," Agamon Toulerak from Kol said, rising to her defense.

"Then what does she need our ships for?" Wilchu countered. "Let her use this super ship of hers."

"The *Audacious* is currently unavailable," Saracasi answered. Revealing the truth about the ship's hyperdrive trouble would probably be more effective as an argument, but she couldn't risk leaking that information, even here.

"What do you mean, 'unavailable'?" Inecki asked.

"Meaning she's not available," Saracasi retorted, her tone far too sarcastic for her own good.

"I think it's clear that Major Ocaitchi has no support from her fellow officers, hence the departure of Major Novastar and his ship and the *unavailability* of the *Audacious*," Wilchu said.

"I move that her petition to be placed in command of the navy be rejected and the matter tabled for now," Lei-mey said from the Sulas table.

The sudden declaration from Lei-mey—someone she thought she could count as an ally—stung Saracasi.

In a whirlwind around her, the motion rejecting her petition was seconded and then voted on. It wasn't until Faide addressed her directly that she realized it was over.

"Major, we thank you for your dedication, but your service as naval commander will not be necessary," her Nothan friend said, kindness in his tone despite the words. "I call this meeting adjourned."

The delegates began filing out of the small room, eventually leaving Saracasi alone with just Lei-mey. The Ronid woman remained at her seat, locking her multifaceted eyes on Saracasi. Once they were alone, Saracasi shook her head at Lei-mey. "I thought you would support this effort. You were the one who began this whole war," Saracasi said.

"No, it was your brother and my supporters breaking us out of prison that started this fight, and you know it. I merely seized that event to rally more support to oppose the Alliance," Lei-mey replied, her tone that of a chiding teacher.

"Either way, I don't think you want to see it end with us just fading away without a fight, and if we don't keep the pressure on the Alliance, that's exactly what's going to happen," Saracasi retorted.

"You think it would be better if Congress had voted to put someone else in charge of the military?" Lei-mey asked, calmly.

"Maybe—depends on who it was."

"Not one with any more experience than you," Lei-mey answered. "Just someone with more political savvy. Because that's almost what happened. You brought this issue of leadership up without thought, and you almost got relegated to an insignificant role and placed under the command of a political lackey."

"Even that might be better than sitting around doing nothing," Saracasi snapped back, though she wasn't sure she believed her own words.

Lei-mey sighed. "You burned much of the good opinion you once had."

"It doesn't look like I had very much good opinion," Saracasi said.

"And your brother always claimed you were the one with the political sense," Lei-mey chided. "Maybe that's the problem. He knew he didn't know anything, so he relied on Lahkaba. Maybe you would have, too, had he been here. But instead, you decided to try to wade in on your own."

A retort came to mind about Lei-mey being the one who had betrayed her on the matter, but she bit it back. Suppressing the urge to continue the argument, Saracasi waited. She could see why many people found the Ronid woman insufferable, but even now, she had to admit that Lei-mey knew what she was doing.

"You're well respected among the members of Congress for your part in starting our move toward independence, and more recently for your defense of Kol. You're seen as a prodigy who does what must be done. Much like your brother, a person of action.

"And right now, that's the kind of person Congress needs. Peace is governed by politicians. War is won by action. Instead of seizing the opportunity and taking action, you came here hat in hand, begging for the authority to do something. Before, you were someone to be feared—now, you were someone to be controlled. Wilchu and Inecki took advantage of that to make you look stupid," Lei-mey explained.

Saracasi frowned at Lei-mey's view of events. She didn't like the conclusion—that her failure had been her own fault—nor the idea that coming to Congress for authority had been the wrong move. She had long advocated a rebellion against the Alliance, but she had never believed in anarchy. "So, what, I was just supposed to take the ships and go out on my own?" Saracasi asked, disbelieving.

"Of course not," Lei-mey chided. "But you were supposed to do what was necessary."

"What does that mean?" Saracasi asked.

Lei-mey smiled in a creepy way, her mandibles clicking. "Nothing is free, Major. You certainly know that."

Saracasi let out an exasperated sigh. She should have seen this coming. "What do you want?"

"Take me to Sulas," Lei-mey said in a tone that made it sound like she was asking for a ride to the other side of town.

"What?" Saracasi exclaimed. "Sulas? There's no getting past that blockade without getting blown up or captured."

Lei-mey smiled again. "You were a smuggler, were you not? Isn't that what smugglers do?"

Shaking her head, Saracasi sat down at one of the empty chairs. "Smugglers slip illegal cargo through customs. Sometimes, they slip through sensor nets. But those are peacetime nets, not occupied planets blockaded by an entire naval fleet."

"Your ships made it through to Ailleroc."

"That was luck and Alliance over-confidence. We seem to be all out of the first, and we've worn out our uses of the second," Saracasi argued.

Lei-mey shrugged. "That's unfortunate. If you can get me to Sulas, all of your command problems will go away. You will have the perfectly legal authority to take command of the ships you need and without begging Congress for it."

Looking at Lei-mey, Saracasi considered her options. Going rogue wasn't really an option. She would never convince the captains of those cutters to follow her without authorization.

"Okay, what's your plan to make that happen?" Saracasi asked.

Lei-mey gave her a Ronid's disturbing version of a smile but said nothing.

With a sigh, Saracasi finally relented. "All right. But if you die, it's your own damn fault."

Lei-mey shrugged. "It always will be."

A week had gone by since the last time a guard had taken him for an interrogation. Or, at least, Maarkean thought it had been a week. It had been several days, he felt sure. Even though he hadn't been tortured during that time, he didn't really have a lot to help him gauge the time.

"Once you get past the repeated torture, this place isn't so bad," Lohcja said from his bunk.

"Right up there with some of the finest resorts I've ever stayed at," Maarkean replied.

As he stood up, Lohcja said, "Twenty-hour-a-day room service. Fine bedding made from only the cheapest material. And a view."

Maarkean began stretching while Lohcja talked. With both of them standing, they didn't have a lot of open space. But with nothing else to do, they had taken to sparring much of the time. Granted, given their injuries, it was a sad excuse for sparring that would have inspired either pity or amusement from anyone who could have seen it, but it still made them feel better somehow.

Ronid bodies didn't work quite the same as Braz, so Lohcja just stood there, waiting for Maarkean to finish stretching. "Come on. I only have all day," Lohcja said with mock impatience.

Maarkean smiled and then moved from his current stretch into an attack, though one accompanied by a bit of a stagger. The move caught Lohcja off guard, and he stumbled back into the wall. Maarkean swung again, and with nowhere else to retreat to, Lohcja hastily tried to block. Then Maarkean faltered from a wave of dizziness, and Lohcja had an opening. After this first round, they broke into a pattern of practice moves, and Maarkean felt the rest of the world wash away into the background.

They continued to exchange blows, though much more gentle ones than they had ever used before their capture and harsh treatment at the hands of the Alliance, until Maarkean felt exhaustion overtaking him. He felt his whole body covered in sweat. Lohcja looked just the same as when the pair had started, Ronids not having a lot of outward physical signs of exhaustion.

"You think we killed four, five hours?" Maarkean joked through gasps for air.

"No, at least eight. The war's probably over now, and we'll be released in a few minutes," Lohcja replied.

The pair collapsed onto their bunks.

Several long minutes went by in silence. Maarkean considered taking a nap but tried to stop himself. He was tired, but he'd been sleeping far too much. There wasn't much else to do here, but he was concerned about the implications of wanting to sleep all the time.

He tried to think of some new topic of conversation he and Lohcja could discuss. They had run out of new ideas a few days ago. Unfortunately, despite being friends, they didn't have a lot in common. They had tried to use that to their advantage, since their knowledge bases covered vastly different areas, but the end result had been one-sided lectures rather than conversations.

"Why have they left us alone?" Lohcja asked into the silence.

The question hung in the air while Maarkean tried to decide whether or not to ignore it. They had been avoiding the topic in an unspoken agreement not to jinx it, but it had been one of the things foremost on Maarkean's mind.

Letting out a sigh and a shrug, which he knew Lohcja couldn't see, Maarkean said, "Probably a new tactic. Psychological torture. Hoping we'll discuss something of vital importance in our boredom. Giving us time to heal for a new round of attempts. Maybe they just got bored and ran out of new and creative ways to make us suffer."

Lohcja let out an unsatisfied noise. "You were once an Alliance officer. What do you actually think?"

"Actual Alliance officers would never do this," Maarkean snapped, resenting the implication. "The ones torturing us aren't Alliance officers. They're the ones we're fighting against."

"Right," Lohcja said cautiously after a minute. "Okay. So why would anyone do this? What can they possibly gain?"

"Revenge," a voice said, startling Maarkean.

Above him, Lohcja let out a noise, and Maarkean heard the Ronid slam his head into the low ceiling. Ignoring Lohcja's curses of pain, he turned to look through the bars of their cell.

A young Braz woman in an Alliance lieutenant's uniform stood outside the cell. She bore a dark blue screfa and an intelligence corps pin on her breast pocket. "The ship's intelligence chief's brother was aboard the cruiser destroyed during the battle. He's been doing all of this just out of revenge," the lieutenant said.

Maarkean frowned. "That's a lot of effort for revenge."

The lieutenant shrugged. "Revenge is a powerful motivator. But the chief has been relieved. I'm Lieutenant Merski, and I have taken over your care."

"So I suppose we have you to thank for our luxurious vacation?" Lohcja quipped.

Merski nodded. "Yes. After the chief's reprehensible behavior was discovered, I decided you both could use a few days' rest."

Lohcja let out an odd laugh. "I think I've seen this one before. What was that show, *Crime and Justice*? Yeah, you're playing the role of the good cop."

"I assure you, nothing of the sort," Merski stammered.

"Save it, Lieutenant," Maarkean said. "We appreciate the break, but we don't buy the story for a second. All of this was done by a single chief out for revenge? That's a lot of power for an intelligence spook to have aboard a warship. We've been 'interrogated' by many different crew-members and treated by the medical staff. There's no way the captain wouldn't be aware of it after this long. That means they're all complicit."

Merski frowned and her shoulders slumped. She glanced over her shoulder at what Maarkean could only assume was one of the cameras monitoring them. Pulling out her comm device, the lieutenant entered a command and then looked back up. "You're right," she said. "I was sent in here to gain your trust so we could try getting you to open up to me. But I really do find what's been done to you reprehensible. You have to believe me about that."

Maarkean studied the young woman. He normally considered himself very good at reading people. There were no obvious signs of deception, but he wasn't sure he could believe her. Intelligence officers were trained to lie, after all.

"That the entire crew has been involved makes me sick," she continued. "But I took this assignment because it gave me a lot of latitude. I was supposed to use it to try to gain your trust. Instead, I'm going to use it to get you free."

A sharp bark came from Lohcja. "That's taking the good cop approach to a new extreme."

Maarkean considered the woman's statement. Odds were good that Lohcja was right and this was just part of her attempt to gain their trust. But what if it wasn't? Many other Alliance officers, himself included, had turned to the Union after seeing the moral decay of the Alliance first-hand. She could be telling the truth.

"I'll play along," Maarkean said. "How do you plan to get us out?"

"I'm not sure yet," Merski said in a tone that sounded sincere. "But I just wanted you to know that help is on the way. Just hold on for a little while longer."

She glanced back at the camera and then hit a control on her comm device. When she spoke again, her tone was more formal. "We'll resume your interrogations once you've sufficiently healed from your injuries. I assure you, this chief will pay for his violation of the Alliance's uniform code."

Turning on her heel, she strode out the door. Maarkean leaned off the cot slightly, peering at the camera. It was clear that she meant for them not to discuss what she had just said. He shared a look with Lohcja before leaning back against the wall. Could he let himself believe they might be able to get out of here?

Chapter Four

Pulling his Razors cap tight on his head, Zeric started down the hallway toward the service elevator that led out of the arena's basement. It felt good to be headed out for some excitement with a rifle in his hands again.

He barely made it ten meters before the feeling vanished.

Waiting for him at the last corner before the elevator was Ymp. She was also decked out in BDUs and combat gear. Despite her diminutive size compared to him, her stance made it clear there was no getting past her.

"Oh, come on, Ymp," Zeric complained. "I outrank you by several levels. Don't try this pushing me around nonsense."

Her expression was serious, though from the way her eyestalks swayed slightly, it was obvious to him that she derived a lot of pleasure from what she said next. "It's my duty as the next senior officer to keep you out of danger. That last raid was a close one. Your presence on this mission would be a liability."

"We're just going to blow up some more Alliance supplies," Zeric countered. "Nothing fancy."

"Exactly, which is why you're not needed," Ymp said, her stance not wavering.

"Who cares if I'm needed?" Zeric argued. "I'm the one in charge here. This is what I do best—blow shit up!"

Getting up close to his face, Ymp said again, her voice comparatively calm, "You're our leader. You die on a worthless mission after we've already lost Generals Numba and Ocaitchi, and morale dies with you. You ceded your actual control of this army to Kantor and Kil'dare, and that's your prerogative, but that doesn't make you any less in command. You're a symbol for the troops, and that means you need to stay alive. And it's my job to make sure that happens."

Zeric hated this talk of him being a symbol. Before, he had been a little jealous that Maarkean had gotten all of that attention, though he had mostly felt sympathy for his friend. Now, any feelings of jealousy were gone. "So, I'm just supposed to sit here for the rest of the war doing nothing?" Zeric asked sarcastically.

"Plan an attack that has an objective worth risking the life of a general for, and you can be the one to lead it," Ymp said.

"All right, fine," Zeric grumbled. "But I'll remember this on your birthday." After a grudging sigh, he leaned his rifle against the wall and unclipped his pack, setting it down. Seemingly from out of nowhere, his aide, Kumus Stryker, materialized and picked them up, then disappeared down the corridor, back toward Zeric's quarters.

Without another word to Ymp, Zeric proceeded around the corner. Careful to conceal his frustration, he greeted the troops assembled there. He took a few minutes to move about them, talking to each of them briefly. It had always boosted his morale when officers had done that to his unit during the Colonial War.

After speaking to each of them, Zeric stopped before Ymp. Suppressing his annoyance at her, he gives her a smile and a salute. "Good hunting, Major."

"Thank you, sir," Ymp replied, returning the salute.

She then led the team of soldiers into the elevator, leaving Zeric alone in the hallway. Still grumbling to himself about Ymp's hardheadedness, and enjoying the irony that her skull was actually softer than his, he went in search of something to do.

In the area of the arena's basement being used as the marines' mess, Zeric found a group of them watching a hockey game. The feed was live from the arena above them. Zeric frowned when he saw that the Razors were down by one.

"General," Lieutenant Sigfa Neith asked, "care to join us?"

Realizing he had nothing else to do, Zeric sat down. One of the marines handed him a beer, and he relaxed. Jairyd and Kantor were taking care of military planning. Ymp was leading the raids. A cold beer and a hockey game weren't a bad way to spend a war.

Zeric watched, chatting with the marines and army soldiers, as the game unfolded. When the period ended, the Razors had come back to tie, and Zeric had forgotten about his situation for a short time. Then Sigfa asked him a question that brought it all back.

"General, any word on how long we'll be down here?" the young Terran asked.

Caught off guard and annoyed that it brought him back to reality, Zeric turned to Sergeant Ocif, the marine who was currently using the cooler as a seat. "Sergeant, how about another beer?"

Obod looked abashed. "Sorry, sir. We're all out. Lieutenant Neith limited us to two apiece since we're up for a mission tomorrow."

To himself, Zeric cursed. Two beers were hardly enough to have even given him the hints of a buzz. But to Obod, he said, "Very sensible, Lieutenant." Then, realizing he probably couldn't dodge Sigfa's question, he equivocated. "As to your question, I wish I could give you an answer. General Kil'dare's plan for a guerrilla campaign will take some time to work. We need to get the Alliance off balance before we can take further action."

He felt bad lying to the troops. There was no plan beyond hitting the Alliance and hoping they just went away. But he couldn't tell Sigfa that.

"We're ready for it, however long it takes," Sigfa said, his conviction making Zeric feel some shame. Sigfa had once been a mercenary but was now more sold on the cause than Zeric was.

"All right, Rogues," Sigfa said to the mix of marines and army troops, "we need to be up early. Let's hit the sack."

Zeric wanted to order them to sit down. The game had just gone into overtime. But he didn't have to go to bed—he would just have to watch the rest of the game alone. Or he could go find Gu'od.

Bidding the others good night and good luck on their mission tomorrow, Zeric went in search of his friend. After stopping by his room for a bottle of more potent liquor and his datapad, he found Gu'od right where he expected: meditating in his small room. Without comment, Zeric activated the datapad and brought up the feed from the game.

After a few minutes, Gu'od stood up, stretched, and took a seat. Zeric handed Gu'od the bottle, and Gu'od took a small swig before handing it back. They sat in silence for the rest of the game, going through the bottle without a word.

"I don't like it," Fracsid argued.

Beside Saracasi, the Braz ex-smuggler drummed his fingers on the tactical holo-projector. They were standing around the device at the front of *Defiant Glory*'s pilot ready room, although, aside from Jerik, none of the ships' pilots were present.

"This won't be like the insertion into Ailleroc," Fracsid continued. "There was still civilian traffic going to and from the planet to blend into. Sulas is completely cut off. The Alliance is not letting any ships planet-side. A few occasionally try, so we might be able to jump into the legal jump zone without getting blown away immediately. But we won't be able to do anything but scan and jump away."

Saracasi shook her head. "No, Lei-mey made it very clear that she has to get to the surface. So that's what we're going to do."

"But why?" Fracsid pressed. "You already have my support for taking the fight to the Alliance. Those cutters barely qualify as warships. Sure, they have a heavy neutron blaster, but they're as frail as paper. Let's just take our chances, with or without Congress's support."

"No," Saracasi said emphatically, surprising even herself. "When Maarkean raided Olan, he did so as a rebel because there was no one else to turn to. When he fought the Alliance on Enro, though, he did so with the approval of the sector congress. We all swore our loyalty to the people of this sector who are represented by that congress. If we start ignoring them because we don't like their decisions, then we're nothing more than anarchist rebels and not the revolutionary patriots we claim."

In truth, she'd been entertaining the notion of going on her own, and she'd been trying to convince herself not to. It helped to explain out loud why she shouldn't.

Fracsid shrugged, but Jerik and Kaars gave solemn nods of agreement. Jerik then asked, "So how do you plan to get past their blockade?"

"We exit hyperspace right in the atmosphere," Saracasi said, keeping her tone mild.

"That's crazy!" Fracsid said but then smiled. "I like it."

Jerik kept a straight face. "That is, indeed, crazy. There's a reason ships exit hyperspace tens of thousands of kilometers away from planets. The gravity field allows you to exit, but it's not a smooth transition. And it will immediately start pulling you down into a death plummet. Then there's the friction from the sudden collision with the air, not to mention if your calculations are off by a fraction, you emerge *inside* the planet instead of above it."

"I know all that," Saracasi said, though she was glad neither of them were just agreeing to her suggestion without comment. It *was* a crazy idea, and it wouldn't be a good sign. "But I've done it before. Well, Maarkean did it before. *Cutty Sark* can handle it."

"Maybe, but is it even worth attempting?" Jerik asked. "What do you expect to gain from this that's worth the risk?"

Saracasi shrugged, feeling awkward that she didn't have a good answer to that particular question. "I've decided to trust Lei-mey on this. She's always had the best interests of the Union in mind. If getting to Sulas is this important to her, then it's worth doing. That it will resolve our problem, so much the better."

Jerik looked like he wanted to argue more but didn't say anything.

Fracsid raised the next important question. "You're going to need one hell of a pilot. I'm good, but I don't think I'm that good."

"That's OK," Saracasi said. "I actually need you to stay here. This has a high chance of failure, so we can't risk two senior officers on it. Jerik, who do you have who can do this?"

Jerik frowned, considering the question.

Saracasi noticed the irony of trusting this plan to Jerik's judgment. Part of her still didn't trust the former bounty hunter. Despite the slight limp he still had, he didn't appear to hold any grudge against her, which was why she had decided to accept him as her CAG: Commander Air Group.

"Well, I could probably do it," Jerik said with no hint of modesty in his tone. "But I should stay here for the same reason Major Relis is. Sienn'lyn I'fu. She's the best natural pilot we have. She just lacks experience. Which is fortunate, since that's the only reason she wasn't on the last mission to Sulas."

Saracasi nodded. They had little hope any of the pilots had survived who been with the two escort carriers sent to invade Sulas. *Defiant Glory* had escaped after the battle without recovering any of her fighters. Some might have landed on Sulas along with the army troop transports, but as it stood now, they had no idea if any had.

"Good," Saracasi said. "She's flown *Cutty Sark* before. We'll keep the rest of the crew to a minimum. I'll just need a gunner."

Fracsid nodded and then said, his tone slightly apologetic, "Specialist Almes has been manning the weapons console since Ailleroc. He knows all the upgrades backward and forward, which is why I kept him over my original gunner."

"He'll do," Saracasi replied, unsure what Fracsid's tone was suggesting.

"The big question is still, assuming you survive reentry, how do you get back out?" Jerik asked. "Exiting hyperspace that close to a planet is rough but possible. Entering hyperspace that deep in the gravity well will destroy your ship."

"We'll just have to do it the old-fashioned way," Saracasi said with a grim smile. She didn't relish that prospect, but it was a lot easier to escape a blockade from the inside.

Turning to the former Alliance intelligence officer, Saracasi asked, "Any suggestions that might help us, Master Sergeant?"

Kaars Aerinstar shook his head. "Unfortunately, no, Major. You've already read my brief on Alliance blockade tactics, which is hardly complete since we don't even know how many ships are still there. If you take me with you, I might be able to use the opportunity to gather some new information."

"As valuable as that might be, you're our best source of intelligence and information on Alliance tactics and personnel, even if it's outdated," Saracasi said.

In truth, she wasn't sure if she could let Kaars go off alone. It had been him and Davidus who had spent more than a month intelligence-gathering on Ailleroc. It had been after that trip that he had convinced General Numba to begin the invasion of Sulas. Everyone assumed that it was Davidus who had made contact with Admiral Sartori, but until they knew what evidence Zeric had, she couldn't rule out Kaars being in on the conspiracy.

"I appreciate the flattery, Major, but I would be more valuable gathering updated information," Kaars insisted.

When it became obvious that Saracasi would not budge on this request, he changed the subject. "If you have the opportunity, depart the surface along a vector that takes you toward a corvette."

"A corvette?" Jerik said, shocked. "They'll tear the *Cutty Sark* up. Better to head toward a big ship with fewer point defense guns."

"You would think," Kaars said. "But the corvettes actually have pretty poor ground sensors. They fight star fighters in the openness of empty space. It will take them longer to identify you as a threat coming up from the ground, and that might give you the time you need to escape."

"I'll keep that in mind," Saracasi said, filing away the information. It seemed to match what she could remember about the *Gallant*'s systems, so she hoped it proved to be true. "All right, gentlemen. Keep the fleet warm until I get back."

Chapter Five

As he set the shuttle down on the deck of the *Gallant*, Solyss let himself relax. The meeting on the Hollis moon hadn't gone at all like he had expected, and that had made him nervous. During the journey back to the ship, he had anticipated countless scenarios that involved Kueth Kahl-Amar coming with them in order to set a trap, but now that they were safely back onboard his ship, Solyss relaxed. Even if Kueth were carrying a tracking device leading a fleet of pirate ships to them, Solyss felt confident his ship and crew could handle anything the crime lord threw at them.

Waiting on the cramped hangar deck stood lieutenants Aly Tess, his blue-hued Camari XO, and Isaxo Mahon, his Notha fighter squadron leader. Isaxo had been with him since before the war started, joining his crew after Maarkean Ocaitchi had busted the young pilot out of an Alliance prison for aliens. In many ways, Isaxo was responsible for Solyss deciding to join the cause.

"How did the meeting go, Captain?" Tess asked. Unlike Isaxo or Ash-eerah, Solyss hadn't met Tess until after he had taken command of the *Gallant*. In this military setting, he tended to think of her by her last name, as was custom.

In response, Solyss continued his climb out of the cargo shuttle, revealing the figure of Kueth Kahl-Amar behind him. Isaxo cocked his head to the side at the sight of the unexpected passenger, while Tess's eyestalks lowered slightly. Kueth's brief pause to study his new surroundings was cut short by Asheerah pushing him out of the shuttle from behind.

"Lieutenant Aru," Solyss said, resuming the use of his formal command tone, "take our guest to the ward room. I'll join you shortly."

Asheerah gestured for Kueth to precede her toward the hangar's exit. From her demeanor, she saw little difference between guest and prisoner. At least she hadn't drawn her weapon, Solyss decided. Gamaly exited the shuttle without a word and followed them.

"Lieutenant," Solyss said, turning to Tess, "break orbit and get us to a safe hyperspace distance from Hollis. Depending on how this meeting goes, I want to be able to jump quickly."

Tess's eyestalks gave a momentary flicker toward Isaxo before she spoke. "Sir, we have two fighter craft on an unauthorized patrol. It will take at least twenty minutes to recover them."

Isaxo said, annoyance evident in his voice, "Unauthorized? *I'm* in command of the fighter squadron, and I authorized their flight."

"Without clearance from the ship's commander," Tess replied, keeping her tone even compared to Isaxo's emotional outburst.

Solyss sighed.

As the ship's XO, command fell to Tess when Solyss was away, which had displeased Isaxo from the start. With Kard Ulis off commanding their old ship, the *Chimopori*, Isaxo had assumed he would be the second in command. Despite that assumption, Isaxo hadn't complained when Solyss had elected to go with Tess, who had more experience working on larger starships. It wasn't until the Battle of Sulas, where Isaxo's brother Owrik had died, that Isaxo had started butting heads with Tess. Solyss felt confident that the antagonism between the two was partially motivated by grief. He'd tried to explain that to Tess, but it hadn't helped. The two just didn't get along. Until now, their disagreements had been minor—mostly sharp words said in the wardroom.

Technically, Tess was correct. As the ship's commander, she needed to approve all flights. But Solyss didn't feel like playing referee or admonishing either of them at the moment. He decided to just ignore it, saying, "Recall the fighters and then get us clear of the moon."

"Aye, Captain," Tess said, though her lowered eyestalk glance toward Isaxo indicated she was not happy.

Before she or Isaxo could say any more, Solyss headed for the hangar's door, leaving them behind. Right now, he had to deal with a criminal in order to save the Union. And the criminal appeared to want to play games with him.

Solyss left the hangar bay behind and entered the ship's main corridor. Despite the hangar being quite cramped—it could hold only the cargo shuttle and one other smaller vessel—it was by far the largest room on the *Gallant*. A heavily modified Alliance corvette, the ship was the smallest full-fledged type of capital ship. The four fighters she carried—the ones Isaxo and Tess had been arguing over—were mounted on external docking ports. Only one at a time could be brought into the hangar when repairs were needed.

The bulkheads lining the corridor shone with a bright gleam. They were a fairly ordinary metallic grey, but with the heavy polish, this particular alloy looked almost white. Solyss made sure the crew kept the ship looking in pristine condition. Not only had there not been a lot to do during their three-month journey, he also felt it necessary to morale. A clean, well-maintained ship meant a strong, united crew.

Located in the ship's aft section, resting above the main engines, the hangar shared B Deck with only a few other locations—mainly maintenance rooms for the weapon systems. Solyss walked the length of the ship to a stairwell and went down to C Deck. From there, he turned and continued walking toward the ship's bow.

Officer quarters were located in their own compartment toward the front of the ship. The only thing between them and the emptiness of space was the main sensor array, though that covered three decks. This left the officer section the farthest away from any of the day-to-day activity aboard ship.

A total of seven rooms were located here: six individual rooms for Isaxo, Tess, the ship's surgeon, the chief engineer, himself, and Asheerah, who had yielded her quarters to Gamaly, and then a cramped wardroom with its own small galley. While the quarters here were individual rooms, compared to the two barrack rooms for the main crew and the three-person bunks for the senior enlisted personnel, they weren't spacious. Solyss spent little of his time in his quarters.

Readying himself for the coming discussion, Solyss lifted his head up in a confident manner and strode into the wardroom. Shaped like an oval, the room had eight padded seats lining the wall. Monitors hung over the seats, capable of displaying ship status reports or entertainment programs. In the center of the room, currently acting as the room's floor, was the table. It could be lowered to the deck, providing a reasonable amount of walking space, or raised to serve as a table for the eight chairs. When raised, it made getting across the room very difficult.

Asheerah stood across from the entrance, resting against the door leading to the small galley. Her weapons were holstered, but she exuded menace nonetheless. Her eyes stayed locked onto Kueth like a predator ready to strike, despite him having been thoroughly checked for weapons.

Gamaly sat on the opposite side of the room from Kueth, chatting amicably with him. From the snippets of conversation Solyss picked up when he entered, they were talking about the colony on the Hollis moon. The conversation stopped and Kueth rose as he entered.

"Captain Novastar," Kueth said by way of greeting.

Solyss nodded his head, acknowledging the man's understanding of naval tradition. Turning to a small counter beside the door, Solyss picked up a bottle and held it up so Kueth could see. The man nodded his head in agreement, and Solyss poured the two of them a glass of cognac. It was a delicacy from his native Terra and not easy to come by in the colonial sectors.

Solyss handed the glass to Kueth and then took a seat beside Gamaly. He never even considered offering a glass to the two women. Gamaly was pregnant and Asheerah always stuck her nose up at his "snobby liquors."

Sipping his drink slowly, he relished the flavor. He hadn't indulged himself in a drink but once since leaving Kol on this mission. That one time had been a memorial service for those lost in the Battle of Sulas.

After giving Kueth a moment to enjoy his drink, Solyss leaned back and gave the man a hard look. The drink had allowed him to release some of the tension he had been feeling earlier, but he still felt annoyed at the situation. He had come out here in a desperate move to save the Union. He wasn't interested in word games.

"All right, Mr. Kahl-Amar," Solyss began, "let's hear it. And no more games. Give it to me straight."

Sitting up straighter, Kueth lowered his glass. "Very well. In exchange for your help in freeing the world of Okaral from Alliance control, and then making the freedom of all worlds in the Trepon sector a condition of any final peace treaty with the Alliance, Mr. Renard will gain control of the *Black Market* and provide it for the Union's use for the remainder of the war with the Alliance."

Solyss considered this for a moment. Gaining the support of the Trepon sector was his secondary objective in coming on this mission. He had no idea what kind of support the people of the sector had, but he had to guess that at least the people of this world of Okaral had an interest in being free of the Alliance.

"Before I agree, I'll need to know what kind of defenses the Alliance has on Okaral," Solyss replied.

"And you'll need to explain where Renard is and why we aren't speaking to him directly," Gamaly interjected.

After casting a nervous glance at Gamaly, Kueth focused his attention on Solyss. "The planet is protected by a small garrison and one ship in orbit, which rotates out every few weeks but is guarded by a frigate. The garrison is mostly based aboard an orbiting space station, with only a small contingent being on the surface at any one time."

One frigate and a space station, Solyss considered. Depending on the armament of the station, that might be a winnable fight. Even though corvettes were usually no match for a frigate, the *Gallant* had received upgrades he felt made her up to the task.

"You said the ship rotates out every few weeks?" Asheerah asked. "Where do they rotate from?"

Kueth shrugged. "I don't know. Food and resources created on Okaral are sent to the orbiting station. From there, I assume they're sent to another Alliance base, but I have no information on where that is."

Rubbing his cheek, Solyss considered that information. They had expected that there would be an unknown Alliance base elsewhere in the sector. The intelligence Kaars Aerinstar had provided to the Union after defecting from the Alliance had indicated that much of the fighting force from Fourth Fleet lay somewhere in Trepon. But it was a big sector, with most colonized worlds being small and scattered.

He had hoped that the Alliance fleet was scattered as well. The single ship rotating in and out supported that. But the frequency of the rotation might indicate a closer, more concentrated presence.

Finally, Solyss said, "Without that information, it would be foolish to try to free this world right now. We'll agree to make Trepon's freedom part of the eventual peace treaty with the Alliance and to come and liberate Okaral as soon as resources become available. Right now, even if we did free them, we couldn't stay here to ensure they remained that way."

Kueth shook his head emphatically. "No. That's unacceptable. Okaral must be freed *before* you leave, and you must do everything you can to make sure it remains that way."

A feeling of frustration started to work its way through Solyss. From the direction this conversation had gone so far, Kueth didn't have the authority to negotiate—just issue demands. If this trip turned out to be for nothing, he would have put one of the Union's few warships out of action for almost six months and for no gain.

"We seem to keep coming back to this point," Solyss said, not suppressing the annoyance in his voice this time. "It's clear these negotiations cannot continue until we meet directly with Josserand."

"I'm afraid that won't be possible," Kueth said simply.

"Why the hell not?" Solyss growled.

There was silence in the room for a moment. He immediately regretted his outburst but decided not to offer an apology.

After a moment, Kueth leaned back in his seat, his shoulders sagging. "Because Josserand is on Okaral."

Solyss let out a dismissive noise. "So what? Just have him come meet with us here. One frigate can't blockade an entire world."

Kueth sighed. "Okaral is a prison planet. The only transports in and out are Alliance military vessels."

Solyss blinked in surprise. Before he could come to terms with this news, Gamaly let out a boisterous laugh. The sound reverberated through the room. Taken off guard by the sound, Solyss found his annoyance dissipating.

"Renard wants us to break him out of prison? Oh, that's priceless," Gamaly said, still laughing.

A grin spread across Solyss's face, and he let out a chuckle. It was nice to see Gamaly laugh and smile. She had been pretty blue for the entire journey, due, undoubtedly, to missing Gu'od.

Then a dark thought crossed his mind. He turned to look at Kueth, his gaze angry. "This was all an elaborate ruse, wasn't it? Josserand just wants us to break him out of prison and is dangling the *Black Market* as bait. But if he really could gain control of the ship, you would have done it by now in order to free him."

Gamaly stopped laughing long enough to add, "That sounds like Renard."

"No!" Kueth said, his voice frantic. "That's not true! We were planning to seize control of the *Black Market* and use it to free Okaral and the other worlds of Trepon while the Alliance was occupied fighting in Kreogh. We were going to be free again. But then Josserand got captured. He's the only one who has the codes and contacts we'll need to take the ship."

The emotion evident in Kueth's voice brought Solyss up short. Whether or not Josserand truly could gain control of the *Black Market* and would loan it to the Union, Kueth clearly felt strongly about freeing Trepon from the Alliance. He started to wonder if he might need to reassess Kueth.

"Our people don't have anything big enough to take on a frigate. All of our fighters are in Kreogh sector and none of them are hyperspace-capable. They were going to be picked up once we seized the *Black Market*. Then we would have taken Okaral ourselves," Kueth continued. His tone took on a note of desperation. "Please, my family lives on Okaral. They're not criminals and were sent there for a trivial offense. So many of the people down there are innocents. Maybe Josserand can't actually get you the *Black Market*. But you're fighting a war against the Alliance in order to stop things like what happened to my family."

Asheerah grunted. "What a waste of time. I say we throw this waste out of the airlock and get back before we miss all the fighting."

Kueth's words struck at Solyss's heart. Despite the deception, he understood what the man must be going through. He'd had hope for his family, even if it had rested with a fiend like Josserand. Now that hope was gone.

"No," Solyss said. "We're going to help if we can. It's the right thing to do. Plus, if there's still a chance we can salvage something useful out of this mission, we have to take it."

"Thank you," Kueth said, relaxing and casting grateful looks to the three of them.

"But know this," Gamaly said, leaning forward, "if you're still lying to us, if we've wasted our time here, you will regret it."

The look in Gamaly's eyes made Kueth lean back in his seat as far as he could go. It also made Solyss suddenly start to question his assumption that Asheerah was the most dangerous Liw'kel in the room.

Try as he might, Lahkaba could not remember a time he had been more uncomfortable. Even though his fur did a wonderful job of regulating his internal body temperature, it couldn't make up for the extremely uncomfortable temperature the Dotran were maintaining. Plus, they had been sitting in this meeting for hours now, and he hadn't said a word almost the entire time.

At Zoeko's suggestion, he and Valinther had allowed her and Lionell to conduct the negotiations. Many times, he had wanted to say something in response to the Dotran foreign minister but had held himself back. Today's discussions were merely preliminary, anyway. He would have a chance to talk with the others before they needed to make any commitments.

As the talks droned on, Lahkaba contented himself with studying the Dotran representatives. Sceglis Amib, their foreign minister and chief negotiator, had so far shown himself to be the embodiment of the stereotype of Dotran bronze: arrogant, dismissive of others, short-tempered, and with a superior attitude. His companions had acted similarly, at least to his team and the Kowwok servants. They were perfectly deferential to Sceglis and Zoeko.

One of the Kowwok servants came in, offering drinks to everyone. After taking a cup, one of the Dotran delegates found a few stray Kow-wok hairs stuck to the outside. He shouted at the Kowwok in native Dotran—words Lahkaba couldn't understand—sending the servant running from the room. He returned a moment later with a clean glass.

He had always found Zoeko to be fairly arrogant and hard to get along with, and until today, he had never realized how accommodating she usually was. Either as a negotiation tactic, or simply because she was among her own people, Zoeko had risen to new levels of arrogance. Every stubborn stance Sceglis took, she matched. She even treated the Kowwok servants in the same manner the other Dotran did.

The whole scene was difficult to watch. If Lahkaba hadn't been in politics as long as he had, he might have taken Zoeko's change in attitude as genuine, instead of the theater it really was. Still, the longer the discussions dragged on, the worst he felt for sitting there, saying nothing.

"We may be willing to share some of our naval technology with you in exchange for any new tech or tactics you develop during your battles with the Alliance," Sceglis said, drawing Lahkaba's attention back to the discussion.

"That's a most generous offer," Lionell replied hesitantly. Unlike everyone else in the room, the Terran was visibly suffering from the heat. Sweat had soaked his clothes, and it ran down his forehead.

"Excellent. Then we're agreed in principle to share military technology," Sceglis said, his tone flat.

Something about the exchange tickled the back of Lahkaba's mind, but he couldn't tell why. The expansive Dotran military surely had some interesting technology that would be very useful to their fight. The Union had only a few cobbled-together or stolen ships, along with commercially available weapons for their troops.

"Now, back to the matter of integration into the Confederacy . . ." Sceglis said.

"You mean treaty between sovereign nations?" Zoeko countered, her tone dark.

The entire discussion so far had revolved around that core concept. They had come here as an independent government negotiating with another independent government. The Dotran kept trying to bring things back to a discussion about merging the Kreogh sector with the Confederacy.

So far, Zoeko had dismissed every attempt. This time, Sceglis had thought to try to offer something valuable first. A clever tactic, Lahkaba thought.

" . . .'s military command structure, should we come to an agreement," Sceglis said, switching his angle of attack seamlessly. "Our commanders are far more experienced fighting the Alliance than any of yours. We would insist on overall command."

"In naval matters, we may be able to accept that," Lionell said.

"But on the surface of any of our worlds, our commanders must have seniority. If any battles occur outside the Kreogh sector, then we would defer to you," Zoeko added.

Lahkaba didn't want to put any troops under Dotran command, but it made sense. The Union's naval forces were laughable in comparison, and their only commanders with any experience—Maarkean and Davidus—were no longer available. As much as he respected Saracasi and Solyss, neither of them were admiral material.

Sceglis paused a moment before replying, as if seriously considering the matter. Then he nodded. "I believe our two positions are not very far apart. We should be able to work out an agreement here. Perhaps we should end for the day and return to the matter tomorrow?"

Resisting the urge to let out a sigh of relief, Lahkaba stood with the others, keeping his expression neutral. Lionell, though obviously trying just as hard, failed to contain his relief at the prospect of getting out of this stifling room. They exchanged pleasantries with Sceglis and his staff, and then their Kowwok guide, Rathalos, led them out of the room.

Once out of the building and in the ground car that would take them to their housing accommodations, the four of them let out a collective sigh. They cranked the cooling system in the car up to maximum, leaning close to the fans. Even Zoeko appeared to relax at the cool air.

"While I enjoy a good heat, that room was too warm even for my taste. Mirthod is far from the warmest planet and quite humid. I guess I've gotten used to a moister atmosphere and less intense heat. Sceglis used it as a dirty tactic to unsettle us," Zoeko said in response to Lahkaba's look.

Her frankness surprised him. She had never been especially friendly, and after the display in the negotiations, he thought she would revert back to even more aloofness.

"Well, that went nowhere," Valinther complained. "Perhaps Lahkaba and I should return to the ship. We would be just as valuable there, and far more comfortable."

"Nonsense," Zoeko retorted. "I admit I was originally against your presence. But it has actually worked to our advantage. Your inclusion means the Dotran have to treat their Kowwok servants better than usual. That's putting them off balance, just as the heat has done to us."

"This was them treating their servants *better*?" Lahkaba asked in disbelief.

Zoeko gave him a pointed look, and Valinther growled, his tone suggesting personal experience. "Yes. You didn't see any of them get beaten," he said.

Disgusted, Lahkaba forced himself to ignore that. They had a mission to accomplish. Freedom had a price. For him, it meant working with the Dotran. Others would be paying with their lives.

He wasn't sure they weren't getting the better deal.

"Even though we seem far from any agreement, I thought things went reasonably well," Lionell said, breaking the moment of tension that had filled the car. "They keep coming back to the idea of merger into the Confederacy, but they also appear willing to entertain other options. They even offered us some of their military tech."

"Yes, as an attempt to butter us up to accept their plans for a merger," Valinther pointed out.

"Sure, but the offer's been made. We could use some more hardware," Lionell said.

Everyone nodded in agreement with Lionell and then slipped into silence. The car drove down the streets of the capital city, the tall buildings looking like the walls of a shiny canyon around them. Fortunately, the windows were tinted against the glare, allowing Lahkaba to get a good look at the city.

Alongside the streets were busy sidewalks full of people. Awash with color, the crowds stood out even against the bright buildings. Even though he despised them, there was no denying that the Dotran were beautiful creatures, especially mixed together in the bright sunlight.

Coming to a stop at an intersection, Lahkaba got a closer look at the crowds. Mixed in with the brightly colored Dotran walked a fair number of his own people. He had no idea how many Kowwoks lived on Dotra, but it appeared to be more than he had thought. Almost a quarter of the people on the street were Kowwoks.

And every single one of them appeared to be filling some form of service role. Many carried packages while walking behind a Dotran. Others worked as waiters in an outside café. One even carried a mirror that he used to reflect the sunlight directly onto a gold scaled Dotran as she walked down the street.

Turning away from the scene that he had a moment before found beautiful, Lahkaba caught Valinther's eye. The other Kowwok said nothing but gave a small nod, acknowledging the realization Lahkaba had just had. To his surprise, Lahkaba also caught a glimpse of Rathalos, the servant the Dotran had assigned to them, looking at him in the rear-view mirror through the partition between them and the driver compartment. The dark-brown-furred Kowwok's expression seemed to be one of appraisal, though it was only an instant before he shifted his gaze.

The brief moment of companionship with his fellow Kowwok stirred something in Lahkaba. Breaking the silence, he said, "We need to be careful. Instead of focusing on what the Dotran can provide us, we should consider what we'll have to give up to the Dotran."

Valinther and Lionell shared a look between them and then nodded at him. Oblivious to the unspoken meaning of his words, Zoeko said, "Wise words. We have made it clear we'll not join the Confederacy, but there are many things the Dotran could demand instead that would be equally harmful to our Union in the long run. Restrictive trade agreements, exclusivity contracts, or making us dependent on them militarily. We must be cautious."

To himself, Lahkaba tried to figure out how much of his soul he would be willing to trade for the Dotrans' help in winning the war.

Chapter Six

Saracasi had just finished securing the last of the systems in the engine room when the hyperspace timer warning went off. It had been set to alert them at ten minutes before reentry rather than the usual five, since this would be anything other than a usual reentry.

Her preparation work across the ship had been surprisingly minimal. She was still used to *Cutty Sark* being in a perpetual state of partial repair. It reminded her how little time she had been aboard the ship that had once been her home in the last few months. Chavatwor had done amazing work on her, and Fracsid had done a remarkable job of keeping everything in pristine condition.

She left the engine room and ran into Almes and Lei-mey in the cargo bay. The Ronid delegate seemed to be the only one in the small crew who could tolerate the unending advances from the Terran. She almost seemed to enjoy them. That was probably because he was making them at all. Few Terrans or Braz or Liw'kel found anything physically desirable about Ronids.

"We secure down here, Specialist?" Saracasi asked.

"Yes, ma'am," Almes said, then winked. "Everything's tied up good and tight, just like you like it."

Saracasi ignored the man's obvious allusion and headed up the stairs to the command deck. The pair followed her up and through the narrow corridor to the flight deck. The ship's only other occupant, Flight Specialist Sienn'lyn I'fu, waited for them. The young Liw'kel woman sat at the helm controls, her eyes closed and her body relaxed. Saracasi recognized her posture as one of the Ni'jar meditation poses. She had gotten so used to thinking of Sienn'lyn as a pilot, she had forgotten her origins as a Ni'jar acolyte.

"We're ready up here, Captain," Sienn'lyn said, coming instantly out of her trance-like state.

"Delegate, you need to return to the crew cabin now and strap yourself in," Saracasi said, turning back to Lei-mey. "This is going to be a bit bumpy."

"Very well," Lei-mey said, her tone suggesting she wasn't a fan of being ordered around by Saracasi.

Putting Lei-mey's annoyance out of her mind, Saracasi moved onto the flight deck and took her position at the operations station. The hard task—keeping the ship from crashing into anything—would fall to Sienn'lyn. But Saracasi would have to keep the ship in one piece during the descent.

"Would either of you lovely ladies care for a kiss before we face our potential fiery deaths?" Almes asked. He must have believed that his tone was deep and sensual, but Saracasi found it grating. "For luck, of course."

She recalled that Fracsid had seemed apologetic about suggesting Almes for the mission. That Almes annoyed Fracsid said something. She had already decided that Almes had better be as good with the guns as he claimed. Otherwise, she would seriously consider leaving him behind on some lifeless moon.

The annoyed glare Sienn'lyn wore on her face suggested that her pilot felt the same way she did. The Liw'kel was normally reserved with her emotions, much like Gu'od. If she was allowing the frustration to break through her Ni'jar training, it must be severe.

"Take your station, Specialist. If I ever have to remind you again not to sexually harass someone, you might find yourself in a very uncomfortable position," Saracasi said, lacing her tone with as much threat as she could manage.

"Aye, Captain," Almes said. He looked slightly shaken for a second, but then a grin crossed his face, and he winked.

Shaking her head at the futility of the situation, Saracasi turned back to the operations controls. She ran another couple of diagnostics, ensuring everything was working at peak efficiency. The descent would rely on the inertial dampeners and maneuvering thrusters more than anything else. Any major failures with those systems and there would be no recovering.

The timer kept ticking down closer to zero. With only a handful of seconds left, Saracasi looked to Sienn'lyn. "You ready for this, Specialist? If not, we can still hit the override and shoot past Sulas."

"This is my Focus," Sienn'lyn said, as if her mind was elsewhere.

Accepting that as a "yes," Saracasi watched the timer hit zero. As soon as it did, she felt the familiar gut-twisting sensation of reversion from hyperspace. This feeling was quickly replaced by a thrust of pressure on her chest and a sharp reverberation through the deck beneath her.

A cloudy blue sky filled the flight deck windows for an instant. In a blur, it was replaced by a dark brown mountain and then a dark blue sea. The sky returned an instant later.

The ship must be tumbling wildly as it fell through the Sulas sky, Saracasi realized. The pressure continued to press down on her, which meant the inertial dampeners weren't fully compensating. She struggled to fight the inertial forces and reach the operation controls.

"Need inertial systems fixed," Sienn'lyn grunted from beside her.

Saracasi redoubled her efforts, struggling to reinitialize the field. If this simple task was so hard for her, she couldn't imagine what Sienn'lyn must be experiencing while trying to right the descent of the ship. With a final grunt of effort, she toggled the settings, and the pressure on her chest released, replaced by a thrust of force on her back and then her side, and finally nothing but the normal pull of the internal artificial gravity field.

The shifts of gravity, perspective, and pressure left Saracasi feeling a sudden urge to curl up, vomit, and then go to sleep. But outside the window, Sulas was still spinning before them. She forced herself to remain focused on the controls, ready to activate the main engines if Sienn'lyn needed them.

They wanted to avoid using the engines if at all possible, to help minimize their chances of detection—and because a burst from them would be just as likely to plow them into the surface of the planet or rip the ship apart as it would be to stabilize them. That was one part of what made the maneuver so difficult.

Several tense seconds went by while Saracasi watched how much closer the surface of the planet looked each time it passed the window. More and more, the view became filled with greens and browns as they got closer and closer to the ground. She felt increasingly sure she could make out details such as individual trees.

It took her a few passes to realize that while being close enough to the ground to see trees was bad, having enough time to recognize them meant that the spinning was slowing down. By the time she realized that, the sky had become a permanent fixture in the window, a cloud bank floating lazily before them above a low hill—a hill that was no longer getting any bigger.

Saracasi cautiously leaned back in her seat, her heart still beating at a rapid pace. She never wanted to do that again. Behind her, Almes was uncharacteristically silent, and she glanced back to see the Terran still gripping his restraint harness with his eyes squeezed shut. In contrast, Sienn'lyn looked as calm as she had earlier, with a passive look that reminded her of Gu'od.

"Nice work, Sienn," Saracasi said, allowing herself to use Sienn'lyn's familiar name. Turning in her seat, she said to Almes, "My scopes look clear. Yours?"

"Nothing, Captain," Almes replied, his tone professional for a change. "No target locks. No scans. No pursuit."

Saracasi allowed herself a quiet sigh of relief, ordering her heart rate to slow down. "All right, go and get Delegate Darshawn and bring her—"

The door to the flight deck slid open. Lei-mey came through and gave an appreciative nod to Sienn'lyn. "My compliments to the pilot."

Sienn'lyn returned the nod without turning around in her seat, still watching the coastline that they were rapidly approaching. They had arrived near the ocean east of the most populated Emerald continent. Compared to the homeworlds, Sulas's land masses were sparsely populated, but they would be nearing signs of civilization soon.

"All right," Saracasi said, facing Lei-mey. "We're here. Barely, I might add. We've completed our part of the bargain. Now it's your turn. How is this supposed to help me gain authority over the fleet?"

"Not you," Lei-mey said crisply. "We find General Dustlighter and bring him back to take charge of the fleet."

Saracasi blinked. She had never thought about that possibility. She had ruled Zeric out as an avenue of help once he was cut off. Even after Lei-mey had convinced her to come to Sulas, she had still assumed that Zeric was captured, dead, or in hiding. "And how do you expect to find him? The Alliance has recaptured the planetary defense batteries. They either defeated our forces here or Zeric abandoned them. If the latter, we have no idea where he might be hiding. If the former, then he's no more reachable than Maarkean," Saracasi said.

"Oh, Zeric is a survivor. I have no doubt he's still alive. And as for finding him, that's why I had to come. This is my home, after all. I have many contacts here."

The plan was weak—and it was annoying to discover that it involved taking Saracasi down a rank—but they had already come this far. She had to trust that Lei-mey knew what she was doing. Otherwise, she had just risked all their lives for nothing. "Where to?" she finally asked.

"Get us as close to Ba'aar as possible," Lei-mey replied.

"Why Ba'aar?" Saracasi asked. "Doesn't the Union have a stronghold in Chuthor?"

"Yes," Lei-mey answered. "But Zeric is a hockey fan."

Zeric lay stretched out on the couch in his small quarters. It had once been an office for some arena supplier. The former occupant had left the couch, and Zeric had happily accepted the stroke of luck.

A video monitor on one wall showed the hockey game that was going on upstairs. The Ba'aar Razors were behind by two against the Ciread Diamonds. On a few occasions, he'd tried to slip upstairs to watch the games in person, but each time either Ymp or common sense had turned him back.

Reaching out to the small table in the center of the room, Zeric poured himself another glass of whiskey. For a hockey game, he generally preferred beer but had started to really like this whiskey. It took the edge off of sitting around worrying about people much quicker than beer.

As Zeric sipped the whiskey, a rapid banging sounded on his door. Annoyed at the interruption, though also glad to have an excuse to look away from the massacre that was happening to his team, he got up. Staggering a little—he must have been laying there too long—he opened the door to reveal Kumus.

"What is it, Kumus?" Zeric asked, not bothering to hide his annoyance.

Kumus, his face flushed from apparently running here, said, "Sir, we have company."

Immediately, Zeric dropped his glass and grabbed the rifle that leaned against the wall. He checked the power level as a surge of excitement started to pump through him. It would be terrible if the Alliance found their hiding spot, but it would be a good fight.

"No, sir—I'm sorry, sir," Kumus stammered, looking wildly at Zeric's rifle. "Not that kind of company. Delegate Darshawn is here! She got through the blockade to see you!"

Zeric's shoulders slouched. Looking at the rifle for a long moment, he contemplated taking it with him. With a resigned sigh, he set the gun down and picked his glass up off the floor. Lamenting the spilled whiskey now soaked into the carpet, he refilled the glass and then gestured for Kumus to lead him to Lei-mey.

Kumus led them through the maze of maintenance tunnels, finally arriving at a small storage room that still held goods belonging to the arena. In the small room, leaning against the boxes of unused souvenir cups, was Lei-mey Darshawn. Her multifaceted eyes stared at him as he entered, giving Zeric a slight chill. Ronids had that effect on him.

There were several other people in the room he didn't recognize, but when he caught sight of the red-haired ponytail dangling from the back of one Braz woman's head, he felt a giant smile spread across his face. Ignoring Lei-mey, he went straight over to her. "Casi!" Zeric said, genuine affection in his tone.

He embraced her, which she was clearly not ready for. Sensing the eyes of everyone else in the room on him, he let go after a second. It generally wasn't appropriate for a general to hug a subordinate, but he didn't exactly care. "Casi," Zeric said again, his tone quieter, "I wish I had good news about Maark. We've tried to find some information about him but haven't found anything. If he made it off *Defiant Glory*, he's likely a prisoner."

Saracasi gave him a weak smile in return. "Thank you, but I already know he's a prisoner. The DeeGee managed to escape after she was captured. Based on your warning to Fracsid, we assume that was orchestrated by Commander Brieni. But Maarkean and Lohcja were removed and taken prisoner before the ship escaped."

"Damn. He's not going to be easy to get to," Zeric said, his mind now racing. Confirmation that Maarkean was alive reignited his interest in staging a rescue operation. He would have to get Ymp on that. Now that they knew where he was, maybe they could slip aboard like they did with *Gallant* or find someone sympathetic to the rebels.

Turning his attention back to Saracasi, he said, "So Brieni did turn out to be the traitor?"

Saracasi gave him a dark frown. "We arrested him based on your warning and the suspicious way *Defiant Glory* escaped. I assumed you had some clear evidence."

Sheepishly, Zeric shook his head. "No, just a suspicion. Ice Company turned on us during the battle. Apparently, they were hired by the Alliance. I had seen Firek and Davidus talking shortly before the attack."

"That's your evidence?" Saracasi exclaimed.

Zeric shrugged apologetically. "It was the middle of a battle. Thought it would be best to warn someone at the time."

As he and Saracasi talked, an odd noise came from behind them. It sounded like a cross between a cough and whistle. Turning, Zeric saw Lei-mey standing there, looking agitated.

"Ah, Lei-mey, how good to see you again," Zeric said with fake sincerity.

"Thank you, General. I'm pleased to find you alive and well," Lei-mey said, her fake sincerity much better than his.

After the Battle of Perth, Zeric had thought that he and Lei-mey had come to an understanding of each other. After all, he had saved her life on several occasions that day. But their few encounters since had featured nothing but a cold shoulder from her.

"How did you get through the blockade?" Zeric asked, hoping for some good news.

"Through the heroic efforts of Major Ocaitchi and crew of *Cutty Sark*," Lei-mey answered. "Unfortunately, as I understand it, it was not an action that should be repeated often."

"Atmospheric jump," Saracasi added.

Shivering at that, Zeric said, "What could be so important that you would risk that to get here?"

"We came to find you," Lei-mey answered. "And to bring you back to take command of the army."

With a confused look on his face, Zeric raised an eyebrow at Lei-mey. "That's what I'm doing here."

"No, cut off as you are here, you're unable to perform the functions of your new position effectively," Lei-mey explained. "While I wish to see the operation here on Sulas succeed, your skills will be better used overseeing the rest of the sector."

"We need you, Zeric," Saracasi added. "We have no leader, and the Alliance is quickly reasserting control across the sector. They've already sent forces to Enro, Dantyne, and Mirthod. That only leaves Kol and Cardine relatively free, and Cardine is still fighting a ground war with the forces already there. I have plans for ways the navy can help, but I don't have the authority to command any more ships. But you do."

For Zeric, getting off Sulas had a lot of appeal, though the thought embarrassed even him. It would be tantamount to running away. While he had no hang-ups about making a strategic retreat when necessary, running away was different. "Well, I'm a general, aren't I?" Zeric mumbled. "I can promote people on the battlefield. So, Saracasi, you're an admiral or something."

Lei-mey shook her head. "We established the Union military based on the Alliance uniform code. You only have the authority to promote Major Ocaitchi to commander and give her the temporary rank of commodore. Only Congress can promote anyone to a permanent flag rank."

"Fine, then I do that. Congratulations, Commander/Commodore," Zeric grumbled. "You're now in command of all naval forces. And marine and army, too. Now you don't need me."

Saracasi smiled and gave an odd look to Lei-mey. Surprisingly, she didn't object to the promotion. Last time he had seen her, Saracasi had shown no interest in fighting, obsessed as she was with fixing ships. In truth, he wasn't sure she could do the job he had just thrown at her. But every other time he had tried to get someone to accept a leadership position in place of him, they had said no.

"That only achieves one of my goals in coming here," Lei-mey said, and then her speech became passionate. "But we still need you. Commodore Ocaitchi will do well with her plans for counter-attacks against the Alliance, but we still need an overall commander. A leader the people respect. Someone to rally the morale of the troops.

"Congress could appoint a new commander, but they would be an unknown. The battle during the invasion of Sulas cost us two well-known and respected leaders. You're the only one left. You need to be seen by the population so they know the fighting is not over and that we can still win."

This was not the first time Lei-mey had tried to use him as a symbol. The last time, before the war had even begun, he had run away as fast as possible. He had never wanted to be a symbol and hadn't wanted to become involved in her rebellion against the Alliance. But now he was already hip deep in the rebellion.

Would it really be that bad? he wondered. Not having to live in the damp basement of a sports arena, constantly fearing the Alliance could show up at any moment, sending people off to fight and die but not being able to go himself? He wouldn't have to see their faces as they left, eager for the fight, and then not see their faces when they failed to return.

After a moment of consideration, Zeric shook his head. "No, my place is here."

Lei-mey clicked her mandibles in a sign of frustration. "I had hoped I wouldn't have to resort to this." She removed a datapad from her pocket and brought a picture up on the screen. When she handed it to Zeric, he saw the image of a Terran baby. He looked at it a second and then shrugged his shoulders, confused.

"This is your daughter," Lei-mey said.

"Yeah, so I apparently have a daughter," Zeric said as he strode into Gu'od's quarters.

Kneeling on the floor in the middle of a meditation ritual, Gu'od remained still. The only indication that he had heard Zeric came in the form of a slight twitch of his antennae.

Taking that as a sign to continue, Zeric told the rest of the story, pacing in a circle around Gu'od. "Apparently, Ceta got pregnant from our little fling after we rescued you from Olan. You remember her, right? Beautiful girl. Lei-mey's adopted sister. Helped us bust you guys out," Zeric rambled. "Well, now she's on Irod. Lei-mey wants me to go back there to be her puppet commander of the Union army and a father.

"Oh, yeah, Casi and Sienn'lyn are here. They brought Lei-mey down here through the blockade. Something I don't think I can ever forgive them for."

Zeric continued to pace in silence for a moment before Gu'od said, "Did they mention Gamaly?"

"Right . . . sorry, I, uh, forgot to ask," Zeric said, feeling ashamed for not thinking of his friend.

Standing up from the floor in a fluid motion, Gu'od locked a stare onto Zeric which made him uncomfortable. It wasn't a new feeling, but it made him very glad Gamaly wasn't here.

"You didn't think to take precautions?" Gu'od asked.

"I didn't exactly have access to a pharmacy," Zeric grumbled. "I figured she was on birth control."

"Was she?"

"I guess not."

Silence returned while Zeric fumed. He hadn't been on Irod much, but he had been there before the invasion on Sulas. He had also seen Lei-mey on a few occasions. Yet no one had bothered to tell him he had a kid. Granted, he hadn't even tried to look Ceta up while he'd been on Irod, and, in fact, he hadn't known she was still there until now.

As if mirroring his thoughts, Gu'od asked, "Why is she telling you this now?"

"Lei-mey wants me to leave Sulas with her and return to Irod. She says it's so I can do my job as the Union military commander, which I can't do while I'm cut off down here. She's right about that, but I think it's just so she can use me as a symbol and her puppet commander," Zeric speculated.

"You don't think she's actually concerned for her sister and niece?" Gu'od asked.

"I'm sure she is, but that has nothing to do with it. If she thought I should be involved with the baby at all, she would have told me months ago. Hell, it's been a year and a half, almost, since I last saw Ceta," Zeric said. "No, she's doing this to manipulate me."

"Perhaps you should let her," Gu'od said, bringing Zeric up short. "You've complained that you're useless here. Ymp won't let you go on any raids, and Minister Kantor and Jairyd have effectively taken over. Maybe it's time to go where you can do more good. For your family and for the war."

The words sank in. "His family." The closest thing to a family he had had in recent years had been Gu'od and Gamaly. He had never had a close relationship with his parents or siblings and hadn't even spoken to them since he was discharged from the Alliance marines.

But now he had a daughter—his own flesh and blood. Did he have a responsibility to her? To Ceta? He had always liked Ceta but knew he'd never loved her. She hadn't told him about the girl, so would she even want him around? Should that matter?

He also had a responsibility to the troops under his command. Would going to Irod be abandoning them, or would it be doing his duty by taking command? He didn't like Lei-mey using him, but if raising morale and recruiting more troops helped them win the war, wouldn't that be the best thing?

All of these questions raced through his head. He hated moral co-nundrums, which was why he preferred a straight-up fight. If some-one was trying to kill you, there was no moral question—you just had to try to kill them right back. Responsibility could be a real bitch.

"What do you think I should do?" Zeric finally asked, his tone pa-thetic and pleading.

"It's my intention to use this opportunity to return to Kol to be with Gamaly and our child. My duty is clear. I suggest you do the same.

I know I would feel better knowing you were out of harm's way," Gu'od said.

Reluctantly, Zeric nodded. Gu'od was the next best thing he had to a conscience. Yet deciding to leave didn't fill him with relief.

Chapter Seven

The journey from Sulas to Irod was not a long one by galactic travel standards, but it still left Zeric with very little to do for several days. When they arrived, he had had plenty of time to drive himself crazy with all the possibilities of how this coming meeting would play out.

For once, Lei-mey cooperated when he asked for Ceta's address, simply telling him where to find her instead of making it a complicated negotiation. Of course, she had been the one to travel all the way to Sulas specifically to bring him back here, but he still wouldn't have put it past her to hold out on him just to be annoying.

The home Ceta lived in was a small, prefabricated structure, like most of the buildings in Lost Hope. Ever since Zeric had delivered the prison refugees here, the small town had seen a population explosion. First the refugees who didn't want to return home had settled here, then the military trainees had arrived, followed by support people, families, and other refugees.

If Irod's location hadn't been kept secret, being divulged only to trusted ship captains, Zeric felt sure the small, dark moon would have been overrun with refugees fleeing the fighting on the other worlds. Granted, even though it was technically a moon, Irod was not much smaller than most habitable planets, so there was a lot of untapped terrain for settlements. As it was, the population explosion was contained to Lost Hope.

Zeric paced outside the small home for several minutes. For some reason, he never felt courageous unless someone was shooting at him. He only had to face a woman he'd slept with and the baby they'd made—something people had been doing since the beginning of time. But, at the moment, he would rather have stormed an Alliance base.

Taking a deep breath, he stepped up to the door and knocked. When the door didn't immediately swing open, he started to turn away, deciding that Ceta must not be home. But before he could completely back away from the door, it opened.

Standing there, looking far less lovely than the last time he had seen her, was Ceta Darshawn. The former stripper had her hair in disarray and wore some of the least attractive, rumpled, old clothes possible. Supported in her left arm, resting against her hip, was a small baby girl.

The baby had small wisps of blond hair, like her mother. She was happily chewing on her fingers and staring curiously at Zeric. Her cheeks were chubby, and a stream of drool ran down her hand and chin.

Despite what he'd heard some new fathers say, Zeric didn't feel an immediate sense of love at the sight of his daughter. To be sure, she was pretty cute, even with the drool. But he felt no more connection to her than any other baby he'd ever seen.

For her part, Ceta stared at him, her eyes wide and her mouth slightly open. She didn't say anything, just continued to stare at him for a moment.

Feeling uncomfortable, Zeric tried a smile but felt it came off rather weak. "Um, hi," he finally said.

"What are you doing here?" Ceta asked in reply.

"Your sister told me about the baby."

"Damn her," Ceta growled. "I didn't want you find out."

Zeric blinked in surprise. "Wait, what? She came to Sulas to tell me and bring me back here. I assumed you asked her to."

"No, I didn't want you to know until after the war," Ceta replied.

"Why not?"

A neighbor opened her front door a crack to peer at the pair of them as their voices began to rise. Grabbing Zeric's arm, Ceta dragged him inside the house and closed the door. The main room was a mess of burp clothes, toys, and other things. Most of the walking space was consumed by a couch, a baby swing and a playmat covered in toys.

Ceta set the baby down on the mat, and the baby immediately grabbed one of the toys to replace her fingers in her mouth. Turning back toward Zeric, Ceta glared at him with her hands on her hips. "You have enough distractions on your plate with this war. You don't need a baby added to the mix," she declared. "Besides, I'm quite capable of taking care of her on my own."

"I never doubted that," Zeric said quickly. He did have his doubts about how good of a mother Ceta would make, but those were far fewer than his doubts about how good of a father he would make. Changing the subject, he asked, "What's her name?"

"Ciara."

"Ciara," Zeric repeated. "Pretty." He stared down at the little girl, unsure what else to do. She continued to randomly grab toys and stuff them in her mouth before dropping them. Then she picked up two toys and banged them together.

"Oh, I got something for her," Zeric said, remembering. He pulled a small rattle out of his pocket, and when Ceta nodded, he bent down and held it out to Ciara. She immediately grabbed it. After the obligatory taste test, she started shaking it around, amused by the sound.

"So, what now?" Zeric asked. "I know you didn't want to tell me, but that's kind of behind us now."

"Well, that depends on you," Ceta replied. "I knew what I was doing when I slept with you. I may have been consumed by excitement after the rescue, but I did do it. Aside from some financial support, I won't expect anything from you."

"Financial support?" Zeric blurted.

"As the head of the military, I'm sure you can afford to send some money to support your daughter. My body isn't exactly in the best shape to return to my old career," Ceta said. "But if you don't want to be involved beyond that, I completely understand."

"I thought you didn't even want to tell me, and now you're asking for money?" Zeric said, annoyed.

"Forget about the money for now," Ceta said with a sigh. "Winning this war is far more important. I can get by. The people here have been more than generous. Before Ciara was born, I found some work helping out on the farms, and I've got financial support from the city government until she's a year old. We're doing fine."

Zeric's head started spinning. At first, he had been confident that Lei-mey was manipulating him, then he had started to think Ceta might actually need help. Then she claimed to be doing fine but then started asking for money. Now she claimed to be fine again. He had no idea what was going on, what was expected of him, or who was trying to manipulate him into doing what.

"I just don't know what to do." Zeric slouched down to the floor, feeling defeated. He looked again at the baby, and something about the sight of her made him suddenly start confessing, "I never wanted a kid, but I also never wanted to be a deadbeat dad. I want to do the right thing for you, for Ciara, and for the Union. But all I can think about is just running away."

Squatting down beside him, Ceta put her hand on his cheek, a slight frown of sympathy on her face. "This is why I didn't want to tell you. We're fine, really. Knowing my sister, she told you because it serves her interests. While that may seem cruel, her intentions are always for the best of others. First Sulas, and now the Union. So if bringing you here helps in some way, then I'm glad you're here."

Ceta sat down completely and then picked up Ciara. She held the baby out to Zeric. For a moment, he stared at the child, unsure what to do. He took her hesitantly and then held her up to get a good look. She laughed and smiled at him.

Maybe this won't be so bad, he thought, unable to hold back a smile in return.

When the shuttle door slid open, revealing the hangar deck of *Defiant Glory*, Saracasi found Jerik and Fracsid waiting for her. The two men looked relieved to see her, which she couldn't blame them for. When she had left for Sulas, she had half expected not to be coming back.

As she started down the ramp, Jerik straightened into a stance of attention and then shouted, "Commander *Defiant Glory*, arriving."

He immediately snapped a salute. An uneasy and uneven wave washed over the crewmembers who were working on the hangar deck. Some snapped to attention and saluted, and some just straightened up slightly, while others just looked confused. Standing beside Jerik, Fracsid looked caught off guard but tried to emulate Jerik's stance.

Maarkean hadn't instructed the officers on proper military etiquette. Davidus, however, had made a point of training them on these kinds of formal ceremonies and procedures whenever he could. During his time in command of *Defiant Glory*, he had drilled certain protocols into the crew.

Saracasi wasn't sure how she felt about the uneven response from the crew. On one hand, she didn't much care for the pomp and circumstance most militaries had. Considering the situation the Union military found itself in, focusing on military ceremony felt like an unnecessary waste of time and resources. However, she also understood the importance of tradition and ceremony to build a sense of esprit de corp, which was especially important for the Union. A little ceremony could be what made the difference between them being a legitimate military and a band of rebels.

Deciding to play along, if for no other reason than to not insult Jerik and Fracsid, once she reached the end of the ramp, she returned the salute. "Permission to come aboard."

An awkward silence hung in the air for a moment as she waited for Fracsid's reply. It took a nudge from Jerik to remind him that, as the senior officer left in command, it was him Saracasi was addressing.

"Of course," Fracsid said, fumbling. "Permission granted, Major Ocaitchi . . . Captain Ocaitchi . . ."

Saracasi grimaced slightly—not at Fracsid's stumbling, but at the confusing nature of it all. With the promotion Zeric had given her, things were even more confusing now.

Trying to recover from his own awkwardness, Fracsid spoke first, his voice more confident than before. "How was your trip?"

"Far more effective than I expected it would be," Saracasi answered, stepping away from the ramp.

Behind her, Sienn'lyn disembarked from the shuttle and, after a quick nod from Saracasi and Jerik, headed for the hangar's exit. Earlier, Zeric had requested that Sienn'lyn remain with him and Gu'od, and knowing how useful a combat-capable Ni'jar would be, Saracasi had been prepared to allow it. To her surprise, however, both Sienn'lyn and Gu'od had protested, citing something about how Sienn'lyn's Focus was to fly.

Once Sienn'lyn was away, Saracasi allowed Jerik and Fracsid to lead her off the hangar. The once-cavernous cargo containers of the converted mining ship now felt small and crowded. Split in half, with another deck below them used for launch and retrieval of fighter craft, the hangar was crowded with fighters and supplies. The shuttle she had arrived on still rested on the elevator, there being no room to move it anywhere else. One corner of the deck lay hidden behind a temporary screen, making the room feel even smaller. Sounds of machinework rang across the metal floor and walls, making conversation difficult, if not impossible.

As they walked the corridors of the ship to the officer quarters, Saracasi filled the others in on her adventure on Sulas. "We were able to find General Dustlighter and bring him back with us. So the command issue has been solved. Congress won't see any need to find a replacement now."

"That's good news. Though I'm surprised the general agreed to be taken out of a combat zone. He always struck me as someone who likes to lead from the front," Jerik said.

Saracasi smiled at that. She knew Zeric well enough to know he had a strong self-preservation instinct. Not to say that he was a coward—far from it—but given the opportunity to get away from people shooting at him, he had taken it. She was glad others appeared unaware of that character trait.

"General Kil'dare is still there and a Sulas native," Saracasi answered. "General Dustlighter understood that his responsibility lay here."

"Did he agree to your plan, then?" Fracsid asked.

"More or less," Saracasi said. "He's promoted me to commander and made me acting commodore of all naval forces. We'll begin the space portion of the plan immediately. Ground deployment may follow once Zeric feels confident in the readiness of the remaining troops and once we have more troop transports."

"All fighters stand ready," Jerik said confidently. "We've been conducting combat drills since your departure. They were raw, but the fight over Kol toughened them up. Now they're ready to fight."

"Good, we're going to need them," Saracasi replied. "How is La'ari's special project coming?"

"She's almost ready," Fracsid answered. "There's not much more she can do until the cutters are ready."

"Good," Jerik grumbled. "That mess is taking up almost a third of the hangar space. We've had to leave half the fighters in the launch bay."

The trio arrived at Saracasi's quarters, and she led them inside. She removed the civilian jacket she had been wearing since Sulas and went to pull a fresh uniform out of her closet. Unconcerned with the presence of the two men, Saracasi began changing. Since the humiliating experience of being stripped naked while at Olan prison, she found nudity didn't really bother her.

"Any reports from the other worlds?" Saracasi asked while stripping off her civilian clothes.

For his part, Fracsid tried to look embarrassed and stared at the wall. "I sent gunships on scouting missions to Enro and Dantyne, both worlds we've previously lost contact with. There are Alliance task forces in the orbits of both worlds, just like we suspected. We can assume reinforcements were on the ground, but neither scout was able to get close enough for a detailed scan."

"How many ships?" Saracasi asked.

"At least three each," Fracsid answered. "They weren't able to do a full orbit, so we can expect more on the opposite side of the planet. Both had an escort carrier and a corvette."

"So, no heavy guns spotted," Saracasi said, referring to cruisers, frigates, and battle carriers.

"Not that we saw," Fracsid said. "Mr. Aerinstar feels Admiral Sartori will keep her main forces over Ailleroc and Sulas until she's ready to move on Cardine or Kol."

"What's his assessment of the Alliance's total forces?" Saracasi asked, slipping into her uniform coveralls and relieving Fracsid of the need to look away.

"He estimates that the Alliance has no more than fifty capital ships in the sector. Most come from the 4th Fleet, with a minimum of six having traveled with the MEF that arrived. Those would mostly be heavies—cruisers, at least one battle carrier, and frigates. Plus, of course, the local defense cutters from Sulas and Ailleroc, which he didn't include in his estimate.

"The good news is that, out of that potential fifty, we've already destroyed one cruiser and one escort carrier, stolen one corvette, and damaged two corvettes and one cruiser. The cruiser we damaged over Ailleroc was months ago, though, so we can expect her to be operational again."

Saracasi paused from pulling on her boots to look up. "That's twelve percent of her potential forces damaged and six percent completely lost."

She had always viewed the Alliance fleet as gargantuan. Which, if put together, it was. The entire Alliance navy consisted of several hundred warships. But those were spread out across eight sectors of space. Most were kept close to the main worlds or the systems that bordered the Dotran Confederacy and the Camari Republic.

"Or more," Fracsid said. "Fifty was his upper estimate."

"That's just the capital ships, though," Jerik said, his tone dire. "We've barely scratched their complement of star fighters. We took out a squadron over Kol and estimates from the Battle of Sulas put the Alliance fighter losses between one and two squadrons. But with two battle carriers and several escort carriers, the Alliance has at least ten more. And that's just the mobile ones. Ailleroc and Sulas both have several defense squadrons."

Fracsid frowned at Jerik. "Don't be so negative."

"I'm just being practical," Jerik replied. "We have two aboard the DeeGee. Chavatwor has managed to build, borrow, or piece together another one back on Kol, but their pilots don't have any experienced staff to train them. Just Lieutenant Ernebee, who's also managing the planet's defenses and *Audacious*."

"One problem at a time," Saracasi said. "We need to focus on pushing the Alliance back and reopening access to Enro and Dantyne's resources and people. Above all, we need to show the Alliance they can't take our worlds without a fight."

Standing up, Saracasi grabbed the jacket she had worn aboard. She pulled a small case out of the pocket. Inside, she revealed two ranks emblems. Instead of the two triangles pointed at a central pip, like Fracsid wore and like had been on her uniform, the emblem had a second set of triangles. These were vertical but also pointed at the central pip, forming a complete cluster.

She had debated whether it was proper to wear the rank emblems of a commodore, since her position was technically temporary, but Zeric had assured her that a brevet position carried the full authority and responsibility of the rank. It would be proper to wear the emblems.

Removing the major emblems from her collars, she tossed them to Jerik before pinning the commodore emblems in their place. "Congratulations, Major Needa. You're the new commander of the *Defiant Glory*. I recommend Sienn'lyn for a promotion as CAG."

Looking surprised at the sudden promotion, probably given their history, Jerik took a moment before nodding. "She's our best pilot. Not much leadership experience, but, then, none of the others have much, either."

"It's your call," Saracasi forced herself to say. She had made this decision out of necessity, but now that it was made, she had to trust Jerik to do the job she was giving him.

Jerik just nodded, and she continued, "Signal the captains of the cutters that I'd like to meet with them later today. I need to inform them of the change in orders and get them ready. Have Lieutenant Coramont join me as well.

"Major Relis, *Cutty Sark* is yours again. She's on the surface of Irod under Almes's watchful eye," Saracasi said, unable to keep the complete disgust out of her voice as she mentioned Almes. "Prepare one ship from your squadron to escort General Dustlighter to Cardine. They'll also be delivering orders to the cutters there."

"Aye, Commodore," Jerik and Fracsid both replied once she made it clear that the meeting was over.

The two men left the room, and Saracasi took a calming breath. She had gotten her wish and was now in charge of the navy. Zeric had been more than happy to hand responsibility for dealing with the Alliance over to her for the time being.

She caught a glimpse of herself in the mirror. The rank emblems on her collar suddenly looked huge. For the first time in a while, she thought about how young she was—not yet thirty. For the last several years, she had been a smuggler aboard a small freighter. Before that, she had failed to complete her university studies. What right did she have to command even a team of engineers, much less an entire navy?

Regardless of the insanity of the idea, she now had to face that responsibility.

Chapter Eight

Solyss waited impatiently at the command station on the *Gallant's* bridge. The timer on the hyperspace clock ticked down at an alarmingly fast pace. When it reached zero, the battle would begin.

Even though this wouldn't be the first time he had been in a battle aboard *Gallant*, it would be the first time since the upgrades and the first time for the crew. And it would also be the first time they'd engaged an arguably superior enemy. The brief battle over Sulas had been corvette vs. corvette—two ships inept at fighting other capital ships. Now, he would be engaging a frigate—a warship specifically designed to kill ships like *Gallant*.

As he watched the timer, Solyss couldn't help but look down at the tactical display. A tiny fleck of something dark brown on the glass had caught his attention the moment he had given the order to engage the hyperdrive. His sense of propriety had kept him from rubbing at the fleck to see what it was, but his imagination had no doubt.

When he had stormed aboard this ship and taken it from the Alliance, her former captain had been standing right where he was now. And he had shot the man. He felt no guilt over the action. It was war, after all, and the captain was the enemy. But he couldn't help but think that small brown fleck had once been a drop of the former captain's blood. Was his noticing it now a sign of something?

Trying to shake the feeling, Solyss instead berated himself for his loss of attention. He was a major in the Union navy, commander of this ship, and a member of the legendary Novastar family. Of course he would survive this mission.

His only mistake had been not making a micro-jump from their reconnaissance position in the system. He hated micro-jumps, thinking them hard on personnel and equipment. So, instead, he had opted to jump five minutes out from the planet of Okaral, and then jump back in, giving the ship and crew time to recover from the effects of hyperspace.

Fortunately, the timer reached zero, and he had no more time to dwell on the brown fleck or anything else. He stood up a little straighter, trying to force as much confidence into his demeanor as possible. The crew needed to know he knew this plan would work.

"XO," Solyss said, keeping his voice level, "launch Operation Mirage."

From her station, Tess nodded and began issuing orders. Solyss trusted her to do her job. He had to prepare himself for his next part.

As expected, the operations officer, Chief Operations Specialist Celay Dar'su, announced they were being hailed after less than a minute. Solyss listened as the Liw'kel told the Alliance frigate and space station that they were also an Alliance warship, here on a special mission.

Also as expected, her message failed to completely persuade them. Fortunately, between them actually having once been an Alliance corvette and Dar'su's faking of a valid identification code, the frigate didn't immediately blow them out of the sky. Instead, they requested to speak to the ship's commander.

Solyss keyed the comm switch at his terminal, activating his headset. "This is *Gallant* Actual. Go ahead, *Tornado*."

The sound coming into his ear was crystal clear, perfectly relaying the gruff voice of the frigate's commander. "Captain, I have no record of your mission or orders to expect you. What are you doing here?"

"Special operations assignment, Captain," Solyss replied, trying to sound like just another Alliance naval officer. "We're here to retrieve one of your prisoners. I cannot reveal any more details than that."

"Spec Ops, eh? That would explain some of the irregularities our sensors are showing. Our data lists the *Gallant* as an ordinary corvette on guard duty in Kreogh Sector. But you're clearly not a standard configuration."

Solyss genuinely smiled at that. "No, we're most definitely not your regular corvette."

On the tactical display, Solyss saw the icon representing their cargo shuttle move away from the *Gallant* and head toward the space station. They had dropped out of hyperspace close to the station, and the transit would take only a few minutes. The frigate had begun moving on an intercept course for them.

"Now, Captain, it has been a long journey and we have another equally long one ahead of us. If you could see to having the prisoner brought up to the station quickly to meet my shuttle, I would be in your debt," Solyss said.

"I'll see what I can do, Captain," the frigate commander said. "But we're still waiting to receive your official orders. Until we can verify their authenticity, we can't let your shuttle dock or make any prisoner transfers."

"Of course," Solyss said. "Transmitting them now."

Without the ability to acquire official Alliance orders, this was where their ruse would start to fall apart. Their appearance as an Alliance ship had kept the frigate from firing on them the moment they entered orbit, but appearances weren't enough. Coded orders and proper identification codes were designed specifically to prevent someone from doing what they were trying to do.

Fortunately, Solyss hadn't expected it to work. As he watched the holographic tactical display, the cargo shuttle crossed the PNR—point of no return. That meant the shuttle was too far away to recover before the frigate could engage, but it also meant that the shuttle had gotten close enough to its destination to begin the next phase.

Turning toward his XO, Solyss said, "Begin Phase Two."

At his words, Tess ordered the helm to change course, moving them away from the station at max acceleration. This prompted the frigate to begin accelerating in response. The frigate's commander began barking at them to change course and return to their previous position.

As soon as the frigate began accelerating, Solyss switched his comm channel over to another frequency. "Isaxo, you're go."

The icon representing the cargo shuttle expanded as Isaxo and his three other fighters broke away from the shuttle's sensor shadow and began accelerating toward the frigate. Solyss allowed himself to smile as he imagined what the frigate's commander must be thinking. One moment, there had been a clunky cargo shuttle—the next, there were four rapidly approaching fighters.

At the same time, the shuttle accelerated toward the station. It had required precise timing, but after only another moment, the shuttle was inside the station's shield perimeter and slamming itself hard against the station's hull. Solyss then pushed the shuttle out of his mind. The fate of the marines aboard was now in Asheerah's hands.

Isaxo's four fighters accelerated toward the *Tornado*, aiming for the frigate's vulnerable engines. With luck, they could pull off the same trick Solyss had used against the cruiser over Ailleroc: using the destabilization effect of the engines to penetrate the shields. If they could disable the frigate with a rapid barrage, this mission might be over quickly.

Unfortunately, the frigate captain appeared to take the approach of armed fighters as a bigger threat than the cruiser captain had. The frigate immediately shut down its main engines. Instead of using a continuous burn, they fired in short, high-energy bursts. This slowed their acceleration significantly, but it also stabilized the aft shields.

Had Solyss been attempting to flee, this would have allowed him to get away. But his goal was not to get away from the frigate, but merely to draw him far enough away from the station that the station's guns would not be a threat. As the frigate slowed and started to turn back toward the fighters, Solyss saw they hadn't quite achieved that goal.

"Helm, reverse thrust. Keep us in weapons range of the frigate. Tactical, prepare a barrage of fire at bearing three three mark two one nine. Full spread. Stand by for my order," Solyss ordered. He watched the sensor display for a moment. "Fire."

The frigate started to turn, angling itself along a new heading. As it did so, Isaxo's squadron flashed across it and zoomed past. With no more enemies behind it, the frigate accelerated again, following the fighters, and ran right into the barrage of fire from all four of the *Gallant*'s main neutron blaster cannons.

Though not as well armed as the frigate, the *Gallant* had four neutron blaster cannons instead of the standard two. They had removed her primary MKPD (mass kinetic point defense) flak turrets. Those weapons were deadly efficient at destroying small fighter craft, but ineffective against capital ships. Their ammo also took up a lot of space aboard.

In order to make room for more supplies and the marine contingent Asheerah was currently using to board the space station, they had removed those guns. In their place, two more neutron blaster cannons had been installed, doubling her effective power. Despite being able to tell that the *Gallant* had been modified, the frigate's commander had evidently missed the firepower upgrade. Otherwise, he wouldn't have been so focused on the fighters.

"Several direct hits," Dar'su reported. "Reading depletion in the *Tornado*'s forward shields—down to 80%."

Solyss smiled. "Tactical, continue barrage. Helm, move us closer."

Moving the *Gallant* closer to the frigate was a calculated risk. Closer meant they had better odds of scoring hits, but it meant the same thing for the frigate. Sudden vibrations in the floor told Solyss that those hits had started.

"Forward shields down to 85%," Dar'su reported.

"Reduce power to aft shield, reinforce forward shield regeneration," Tess ordered. Solyss had given her the role of managing the ship's systems while he concentrated on maneuvering and weapon fire.

"Ion Squadron, come about and prepare for another strafing run from behind us," Solyss said, giving orders to Isaxo's squadron.

The two big ships continued to close on each other, unleashing deadly waves of energy across the empty space in between. As the *Gallant* passed the frigate, they started to receive fire from the space station as well. Fortunately, due to the long distance and the need for careful aim to avoid hitting the frigate, those shots were limited.

"Come about, full burn," Solyss ordered. He risked putting his vulnerable aft section toward the station—with the weakened shields and then engaging the engines, it gave the station an excellent target.

"Shield weakening, below 60%," Dar'su reported.

"We're losing power to gun three," Wes Lar, the ship's gun chief, reported.

Solyss registered and then pushed those updates aside. Tess would handle them. He had to figure out a way to finish off the frigate before the damage to them became severe.

"Ion Squadron, begin strafing run and then immediately reverse and fly in pattern with us," Solyss ordered.

Bracketed by the *Gallant* and the fighters, the frigate was weakening but managing to hold its shields steady. As the fighters passed over the frigate, peppering her with a barrage of blaster shots all along her hull, Solyss unleashed another full spread from the *Gallant*'s guns. As soon as Ion Squadron had passed, they reversed their engines, redirecting their flight path back toward the frigate.

The sudden combination of fire from only a single vector proved enough to penetrate the frigate's depleted shields. Dar'su's voice had a triumphant tone as she reported that the frigate's forward shields were down and their main gun batteries disabled.

Solyss allowed himself a brief smile before he turned to Tess to find out the final tally from the battle. No fight came without a cost. His mind had been focused on fighting the ship, registering only information that was relevant to that.

"Damage report," he asked.

"One neutron cannon and one plasma turret disabled. Forward armor depleted in several locations, minor structural damage to the bow, hull breach in the wardroom galley. Minor damage to docking port two. Fuel reserves depleted 10%," Tess reported.

"Casualties?" Solyss asked, not wanting to hear the answer.

"No fatalities," Tess said straight off, relieving his main concern. "Dr. When reports that three crew suffered severe plasma burns when the plasma turret was disabled. Five other crew are in sickbay for various minor injuries."

Solyss nodded. Plasma burns were no minor injury, and those three crew would have a difficult road ahead of them. But overall, they had weathered the fight well.

Turning away from Tess, Solyss reactivated his comm. "Ion Leader, report the status of your squadron."

An uncomfortably long period of static came before Isaxo finally responded, "We lost Ion Three. I'm not reading any emergency beacon. I don't think he managed to eject."

After the relatively good news from Tess, this information hit Solyss like a sucker punch. The PF-56s that Ion Squadron flew weren't top-of-the-line fighters. They had minimal shielding. Small and light, they used their low mass for their one advantage: maneuverability, with rapid acceleration. But one solid blast from the main guns of a capital ship would likely do them in.

"Ops," Solyss said, recovering himself, "begin scanning for an emergency beacon."

The bridge crew all turned their heads at his order. They would all be just as concerned as he was about a lost fighter pilot. Even with the marine contingent and pilots, the total crew aboard was less than seventy. Ion Three was Ardeth Masaque. None of the crew were faceless or nameless.

While Dar'su scanned, Solyss couldn't help but rethink the battle in his head. Ion Squadron had made several passes against the frigate without a scratch. It then occurred to him that the loss hadn't occurred until he had ordered the squadron to reverse thrust and combine fire with *Gallant.* That had cost them their maneuverability advantage. Beyond just the abstract sense of responsibility he bore as their leader, the loss was his fault.

"No beacon signals, sir," Dar'su replied quietly.

Solyss bowed his head for a moment and then straightened himself up. As much as it hurt to lose a crewmate, and as much as the feeling of guilt started to weigh on him, he knew the battle wasn't over. The marines were still engaged in a battle over on the space station.

Keeping his voice calm and level, Solyss ordered, "Ops, try to get me a line to Lieutenant Aru."

After an agonizing minute, Dar'su connected him to Asheerah, who answered him with an excited tone. "We've secured the central command center. We had to blow the atmosphere in several compartments on the way, so the station's kind of a mess for now. Alliance forces are contained but not subdued. Four injuries, no fatalities."

Solyss grinned. Asheerah became the most vivid and alive during a fight. He loved seeing her happy. She also became quite amorous afterward. He loved that, too.

"Acknowledged, Lieutenant," Solyss replied. "Status of the frigate?"

"Primary weapon systems are still offline. But it appears they managed to boost their velocity beyond escape velocity. They will clear the gravity well in ten minutes."

Solyss felt the desire to curse. If the frigate escaped, it could warn other Alliance facilities in the area. It would take at least another half hour, probably longer, to catch up, engage her before she could escape, and then return to the station. Asheerah claimed that the Alliance forces on the station were contained, but a lot could happen in that time.

"Helm, bring us back to the station. Ops, let the marines know we're coming to assist," Solyss said, deciding.

After issuing his order, Solyss leaned against his console. The battle had lasted barely half an hour, but he felt that it had gone on for hours. It would take more than ten minutes to get back to the station. That left them free from threats for at least a brief period.

"Tess, you have the bridge," Solyss said, turning and heading for the bridge's exit.

"Aye, XO has the bridge," Tess replied.

Stepping out into the corridor, Solyss leaned against the bulkhead and closed his eyes as soon as he verified he was alone. It would be improper for the crew to see the commander looking tired. He regretted his decision to ban beverages during battle stations. Coffee would have gone a long way toward easing the weariness.

Solyss allowed himself a total of five minutes to rest his eyes before returning to the bridge. As he stepped through the door, he immediately realized that he had been gone too long. Tension filled the room—and not the tension of combat or even the anticipation of more to come. The crew was keeping their heads down, and Lieutenant Tess, standing in the void of attention, was speaking sharply into the comm microphone. "Ion Lead, you've been ordered to return to *Gallant*. You're to immediately break off your attack."

As Solyss returned to his place beside Tess, Isaxo must have responded, though Solyss could not hear what he said. Tess then said, her tone laced with frustration, "Don't engage! I say again, don't engage!"

Glancing down at the tactical display, Solyss saw that in the time he had been gone, Ion Squadron had left their escort position around *Gallant* and pursued the Alliance frigate, *Tornado*. The three remaining fighters in the squadron were buzzing the injured warship.

At first glance, Solyss approved of Isaxo's decision to attack the *Tornado*. Keeping the frigate from warning other Alliance bases about the attack here would give the people more time to either evacuate or prepare to defend themselves. Engaging the enemy was the responsibility of every officer.

Watching the battle play itself out on the tactical display, though, Solyss saw why Tess had ordered the fighters to fall back. While the frigate's main weapons were still offline, her point defense systems were still active. Barrages of defensive fire filled the space around the wounded warship. One sweep from a plasma beam battery gave Ion Four a glancing blow. The fragile fighter's weak shields were stripped away, but fortunately, the pilot kept the ship intact and got out of the line of fire.

"Ion Lead, this is *Gallant* Actual. Return to the ship," Solyss ordered, keeping his voice calm and lacing it with as much authority as he could manage.

"Solyss, these bastards killed Masaque! We can't let them get away!" Isaxo replied, an unfamiliar edge of hatred in his voice.

Solyss cast a glance toward Tess. She had tried to warn him that Isaxo's insubordination would be a problem. He had ignored it, thinking it merely a personality conflict between the two of them. Now, he realized there was more to it than that.

Keeping his voice quiet and level, Solyss said, "Sax, you've already disabled their engines. You don't have the fire power to do much more to them. Their momentum is already enough to get them clear of the gravity well. There's nothing you can do to stop them from jumping, and your ships are getting torn apart. Four's already taken heavy damage. Don't lose another good pilot."

For a long moment, no reply came. Solyss debated saying more but forced himself to remain quiet. Ordering Isaxo to turn back again would not do any good if he had already decided to ignore him. Short of sending the *Gallant* after them, or ordering Ion Two and Four to turn back without Isaxo, there was nothing else he could do but hope his friend listened to reason.

Finally, the reply came. "Ion Squadron, break off and return to base."

Solyss let out a sigh of relief. The three remaining fighters broke off and were soon outside the weapons range of the fleeing frigate. Several minutes later, the frigate itself vanished into hyperspace.

That was one problem out of the way. Now he just had to deal with a space station full of Alliance troops and an unknown number on the planet's surface—all before reinforcements could arrive. And, of course, he had to decide what to do about Isaxo.

Chapter Nine

The last few weeks had been a whirlwind of travel for Zeric, from Sulas to Irod and then almost immediately off to Cardine. Originally, he had planned to remain on Irod and assess the remaining forces there, or maybe to accompany Saracasi on her plan to attack the Alliance forces at Dantyne, but Lei-mey had made it clear he was needed elsewhere. Zeric hadn't argued much. The meeting with Ceta and the baby had been pretty uncomfortable. He knew only more meetings would help ease that tension, but he didn't mind a delay before making another attempt.

Eri'dos Ar'cher and his *Durandall II* had taken him and his "staff" on the two-week journey to Cardine. Up until now, he had liked pretty much every Liw'kel he had met. But the *Durandall II* had an unrelenting stink to it. Eri'dos took offense when he mentioned it, and they hadn't gotten along well since.

His "staff" consisted of Gu'od, who had elected to stay with him rather than sitting on Irod for a few months waiting for Gamaly to return, Kumus, whom he had brought with him from Sulas, and Lei-mey, acting as his *political* advisor. Which, to him, meant she was there to tell him where she needed him to go. He had tried to get Sienn'lyn from Saracasi, under the belief that when one Ni'jar was good, two were better, but he had dropped that idea at Gu'od's urging. Taking along their resident intelligence expert, Kaars Aerinstar, had occurred to him, but he decided the man's knowledge could be put to better use by Saracasi, at least in the short term.

As the ship approached Cardine, Zeric went to the flight deck. There, he overheard Eri'dos yelling into the comm. Unexpectedly, Eri'dos brightened up at the sight of him. "Oh, good, you can straighten these lazy assholes out."

"You're going to have to fill me in," Zeric said, unsure whom Eri'dos was talking to. He didn't want to get in the middle of some argument.

"The defense cutters aren't acknowledging the order to accompany me," Eri'dos explained. "I sent them Saracasi's orders, but they're refusing to acknowledge them."

Zeric grumbled and moved up to the operations station. He hated BS like this, but for once, he was in a position to do something about it. Being the commander of all the Union forces had to have some advantages.

"This is General Dustlighter. Who am I speaking to?" he said into the comm.

After a moment, a suspicious voice said, "This is Captain Haarod. Please verify your identity."

"Switch to video," Zeric grumbled.

"Stand by."

One of the monitors on the control panel came to life, showing a yellow-shelled Camari. He wore a different uniform than the official Union navy ships. Instead of a fairly close-fitting dark-blue ship jumpsuit, he wore a flowing set of blue-green robes. Used to reading Camari expressions—thanks to his time with Ymp—Zeric saw surprise clearly evident on his face.

"Now that we've established my identity, I'm ordering you to comply with the instructions transmitted to you moments ago by Captain Ar'cher. Your ships have been drafted into the Union navy," Zeric said, making his tone as authoritative as he could manage. "Fail to comply, and I'll be forced to come over there and transfer command to someone else. And I won't be happy about it."

The unease the captain must have felt at being ordered to take his ship to a potential battle played right into Zeric's hand. A potential future battle was an abstract possibility, but Zeric was here now. And he had, he hoped, a fearsome reputation.

"I'm sorry, sir," Haarod said hesitantly. "The order was said to come from Commodore Ocaitchi, but we were under the impression that Maarkean Ocaitchi was a prisoner of the Alliance and that you were as well."

"I'm clearly no prisoner and never was," Zeric grumbled. "The order comes from Saracasi Ocaitchi, currently in command of all naval forces, including you. Now make preparations to depart along with the *Durandall II*."

"Yes, sir," Haarod replied. Zeric shut the comm off after that and turned to Eri'dos. "Let me know if he gives you any more trouble."

Eri'dos gave him a mischievous smile in reply. "Maybe having you along isn't so bad after all."

"Your ship still stinks," Zeric replied, though he did it with a smile this time.

Taking the insult with a nod, Eri'dos returned to bringing the ship down through Cardine's atmosphere. They had been forced to make a long orbit around the planet to avoid a defense battery that was still under Alliance control. The orbit gave him a chance to get a good look at Cardine, though.

Like most habitable worlds, Cardine featured a broad selection of environments. Like his home of Terra, the planet had a fairly extensive ocean covering the largest portion of the surface. Compared to the rest of the planets in the Kreogh sector, Cardine's ocean was the biggest— something that Zeric got a good sense of. During the orbit, they only passed over one land mass large enough to be identified as such.

This feature was what made Cardine such an attractive planet to the Camari. Although they lived their entire lives on land, Camari were amphibious. They preferred a moist environment and were expert aquatic farmers. The smaller areas of arable land here proved to be no hindrance to a thriving population—it was third in the sector only to Ailleroc and Sulas, and then not by much.

As the ocean gave way to a large continent, Eri'dos skimmed the coastline until they came to a large bay that was fed by several rivers. All around the bay, signs of civilization could be seen. Buildings of glass and metal towered along the coast, some even emerging right out of the water. One area, separated from the tallest buildings and covered in lights and docking pads, was the city's starport.

With their destination in sight, Zeric turned away from the viewports. Only then did he notice Lei-mey standing behind him. He had no idea how long the Ronid woman had been standing there. She had been uncharacteristically quiet.

Making no comment to her, Zeric moved past her and into the narrow corridor leading away from the flight deck. For a few seconds, he thought maybe he would make it out of there without a word, but he proved unlucky. She followed him, and once the door to the flight deck sealed behind them, she spoke. "That was a foolish action."

"Watching the landing?" Zeric asked, not sure what she was referring to. Knowing Lei-mey, she could mean any of a number of things he might have done.

"Strong-arming the other ship captain. You should have let Captain Ar'cher handle it. The navy is not your concern at the moment," Lei-mey explained, her tone like that of a schoolteacher.

"Eri'dos is no diplomat," Zeric said. "He might have tried once more, but then he would have given up and returned to Irod without the ships that Casi needs. It's a long trip between here and anywhere else. If she had to send someone else, or come herself, she would have lost another month of time."

"But you've undoubtedly offended the leaders of Cardine. There's a good chance your order will still be ignored. The only thing you'll have accomplished is generating animosity, making our job of getting more support from Cardine that much harder," Lei-mey explained.

Zeric frowned, considering her words. He could see her point. The Cardinians hadn't been the most enthusiastic about the rebellion at the outset. From what Maarkean had told him, they had only supported the formation of the army because one of their own, General Numba, had been placed in command. Now Numba was dead and Zeric was his replacement.

Despite seeing her point, Zeric argued, "I can't be an effective commander if I have to ask everyone to follow orders. Soldiers who don't follow orders on the battlefield get shot, and not necessarily by the enemy."

"That may be true for a professional, well-trained military. But you know as well as I do that you don't have that. Everyone is here by choice. Authority is much more nebulous in a rebel army. You have to understand that," Lei-mey said, her tone slowly becoming more informative and less of a reprimand the more she talked.

Zeric thought back to the disastrous meetings he had sat through on Sulas. Despite his formal position of authority, Jairyd and Kantor had taken over from him with ease. At the time, he had been fine with it, thinking it just natural. But now he realized it had been partly because of his mismanagement, not just their efforts.

"All right," Zeric said reluctantly. "Assuming you're right, what do you recommend?"

"Start off by offering to help them. Look over the combat situation and see if there's anything you can do or suggest. As difficult as it will be for you, you need to get them to like you," Lei-mey said.

"I thought that was your job. I'm supposed to be here to help them like *you*," Zeric said, confused.

Lei-mey shook her head. "You're here because they respect you. But you also replaced their well-liked leader. We need to show them that he hasn't been forgotten and that Cardine's interests are still going to be important to the Union."

While Zeric mulled over what Lei-mey had told him, the ship touched down on the planet's surface. A moment later, Gu'od and Kumus arrived in the cargo bay. The bay door opened, letting in a waft of air full of the smells of the sea.

The ship's internal intercom clicked on. "Have a good trip, General. We'll be departing immediately in order to make our rendezvous. I trust you can find your own way back."

Eri'dos wasn't lying about his intention to depart immediately—before they were down the boarding ramp, the ship started to power up again. Zeric led the group down in a hustle to get clear of the thrusters. When they were barely clear of the blast radius, the *Durandall II* lifted off the landing pad and back into the air.

"An insufferable man, Captain Ar'cher," Lei-mey complained.

"I dunno. He's starting to grow on me. Doesn't waste time," Zeric commented. The ship had stunk, but he had had a well-stocked bar onboard. He hoped Kumus had found room for the bottle he had pilfered.

They waited on the tarmac for a moment. Zeric had expected some kind of reception to greet them. Their visit had been no secret. It wasn't until they had started walking toward the terminal that a stream of ground vehicles appeared and drove up to them.

The vehicle stopped and several people got out—all Camari except for one Ronid. Several wore the blue-green robe uniform that the cutter's captain had worn. One of the Camari who wasn't wearing a uniform led the group.

"Delegate Darshawn, Lieutenant General Dustlighter, I'm First Lord Reynol," the man said, his Standard heavily accented with a lilting flow. His rubbery skin was a dark shade of blue.

Remembering that Lei-mey had instructed him to take the lead in conversations, Zeric extended his hand and said, "First Lord, it's an honor. May I present my companions, Master Sergeant Gu'od Dos'redna and Specialist Kumus Stryker."

Reynol grasped Zeric's outstretched hand with his limp fingers, tightening them slightly for a momentary handshake. He then nodded to Gu'od and Kumus. He made no effort to introduce the people with him, which was something Lei-mey had warned Zeric about. She had told him not to introduce anyone else with them, but Zeric had ignored that, finding it a fairly rude practice.

"I'm surprised by your visit to our world, so far from the front lines," Reynol said. Then his voice took on a tone of fake indignation. "Did none of our delegates to Congress offer their hospitality in escorting you to our world? I would be ashamed of their rudeness."

Zeric shook his head. "No, First Lord, nothing of the sort. This is a military mission. Delegate Darshawn is only here as my political advisor because of our history of working together. Besides, the Cardine delegation is quite busy with matters of utmost importance to the Union. I didn't want to pull them away."

Most of the Cardine delegation had actually gone on the diplomatic mission to the Camari Republic. Zeric didn't want to discuss it out here in the open, but since they had traveled aboard a Cardine ship, he felt sure Reynol knew about it.

"I see," Reynol said. "And what's this military mission you're on?"

Again taking Lei-mey's advice, Zeric said, "I'm here to see if there's any way I can help in getting rid of your Alliance problem."

"How considerate. We would, of course, be grateful for your experience in this matter. Your effort in removing the Alliance from Enro was quite effective," Reynol said, making no effort to hide the backhandedness of his compliment. "Though I must wonder why your first act was to order our defense cutters away. Without them, we have no naval presence, besides a few captured fighter squadrons."

Zeric cursed to himself. He hated it when Lei-mey was right. "Those ships were needed for another operation. If the Alliance did come here with a sufficiently powerful naval force to get past your planetary defense guns, those cutters would have been cut to ribbons. They will be far more effective where they're going."

"I see," Reynol said again, his eyestalks ridged and fixed on Zeric.

"Now, if I can be shown to whomever's in command of your defense forces, perhaps I can provide them some assistance," Zeric said, trying to change the subject.

Reynol remained staring at Zeric for a second before turning to one of the robed figures. "Marshall Teev is in command of our home defense forces."

Despite the Union military having adopted the Alliance military structure, Cardine had stuck with the Camari system. Zeric knew that, like general, there were several grades of marshalls. Unfortunately, he wasn't familiar with the rank emblems or if the grades were abbreviated to simply "marshall" the way "general" was.

However, even if Teev's brand of marshall technically outranked a lieutenant general, Zeric was now the supreme commander of all Union forces, including planetary defense forces. But taking Lei-mey's advice to heart, he decided to strike a tone of cooperation, rather than simple authority.

"Marshall, a pleasure."

"Likewise, General," Teev said, extending his limp red hand. Unlike Reynol, Teev hadn't added the "lieutenant" portion of Zeric's rank. While technically correct, it was usually omitted when spoken. Reynol had included it either out of ignorance or to be an ass.

Zeric shook the man's hand, careful not to squeeze too hard. "I'm eager to get started whenever you are. I want to see Cardine free of the Alliance."

"Then let's head to my command post," Teev said.

Based on the man's skin shade, a once-bright red that now appeared to be losing its shine, he was a Camari approaching his middle years. Zeric judged them to be about the same age. Also like him, Teev would be old enough to have participated in the fighting during the last war.

"Sounds good," Zeric said, now ignoring Reynol and following Teev. They climbed into the cars and headed off without another word.

"Maark, wake up."

Groggily, Maarkean looked up to see Lohcja standing beside him. Not looking at him, the Ronid stared at something outside their cell. Following Lohcja's gaze, Maarkean saw Lieutenant Merski, in the process of opening the cell door.

Pulling himself up to stand beside Lohcja, Maarkean tried to decide what this meant. They hadn't seen Merski since that first encounter, nor had they discussed whether or not they believed her claim of wanting to help free them. Based on the lack of other guards in the room, he felt sure they would find out soon.

"We don't have much time," Merski said. "Put these on, quickly." She tossed two naval uniform coveralls into the room and then looked down at her comm device. Maarkean got a glimpse of a timer counting down on the screen. He took the uniform and started pulling it on.

"These weren't exactly designed with Ronids in mind," Lohcja said, holding up his uniform.

"I got you a bulky one. And it doesn't have to fit well, just enough to help you blend in a little," Merski said, clearly impatient.

Lohcja clacked his mandibles but started to pull the coveralls on. While he struggled to fit them over his carapace, Maarkean leaned in and whispered, "Looks like something's about to go down. What do you think?"

"I think it's an elaborate game and we're going to get shot attempting escape," Lohcja said. "But, even if it is, maybe we'll find a chance to really escape."

"I'm not so sure," Maarkean said. "I think I believe her."

"It doesn't matter if you believe me or not," Merski said, overhearing. "We need to move now." She moved to the door of the brig and stepped outside, walking with her back straight.

Sharing a glance with Lohcja, Maarkean shrugged and followed. Lohcja hastily zipped up his uniform and joined him.

They passed into an empty control room. A monitoring station showed blank screens, but no one sat in the seat. As they moved to the exit door, the monitors flickered back on, showing two cells. Both sat empty.

Moving into the ship's corridors, Merski led them at a brisk pace. They didn't pass any other crewmembers directly, but Maarkean did catch sight of a few down other branches of corridor. He hoped Lohcja's uniform would be enough to keep any of those crew from taking a closer look.

After traveling down two flights of stairs, Maarkean started to get an idea of where they might be headed. His suspicion proved correct when they turned a corner and stopped at a door marked "Shuttlebay." Merski hastily entered a code into the keypad and the doors opened.

Two shuttles occupied the bulk of the room. He recognized them as TU-17 cargo shuttles, which gave him a sliver of hope. TU-17s came equipped with hyperdrives, even though they had a fairly limited range. The ship could be anywhere at this point, and having a hyperdrive would give them a lot more options on where to go.

Merski strode purposefully toward one of the shuttles, but a voice brought her up short. "Can I help you, Lieutenant?"

A young Terran male crewmember stood over a piece of equipment behind the shuttle Merski had been approaching. He looked up at her, a look of surprise on his face. Maarkean spotted a ration pack open on the floor and could faintly hear the sounds of music.

Food in the shuttle bay was against regulations, and Merski clearly hadn't anticipated anyone being here. Maarkean assumed the crewmember hadn't expected anyone else to walk in on him doing whatever he was doing, either. An awkward moment passed before Merski recovered.

"Specialist, what are you doing here with an open ration pack? This area is off limits," Merski said, clearly trying to sound authoritative.

"I'm working on Shuttle Two's transponder system. I'm part of the deck crew," he said, his voice wavering.

"With an open ration pack? No wonder the hardware's having trouble," Merski snapped.

The specialist looked nervous, and Maarkean thought Merski might be able to overcome this obstacle. But then the young man turned and saw him and Lohcja. His eyes grew wide at the sight of a Ronid.

Reacting immediately, Maarkean leapt forward, grabbing the Terran in a choke hold. He applied pressure, and the specialist dropped unconscious without putting up much of a struggle. All the time he'd spent practicing in his cell was paying off.

"Why did you do that?" Merski said, surprised.

"There was no way you were going to be able to convince him not to report a Ronid in a uniform, lieutenant or no," Maarkean said, lifting the specialist onto his shoulder.

Walking toward the hangar's control booth, he put the Terran on the floor and sealed the room so that he wouldn't be sucked out into space when they opened the bay doors. Being in the wrong place at the wrong time was not a reason to die.

Merski gave him a long look as he emerged from the control booth. For the first time, he got a sense of genuine emotion from her, unmasked by her intelligence training. She looked relieved, and he felt sure his action had surprised her.

Not wanting to waste time figuring out what that meant, Maarkean moved toward the shuttle. Lohcja had already gotten onboard, giving the all-clear sign. There would be no more unexpected visitors.

Maarkean boarded the shuttle and took a seat at the pilot controls. He started the power-up sequence. With the transponder system uninstalled and in pieces on the hangar deck, he felt fairly confident in their chances—it would be harder for any Alliance ship to track them as they attempted to escape.

"I'll go set the bay doors to auto-open in two minutes," Merski said before turning and stepping off the shuttle.

As soon as she left, Lohcja leaned in. "This is our chance. Where would they keep a weapon aboard this thing?"

"For what?" Maarkean asked.

"To use on Merski," Lohcja said incredulously. "If this is some elaborate hoax, if we arm ourselves, we can still turn it to our advantage."

"I don't think it's a hoax," Maarkean said. "The transponder has been removed, and we're aboard a hyperspace-capable craft that's fully fueled. That specialist working on it surprised her. She must have disabled the transponder in preparation for our escape. He just noticed the problem and came to fix it. I think she's legit."

Lohcja paused in his search of the shuttle. "Maybe, but I'd still rather be armed than not."

"Unfortunately, shuttles don't typically come with a supply of weapons. They're only used for moving supplies to and from the ship. It's not a combat vessel," Maarkean replied.

Shrugging his antennae, Lohcja resumed his search. Maarkean turned back to the forward window and saw Merski emerging from the control booth. As she started back toward the shuttle, a blast rang through the hangar. Something hit Merski in the back, and she tumbled forward.

Once Merski fell, Maarkean saw a squad of marines dashing into the shuttle bay. They had their blasters raised, and they immediately fanned out. Turning away from the pilot controls, Maarkean looked at Lohcja. "Any luck finding a weapon?" he asked.

"No, I thought you said we . . ." Lohcja stopped as he looked out of the viewport.

Seconds later, three marines came around the back of the shuttle. Reluctantly, Maarkean raised his hands, followed a second later by Lohcja. As the marines led them out of the shuttle and back toward the brig, Maarkean caught sight of Merski's motionless body laying on the shuttle bay's floor. In the center of her back, the black burn mark of a blaster bolt stood out. The marines hadn't been set to stun.

Whatever doubts he'd had about Merski's sincerity faded away, replaced by guilt at her death.

Chapter Ten

Saracasi's first major command decision weighed on her. Eager to begin taking the fight back to the Alliance, she had decided to take what ships she had and begin the campaign. She would have had better odds of success if she had waited for Eri'dos and the cutters from Cardine to arrive, but that would have added another month of delay—a month more for the Alliance to entrench themselves.

Fortunately, Fracsid and Chavatwor had kept busy, and she still had five gunships available, even with Eri'dos gone. The gunships and the two fighter squadrons aboard *Defiant Glory* would be their main strike force. It wasn't much against an Alliance taskforce, but then, she'd beaten one before with less.

"All fighters report ready for launch," Jerik said beside her. "Reserve fighters are prepped and ready to move into position the moment the bay is clear."

"Thank you, Captain," Saracasi said.

One of *Defiant Glory*'s biggest flaws was the inability to fit more than twelve fighters in the launch bay. She carried another six, but they would have to be moved to the launch bay once the others launched—an operation that meant a lot of time spent without their full complement of fighters available. It also meant they could only recover twelve fighters at a time, making a quick exit difficult.

"Hyperspace exit in one minute," Tadashio reported from the operations station.

Saracasi tried to keep calm, but the approaching battle kept intruding. Her palms were sweaty, and she debated wiping them off on her uniform. Would that look unprofessional? Would it look bad for the commodore to appear nervous? Or would it just show good sense?

While debating this in her head, she completely missed the final countdown. Suddenly, the fleet had left hyperspace, and Tadashio was already reporting on sensor contacts. She quietly berated herself and refocused her attention.

"Picking up one Alliance escort carrier, one frigate, and one corvette," Tadashio reported as the images appeared on the tactical hologram. "One flight of two fighter craft appear to be flying CAP."

The Alliance ships were arrayed in a loose formation covering the northern hemisphere of Dantyne. Given their positions and altitudes, they had complete coverage over half of the planet. Saracasi guessed that more ships would be on the other side of the planet, hidden from their sensors.

Without any direction from her, Jerik went about his duties, commanding *Defiant Glory*. The fighters launched and the reserve fighters moved into position. The twelve fighter craft spread out in pairs, taking up a point position in front of the carrier and three gunships that accompanied her.

Tuning out the background noise as the bridge crew went about their duties, Saracasi activated the comm array. "Alliance fleet, this is Commodore Ocaitchi of the Union 2nd Fleet. You're in an illegal orbit of a Union world. You're ordered to withdraw immediately, or we'll be forced to open fire."

Her force of ships hardly constituted a fleet, and in truth, they didn't have a proper designation, but Saracasi thought it sounded more impressive that way. Let the Alliance sort out what it would from the term. No need for them to know that she had chosen "second" only because they had already destroyed the equivalent of the Union's first.

"Rebel fleet," came the reply from the Alliance, "this is Commodore Dolan of Alliance Task Force 413. You're in possession of illegal military hardware. You're ordered to stand by and prepare to be boarded. Comply now. You will not get a second warning."

Saracasi identified the ship where the order had originated. Unexpectedly, it had come from the frigate. Most Alliance officers commanded from onboard carriers. She switched her comm over to the gunships' channel. "*Cutty Sark*, take your ships and head for the frigate. Concentrate on disabling her communications."

"Aye, Commodore," Fracsid replied.

The three gunships broke out of formation and accelerated toward the Alliance frigate. Three gunships against a frigate should put the gunships at only a slight disadvantage, if the fighters were kept out of the mix. Satisfied that Fracsid could handle the assignment from there, she turned her attention to the fighter deployment.

Jerik had the fighters in a screening defensive formation. The fighters were far enough ahead to intercept incoming projectiles and enemy fighters, but not too far away to be outside the coverage of *Defiant Glory*'s defense batteries. It was a common tactic for carriers. Unfortunately, it also tied up their primary offensive tool for defense.

"Captain Needa," Saracasi said, "designate the Alliance carrier as the primary target for the fighters. Minimal defenses for us. We're going after the corvette."

"Aye," Jerik replied. "Mr. Gotit, plot an intercept course for the corvette. Valour Squadron, designate priority target Alliance carrier. Wildcard Squadron, provide cover. Reserve fighters, launch and reform defense screen."

Several minutes went by as the two fleets moved closer together. Though they hadn't jumped in at an incredible distance, the Union ships were still further from Dantyne than a normal jump would dictate. Dantyne didn't have full planetary defense coverage, and their weapons were light, but unlike on Enro and Mirthod, there *were* defense batteries to worry about. Keeping those from tipping the balance in the battle would be important.

"Alliance fleet is firing torpedoes at us," Tadashio announced, the first hint of concern in his voice.

Saracasi glanced at the tactical display, relieved to see that some of their reserve fighters had already been launched. Jerik calmly ordered, "Defense fighters, engage torpedoes."

Torpedoes were dangerous weapons, capable of doing a lot of damage to a capital ship. Fortunately, they were also expensive, so they weren't wasted on small craft that could keep up with their ability to maneuver. Unfortunately, that meant *Defiant Glory* was the only ship worth shooting them at.

"Point defense batteries, stand by," Jerik ordered.

A tense minute went by while their fighters and the torpedoes moved closer. On the tactical display, they converged, and the sensor data became confused for a moment. Then the response from the fighters came. "All but two down," the flight leader reported.

"Point defense batteries, engage," Jerik said. "Fighters stay clear."

Defiant Glory didn't match up to regular warships, but as a former mining ship, she had a few advantages. She had been built tough, as stray asteroid fragments could be dangerous. And her original complement of mining equipment had been easy to convert to point defense weapons. She had far better coverage in that area than most warships.

Their plasma beam turrets lanced out into space, converging around the evasively moving torpedoes. Before the lead one could get close enough for Saracasi to feel concerned, the beams found their target and detonated the warhead. One of the torpedoes vanished from the display.

"Final torpedo is changing targets!" Tadashio shouted. "And it's out of range of our defensive guns."

The sudden change in tactics took Saracasi off guard. *Defiant Glory* was the biggest threat, but the Alliance commander had apparently decided she was also too well defended. While Saracasi watched helplessly, the final torpedo moved away from her ship and toward the mostly defenseless cutter flying escort to them.

With a sudden finality, the torpedo detonated against the cutter's shields. Several long seconds went by as the sensors tried to sort out the results. When the energy surge faded enough, Tadashio relayed the grim news. "Reading complete destruction of *Ocean Mist*. I'm not picking up any escape pod beacons," the Kowwok operations officer said, his voice quavering.

The bridge faded to silence for a long moment, and Saracasi felt the gaze of everyone in the room on her. Taking the cutters had been her decision. Now, one had been lost with all hands within the first few minutes of their first engagement.

"*Defiant Glory*, we're engaging the enemy," Fracsid voice said into her earpiece, taking her away from being able to mourn this loss.

Putting aside the cutter's destruction, Saracasi watched the display as the ships started firing at each other. The frigate had the clear advantage in firepower and defenses over the gunships, but they carried limited point defense weapons. The gunships could withstand the defense weapons while also being able to outmaneuver much of the fire from the heavier weapons.

Forcing herself not to focus too much on one segment of the fight, Saracasi surveyed the battlefield. The six fighters from Wildcard Squadron had just engaged the approaching Alliance fighters. This had allowed the ships from Valour Squadron, led by Sienn'lyn I'fu, to slip past and beeline for the carrier. A small miracle had granted them a slight advantage in total fighter craft.

"New contacts!" Tadashio reported. "One Alliance frigate coming around the planet's horizon. Correction, one frigate *and* one corvette."

Though she had half-expected it, Saracasi mentally cursed. The battle so far had been fairly balanced, even with the loss of the *Ocean's Mist*. Now she would have to find out if the ace up her sleeve was really worth anything.

"Mr. Clemyo," Saracasi said, trying to sound calm, "send a signal to the Phantom. Calculate a position at extreme weapons range of the new frigate and give them those jump coordinates."

"Phantom" was what she had designated the four remaining cutters and their two gunship escorts. Waiting at a point five light-minutes away from Dantyne, the ships were outside effective sensor range but close enough that a comm signal followed by a micro hyperspace jump could bring them into the fight with minimal delay. The ships could potentially still be seen with a deep space scan, but the vastness of space kept the odds of that very low.

While she waited for the signal to travel through space, *Defiant Glory* moved within range of the first Alliance corvette's weapons. Jerik redeployed the remaining fighter screen to stay behind them, away from the potentially deadly fire from the corvette. Exchanges of fire began flying between the two ships. Saracasi felt the slight vibration as kinetic energy, not fully absorbed by the shields, transferred to the ship.

Unlike in previous engagements, *Defiant Glory* weathered this first exchange of fire with little ill effect. After the Battle of Sulas, the main reactor had been rebuilt and replaced, and she now had a power supply adequate for her role as a warship, and her heavy weaponry outclassed that of a corvette, though not by much.

Jerik slowed the ship and reversed course, keeping the carrier between the corvette and the rest of the fleet. Saracasi turned her attention away from this immediate battle and reassessed the overall battle. Fracsid's ships were still trading fire with the frigate, though *Chimopori* looked sluggish. The Alliance fighters had rallied and intercepted Valour Squadron before they could reach the Alliance carrier. This left the carrier untouched but had allowed *Wildcard* to give the Alliance fighters a solid strike.

Spread out as they were, the fleet was not able to bring very much firepower to bear against any particular enemy target. This proved the same for the Alliance, though their individual ships were slightly more powerful. She could either continue the broad focus or close ranks.

Making her decision, Saracasi began issuing orders. "*Chimopori*, break off and move to engage enemy fighters. Valour Squadron, disengage fighters and move to intercept Alliance Frigate F1. Defense fighters, advance to back up *Wildcard*. You're clear to engage Carrier CV1 if the opportunity presents itself, but your primary focus is keeping those fighters occupied."

The ships of her fleet started to move in response. It would take some time for the redeployment to occur. How quickly Phantom Group responded to their order would determine whether all the pieces got into place before the Alliance reinforcements arrived. Ground-based fighters had started to appear on the sensors as well, though they were still a significant distance out.

"New contacts!" Tadashio shouted again, this time with a note of cheerful shock in his voice. "Reading contact as our gunships and . . . *Audacious*!"

Saracasi allowed herself a wide smile. Using the remains of *Defiant Glory*'s old reactor, generous amounts of spare hull plating, and flexible support struts, Saracasi had devised a false framework for their cutters. Flying in a tight formation, the cutters would appear on sensors to be the shape of the *Audacious*. The addition of the old reactor, along with the cutters' own power sources, would provide a strong enough energy reading to mimic the anti-matter reactor of the experimental frigate.

She had told very few people about this plan. Only La'ari, responsible for assembling the frame, Lieutenant Sheanna Coramont, who commanded the group, and eventually the cutter captains had been told the full details. She hadn't wanted to risk any potential leaks. For this to work, the Alliance had to believe that those cutters were indeed the unkillable frigate.

"*Audacious* is firing! Alliance frigate and corvette are going evasive and altering course," Tadashio reported.

This news was both good and bad. By changing course, those ships would not join the current battle, providing no relief to the currently engaged Alliance ships. But the closer they got to the fake *Audacious*, the more likely it was that they would see through the deception. It would also increase the risk to the cutters, as they didn't actually have an impenetrable shield to protect them from enemy fire.

Nervously, Saracasi watched the battle unfold. At this point, there was very little for her to do but watch. As the fleet commander, she was responsible for everything and everyone. Part of that responsibility was staying out of their way and letting them do their jobs. Unless something changed, she could only sit by and hope they did them well.

"Commodore," Tadashio said via her earpiece, "I've been able to positively identify the frigate designated F2. She's the *Typhoon*, the same ship you fought over Kol."

"Thank you, Tada," she said with a grim smile. If she played her cards right, that fact could be used to her advantage.

"Phantom lead, signal the frigate you're engaging. Let them know you're glad to see them, as you're sad she got away from you at Kol," Saracasi said.

"Understood," came the simple reply from Sheanna, who was onboard one of the cutters. She would not understand the full details of the order, but she was quite perceptive. She had been aboard *Audacious* during the previous battle with the Alliance frigate.

While she awaited the relayed response from the frigate, the tide of the battle suddenly shifted. The additional firepower from Valour Squadron, working beside Fracsid's two gunships, penetrated the shields on the first frigate, disabling her engines and, more importantly, her communications gear.

Not waiting for fate to balance out the battle, Saracasi began issuing orders. "*Cutty Sark*, Valour Squadron, break off and move to intercept the carrier. Captain Needa, break off from the corvette and move to intercept the carrier.

"Captain Coramont, transmit another message to the frigate. Let them know you've already had one carrier kill to your credit, so the others can have this next one. You're hungry for a frigate."

The ships responded to her orders. The gunships and fighters moved quickly away from the disabled frigate, putting her out of the engagement. While far from finished, without her main engines, the Alliance frigate was unable to maneuver to keep up. She would also make an easy target to mop up later.

Tense minutes went by as her fleet again repositioned themselves. The Alliance corvette followed *Defiant Glory*, continuing to fire on them. *Typhoon* and the second corvette got closer and closer to the phantom *Audacious*, but Sheanna did an admirable job of keeping their distance without being obvious about it.

Just before they got into firing range of the Alliance carrier, Tadashio gave an excited report. "Alliance ships are breaking off! Frigate F2 and Corvette C2 are accelerating away from Dantyne. Remaining fighter craft have begun making emergency landings aboard the carrier. Corvette C1 is accelerating to run interference between our fighters and the carrier."

Saracasi smiled. "All fighters, break off from the carrier. Keep a safe distance from the corvette. Captain Needa, continue firing on the corvette but let the carrier go. Captain Coramont, make a show of pursuing the fleeing Alliance frigate but break off once you reach max weapons range."

Despite the loss of *Ocean Mist,* her second battle had gone better than she had hoped. One cutter in exchange for one Alliance frigate and retaking Dantyne. Maybe this war wouldn't last as long as she had once feared.

Chapter Eleven

"I'm not looking forward to another day in that room," Valinther grumbled as he gave his clothing a final check in the mirror.

Lahkaba nodded his agreement. They stood waiting in the common room of the quarters the Dotran had given them, waiting for Rathalos to arrive and transport them to the next meeting. None of them looked excited.

When the door to the apartment finally opened, their Kowwok guide came in, escorted by Lt. Commander Bryel Prytoker. This was the first time they had seen Bryel after the initial greeting at the starport, even though he had been the Dotran representative to Congress.

"Commander Prytoker, what a surprise. Your presence at the meetings has been missed," Lahkaba said, surprising himself with the sincerity in his voice.

"I apologize. My duties have kept me elsewhere," Bryel responded, his tone evasive. "I'm here to inform you that Minister Amib will not be able to meet with you today."

"That is . . . unfortunate," Lionell replied. "When will we be rescheduling?"

"For tomorrow," Bryel answered. "In the meantime, I can provide you with a tour of some of the city's best cultural icons, if you don't desire to stay here all day."

"You mean we can't go anywhere on our own?" Valinther asked, sounding accusatory.

For his part, Bryel had enough tact to look embarrassed as he replied, "Unfortunately, not without military escort. For your safety. There are undoubtedly Alliance spies on the planet, and your safety is our responsibility."

"Right," Lionell replied.

Speaking up for the first time, Zoeko said, "Commander Prytoker is quite correct. Did we not confine his movements while on Irod?"

Zoeko's point was met by silence by the rest of the group. She had a point.

"Very well," he said. "Since I don't want to be locked up here, perhaps this tour of yours would be enlightening." The idea of seeing Dotran cultural hotspots didn't really appeal to him, but he agreed to Bryel's tour merely to get out of sitting in the apartment for the entire day.

When he had remarked it could be enlightening, he hadn't really meant it. Several hours later, he was forced to change that assessment.

They made several stops, but the art museum proved the most interesting. The first piece they viewed upon entering the museum was a giant statue of a Dotran warrior. Suitably, the statue was made out of bronze and depicted a legendary hero from Dotran myth: Scarlo, Champion of Azar.

From there, they toured the museum, seeing a magnificent painting of the Queen Jeliana, considered to be the most beautiful Dotran to ever live. She was, of course, a gold. By the time they had gotten through half the museum, Lahkaba hadn't seen but a handful of paintings or statues that depicted anything other than gold or bronze Dotran. Those that did showed reds and oranges. The only blues and greens he saw were background figures, usually looking up in admiration at some gold or bronze hero.

As they walked, he remarked to Bryel, "Your people certainly aren't subtle about the golds and bronzes being in charge."

"Of course they're in charge—they're superior mentally and physically," Bryel replied, sounding as if he were repeating something from memory. As he spoke, Lahkaba saw him cast an almost imperceptible glance down at his blue-scaled hands.

Stopping before a large painting, Bryel said, "Take this one by Moresala. It depicts the hero Scarlo after he defeated a barbarian horde assaulting his city."

The painting showed the same well-muscled and intimidating Dotran that Lahkaba had seen from the statue in the main foyer. His bronze form stood over a decapitated Dotran with orange scales, while a swarm of other Dotran rode away on some kind of four-legged creature in the distance. A crowd stood on the walls of a city, cheering.

"Of course, some historians believe Scarlo was actually a blue," Bryel said, his tone quieter than it had been a moment before. "They say that the belief that Scarlo was bronze emerged a few hundred years later, due to the famous statue of him being made of actual bronze, a common building material in the time it was made."

The statement from Bryel took Lahkaba off guard. He cast a look around to see what the others thought and only then noticed that the rest of the group had moved on to the next painting. Before he could give a response, Bryel, too, moved on to join them.

Lahkaba followed, still contemplating Bryel's statement. As he got closer, his thoughts were interrupted by the sounds of an argument. Zoeko and Valinther were glaring at each other.

"Worshiping the Great One didn't cause my people to become subjects of the Dotran!" Valinther said, his tone defensive.

"You must admit that your people's foolish belief in non-violence kept you from putting up a fight when we arrived. And that's a tenant of your religion, is it not?" Zoeko asked, her tone surprisingly calm.

Bryel and Lionell both started speaking at once, trying to ease the tension. Confused by the sudden argument, Lahkaba turned to Rathalos. "What happened?"

"Ambassadors Lide and Valinther are in disagreement over the meaning of this painting," Rathalos answered.

The painting in question showed a tall, glowing Kowwok with bright golden fur. Lahkaba recognized it as an image commonly used to represent the Great One. The Great One was bowing, as if in submission, before an even brighter golden Dotran. Despite his general distaste for his people's religion, the image offended even him.

"Ambassador Lide asserts that this painting shows how our religion has made us slaves to the Dotran—a statement Ambassador Valinther objected to," Rathalos explained.

Looking at the painting again, Lahkaba reassessed his initial reaction. At first, he had thought as Valinther probably did—that the painting merely represented the conceited view of many Dotran that they were greater than even the gods. But he could see the hidden meaning now.

He was impressed that Zoeko had. In a way, the painting could almost be seen as a statement for the Kowwok to resist the Dotran. Taken in that light, it seemed unusual that the painting was hanging here.

While the others argued, Lahkaba asked Rathalos, "And what do you think it means?"

Looking startled and uncomfortable, Rathalos squirmed slightly before answering evasively, "It's not my place to judge such things."

Disappointed in the response, Lahkaba sighed. He knew he shouldn't expect more from someone like Rathalos. Being a faithful servant of the Dotran must have been his entire life.

But when he started to move to try to help cool the argument, he was stopped by Rathalos's hand on his shoulder. Leaning in, the big Kowwok whispered, "Don't accept the agreement to share military technology. You would be giving away more than you can gain."

Puzzled by the cryptic comment, Lahkaba studied Rathalos. The servant looked back with intensity before letting go of Lahkaba's shoulder, and his expression returned to his usual passive one, as if nothing had just occurred.

When it became clear Rathalos would say no more, Lahkaba reluctantly moved to help end the argument between Zoeko and Valinther.

During the next meeting with Minister Amib, Lahkaba found himself spending another long day in a hot room. Like before, his entire role in the negotiation involved sitting there, making the Dotran uncomfortable with his presence. All in all, he found it a terrible way to conduct a negotiation.

Toward the end of the day, Sceglis produced a document for them, saying, "As a show of good faith, we have gone ahead and drawn up this minor agreement for the sharing of tactics and military technology. We'll offer you our knowledge of fighting the Alliance and some of our weaponry to help your Union keep fighting while we work out the rest of the details for our treaty."

Copies of the agreements appeared on each of their personal datapads, and Lahkaba started scanning it while Sceglis kept talking. "I believe you'll see it matches the principles we discussed before. If we sign it today, we can dispatch a transport with weapons and tacticians as soon as tomorrow."

As Lahkaba scanned the document, he saw how beneficial this could be to the fight. They had been subsisting on stolen or commercially acquired weapons. Their remaining senior general had only ever risen as high as a corporal beforehand. Even though he despised the Dotran, and even though they had lost the war, they had the most experience fighting the Alliance.

But the warning Rathalos had given him the other day in the museum kept repeating itself in his mind. He had said that they would be giving away more than they would gain with this agreement. The fact that Sceglis had drawn up this agreement as a separate treaty was warning enough to be cautious. No one gave anything away for free.

Continuing to scan, he came across a section that detailed how the Union would be required to share "all technology captured or developed." On the surface, it seemed like a reasonable request: to share details about technology that the enemy used or which worked well against them. But then it hit him.

Audacious. The advanced shield and hyperdrive technology aboard the captured frigate had proven strong enough to allow that one ship to survive an engagement with an entire Alliance task force. The Dotran would be all over themselves to have that kind of ability.

Despite all the problems Saracasi claimed the *Audacious* had, the potential for the tech was clear. A Dotran armada equipped with that kind of shield? They would be a great asset in crushing the Alliance and freeing the Kreogh sector. But at what cost?

"This agreement appears most generous," Zoeko said, bringing Lahkaba's attention back.

He hadn't told any of the others about what Rathalos had said. The man had been very careful to say it when Lahkaba was the only one around, and in a public place, as their apartment was undoubtedly bugged by Confederate Intelligence.

Deciding he had to do something quickly, Lahkaba said, "But, unfortunately, we cannot accept it at this time. We'd prefer to work out a complete agreement, rather than conducting matters piecemeal."

Sceglis turned to him for the first time, with a look of contempt that wasn't very well hidden. "I assure you, this will in no way dampen our resolve to finalize a more permanent and complete treaty."

"Of course not," Lahkaba replied, not believing him for a moment. "But still, we would not want to take advantage of your hospitality and start our relationship off poorly. We hope to be partners."

While Sceglis stared at him, clearly trying to ascertain Lahkaba's strategy, the other three members of Lahkaba's party cast him confused looks, though Zoeko's gaze was more of reprimand and agitation. He hoped that was just part of her act as a gold, but he doubted it. Their discussion after leaving here wouldn't be fun.

"I can see you're not seriously interested in a treaty," Sceglis said sternly. "Perhaps some time to discuss this with your fellow delegates will change your mind. As it stands right now, you clearly want more from us than is reasonable. Good day."

With that, Sceglis and his party stood up and departed the room, leaving Lahkaba alone with nothing but the confused and angry looks of his people.

"You had better have a damn good explanation for that!" Lionell demanded once they were back in their transport car. He had activated their jamming device, preventing any eavesdropping, though Lahkaba thought it might be better for the Dotran to hear that he had acted alone.

"Yes, I would like to hear this as well, though I suspect it's merely foolish Kowwok pride," Zoeko hissed.

Valinther cast her a dark look but then turned it on Lahkaba. That made three sets of eyes boring into him. It made him feel like a kid again, caught doing something wrong. What he had just done might be much worse than stealing a sweet without asking, though.

Deciding that his best explanation was a full offensive, he reached over and hit the button that lowered the barrier between the passenger cabin and the driver. The glass partition lowered, revealing Rathalos operating the car's controls.

Lahkaba stared at the other Kowwok's back for a long moment and then said, "They all have good questions. Why did I just do that?"

Rathalos's fur stiffened, but he didn't turn back toward them. "You did it to prevent the Dotran from getting their hands on your unkillable warship."

The cabin became dead silent for a minute. Lionell, Valinther, and Zoeko all exchanged glances as they processed the announcement. They wouldn't want to see the Dotran become equipped with the *Audacious*'s regenerative shield technology, either.

"Yes, that would be an unfortunate side effect of that deal, but the price might be worth it. They were offering things we desperately need," Lionell finally said, his tone reluctant.

"It's a great bargaining chip," Zoeko said, her voice ecstatic. "You were right to refuse the agreement. We can use this to gain much more than they were offering."

"We can't let them have that shield!" Valinther retorted. "Once we equip the Dotran with those shields, they'll be unstoppable!"

"She may be right, Val," Lionell said. "The ship doesn't even work."

"Tell that to the Alliance task force it destroyed defending my planet," Valinther snapped back.

Zoeko let out a hissing growl. "We're fighting over a side issue. The question we must address now is what does our driver have to do with this?"

"He was the one who brought my attention to what we would be giving away," Lahkaba answered simply. "Though he didn't tell me *why* he did that."

Everyone's attention shifted off of Lahkaba, filling him with relief, and settled on the Kowwok driver. Rathalos remained facing forward, avoiding the brunt of the stares. Silence was the only reply for a minute.

When it became obvious that the attention wasn't going to go away, Rathalos dropped his shoulders slightly. "It would not be in our best interest to allow the Dotran such a tactical advantage."

"Who is *we*?" Lahkaba asked, glad to finally be able to ask that question. He had only hopes and suspicions.

Rathalos hesitated again, but after a moment his voice was filled with pride. "The Kowwok Resistance."

A surge of excitement washed through Lahkaba. When Rathalos had first spoken to him, a tiny voice in his head had imagined this possibility—his people fighting back and resisting the Dotran. But he had suppressed that idea immediately.

The Kowwok had been subjects of the Dotran for hundreds of years. Most of his people were still devoted to the non-violence taught by the Great One. But as Valinther and himself demonstrated, not all of them were.

"There is no Kowwok Resistance," Valinther said. "I grew up on the homeworld. Anyone who thought of resisting was shunned. That's why I left."

Rathalos nodded. "That was true, and for many, it still is. But many among our people have been starting to feel that the pacifistic tenant of our faith is outdated. During the Colonial War, when the Dotran forcibly conscripted many Kowwok to fight, things started to change. The number of Kowwok opposed to any form of violence started to shrink at a faster pace. There are more and more of us who are ready to fight for our freedom."

Still driving, Rathalos continued, "When we learned you were coming, I was inserted as your servant so I could help ensure that the negotiations succeeded. I decided warning you about the potential consequences of the deal they were offering was worth risking my cover. I never thought Sceglis would walk away from the table over this issue."

"Why would you want the Dotran and us to form a treaty?" Lionell asked. "I'd think the resistance would be better served looking to us for aid rather than making us dependent on the Dotran. If we form a treaty, helping your people would be outside of our power."

"We considered that," Rathalos confessed. "But in the end we settled on a plan that required the Dotran sending a fleet to Kreogh Sector. We've been putting pieces into place since the news of the first uprising there occurred. We knew the Dotran would eventually send a fleet, one way or another, and better as a friend to you than as a conquering force."

"You're planning an uprising when the fleet departs?" Valinther asked, excitement creeping into his voice.

Lahkaba could appreciate the sentiment. A Kowwok uprising occurring at the same time that a Dotran fleet came and aided their efforts to be free from the Alliance—it would be the perfect event. Due to the travel delay, they would have several months of use out of the fleet before it got called back.

A selfish part of him also thought of the second benefit—if the Dotran fleet got called back to deal with an uprising at home, it wouldn't become a permanent fixture in Kreogh. That was the major potential drawback to any treaty involving military aid.

"Not exactly," Rathalos said, clearly hesitant.

"What do you mean, not exactly?" Lionell asked insistently. "What other benefit could a Dotran fleet being away provide to your resistance?"

"I'm not authorized to share that," Rathalos replied. "I really shouldn't be talking to you at all, but it was my advice that disrupted the talks, and I need to ensure they get back on track."

Lahkaba wished Rathalos would tell them everything, but he could appreciate the position the other Kowwok was in. A resistance movement survived through secrecy. He didn't want to jeopardize their chances by forcing him to say too much.

"So, how do we do that?" Lahkaba asked. "We can't give them the shield technology. Even if it has problems, the potential threat is still too high. And it sounds like they're going to hold out for either that or our submission to joining the Confederacy."

"Neither one of which we can give them," Valinther stated emphatically.

"We have only what we came here prepared to offer them," Zoeko said, her tone surprisingly calm. "Trade agreements and resources rights."

"That's not insignificant," Rathalos said. "The Dotran have a strong desire to gain access to the mineral wealth on Kol and the biodiversity on Mirthod."

"We'll just have to hope it's enough," Zoeko said. Something in her tone disturbed Lahkaba.

Chapter Twelve

Walking along the perimeter battle line between the Cardine and Alliance forces left Zeric feeling exposed. More than a kilometer of ground separated them, but it was mostly open ground. He could see the walls of the Alliance base, with guards standing watch.

Despite the appearance of danger, and his usual sense of self-preservation telling him to get behind something, Zeric knew the Alliance base presented no immediate danger. Protective shields protected him from any weapons fire from the Alliance. A similar field protected the Alliance, in turn.

As Zeric walked along with Marshall Teev, he greeted the mostly Camari soldiers manning the line. The shield protected them from long-range weapons fire, but due to the uneven nature of the ground, there were plenty of gaps large enough for soldiers to get through. That was the nature of portable shield generators, and he remembered being one of the soldiers having to sit right on the edge, watching for an attack.

The response from the soldiers holding the line made Zeric very uncomfortable. Most of them greeted him warmly and with a glow of excitement. He tried to recall if meeting any big-name generals had made him act like that, but he couldn't recall a time he had met any big-name generals on the front lines.

What surprised him the most about the tour was how the troops responded to Marshall Teev. The troops greeted the man like a friend, and while they showed pleasure at seeing him, they didn't treat it as a special event. Apparently, it wasn't unusual for them to see their leader on the front lines.

"You've got an impressive set-up here, Marshall," Zeric said as they moved between two units of troop.

"Thank you," Teev responded, genuine pride evident in his tone. "They've served their planet well, defending us all. I only hope I can repay them for their courage by finding a way to end this detestable stalemate soon. Any suggestions you might have would be welcome."

Zeric gritted his teeth to hold back his first, natural response. The previous night, he and Gu'od had discussed a number of potential plans to breach the Alliance's defenses and end the current standoff, but Lei-mey had been insistent on preserving the situation.

"Actually, Marshall, I would recommend that you keep up the stalemate as long as possible," Zeric said, half regretting it even as he spoke.

Teev gave him a startled look, and Zeric continued, "Right now, you've got the Alliance in a weak but defensible position. You can resupply; they cannot. A prolonged siege benefits you more than it does them."

Teev looked thoughtful but shook his head. "That would be unfair to my forces, making them sit. Idleness is the bane of any army."

"True." Zeric hated the old routine of "hurry up and wait." He went on, "But you have another advantage—you can rotate your forces off the front lines; the Alliance cannot."

"Not unless they send reinforcements, and as long as the Alliance has a foothold on Cardine, the easier that will be for them," Teev said.

"Also true," Zeric said. "But no Alliance commander is going to call for reinforcements as long as he thinks he has a chance of winning on his own. Your two forces have been sitting here for weeks now, facing off against each other. While the wait is annoying and damaging to morale, it also boosts the confidence of their commander.

"If you could finish them, why haven't you done it by now? he's thinking. He's got a powerful enough comm system to break through planetary jamming, so he can send messages to any Alliance spy ships that might appear. He's got months of supplies. Show him a few signs of your troops weakening, and he'll be ready to keep this siege going without calling for assistance.

"Admiral Sartori has an entire sector in rebellion, and Cardine has planetary weapons capable of defending itself. As long as the Alliance commander on the scene believes he can hold out, Sartori won't risk sending forces here that she can use elsewhere. The moment you remove that option is the moment you need to start getting ready to repel an invasion."

Despite his distaste for pushing Lei-mey's plan on Teev, he didn't disagree with it. None of it was a lie, which he hadn't expected from her.

Even though it wasn't a plan he would have endorsed on his own, it was a sound military strategy. He just hated waiting as much as the soldiers here holding the line did.

"Perhaps you're right," Teev finally said, still looking thoughtful.

Seizing this, Zeric decided to throw in a little of his own perspective. "Trust me, Marshall, I wouldn't want to prolong a siege any more than you. If it were just me, I'd charge the Alliance base now—to hell with sitting around waiting. But, unfortunately, you and I don't have the luxury of indulging our own personal desires."

Teev gave a small chuckle. "That we don't."

Taking in a deep breath, Zeric prepared for the unpleasant part of the conversation—the entire reason Lei-mey had suggested this plan, and the reason he had come to Cardine in the first place.

"Now, the other benefit of a prolonged stand-off is that it frees up a lot of your forces," Zeric began. "You can maintain a strong defensive perimeter with less total strength than you would need for a frontal assault. That would allow you to dispatch forces with me to join the fight on other worlds in the sector."

Teev frowned at that last comment, a look of disappointment on his face. The subtle accusation stung Zeric, but he had come this far. He pushed forward. "I know how that sounds, a Terran coming here with a pushy delegate from Sulas asking for more troops. But the truth is, the rest of the sector needs Cardine's help. Kol is the only planet in a similar defensive position as Cardine, and that's thanks to the navy. Dantyne, Sulas, and Enro are all under invasion already and need help pushing the Alliance back. Ailleroc is under a stranglehold, and we can't even think about helping them until we push the Alliance back everywhere else, including here.

"But to start, we need to push the Alliance back. Right now, Cardine can do that, but if you're the only one who does, you're the next target. If, together, we push the Alliance off the other worlds in the sector along with Cardine, they won't be able to respond and crush you alone."

Still looking unconvinced, Teev said nothing. Zeric decided he had only one more card to play. "You have my personal assurance that if the Alliance makes a move on Cardine, I'll lead whatever troops I can back here as fast as I possibly can. This isn't an empty promise of a politician, but from me to you. One military officer to another."

Teev's eyestalks rose up in a look of surprise. Lei-mey had told Zeric not to make any kind of promises, and for good reason. He knew perfectly well that if the Alliance made a move on Cardine, he wouldn't likely be in a position to help. But he would still try.

Finally, Teev nodded. "Coming from a politician, I would take that as an empty platitude, but even if those reinforcements just end up being you, I actually believe you'll do it. Very well, I'll detach a regiment with you. I believe they'll be put to good use in ensuring the freedom of our fellow Union worlds."

Zeric shook Teev's outstretched hand, giving him a grim smile. Even though he had gotten what he wanted—what he needed—he still couldn't shake a dirty feeling inside.

Katerina didn't often feel like yelling. Especially at her staff, many of whom had been with her for a number of years. But sometimes the news delivered was so infuriating that you still wanted to blame the messenger because they were the one telling you about it.

Controlling herself, Katerina said, "Please repeat that, Major."

"Taskforce 413 has returned from Dantyne after fleeing a rebel attack force," Major Anderson replied in an emotionless tone. "Commander Maritski reports that they were outnumbered by rebel forces and that the fleet contained the FX-21. They report one lost frigate, with Commodore Dolan aboard, presumed captured by the rebels."

Unfortunately, the news hadn't changed on the second telling. It rarely did. What she had originally assumed to be a poorly organized band of opportunist rebels had now managed to capture or destroy four of her warships. Granted, in comparison to the last war, those were light losses. But then she'd been fighting a well-trained and well-equipped military of equivalent power.

"Commander Maritski says she departed in order to gather additional forces before returning to Dantyne," Anderson added.

Katerina scoffed. "I'm sure. Tell the commander to prepare a full report on the battle over Dantyne. Let her know I want her to present it to me personally." That would help her decide if this recent loss was due to incompetence, cowardice, or just bad luck. She wanted to believe in the latter. One of her Braz peers would have probably called it cosmic balance for her overwhelming victory in ambushing the rebels over Sulas.

"Something else, Major?" Katerina asked when Anderson didn't immediately depart.

"Yes, Admiral. I hesitate to mention it since it's an unconfirmed report," Anderson said, "but the preliminary indications are that the rebels were led by a Commodore Ocaitchi."

Katerina considered the information. "You believe this is the same Ocaitchi who led the defense of Kol? Maarkean's sister?"

"It would make sense, Admiral."

"I thought our operative's report described her as an idealist engineer with no will to fight?" Katerina asked.

Anderson nodded. "It did. Though he did make clear he had only had limited contact with her up until that point."

"And nothing from him recently?" Katerina asked. "It was his plan to reinsert himself with the rebels by releasing that freighter. Now it's already cost me a frigate and Commodore Dolan."

"No recent updates. Though if he was identified, it might be some time before we learned of it. He could also be with this assault fleet and unable to break cover," Anderson theorized.

"Possibly," Katerina said quietly. "But we can't keep waiting on his report. Dispatch a recon ship to Kol. Confirm that the FX-21 has indeed departed the system. Then dispatch a message to Taffy 422—order them to depart Mirthod."

"Long range recon or active scan?" Anderson asked.

With the openness of space, it was possible to appear anywhere in a star system and through a long-range, passive scan, observe a planet using telescopes and other passive sensors, keeping yourself out of danger. This means of intelligence gathering was limited, however. Identifying an object as small as a ship from millions of kilometers away while it was backdropped by a bright planet could be difficult. It was also incredibly easy to fool this type of surveillance with decoys or simply keeping vital items inside another structure, such as the ground or the orbital shipyard they knew the rebels had at Kol. Confirming the readings of a passive scan required getting close and using an active sensor scan.

"Active scan," Katerina decided. "But have them scan and depart only. I want that gunship coming back in one piece."

"Understood, Admiral," Anderson said and started for the door.

"Also," Katerina added, stopping Anderson, "I think it's time I had a chat with our resident rebel. Major Ocaitchi has been sitting in a cell giving us nothing useful for long enough. But he will be our best source of information on his sister, since it appears our operative's assessment of her as 'unwilling to fight' isn't exactly accurate."

"You want to speak to him yourself?" Anderson asked, unable to keep his incredulity out of his voice.

Katerina nodded. "Yes. I need to get to know my enemy. I've been striking at them from the dark for long enough."

If an untrained engineer who had been marked as a non-combatant could defeat her former adjutant, then these rebels were a much greater threat than she had previously judged. She would need to start taking a completely new approach.

"Sensors reading one Alliance escort carrier, one corvette, and two gunships," Tadashio reported. "No fighters are currently deployed."

The news surprised Saracasi. They had delayed longer at Dantyne than she had wanted, so she had expected to find Mirthod heavily reinforced. Instead, she faced a task force smaller than her own, even discounting the decoy *Audacious*. The addition of the captured Alliance frigate, *Hurricane*, and the return of Eri'dos with his *Durandall II* and four cutters had boosted their strength significantly.

"Plot an intercept course," Saracasi ordered.

The trajectory of the Alliance ships would take them out of Mirthod's gravity well. By the look of it, she had arrived just as they were departing. At least, that's how it looked.

She tried to figure out how their course could be used as a trap for her fleet. With the Alliance ships moving away from Mirthod, any other ships hiding around the curve of the planet would have a long journey to come around as reinforcements. Mirthod itself had no planetary defense weapons. Even if the Alliance had installed any, she could easily keep her ships out of effective range.

Though she hated to admit it, it looked like they just got lucky. A small Alliance fleet caught alone, fleeing before a superior force.

That the phrase "superior force" could describe her collection of banged-up, refitted, and overused ships almost made her laugh.

The fleet altered its trajectory along a vector that would intercept the four Alliance ships just before they were at a safe jump distance. It wasn't likely that they could do enough damage to the ships to prevent them from escaping, but she didn't feel like letting them go without a show.

As they moved closer, Saracasi allowed herself to finally feel some relief. They would likely avoid a full battle yet would still be able to claim that they had chased the Alliance away from Mirthod. A public relationships victory was still a victory.

With the damage the fleet had taken at Dantyne, the engineer in her had wanted to turn back for Kol and make repairs. La'ari had actually been fairly insistent on that point. *Chimopori* needed structural repairs that required a shipyard. Their captured frigate was not capable of combat maneuvers, and half the weapon systems were offline.

Defiant Glory had been spared too much damage, and all of her fighters could be repaired en route. That fact had convinced the warrior in her to press forward. The only thing the Union fleet had on its side was surprise. She had to keep pressing the attack before the Alliance figured out her ruse and sent a powerful enough force to stop them.

Without warning, the lights on the bridge suddenly started flickering. The tactical holodisplay winked out, as did several consoles around the bridge and CIC. She exchanged a look with Jerik and Kaars beside her. Power issues on a warship were never a good sign.

After a few seconds, everything came back on. Before the replacement of the power reactor on *Defiant Glory*, small power issues had been common, especially when she was powered up for combat. But since the upgrade, they hadn't experienced any such problems.

If her flagship was experiencing trouble and had been the least damaged ship in the previous battle, what could the other ships be experiencing? Reluctantly, Saracasi came to the conclusion that she needed to find out.

"All ships, reduce speed. The Alliance is running. We'll follow them out, but if they want to flee at the sight of us, I say let them," Saracasi said after activating the fleet-wide comm. She hoped that playing it up as being merciful to a cowardly Alliance wouldn't affect morale negatively.

She then sent a less public request for ship status updates to all captains. Several minutes later, updates came in. Everything appeared to be standard. The frigate, *Hurricane*, had the most issues, but all were known and unrepaired battle damage. The gunships and cutters all reported full status. *Defiant Glory* had been the only ship to experience any unexpected problems.

"Captain," Saracasi said turning to Jerik, "do you have a report on that power issue?"

Jerik nodded. "We suffered a low-grade power spike. La'ari is still trying to ascertain why, though. In addition to the lights flickering and console trouble, our comm unit surged and the navigational computer temporarily went offline before rebooting. No major systems were affected. *Defiant Glory* is still combat capable."

"Thank you, Captain," Saracasi said. Though the news sounded positive, even secondary systems didn't break for no reason. Plus, she recalled their escape from Sulas. They almost hadn't made it to safety due to the original programmers' designation of the hyperdrive as a secondary system that wasn't checked on a standard diagnostic.

The Alliance task force had gained ground. With her order to slow down, her fleet would no longer intercept before the Alliance ships could jump to hyperspace. Had her caution just cost them an easy victory?

Before she could start to relax or drive herself crazy overthinking her decisions, a priority message came in from the faux-*Audacious* Phantom group. Sheanna's voice came through her earpiece. "Commodore, we've been intercepted by a civilian mining scout. They managed to get close enough to get a close look at my ships. I estimate high probability his sensor data is accurate enough to see through our ruse. We're currently jamming his comm system, but he'll be out of range shortly. Our tractor beams cannot operate while linked together and the ship will be outside of weapon and jamming range in six minutes from your receipt of this message. Your orders?"

Saracasi cursed to herself. The worse of all possible scenarios had occurred. Sheanna could not communicate with the civilian ship without dropping the jamming system. If he did, and the ship proved to be loyal to the Alliance, the civilian would have time to transmit a distress signal, including sensor data, to the fleeing Alliance task force.

Faux-*Audacious* and the civilian were four light-minutes away. The Alliance fleet was still twelve minutes from jumping away—plenty of time for them to receive a signal. If the Alliance learned of her ruse with the cutters, her main tactical advantage would be gone. She could either let the civilian go and risk that, or destroy him to preserve her secret.

The time on the clock ticked down at an unnaturally rapid pace. Her order to Sheanna would take four minutes to arrive. They had less than two minutes for her to decide and for him to take action.

"Disable that ship if you can. Destroy it if you must," Saracasi finally said in a rush into her comm.

A twist of guilt stabbed at her insides the moment the words were out. She almost rescinded the order, but she knew she had made the right call. Her duty was to protect the people under her and to beat the Alliance. This was one of those tough calls a leader had to make. Her brother would do the same. Wouldn't he?

The next ten minutes passed at an agonizing crawl. Her fleet and the Alliance task force got closer together. No transmission came from Sheanna, and the Alliance gave no indication of having received one themselves. When they reached the edge of the gravity well, they jumped away.

Finally, fourteen minutes after she had received the first message, a follow-up came in from Sheanna. "The civilian ship has been destroyed, Commodore. We attempted to disable, but he went evasive, reducing the accuracy of our weapons fire. SAR operations are now in effect, but no emergency beacons have been detected. No transmissions were made from him before the destruction."

Letting out a heavy sigh, Saracasi felt her shoulders loosen. It had been a horrible call to make, but the safety of her fleet had been preserved. She put the incident behind her and ordered the fleet to stand down. They could afford to spend a few hours showing the flag over Mirthod and making a few more repairs.

Chapter Thirteen

Maarkean had never thought he could miss light. Their Alliance captors had taken to a new form of torture the last few days: three days of non-stop bright lights, followed by three days of complete darkness.

At first, the darkness had felt like a blessed relief from the lights, but that hadn't lasted long. Ronids had excellent night vision, but unfortunately for Maarkean, Braz required at least a little light to see.

The only bright spot—he enjoyed thinking of it that way, since the pun amused him—in the whole ordeal of imprisonment had been Lohcja. Despite the adventures they'd shared, he had never considered himself all that close to the man before, at least not like Zeric or Lahkaba. Maybe the Alliance bigotry against other alien species was more ingrained in him than he had thought.

Whatever subtle revulsion he might have had toward Ronids, he felt sure it was gone now. Having Lohcja here had kept him stable. He had no idea how he would have coped for so long alone, especially after getting so close to escape, only to be defeated and recaptured. Plus, the added guilt over Merski's death weighed on him.

"Kaars. Kill. Betrayed." Lohcja's mumbling caught Maarkean's attention.

Many nights, Maarkean awoke to hear his friend mumbling something similar. The sounds of Lohcja expressing the desire to kill in his dreams unsettled him, though he could hardly blame him. As Lohcja had explained early in their captivity, Kaars Aerinstar had betrayed them.

Maarkean didn't fully understand the nature of their relationship, but he knew the two men had been friends. The betrayal had unsettled Lohcja severely, and the time in captivity and torture had done nothing to stymie his growing hatred.

"LJ," Maarkean said, and then repeated the nickname a few times. He had learned the hard way not to touch the Ronid when he was dreaming.

"Hmm . . . I'm awake . . . what?" Lohcja said groggily. "Is it morning already?"

"I think it's actually yesterday," Maarkean joked.

"That's not very damn funny."

Before the two could continue their banter, bright light flared, blinding Maarkean. He automatically shut his eyes, but he could already feel the pain from the sudden light. Grimacing through the pain, he tried to open them again, but could only see a bright glow that still stung. Squeezing his eyes shut, he tried to listen.

The sounds of voices and boot steps on the metal deck could be heard. The voices were muffled at first, but one rose above the others. "Explain to me, Specialist, how two of your prisoners have gotten into this condition?"

"Injuries sustained when they were captured. Ma'am," an uneasy voice replied. It took Maarkean a moment, given the drastically different tone, but he soon identified the speaker as one of the Alliance crew in charge of the brig.

"Really? Injuries sustained months ago have been left untreated for all that time?" the first voice asked. The tone was clear and commanding, making Maarkean suspect a high-ranking officer.

"No, ma'am, of course not. They've been well tended to, per the LT's orders," the brig crewman replied.

"I see. Why don't you go and tell the lieutenant I want to see her."

The sounds of hasty steps and the brig door opening followed the order. Maarkean still wasn't sure exactly what was happening, but the mental image of one of their torturers being verbally abused and made to run around gave him no small amount of pleasure.

Several minutes passed while Maarkean tried opening his eyes. He suddenly thought how much more unbearable this must be for Lohcja, who didn't have eyelids. Slowly, vision returned to him, though he had to squint, and it helped to look through small cracks in his fingers.

A tall, intimidating Terran female with light brown skin stood outside their cell. She wore the uniform of an Alliance naval major. On the right shoulder of the dark green uniform jacket hung a gold cord of office, which identified her as the adjutant of a flag officer. That meant her words carried the same weight as the admiral's.

The major stood there in silence, studying them. Her facial expression gave no hint as to what she was thinking. The only thing Maarkean could derive was a sense of intelligence.

"Ah, Major Anderson, congratulations on your promotion. How can I help you?" a young lieutenant said as she came into the brig. It took Maarkean a minute to place that voice, and he thought his eyes must still be suffering, but the lieutenant was indeed Merski.

At first, Maarkean felt a wave of relief at the sight of Merski alive. That was quickly followed by an overwhelming sense of anger. Lohcja had been right from the beginning—the escape attempt had, indeed, all been a trick. So had staging the woman's death. But why? What purpose had it served?

"You can explain to me how your prisoners got into the state they're in," Anderson said flatly.

"When they were captured aboard their ship, they were already in pretty bad shape—" Merski began, but Anderson cut her off.

"That lie isn't going to work with me. Try again."

Merski visibly gulped and then said, "The process of interrogation can sometimes be a messy business with uncooperative individuals. They require some more, umm, enhanced techniques."

"You mean you tortured them," Anderson said, her voice still unemotional. Maarkean found himself admiring the woman. She had an almost Braz-like detachment.

"Of course not," Merski said unconvincingly. "That would be a violation of Alliance rules governing the treatment of prisoners."

"Yes, it would," Anderson said.

What she left unsaid hung in the air between the two women.

"Admiral Sartori wishes to speak with the prisoners," Anderson said after a long moment of silence. "Take them to the showers and then get them clean uniforms."

"Aye, Major," Merski said, concern evident in her voice. Her face dropped at Anderson's next command.

"You and Major Barshan will be accompanying me back to the flagship."

The idea of some justice being delivered for what had been done to him and Lohcja gave Maarkean a small amount of relief. Merski would pay for what she had done, even though he knew her punishment would not match the scale of her crime. But this was far overshadowed by the news that he was about to be brought before Admiral Katerina Sartori. Whatever she wanted with him, it couldn't be good.

Saracasi watched Commodore Dolan through the video monitor. Previously, she hadn't paid much attention to the Alliance personnel they had captured at Dantyne, because they were trained officers, loyal to the Alliance, and she had assumed no reliable information could be obtained from them. Then she had learned that Commodore Dolan had previously served as Admiral Sartori's adjutant. That gave him invaluable insight into how the admiral thought, which she desperately needed.

She listened as Kaars asked, "Why would Admiral Sartori withdraw her forces from Mirthod?"

Dolan just sat there, saying nothing, like he had in response to every other question.

She wanted to get something from him, anything that would help separate the legend that was Admiral Sartori from the woman, but the only sign of emotion the man had revealed had come when Kaars had first entered the room. She had taken that as a sign that he knew the intelligence officer and had hoped it might help bridge a connection.

After more silence from Dolan, Kaars contacted her on a private channel. "He's not talking, Commodore. Standard interrogation tactics won't work. He's too well trained."

"Keep trying as best you can," she said.

"Commodore," Kaars said hesitantly, "I could try more advanced techniques."

Saracasi frowned. She disliked torture. It was barbaric and rarely effective. She considered the option for a moment but then shook her head. "No, Master Sergeant. The Alliance has rules against the torture of enemy soldiers. We won't be the ones to cross that line."

"Ma'am," Kaars hedged, "they've already crossed that line. General Kil'dare was tortured after being taken prisoner in the Olan raid."

She had forgotten about that fact. Had the Alliance already broken the rules of war, freeing her from any obligation to follow them? At the time, the Union hadn't existed, so Jairyd would have been considered a terrorist, not an enemy soldier. But did that matter? She didn't think so.

"We're fighting the Alliance for that very reason. They've abandoned their principles. That doesn't mean we will. Conventional tactics only. Treat him well," Saracasi ordered.

"Aye," Kaars responded.

Saracasi shut down the monitor feed to the interrogation. A few moments later, Fracsid, Jerik, La'ari, and Sheanna came in and sat in the first row of the briefing seats. For the first time, she regretted their earlier decision to convert this room into a pilot briefing room. It had once been a corporate conference room, back when the ship had been a commercial mining vessel. At the time, the conversion had made sense. That had been before she had had a need to sit down and meet with people on a regular basis. Now, instead of sitting around a table for a discussion, she had to either stand at the front, like a teacher lecturing a class, or have everyone sit in a single row, making communication awkward.

"When was your recon report on Enro?" Saracasi asked.

"Just under two weeks ago," Fracsid said, standing up to join her at the front projector. "*Bright Blade* checked in while we were in transit to Mirthod."

"What do you make of those forces?" Saracasi asked.

Fracsid replied, "Based on that report, I would estimate the fleet to be the main force of a Marine Expeditionary Force. One fleet carrier, one cruiser, and several support ships, including at least one frigate and corvette. At least four ships, most likely eight or ten."

"That's against our fifteen. We outnumber them almost two to one," Jerik said enthusiastically.

"That's assuming one-to-one ship parity," La'ari said, her tone grumpy. "Our ships are converted freighters and patrol cutters. Those are actual warships."

"We've done pretty well so far. And we have a captured frigate now, too," Jerik exclaimed.

"Which, sad to say, is still in need of a lot of repairs," Sheanna added. Saracasi had moved her from commanding the phantom squad to captaining the captured frigate.

"Exactly!" La'ari added. "All of our ships are in need of some kind of repair. I still haven't tracked down what caused the power spike aboard the *Defiant Glory*, which means it could happen again at any time."

"Or it might not," Jerik argued. "We need to move fast if we're to keep the Alliance off balance. The trick with the phantom squad won't work forever."

"With this fleet, I don't think that trick will work at all. They've got enough firepower to take *Audacious* on," Sheanna added.

Saracasi's first thought was to argue with Sheanna. The Alliance had outclassed them at Dantyne and had still run. If their trick with the phantom squad was now useless, had she ordered that civilian mining ship destroyed for nothing?

No, she decided. Their secret was safe and the trick could still work—just not against such a powerful enemy fleet. She had intended the trick to help her tip the balance when fighting a fleet of comparable strength to hers. The fact that it had worked the first time against a much more powerful one had been a fluke.

"Sheanna's right," Saracasi said, interrupting Jerik's argument. "The phantom squad would be discovered and those cutters would be torn to shreds against the MEF."

"So we're not going?" Jerik asked, disappointment in his tone.

"I haven't decided," Saracasi admitted.

"You'd be a fool to attack," La'ari said angrily. "Your brother let an attack against a superior enemy go forward, and it got my brother killed. You're an engineer. I thought you were smarter than that."

The sudden vehemence in La'ari's tone took Saracasi off guard. The Notha engineer had never been shy about sharing her opinion, but while she had never officially agreed to join the military, she had always conducted herself respectfully. This outburst went over the line into insubordination.

Saracasi's initial shock quickly gave way to anger. How dare La'ari say those things about her brother? Maarkean had done everything he could to save the fleet, and he had gotten himself captured in the process. La'ari was just a civilian engineer without a bit of military training.

Of course, Saracasi was just an engineer with a handful of platitudes and lectures from disgraced former officers.

While Saracasi sat there deciding how to respond, Jerik barked out a sharp order. "That's enough, Engineer Mahon. Your tone is unbecoming of an officer on this ship. You're dismissed."

La'ari glared at Jerik for a second and then turned to Saracasi. For a moment, she seemed to be waiting for her to countermand Jerik. When Saracasi said nothing, La'ari slouched and then said, her voice almost a growl, "If you'll excuse me, Your Highness, I have to go finish fixing the ship before you break it again." La'ari turned toward the exit.

As she watched the Notha leave, Saracasi considered calling her back and dressing her down for that tone. She knew it could be detrimental to military discipline if insubordination and disrespect went unchecked. But she knew La'ari, and she knew the grief the woman felt over the loss of her brother. She could even understand it on a personal level, recalling how she had felt when she had thought Maarkean had also died at Sulas. If she weren't trying to pretend to be a professional military leader, would she have yelled back at La'ari?

While trying to answer that question, Saracasi forced herself to keep listening to the others around her. Fracsid and Jerik had picked up with planning the next battle as soon as La'ari had left. Sheanna wasn't contributing anything to the discussion so far and wore a neutral expression.

"Even with *Chimopori* damaged, if two gunships don't have to play escort to the phantom squad, we'll be more than a match for one of the Alliance's frigates," Fracsid said.

"And the cutters can form two squads and take on any corvettes," Jerik said, sounding excited. "Together, they have more firepower, and corvettes don't have enough to be much of a threat to them. That will keep them off our fighters as well."

"Which will be a problem. That carrier will have a lot more fighters than we will," Fracsid said, showing the first sign of reluctance.

"True, but it's a marine carrier. They're likely carrying mostly ground attack craft and bombers. Those are no match for space superiority fighters. We'll tear them up," Jerik said confidently.

"We should be able to get the *Hurricane* battle-ready in two days. Together with the *Defiant Glory*, we can probably take on the carrier itself. That will just leave the cruiser," Sheanna added.

Saracasi looked around at the three officers. With La'ari gone, the discussion had completely shifted. Now everyone was assuming that they would resume the assault, which was a relief. She wanted to continue the fight, and she didn't want to have a debate about it.

That thought suddenly made her frown, recalling the battle over Kol. Right before they had launched, she had decided to make Arzesaeth her executive officer instead of Sheanna. She had done so because the man thought differently than she did.

Now, the lone voice of dissent against continuing their offensive had left. Had La'ari been wrong in her assessment? Was this a foolish idea? Or was it bold and necessary?

"No," Saracasi said, deciding. "We're returning to Kol to finish repairs on all ships, especially *Hurricane*. Major Relis, dispatch your squadron for another recon mission before returning to Kol. I want eyes on Enro, Dantyne, Sulas, and Ailleroc. Let's make sure the Alliance hasn't come right behind us with another task force."

Growing more confident with her decision, Saracasi added, "Lieutenant Coramont, contact Phantom squad. Have them make a buzz of Sulas before returning. I want the Alliance to see them. Make it look like *Audacious* taunting them. Make sure the cutter captains know it's just a fly-by. Stay at extreme range, and keep it short, but let's keep the Alliance guessing."

Sheanna and Fracsid nodded without an argument, but Jerik said, "But Commodore, we have a chance to help free Enro."

"Not yet," Saracasi said, trying to make her tone confident. "Major Novastar will be back from Trepon by the time our ships are repaired. Even if he doesn't bring the *Black Market* with him, his ship will be back to add to our firepower. By then, General Dustlighter will also have another army force ready to deploy. Then we won't just be scaring the Alliance out of orbit—we'll actually be able to retake the planet."

Chapter Fourteen

As Katerina looked through the one-way glass at the traitor Maarkean, she couldn't help but feel a touch of sympathy for the man. Bruises almost hid the purple screfa on his cheek, and a deep gash on his forehead bore signs of fresh stitches.

The man had betrayed his oath to the Alliance. By every reasonable measure, he was a traitor and would die for his crimes. But even that didn't justify torture.

What bothered Katerina the most was knowing that it had been her people who had done this. She had left Maarkean in a brig for months, expecting the intelligence division to do their duty: interrogate him for any useful intelligence and then confine him until he could be tried for his crimes. Instead, they had made him pay for their outrage for the losses the Alliance had suffered in this rebellion. Their other prisoner, the Ronid, had suffered even worse. And it had happened on her watch. The frigate's captain and intelligence officer and the crew involved would all be court-martialed for this. But Katerina wouldn't suffer any consequences, despite feeling the responsibility.

Quietly, she berated herself for allowing this line of thought. The torture was a tragedy, yes, but she was here to interrogate the leader of a terrorist rebellion. She couldn't start that process by feeling sympathy for him—unless she could use it to her advantage.

Nodding to herself as a strategy formed in her mind, Katerina walked over to the door and entered the interrogation room. Maarkean sat bound to a chair with chains, a wide table in front of him. As she came in the room, he looked up, and she felt a sudden sense of familiarity. Instead of the cold look of hatred she would have expected from a terrorist, the look he gave her reminded her of how every new officer she met looked at her. Respect, admiration, worship.

Unsettled by this familiarity, Katerina pushed forward. "Major Ocaitchi, I wish to apologize for the way you've been treated. The manner in which Lieutenant Merski handled your interrogation was disgraceful and unacceptable. All those involved will be court-martialed for this crime, I assure you.

"I'm glad to see that your wounds have been seen to. When Major Anderson told me what had been done to you and Mr. Cargon, I was shocked. The Alliance doesn't torture its prisoners under any circumstances."

Maarkean remained silent. His initial look of respect slowly started to disappear behind a passive expression. Using sympathy to gain his cooperation might prove harder than she had hoped. But she should have expected that. Braz tended to hold their emotions close to the chest.

"As deplorable as this situation may be, it's a good analogy for why I'm here. The Alliance made some mistakes in how we managed the colonies. Much like Lieutenant Merski did with how she treated you. She forgot what it meant to be an Alliance officer. But I haven't. That's why they sent me. To try to mend the wounds, metaphorically, between the colonies and the Alliance."

Switching tactics, Katerina sat down and settled into a relaxed, conversational posture. "Did you know I was about to retire? I had already stepped down as the commander of Second Fleet. I was going to return home to Terra, spend time with my grandchildren. But a few days before I left, we learned about the prison break on Sulas.

"As much as I wanted to continue with my plans, I knew it was my duty to return here to try to stop any more blood from being spilt. I left this sector sixteen years ago after a violent and ugly war, but I left it in peace. When the Alliance called me to help restore that state of peace, I knew I had to come."

Leaning forward, Katerina looked Maarkean in the eye. "It's the sworn duty of any Alliance officer to uphold the law and preserve the peace. Some bad apples, like Lieutenant Merski, had forgotten that. You saw those violations of their oath, and I know how it must have disgusted you. They were betraying their oath and duty. You wanted to address that. Believe me, I understand.

"But the way a loyal officer addresses injustice is within the law, not by violating it more. By all accounts, you were a good officer. You even served with me onboard the *Enterprise* during the war. Why would an exemplary officer such as yourself decide to violate his principles in order to fight others for violating theirs?"

Katerina stared intently at Maarkean, making it clear that she expected an answer. She tried to hide any contempt she felt, instead focusing on the genuine curiosity she had. She really did want to know the answer to that question.

Several minutes went by, and Maarkean remained silent. Deciding another shift in tactics was called for, she activated a holoprojector in the table. A translucent hologram of a Braz female appeared: Maarkean's sister, Saracasi.

"I've looked into the history of your family. Your sister has quite the reputation as a radical. Very extreme viewpoints. But something didn't sit right with me. Before this whole mess started, she had an arrest warrant out for treason for a riot that occurred on her campus. A riot that resulted in several deaths, including several AIS officers.

"In looking at the evidence, there doesn't appear to be any indication that she was directly responsible for any of those deaths. Had she not run from the law, and instead gone through the process the way it's supposed to work, I expect that treason charge would have been overturned with something minor."

Katerina paused, looking Maarkean over. When the hologram of his sister had appeared, she had seen the first indication that his emotional shell might be cracking. His eyes had tightened and he'd sat up just a little straighter.

Continuing to try to exploit this vulnerability, Katerina went on, "Our early intelligence reports pegged her as a non-combatant. Supporting a rebel army, even fixing their ships, is still treason. But it's a far cry from taking up arms. Sadly, it seems our initial reports were mistaken. Our latest reports indicate that she's followed her brother's example and is now leading the rebel navy in direct conflict with the Alliance."

Maarkean's eyes widened slightly and then drooped. If she had to guess, she would say that bit of news surprised and disturbed him more than anything else she had said. Her hunch about his sister being a weak point appeared to be true.

"Unfortunately, this means we'll have to hunt her down. Your rebels are surprisingly well equipped, but in the end, they're no match for my fleet. It's only a matter of time," Katerina said, her tone trying to indicate regret. "What a terrible way for a young woman to meet her end. So much life ahead of her. So much potential. I'm told the restoration of the scrapped experimental frigate you stole was, in large part, her work. What brilliance. Wasted. To die in a pointless battle."

She let that last statement hang in the air for a long moment. Maarkean blinked a few times. She had him thinking about the consequences of this war. Now was the time to give him an out.

"But it doesn't have to end that way. If the rebels lay down their arms, I have it in my power to pardon them for these crimes, as terrible as they've been. The leaders, of course, people such as yourself, would have to pay the price. But others, such as your sister . . . Maybe our intelligence is wrong, and she's still just a misguided mechanic. People like her wouldn't necessarily have to die if the war ended now."

Maarkean cast a considering look at the hologram and then at Katerina. For a brief moment, she thought she might have broken through. But that moment passed, and what little emotion had shown on his face vanished, replaced by a passive expression yet again.

She had to admire his determination. Despite what he'd been through, despite the danger to his sister, he still wouldn't give up. That was an admirable trait, even in an adversary.

But everyone had their limits. He'd shown chinks in the armor. She just hoped she had more time than he had determination.

"I'll let you think about that for a while," Katerina said, standing up. "I just hope you don't think about it too long. Who knows how long we have before your sister's luck runs out?"

She left the interrogation room, leaving Maarkean to dwell on the somber thought. You didn't break someone in one interrogation, but she had planted the seed.

Major Anderson met her outside the interrogation room. She held out a datapad to Katerina as they walked. "I thought you would want to see this right away, Admiral."

Curious, Katerina glanced down at the datapad, reading over the first-page summary. A dark smile crossed her face. "It seems our spy has finally delivered. We have the location of the rebels' secret planet, and details about how they've been tricking our ships into thinking the FX-21 is with them. Very clever, I must admit."

"The report matches what our recon scout found when visiting Kol. The FX-21 is still in orbit there," Anderson added.

"Good. And it can continue to sit there, useless, while we destroy their leaders," Katerina said, beginning to plan.

When Maarkean returned to his cell, Lohcja stood up immediately. For the first time since their imprisonment, his Ronid friend didn't almost fall in the process. During their previous "interrogations," Lohcja's antennae had been injured, which damaged how he saw the world around him. While he still wavered, the medical attention he had received had repaired at least some of the damaged nerves.

The sight of his friend's improved condition should have made Maarkean happy. Instead, it just added to his confusion. Ignoring Lohcja's questioning look, he shuffled over to his bed and lay down. Turning to face the wall, he said nothing, hoping Lohcja would take the hint.

"Well, I don't see any fresh bruises and your stitches are still intact. So I'm guessing the beatings to improve our morale haven't resumed?" Lohcja quipped, not taking the hint.

Maarkean remained silent. Lohcja's jokes had once been unstoppable, but until now, he hadn't made one since the failed escape attempt. Things had definitely improved for them since their rescue from their previous brig cell.

Maybe Sartori was telling the truth. She did have a reputation for fairness as a commander. She had offered to help end the war peacefully and offer leniency to his sister. She could be lying about that, though. This could be another psychological torture technique, just like what Merski had pulled on them.

But the one thing he knew for certain was that, given a battle between Sartori and Saracasi, Sartori would win. He had confidence in his sister's abilities to do many things, but defeating a tactical genius like Sartori wasn't one of them.

He had started this war because of the corruption within the Alliance. People like the officers who had beaten and tortured him were the enemy. Hadn't Sartori arrested them? Did that put them on the same side?

Maybe. He'd actually started this war to save Saracasi. Shouldn't he end it if it meant doing that again? Her safety was his top priority.

All of these ideas and questions swirled around inside Maarkean's head. He knew Sartori was manipulating him. Despite his confusion, there could be no doubt about that. But everything she had said had sounded true.

As Maarkean tried to straighten everything out, he realized that Lohcja hadn't stopped talking. The Ronid had continued to ramble on about something, even without any feedback from him. Had the man fallen further off the cliff of insanity?

"So there I was, being yelled at by a Terran who was irate about us no-good aliens taking all the jobs. I hadn't been working as a cabbie for long, so I wasn't doing very well handling the situation. But that guy was doing an excellent job of scaring away any potential customers," Lohcja was saying.

Maarkean tried to figure out what he could possibly be talking about. Lohcja didn't like to talk about his last job as a cabbie. He felt it undermined his position within the Union army.

"This went on for a good five minutes. I asked the man several times if he would either get in the cab or step away. He never stopped ranting long enough for me to push the issue. Plus, an AIS officer was amongst the onlookers, and I didn't want it to become physical.

"Anyway, in the middle of this guy's rant, out of nowhere, Lahkaba walks up, slips right past him, gets in the cab, and closes the door. Now, we'd never met before. This shut the Terran right up, and he cast a glare down at Lahkaba through the glass. His face got all scrunched up, and he hollered, 'How dare you take my cab!'

"And Lahkaba, just as casual as could be, looks up and replies, 'That's right—a dirty, no-good alien stole the cab driven by the other dirty, no-good alien that stole your job.' He then looks at me and says, 'I'm ready to go.' I hop over into the driver seat and we leave. That's how we became friends."

Lohcja trailed off there, apparently satisfied that he had succeeded in getting Maarkean to turn around.

He'd never known how Lohcja and Lahkaba had met. They had just always been friends. It made a better story than how he had met Lahkaba or Lohcja or Zeric. All had been at gunpoint.

"What was the point of that story?" Maarkean asked.

Lohcja gave the Ronid equivalent of a shrug using his antennae. "Thought it would be interesting. Sometimes it helps to think about friends while in a place like this. To remember those who are still out there, and what it is we're fighting for."

Maarkean lay back down on his bed. He agreed with Lohcja. It would be good to remember what he was fighting for. Unfortunately, he just couldn't be sure anymore.

Chapter Fifteen

Early the following morning, Lahkaba was awakened by a knock on the door to his room. Grumpily, he crawled out of bed and opened the door, revealing Zoeko. She held their jamming device in her hand.

Groggily, Lahkaba sat down in one of the room's chairs. He said nothing. Something important had clearly brought Zoeko here. It was too early in the morning to try to reason out what it was.

"I need you to do something," Zoeko began.

Rubbing sleep from his eyes, Lahkaba remained silent.

After a moment, Zoeko continued, "I need you to find out what Rathalos is planning to do once the Dotran fleet departs."

"Why are you coming to me with this? And in such secrecy?" Lahkaba asked.

Zoeko hissed quietly. "The others are already planning to get closer with our new rebel friend. But I don't believe they'll share what they learn with me."

"And you expect me to?"

"Yes," Zoeko said flatly.

"What makes you think he'll share anything with me?" Lahkaba asked.

He didn't like the idea of there being secrets among the members of their delegation. They were all supposed to be on the same side. But Zoeko was right—Valinther would surely attempt to hide what he learned from her.

"Isn't it obvious?" Zoeko asked. "Rathalos clearly respects you. You're a Kowwok who stood up for justice. You were the one he first revealed himself to. And it wasn't until you all but ordered him to that he spoke to us.

"Valinther may understand him and may even support their resistance efforts more, but he's just a politician. You've fought on the front lines. You were part of the group that started our war for freedom. You're who Rathalos wants to be."

Zoeko's reasoning brought Lahkaba up short. He had never thought of himself in those terms. In the story of the rebellion in the Kreogh sector, Maarkean and Zeric had always been the ones viewed as heroes. He had received his share of praise and respect, but the way Zoeko described his role sounded much more heroic.

He wasn't sure he agreed. She assumed that Rathalos knew far more about him than was likely. But then, half truths were often easier to worship than reality.

"Assuming you're right, isn't getting closer to him dangerous? If the Dotran find out we're consorting with people hell-bent on overthrowing them, it will mean the end of any hope for a treaty. And probably our lives," Lahkaba said.

"Yes, but if you can learn what the rebels are planning, we can use that knowledge as a bargaining chip with the Dotran," Zoeko said with a dark smile.

"Betray the rebels?" Lahkaba said, disgusted. "Why would I do that? They're my own people!"

Zoeko let out a sharp hiss. "No, they're not. *Your* people live on Sulas and all the other worlds in the Kreogh sector. It was you who said we must stand together as a sector to win our freedom from the Alliance. That means putting the needs of the Union ahead of that of the people of Kowwa."

The words stung, making him angry. Without thinking, he snapped, "So I'm just supposed to obey, like a good little Kowwok?"

A deep growl emerged from Zoeko, and she flashed her teeth. Instead of saying anything, though, she leaned back against the dresser behind her and took a deep breath. When she next spoke, her tone was more moderate. Her thick tail still thumped against the dresser—a sign of agitation.

"I don't expect this to be an easy decision for you. And I apologize if I implied otherwise. But you must know that the odds of this resistance group succeeding are small."

"So are the odds of the Union succeeding. Doesn't mean we're not trying," Lahkaba countered.

Zoeko shook her head emphatically. "That's different. My people keep a much tighter leash on the Kowwok than the Alliance ever did on any of our worlds. There's also no history of resistance among your people.

"Yes, drafting Kowwoks into their military has opened the door to Kowwoks learning to fight. And yes, someday, that will probably lead to a revolution. But the odds of it succeeding will be higher *if* the Union gains its independence and can be there to provide support. Right now, we need the Dotran. In ten or twenty years, we might be in a position to help."

Lahkaba's first instinct was to argue, but he held his tongue. The Union needed Dotran help to gain their freedom. The Kowwoks would need help to gain theirs. Right now, he couldn't give it to them.

"All right," Lahkaba conceded. "I'll try to find out more about them. *But*, this doesn't mean I'm going to betray them. I want to try to convince them to wait."

Zoeko looked like she was about to argue, but instead she nodded her head. "Very well. That will be good enough for me. I trust you to do what's right for the Union."

She left his room, leaving Lahkaba feeling guilty. He wanted to help the Kowwok resistance succeed, but he also agreed with Zoeko.

Watching out the shuttle's window, Solyss saw the main city on Okaral start to take shape. The buildings of the settlement looked like nothing more than small rectangles from this height. They were built in the center of a wide ring of cultivated land. Even rows of different colored fields surrounded the city, extending a great distance. A few kilometers away, a massive hole had been dug into what had probably once been a mountain.

Turning away as they entered a cloud bank, Solyss looked over the other people in the shuttle. They were seated in an Alliance assault shuttle that had been acquired from the orbiting space station. Once the *Tornado* had fled and the *Gallant* had taken up a guard position near the station, resistance onboard had collapsed. The station's commander had been killed in the marine assault on the command center, but her XO had surrendered.

Now, Solyss rode down to the surface, accompanied by a squad of marines led by Asheerah. Gamaly and Kueth had also insisted on joining them. Even though the Alliance forces on the station had surrendered, they hadn't been forthcoming about how many troops were planet-side. No one knew what kind of resistance they would find below.

Noticeably absent from the group was Isaxo. Beside Solyss, Soo'bim Bidi'kyre sat at the pilot station. The Liw'kel man normally flew as Ion Two. Isaxo had wanted to fly the team down to the surface, but Solyss had been forced to confine him to quarters for the time being. He hadn't yet decided what to do about his young Notha squadron leader.

As Bidi'kyre set the shuttle down on the surface of Okaral, Asheerah readied her marines near the shuttle's door. Solyss had allowed them to rest for a few hours after the assault on the space station, but he knew it hadn't been nearly long enough. Hidden by their full-body suits of armor, they showed no outward signs of fatigue, but he knew it must be there.

Behind the marines, Kueth sat with his left leg shaking nervously. Solyss could sympathize with the man's desire to reunite with his family. It had been years since he had seen his.

The shuttle door dropped suddenly, forming a ramp. Asheerah led the marines out onto a hard-packed dirt street. Solyss remained where he was, Asheerah having already hammered home the point that he was not to leave the shuttle until she gave the all-clear. After several moments of silence, she gave it.

Solyss, Gamaly, and Kueth stepped off the shuttle. Overhead, the system's dual suns beat down on them with savage intensity. The planet's orbit placed this latitude in the middle of summer, and it was clearly not a pleasant season.

Before them lay the city. The square buildings he had seen from the air now revealed themselves to be shoddy, pre-fab, grey buildings. The dirt street cut a path between the buildings. Everything looked dirty and dilapidated.

The marines stood behind several crates and a parked vehicle that sat near the two buildings on the edge of the town. They were the only signs of life. Completely empty, the streets gave the city the look of a ghost town.

"Where is everyone?" he asked, looking at Kueth.

The other Terran bore a confused expression. He shrugged. "I have no idea. Hiding, maybe?"

As if in answer to his question, a blaster bolt flew out and struck the ground near Solyss's feet. Solyss and Kueth both stood there, momentarily shocked. It took Gamaly grabbing his arm as she ran for cover to bring him back to his senses.

He followed Gamaly to the side of the nearest building. A marine—in the armor, he couldn't tell which one—stood at the edge of the building. The marine had his rifle at the ready but was crouched down, presumably out of the line of fire. Despite feeling that it wouldn't do him much good, Solyss decided to draw his pistol and move up beside the marine, even as he heard more blaster fire coming from around the corner.

"Report," Solyss said.

"At least two shooters, sir," the marine said. Solyss recognized the voice as belonging to Staff Sergeant Wurth Yuly.

Yuly leaned around the corner and fired a quick barrage from his rifle. He came back a second later, tilting his head slightly, as if listening to something. Sitting there, Solyss felt useless. He didn't want to give any orders, knowing Asheerah could handle the situation herself. He would just get in her way.

Beside him, Gamaly looked as uncomfortable as he felt. She was similarly armed with a pistol but had made no move to join the fight. Solyss knew her proficiency with firearms, but the pregnancy limited her.

After an agonizing few minutes, the blaster fire ceased. Yuly leaned around the corner again and then said, "It's clear, sir."

Solyss followed the armored marine out from behind his cover. They found the corpse of a Ronid female in the center of the street. She was dressed in civilian attire, and it was unlikely she had been a member of the Alliance force planet-side.

"Both shooters were civvies," Asheerah said flatly.

"Not the welcome I would have expected from a prison colony. Well, not for their rescuers anyway," Solyss said, casting a meaningful glance at Kueth.

The man shook his head. "I don't understand it. They shouldn't have access to weapons. The Alliance made sure of that."

Asheerah picked up the rifle next to the woman. "RE-112. Alliance standard issue. It looks like they changed their mind about arming the locals."

Looking down at the dead woman, Solyss considered their options. They clearly weren't welcome, at least on first sight. But the locals likely had no idea what had occurred in orbit. The Alliance troops might not even know, and if they did, they could have told the people anything. Perhaps these people had merely been defending themselves from invaders.

"We keep going," Solyss ordered. "Keep on the lookout. From now on, non-lethal force if at all possible."

Though hidden by her armor, Asheerah cast him a glance he felt sure was one of annoyance. She hated using the stun setting. Nevertheless, she gave the order to the marines.

The group continued down the road leading into the city. Marines took positions in the vanguard and brought up the rear, with the unarmored people like Solyss in the center. Eerie silence surrounded them as they walked. After a few blocks, the marine in the lead threw his hand up, signaling them all to stop.

Before Solyss could move away from the center of the street, windows and doors in the buildings around them flew open and people appeared in them, all holding weapons. At a wordless order from Asheerah, the marines collapsed into a tight group surrounding him and the two civilians.

For a long moment, no one moved. Despite the armored marines forming a wall between him and their attackers, Solyss felt vulnerable. Their armor would protect them from some limited fire, but the concentrated attack that could come from those around them would be more than the armor could withstand.

"Mirel?" Kueth said and then suddenly stood up over the crouching marines.

Another shout came from among their ambushers. "Kueth?!"

At the sound of the woman's voice, Kueth pushed himself forward and out from behind the marines. A middle-aged woman came running out of the building to their left, and the two embraced.

No one else quite knew how to respond. After a moment, the weapons held by the civilians started to lower, though not very far. The marines kept theirs raised and aimed.

The realization that they were still surrounded by a bunch of people with guns must have finally intruded on Kueth and Mirel, who Solyss assumed was his wife. The pair of them broke apart, though not going far.

Kueth turned to Solyss. "Major, this is my wife. These people won't hurt you," he said, a wide grin still on his face.

"That depends on what His Lordship decides," Mirel replied. "They've already killed two of our lookouts. Who are they, Kueth? How did you get here?"

Looking confused, Kueth said, "Mirel, this is Major Solyss Novastar of the Union navy. He's come to free us from the Alliance."

"Lord Renard has already freed us from the Alliance. And now he'll decide your fate," one of the Terran men in the windows shouted back.

Beside him, Gamaly groaned.

Ignoring her, Solyss stood up, holstering his pistol as he did so. He surveyed the group of armed locals and was surprised to see that a majority of them were Terrans and Braz. Upon reflection, he decided that shouldn't be surprising. Josserand and Kueth were both Terran. This planet might be a prison, but it was nothing like the Olan prison on Sulas. Here, people would have been free to move about and live their lives, to a certain extent. He turned to face Kueth and Mirel. "I think now's a good time to go see *Lord* Renard."

"Throw your weapons to the ground," said the man who had spoken earlier. "Then we'll take you to Renard."

Solyss started to move his hand to drop his pistol but stopped when Asheerah said, "Not gonna happen."

Stopping, he rested his hand on the pistol's grip as if that had been his intention all along. He had no worries about going unarmed to this meeting. With *Gallant* and the space station in orbit, the people here were at his mercy. But he also recognized that tone in Asheerah's voice. An order from him wouldn't change her mind. He didn't want to have to reprimand another one of his friends for insubordination.

"You're going to drop your weapons, or we're going to make you drop your weapons," the man in the window threatened.

"Good luck with that," Asheerah said, her voice icy calm. Solyss could imagine the satisfied smile on her face at the prospect of showing her skill.

"Boci," Mirel said, stepping away from Kueth and in front of Asheerah. "These people brought Kueth back to me. They're not our enemies."

For a moment, Boci kept his rifle ready, now aimed at Mirel. She continued to give him a determined look, and he eventually lowered the weapon. He gestured to the others. "They can keep their weapons. For now. We'll let His Lordship decide their fate."

Once the locals lowered their weapons, Asheerah ordered the marines to do the same. She kept them in a tight defense formation around Solyss and Gamaly as they were led through the city.

While they walked, Solyss tried to keep an eye on Kueth. The man stayed close to Mirel, the two quietly talking together. Their pleasure at seeing each other was obvious, and Solyss felt slightly better about agreeing to help Kueth. His team still might not achieve their goal by coming here, but at least Kueth hadn't been lying about his family being trapped here. That counted for something in Solyss's book.

They walked through the city streets, taking only a few turns. A large, clean building came into view after a few minutes. The structure looked much more stable and well-maintained than anything else he had seen. As they got closer, he decided it would most likely be the Alliance's ground headquarters.

Once inside the building, Solyss recognized signs of a battle. Burn marks marred the walls, doors were crumpled in, and shattered glass littered the floor. Either the battle had occurred very recently, or the locals didn't have any interest in cleaning it up.

Their journey ended in a small courtroom. The judge's bench towered above them at the front of the room. The room held no jury box, which Solyss knew to be typical for Alliance courts that dealt mostly with aliens, who weren't entitled to trials by jury.

Solyss and the marines squeezed into the center of the room, where the accused would typically stand. The locals lined the walls, still holding their rifles ready, though they remained pointed at the floor.

The man who had spoken to them earlier, Boci, shouted, "All bow in honor of His Lordship Josserand Renard!"

Boci bowed low as a door opened behind the bench. Some of the others in the room bowed, though most merely bobbed their head. The marines, if they did anything, stood up straighter.

A middle-aged man dressed in an ill-fitting Alliance officer's uniform came through the door and took a seat behind the bench. He matched the description Solyss had been given for Josserand. He waved his hand in a sweeping gesture toward those in the room. "You may rise. Now, tell me, what do we have here?"

"My lord," Boci said, "these invaders landed in an Alliance shuttle. They raided the town, killing two of our people. They don't wear Alliance uniforms, but they're clearly mercenaries hired by the Alliance to assassinate you and take back the town."

"Boci, you idiot, they aren't with the Alliance. Kueth brought them here to help us," Mirel said, her tone impatient.

"Is that really you, Kueth, my loyal servant?" Josserand said, surprise evident in his voice.

"It is . . . my lord," Kueth replied, hesitating on the honorific. "When you were taken by the Alliance, I made contact with the Union military. They agreed to help free you in exchange for your help against the Alliance."

Josserand frowned at Kueth's statement, but the man continued, "We arrived here and took control of the orbiting space station, driving off the naval ship defending this world. We're free of the Alliance occupation."

"A mighty deed you've accomplished," Josserand said, his tone icy, "but unnecessary. Thanks to my leadership, the people of Okaral have already thrown off the shackles of Alliance oppression."

"We liberated ourselves this morning, without your help," Boci added.

"Convenient timing," Gamaly whispered beside Solyss.

"Now, now, Boci," Josserand chastised. "They've saved us the trouble of having to take the station ourselves. In exchange for that, we can forgive them the unfortunate incident with our two sentries. We'll call it a mere misunderstanding."

Gamaly pursed her lips at that and then leaned over to whisper to Solyss, "Offer to take him up to the station as compensation."

He cast a curious look down at her but shrugged and turned back to Josserand. "Sir, as further compensation for the unfortunate death of the townsfolk, allow us to provide you transport up to the space station."

Josserand smiled, his eyes flickering to Gamaly briefly. "A worthy offer. I accept. Boci, prepare my transport."

Chapter Sixteen

For the first few days after returning to Kol, Saracasi had avoided the UDF headquarters building. At first, she had told herself she simply had a lot of work to do, which was true. But after all the logistics had been ironed out and repairs to her damaged fleet had begun, she had run out of excuses.

In truth, she admitted to herself, she wasn't sure what she wanted to happen when she saw Asirzi. She definitely had no idea what would happen. She had forced herself to bury her feelings for the last few months. But the sense of loss, hurt, and, yes, she admitted, love, still bounced around in her subconscious.

She finally went down to the HQ building with an excuse to see Chavatwor. She made no effort to find Asirzi, though she half hoped they would run into each other. When that chance encounter didn't come that day, nor the next day, she finally admitted defeat. This time, she would seek her old lover out. Then she could find out where they stood.

As luck would have it, as Saracasi entered the main lobby, Asirzi came out of a meeting room. She glanced up from a datapad she was reading and then stumbled to a halt when she caught sight of Saracasi. For a long moment, both of them stood there.

Forcing herself not to stand around like an idiot, Saracasi approached Asirzi, a tentative smile on her face. Asirzi didn't return the smile, instead merely looking cautious.

"Hi," Saracasi said awkwardly.

"Hello," Asirzi responded, her tone polite but neutral.

The tense greeting hung in the air. Saracasi tried not to read much into it. She had caught Asirzi off guard, after all. They continued to stand there in silence for a moment, Asirzi rubbing her artificial arm and Saracasi trying to decide where to put her own hands.

Finally, Saracasi decided that since she had sought this meeting out, she should start. "I'd hoped to run into you one of the times I've been here."

"Really? I never hid myself," Asirzi said, her tone disbelieving.

"I had hoped it would be a chance encounter. I wasn't sure if you'd want to see me," Saracasi admitted.

"You're the one who walked out on me," Asirzi said, a bite to her tone, though her face softened immediately after she said it.

The jab stung Saracasi. She didn't think it was entirely accurate, but she hadn't come here to argue. Instead, she said, trying to fill the words with as much of her true emotions as she could, "I've missed you."

Asirzi's face and antennae drooped slightly in a look of sadness, though her eyes betrayed a hint of pleasure. She said, "I thought . . . no . . . uh . . . I've missed you, too."

The flustered stammering between what Asirzi said and was going to say made Saracasi smile. It gave her hope to think that Asirzi's feelings might be just as confused as hers. Maybe she hadn't ruined everything irrevocably before.

As the thought crossed her mind, Tadashio came barreling into the lobby. The shaggy Kowwok breathed a heavy sigh of relief at the sight of her and ran over to her, calling, "Commodore! I'm glad I found you!" He sounded somewhat alarmed.

A flash of anger at the distraction flared up in Saracasi. Her sense of duty and desire to fight had been the wedge that had been driven between her and Asirzi. She had come here not dressed in uniform specifically to avoid reminding Asirzi of that. The issue wouldn't be resolved that easily, but she knew she had to start somewhere.

Instead of Asirzi getting mad, though, she laughed. With the first smile Saracasi had seen on her face, Asirzi said, "The universe has it in for us, doesn't it?"

Saracasi chuckled at the thought. "It would seem that way. The universe can't win forever, though. The war will eventually end. And so will my duty to the Union, along with any desire of mine to remain in uniform."

"Well, maybe we should continue this conversation then," Asirzi said, her brief look of mirth replaced by another sad smile.

"I would like that," Saracasi said, ignoring Tadashio, who was practically bouncing beside her.

"Until then," Asirzi said, turning away and disappearing down a hallway.

Taking a deep breath, Saracasi watched her go and then turned to the upset Kowwok. "Yes, Chief?"

"Commodore, I've been going over the communication system as part of the effort to track down the cause of the power surge we had," Tadashio explained. "In the process, I discovered an improper computer program."

"Improper?" Saracasi asked. Software was her biggest weakness with ship design. She had no idea how to program any of the systems on a ship.

"One that shouldn't have been there," Tadashio said.

"A remnant from the DeeGee's days as a miner?" Saracasi asked, a dark suspicion welling up inside her.

"No, it was a recent program. I checked it over and was the cause of the comm array transmission during the surge. It might have even caused the surge, though I can't be sure," Tadashio said.

"What did it transmit? I thought that it was just a burst of static that went out," Saracasi said, already moving toward the building's exit.

"That's what it looked like, but it was actually a coded transmission. I still can't decipher what it said, but, Commodore, I was able to decrypt some of its programming. Before transmitting, it accessed our navigational computer logs. Whatever else it sent, it included the spatial coordinates of the DeeGee's last ten jumps," Tadashio said, his tone fearful.

"Irod," Saracasi said, putting the pieces together.

Tadashio nodded as they stepped out into the bright Kol sun. All thoughts of Asirzi vanished from Saracasi's mind. They still had a traitor in their midst.

"Who else knows about this?" Saracasi asked.

"No one," Tadashio answered. "I didn't tell anyone what I found. Though probably a lot of people knew I was working on the comm system."

"Get back to the ship. Go over every system. Look for more viruses or other signs of tampering, both related to this problem and potential other ones," Saracasi ordered.

Tadashio saluted and then rushed off across the sand. Saracasi pulled out her comm and followed at a more deliberate pace. She tried to raise Kaars Aerinstar but got no response. After several attempts, she gave up and signaled Master Sergeant Deja'z'reth Adat'to, the marine training commander. "Master Sergeant."

"Aye, Commodore. What can I do for you?" said the voice of Deja'z'reth.

"Assemble a team of marines. Bring Davidus Brieni to me aboard the orbital dock," she ordered. After a second, a discomforting thought occurred to her. "Also, find Master Intelligence Specialist Kaars Aerinstar. He's not answering his comm."

"Aye, Commodore," Deja'z'reth said without any hint of hesitation in his voice.

She shut down the comm and immediately established another link. Once she had a connection, she said, "Arz, start powering up *Audacious*."

"Commodore?" Arzesaeth Ernebee asked over the comm, clearly surprised by the order.

"We're taking a little trip. Recall all crew and get Chava's work crews off. I'll be there shortly," Saracasi said and then cut the transmission, moving faster now toward the launch pads.

Watching out of the window of his cabin as the transport came in for a landing outside Lost Hope, Irod, Zeric sighed. After finishing up on Cardine, Lei-mey had directed their transports to a meeting on Mirthod. The last month or so had been nothing but talking to politicians, meeting recruits, and pretending to smile—all things he hated doing.

Fortunately, there had been no shortage of people willing to offer him a drink. He had tasted almost as many different liquors as people he had met. That was probably the only thing that had gotten him through it. He never thought he would actually miss combat.

Even sitting around the arena on Sulas had been better. At least there he had participated in planning actual military operations. He still hated doing that, but he hated smiling for people he couldn't care less about even more.

Zeric took a swig from his last bottle of a type of wine he had been given on Cardine. He'd never cared much for wine, but this stuff had been much stronger than anything he'd tasted before. It was sad to see it gone, but walking down to meet the troops with a bottle in his hand wouldn't look good.

Finishing the bottle, Zeric looked at himself in the mirror. He had neglected shaving on the journey to Irod. The troop transport didn't have many places to go where he'd have been seen. Most of the troops remained in a large barracks-style compartment, while Zeric and the other senior officers had their own rooms. Aside from a few meals with the officers and one with the troops, he had remained in his cabin, only seeing Gu'od and Kumus.

He considered shaving and also finding a clean uniform, since a smudge of something from his last meal could still be seen on his jacket. But the thought of going through the hassle annoyed him. He never would have bothered with either of those things before the war. Not unless he was going out for some fun. Women didn't tend to like being picked up by slobs.

Zeric let out another sigh and looked at the empty bottle mournfully. That was another thing he hadn't done in a long time: find female companionship. The troop transport had a large number of women, some of them even Terran, but even he wouldn't stoop so low as to sleep with his subordinates.

And now he had a daughter to go home to. Even if this damned war ended with him alive and free of an Alliance prison, he couldn't go back to his life of carousing. Responsibility would follow him forever.

Brushing aside the issues with his appearance and his future, Zeric left his cabin and went down to the barracks. When the ship touched down, he spoke to some of the troops as he made his way to the boarding ramp. He didn't mind this part of his job—he just would have preferred not having to order these same people who spoke so kindly to him to go get themselves killed.

He was joined at the boarding ramp by Lei-mey and Gu'od. Lei-mey gave him a dark look, which he ignored. The number of things she disapproved of was a number higher than he could count to—at least, after finishing that bottle of wine—so he didn't care what she took issue with now.

At the bottom of the boarding ramp, Faide Darkthorne and Mayor Reva Shim waited for them, along with the Notha brigadier who was in charge of the remaining division on Irod. Zeric couldn't remember the woman's name. He'd never been good at remembering names.

"General," Faide said. "It seems your recruitment efforts were successful."

"Something like that," Zeric replied. "We've got another three thousand troops—"

A thunderous explosion drowned out the rest of his sentence. The boarding ramp shuddered, as did the ground beneath it. Zeric stumbled but managed to catch himself on one of the support struts. Some of the others weren't as lucky and fell to the ground.

Silence filled the moment after the unexpected explosion. Zeric was trying to figure out what had happened when more sounds of danger appeared. Loud clangs rang out as objects struck the transport above him. Other objects fell from the sky, slamming into the ground beyond him. Plumes of dirt cascaded into the air.

Zeric was suddenly drawn back to the Colonial War. His unit had been trapped outside the protective bubble of a shield generator. Artillery fire had saturated the area, creating plumes of dirt not unlike what he was seeing.

Reacting instantly, Zeric dropped to the ground, remaining underneath the protective hull of the transport. After a few seconds, the rain of objects striking the ground ended. Aside from that first one, there had been no other explosions. The dirt plumes hadn't been artillery, he realized.

Reluctantly, he picked himself up off the ground. His uniform was now smeared with mud from the damp ground, which hid the food stains well. And he had almost changed into a clean uniform.

Cautiously, Zeric stepped out from underneath the transport and looked up. A giant cloud of smoke and gases filled the air a few kilometers above them. It took him a moment to realize that the cloud and the pieces of debris strewn around him were the only things remaining of one of the other troop transports.

One thousand. That had been the number of troops on each transport. One thousand people. Dead in a fiery explosion.

Transports didn't just explode for no reason. Had it malfunctioned? No, ships were designed not to explode like that, even if they failed catastrophically—for some reason, engineers thought that losing power and suffocating in the cold blackness of space was preferable to a quick death.

"Everyone get off the transport!" Zeric yelled as his mind clicked. "Move! Move! Move!"

To match words to action, Zeric started running as quickly as he could away from the transport. Gu'od and the others were already right behind him. Once they got moving, Zeric paused and looked back. Troops had started making their way down the boarding ramp, but at a pace that was far too slow.

With a low growl, Zeric headed back toward the transport, shouting, "Double-time it, people! Bloody run! Move it! Come on!"

At his encouragement, the troops starting streaming off at a faster pace. The trickle turned into a stream. Finally satisfied that they were all coming, Zeric turned and resumed his run away from the transport. It wasn't cowardice now, he decided. He would just be in the way if he kept standing there.

He quickly reached Gu'od and the others, who had slowed about a hundred meters away. Waving his hands, he shouted at them to keep moving. The stream of troops followed him, and he felt that the group of them must have done the fastest team kilometer dash on record.

Reaching the periphery of the town of Lost Hope, Zeric allowed himself to slow down. Breathing heavily, he looked at the transport in the distance. The bottom of the vessel was obscured by a rise in the land between them, but he could still clearly see the top. As he watched, fiery bolts of energy lanced down from the sky. The blaster bolts pummeled the transport and the ground around it.

After only a few seconds of bombardment, the transport's fuel lines ruptured and it exploded. A shockwave flashed out across the ground. Zeric and all the others were knocked to the ground.

He wasn't sure whether the distance or the slight hill had saved them, but he let out a sigh of relief when his insides weren't turned to jelly by the concussion wave.

Looking around, he made a quick estimate of those who had made it off the ship. Even with a generous estimate, he came up far short of the thousand who had been aboard, but at least they hadn't all been vaporized.

He saw no sign of the final transport. It had been the last in line for landing, and that probably gave it the best chance of survival. Still in flight, it might have picked up the attack force and had time to go evasive and raise its shields. There was a good chance that wouldn't have saved it, though.

Picking herself up, Lei-mey stared in horror at the smoking wreckage of their transport. Her antennae quivered nervously. She turned to Zeric and said, "What the hell was that?"

"That, Madam Delegate, was the Alliance. It looks like they've found us."

Chapter Seventeen

As Solyss entered the wardroom, he flashed back to a few days earlier when he had met Kueth here. Like before, Asheerah and Gamaly waited in the room. Also like last time, his mind was preoccupied with the disagreement between Tess and Isaxo. His XO wanted to bring Isaxo before a court martial.

Fortunately for Solyss, the differences proved great enough to bring his focus back to the situation at hand. In addition to Asheerah and Gamaly, the cramped wardroom held two more marines. Gamaly thought no precautions too great when dealing with Josserand.

Compared to his minion, Josserand himself was striking. Kueth sat nervously, but determined. Josserand sat there in a supremely confident and smug fashion. He had helped himself to a large glass of Solyss's cognac.

"Well," Solyss began, trying to hide his irritation, "now that you've made yourself at home, we can get down to business."

"Wonderful," Josserand said with a wide smile. "I'm quite anxious to learn what help I can be to the grand Union that you would come all the way out here to save little old me."

Gamaly frowned at him, but before she could say anything, Solyss said, "We know about your plan to capture the *Black Market*. But you got arrested before you could carry it out. You help us gain control of it, and you get your freedom back."

A momentary frown crossed Josserand's face before the smile returned. "What makes you think I have the power to accomplish such a lofty task?"

This time, Gamaly spoke before Solyss could. "Don't play coy with me, Renard. You're not surprised that we know about your plan for the *Black Market*."

Unfazed by Gamaly's statement, Josserand took another sip of co-gnac before replying, "No, of course not. How else would Kueth have convinced you to come here? What I'm surprised about is that Maarkean decided to take the chance to trust me. And that he's not here himself."

"General Ocaitchi is a very busy man," Solyss answered quickly. Almost too quickly, he thought in retrospect. There was no way word could have preceded them about the defeat at Sulas and Maarkean's captivity fast enough to have made it to the ears of a prisoner. Then again, Josserand always seemed to be more informed than he should be.

Josserand smiled again. "I'm sure he is. I guess he decided he had to find something for Ms. Dos'redna to do. She's clearly of no more use to her husband."

Asheerah started to step forward, and Solyss got a flashback to the Liw'kel man in the cantina on Hollis. As much as he might see the appeal of breaking Josserand's nose, it wouldn't help them any. But before he could do anything to stop Asheerah, she paused and returned to her position against the bulkhead.

Confused, he cast a glance at Gamaly and noticed the Liw'kel women's antennae twitching rapidly. Something must have been said between them to stop Asheerah. He wished he had that kind of pull over her once she had decided to act . . . or over any of his crew.

Proceeding as if nothing had happened, Gamaly said, "It's not just Maarkean who doesn't trust you, Renard. I'm here to make sure you keep up your end of the deal."

Josserand let out a soft chuckle. "What deal is that, my dear? I've made no deal."

"The deal was that we would free you in exchange for control of the *Black Market*," Solyss said levelly. "The arrangement was made on your behalf by your employee, in good faith. Now, can you get us the ship or not?"

Standing up from his seat, Josserand squeezed over to the small table that held the liquor. He poured himself another large glass of cognac. When he put the bottle back down, only a small amount of the expensive liquid remained.

"You don't expect me to feel constrained by an agreement which I had no part in, do you?" Josserand asked, his tone feigning shock. "Should you be held to an agreement Ms. Aru makes on your behalf, Captain?"

"If the deal was made for my benefit by someone I trusted, such as *Lieutenant* Aru, then yes, I should," Solyss answered honestly.

"Well, that's good to know," Josserand said, his eyes predatory. He took another sip before continuing. "I, however, feel no such compulsion. Any deals you made with Mr. Kahl-Amar are between you and him. He definitely benefited a great deal from this transaction. I hope you got your money's worth."

Quietly, Solyss fumed. He had feared something like this would happen. It was the entire reason he had persuaded Gamaly to join the mission.

"You never answered his question, Renard," Gamaly said, her tone revealing no sign of frustration. Considering the wild emotions she had been showing ever since leaving Kol, Solyss felt his respect for her climb.

"No, I didn't," Josserand replied. "And if we're done with this façade of me already being beholden to you, then I'm more than happy to begin the actual negotiations."

Solyss considered the statement. Maybe gaining control of the *Black Market* wouldn't be just a simple matter of liberating an Alliance prison planet, but maybe there was still a chance. "That depends on whether or not you *can* gain control of the *Black Market*," Solyss replied.

"Yes, I can," Josserand answered. A dark smile touched his eyes, though he kept his mouth flat. "What would that be worth to you?"

"We'll offer you the same deal we offered the Fox," Solyss answered. "For the use of the ship for the duration of the war, the Union will grant you free and unmolested trade anywhere in Union space, along with docking permissions on any world, free from inspection. Plus, all damage sustained as a result of battle will be repaired at our expense."

"No wonder the Fox turned you down," Josserand said with a laugh. "That's a terrible deal. The Fox already has all of that, minus the docking permissions. I will as well, once I'm in control. What else do you have?"

Solyss nodded, as if he had expected this. In truth, he didn't know what else he could offer. Legitimacy under the law was all the fledgling government of the Union could provide. Maintaining and repairing the *Black Market* would be an astronomical cost by itself, but adding credits to the deal seemed to be the only option available to him.

"What do you want, Renard?" Gamaly asked, impatience appearing in her voice for the first time. "You're just going to reject whatever offer we make. So just tell us."

"You never could hold out very long," Josserand said with a look toward Gamaly. "Very well: autonomy. As payment for the use of the *Black Market* during the war, the Trepon sector will be included in the peace with the Alliance. The entire sector must be granted to me. And I want to be an admiral in your navy. Something higher than Maarkean, but beyond that, it doesn't matter."

Gamaly laughed. Solyss looked over at her. She'd done the same thing upon learning Josserand was in prison. Apparently, something about the man amused her. "You don't think small, do you, Renard?" Gamaly said after a minute.

"Thinking small doesn't get you where I am in life."

"Freshly freed from an Alliance prison by a rebel army?" Gamaly quipped.

Before the two could continue the exchange, Solyss intervened. "We can't offer you the sector. The people here are free to choose their allegiance. Freeing Trepon from Alliance control we can do, but we won't set you up as a tyrant."

"Of course not. I misspoke," Josserand said, his tone indicating he hadn't. "I will be given a free hand in Trepon, and the Union agrees not to interfere with me or any world that agrees to join me."

For some reason, this description made Solyss feel worse about the proposition than he had a moment ago. He didn't like Josserand. The idea of giving the man any freedom with people, even ones who willingly agreed to follow him, didn't sit well with him. The people of Okaral appeared to have made that choice, and it didn't look good for them.

On the other hand, the Union needed that warship. He didn't think Congress had any interests in Trepon, aside from finding aid and undermining the Alliance. Giving Josserand a free hand here wouldn't really mean much.

"OK," Solyss said. Gamaly cast him a shocked look, which he ignored. "Trepon will be included in the negotiations with the Alliance. All worlds will be free to choose their own destinies. The Union will not interfere."

"And the admiralcy?" Josserand asked.

"That you won't get," Solyss said, his tone brooking no argument. "If you decide to swear loyalty to the Union, Congress may see fit to grant you a commission, and *General* Ocaitchi may even decide to assign you to serve aboard the *Black Market*. But that's as close as you're going to get to a flag rank. You'll be welcome to remain aboard the ship as a civilian observer, otherwise."

Josserand stared intently at Solyss for a moment. Then he downed the last bit of cognac before standing up. "Then our negotiations here are over. I'm ready to return to my space station now."

"You mean our space station," Solyss said, not falling for the tactic Josserand was clearly trying to employ. "We captured it from the Alliance. Under prize laws of war, it now belongs to the Union."

For a moment, Solyss got the sense that Josserand wanted to growl a curse, but he managed to maintain his air of calm. "Very well, to the surface, then."

A look passed between Gamaly and Asheerah, along with more antennae movements. A smile spread across Gamaly's face as she looked at Josserand. "Certainly."

Gamaly's smile sent a chill down Solyss's back. He turned back to Josserand and saw that it had had the same effect on the other man, whose eyes narrowed as he studied Gamaly. A minute went by before Josserand responded. "Please return me to the same place we departed from," he said coldly.

Catching on to what Gamaly implied, Solyss seized the opportunity. "We can certainly open that up to negotiation. But how about this: instead of taking you down to the surface of a backwater planet with no hyperspace-capable craft, we instead provide you transport all the way back to the Kreogh sector. We'll add that to our previous offer."

A tense moment went by while Josserand considered the offer. The prospect of living the rest of his life on Okaral could not have held much appeal for the crime lord. Even though he had the people of the city eating out of his hand at the moment, it wouldn't last forever.

Gamaly continued to smile. "Oh, come on, Renard. You get everything you were planning before your imprisonment. More, in fact, since Okaral is already Alliance-free and the Union will now pay to fully restore and repair the ship. Plus, you really wouldn't want to get stuck down there for the rest of your miserable, yet short, life."

After another long moment, one Solyss thought Josserand held purely out of spite, the man nodded his head. "Very well, Captain Novastar, you have a deal."

Getting out of their apartments proved easier than Lahkaba had expected. He and Valinther had merely requested an opportunity to visit a place frequented by Kowwoks, and Bryel had agreed to escort them. The naval officer's willingness to accommodate them made Lahkaba feel slightly bad for using him like this, but only slightly.

At Rathalos's suggestion, they went to a vartras hall, a form of sports bar. Rathalos himself would not accompany them, as the Dotran would view it poorly for him to fraternize openly with those he was supposed to serve. While Lahkaba couldn't care less, he didn't want any suspicion to fall on the man.

When he and Valinther entered the vartras hall, his vision darkened and his other senses were overwhelmed. Removing the tinted shades from his eyes, Lahkaba took in the room. Plants of every shape and size lined the walls and hung from the ceiling. Only now, confronted with so many, did he realize he had seen very few in the city. Cities lacked an abundance of greenery by their very nature, but most species preferred to have at least some small reminders of the natural world.

The sun still shone outside, and the building had several large sky-lights bathing plant pots in sunlight, but they were the only source of illumination. Normally, he enjoyed bright natural light, but the over-whelming brightness of Motinor had made him crave darkness. He could only imagine that the Kowwoks who lived here felt much the same way.

After a moment of taking in the sights, smells, and sounds, Lahkaba moved further into the bar. As he did, Bryel came in behind him. The ap-pearance of a Dotran made the crowd of Kowwoks suddenly stop talk-ing, almost all at once. It would be illegal for the bar to ban Dotran from coming in, even though the reverse would be true at many Dotran busi-nesses, but that didn't mean the sight of one was welcome.

"I'll wait over here, out of the way," Bryel said, gesturing toward a stool in the corner near the door.

Lahkaba nodded in reply, feeling sympathy again for the blue Do-tran. He was a Dotran, but his position in society was only one step above that of Lahkaba's own people. Well, maybe more than one.

As they moved deeper into the bar, the crowd parted for them with-out comment. Conversation slowly returned to the room, but he and Valinther had already been marked as the people who had brought a Dotran into their bar. He hadn't counted on that when he'd come up with this plan. Rathalos had arranged a meeting with some of his other asso-ciates, but after they'd gotten this kind of attention, it might not happen.

After ordering a drink, Lahkaba stood at the bar, taking in the scene. Being surrounded by fellow Kowwoks reminded him of home. Sulas had a diverse population, but his section of his hometown had consisted mostly of Kowwoks. There probably had been bars like this one, but he had moved before he had gotten old enough to go in one.

"So . . ." Valinther said beside him. While the gathering gave Lahkaba a sense of nostalgia, Valinther looked nervous and uncomfortable. Clandestine meetings in a public place could do that, but it looked like something more. If anything, since Valinther had grown up on Dotra, he should have been feeling even more nostalgic than Lahkaba.

"You boys made quite an impression," a voice said beside him.

Turning, Lahkaba saw a Kowwok female with soft, short, black fur. In the darkness of the bar, she should have been hard to see with that color, but instead of blending into the darkness, her fur glistened.

It took him a moment to realize he was staring.

"We, uh, we're . . . not from around here," Lahkaba babbled.

His twisted tongue took him by surprise. It had been a long time since a beautiful woman had had that effect on him. Granted, it had been a long time since he had talked to a beautiful woman when he wasn't working. But, he forcefully reminded himself, he *was* working right now.

The woman smiled. "I gathered that from your escort over there. You must be Lahkaba and Valinther."

Lahkaba's ears perked up at the mention of his name.

The woman continued, "The whole city's talking about you two. Kowwoks from the Kreogh sector, greeted as equals by the Dotran. Some people call you heroes, an example of what Kowwoks can achieve."

Though the words were flattering, something in her tone made Lahkaba doubt that she included herself among those she mentioned. "I gather you're not one of them?"

She gave him another smile, this one more eerie. "Why would you say that?"

He exchanged a glance with Valinther, but before either of them could decide how to respond, the women tilted her head toward the nearby tables. "How about a game of vartras?"

"Sure," Lahkaba said. He didn't know how to play, and despite the woman's beauty, he was doubtful about talking to her. But they had to blend in if there was any chance of Rathalos's compatriots making contact—assuming she wasn't one of them.

The three of them moved through the crowded bar to an open vartras table. The table itself was a complicated maze of doors, barriers, and holes. Lahkaba knew the basic objective of the game—get the ball in the hole worth the most points—but that was where his knowledge ended.

Fortunately, it seemed Valinther had played before. He grabbed a long pole from the wall while the woman set up a group of five balls at one end of the table. After setting up the balls, the woman gestured to Valinther. "Guests first."

Valinther nodded to her and then started tweaking the arrangement of the moveable doors and barriers on the table. When he finished, he handed the pole to the woman, and she proceeded to hit each of the five balls in turn. They bounced around the table, ricocheting off the barriers. One went into one of the holes on the side of the table.

Once the balls finished moving, she handed the pole to Valinther and then stared at the table for a moment. She reached out and moved one of the barriers about forty-five degrees. When she did, Valinther laughed.

"Clever," he said, and then took his turn hitting each of the four remaining balls.

None of what they did over the next few minutes made much sense to Lahkaba. While he thought the goal was to get the balls in the holes, sometimes they seemed pleased when the balls didn't go in. Sometimes they would manipulate the gates and barriers. Other times, when it looked like they should rearrange them a certain way, they wouldn't change anything.

After about ten minutes, Valinther knocked the last ball into a hole. He sighed and then turned to the woman. "You play very well. I used to be pretty good, but I haven't had the chance to play in many years."

"It doesn't show. You're better than many of the opponents I've played lately," the woman said. "Now, shall we get down to business?"

So his suspicion had been correct. Taking the change of topic in stride, Lahkaba said, "Yes, let's. I think we've played enough to bore our escort."

A casual glance at Bryel showed the Dotran sitting and staring at the glass of water in front of him. He would look toward them occasionally and then quickly survey the room. Clearly, he was not an intelligence or security officer—or, at least, not a very well trained one.

"Our friend says you have questions," the woman said.

"We do," Valinther said.

"Let's start with your name," Lahkaba said, smiling and taking one of the poles off the wall. "I don't like talking to strangers."

"You can call me Mella," she said, resetting the five balls on the table.

Lahkaba frowned. The name was too short to be genuine, but he decided that pressing for her real name would be pointless and unnecessary. "Very well, Mella, let's get down to details. Why do your people want our Union's negotiations with the Confederacy to succeed?" he asked.

"Having a free state open to independent Kowwoks would be a great benefit to us," she said, giving the same response Rathalos had.

"Maybe. But that's not the reason. Let's put the games behind us," Lahkaba replied. Then, to add a layer of irony to his words while also maintaining their cover, he bent over and hit one of the balls with the pole. He didn't watch where it went, instead keeping his eyes up, on Mella.

"All right," Mella said, moving forward to take the pole. "Once the fleet leaves Confederate space, we're planning a mutiny to seize control of it."

The sudden revelation brought Lahkaba up short. He stared at Mella for a long time. The sheer audacity of the idea left him speechless.

Valinther was the first to speak. "Why wait for it to go all the way to Kreogh Sector? I assume this is going to be carried out by the Kowwok personnel aboard. Why go so far away?"

"So that it takes the Dotran longer to respond," Mella said, her tone matter-of-fact. "Anywhere in the Confederacy is just a few days away from reinforcements. But if we act during the long hyperspace journey, when each ship is out of contact from each other, our people will have plenty of time to gain full control of the ship.

"There aren't enough Kowwoks aboard every ship to get them all, but we can get most of them. By the time the fleet emerges from hyperspace, we'll control the majority of them. Then we can force the rest to surrender, or destroy them. And it will be months before high command knows anything about it. We can take the fleet and expel the Dotran from Kowwa before they know what's happened."

"That's a bold plan," Lahkaba said, unsure what else to say. It had a certain simplistic elegance to it. And he had to admit that it did have a higher chance of success in hyperspace than in port.

"I like it," Valinther said, his tone excited. "Though it does beg the question, how quickly do you plan to return the fleet to Kowwa?"

The question hung in the air like an accusation. It pleased Lahkaba that Valinther had been the one to ask it. He had felt sure his fellow delegate was becoming wrapped up in the idea of Kowwok independence and forgetting about the Union fight.

"Originally, we intended to return immediately," Mella admitted. "But, now that we're working together, we can take a little time to help you with your Alliance problem."

"I'm glad to hear it," Valinther said with a wide smile. "Then, maybe, together, our two fleets can liberate Kowwa."

"Wait a minute, Val," Lahkaba said. "Let's not get ahead of ourselves. Right now, the Dotran have halted negotiations until we agree to give them the regenerative shield tech. So there's no fleet coming to help either of us."

The group descended into silence for a minute. Lahkaba took his turn at the table while he thought about the new information. An entire fleet of Confederation warships controlled by Kowwoks? Would that even be enough to liberate Kowwa? Maybe, since they would arrive as friendlies. But then, could they hope to hold it?

Kreogh Sector had one main advantage against the Alliance: distance. The core worlds of the Alliance were months away. They couldn't just dispatch large numbers of warships and personnel on that kind of journey without risking their other borders.

But Kowwa was only a few days from Dotra. The Confederacy might be weakened by losing some of their warships to the rebels, but they wouldn't have to dispatch others for a multi-month journey. It would be a costly fight for them, assuming the rebels managed to take Kowwa with its planetary defense guns intact, but a winnable one.

"I think I have a way around that," Valinther said, returning to the topic Lahkaba was supposed to be thinking about. "We offer them the shield tech in exchange for a fleet of warships, but we don't agree to give it to them until the fleet arrives. Then, our friends here take over the fleet while en route. We won't be obliged to turn over the technology, because no Dotran fleet will ever arrive to assist us."

Lahkaba frowned. He hated deals that hinged on backstabbing the other party. Granted, it was all too common in politics, but this was a new level of underhandedness. But, it might free both his home of Sulas and his people's homeworld of Kowwa. Wouldn't that be worth a little underhanded negotiation and some risky actions?

Before he could answer that question for himself, the sounds of a commotion drew his attention. The doors to the club flew open, and a group of armored Dotran streamed in. Another sound alerted him to a similar group coming in the back entrance. The two groups plowed through the club, making no effort to wait for people to get out of their way. They converged on Lahkaba and his small group.

The first Dotran there grabbed Mella and slammed her against the vartras table. Restraining her arms behind her, another Dotran put metal cuffs around her wrists. They hadn't been gentle, and a trickle of blood flowed from Mella's nose, matting her fur. Despite the injury, no look of pain crossed her face. The only emotion he saw in her eyes was contempt. And she wasn't looking at the Dotran.

Still staring helplessly, Lahkaba watched as they hauled Mella away. The other guards fanned out around the club and began arresting all the Kowwoks present—all except him and Valinther.

Bryel approached them once Mella was clear. "You did excellent work, Ambassadors."

The statement sent Lahkaba's head spinning even more. Everything had happened so quickly. Bryel's statement clicked into place. This hadn't been a random raid or because Mella had been under surveillance. He had been the one under surveillance.

"We did what?" Valinther stammered. "What just happened?"

Lahkaba realized that Valinther hadn't made the connection, so he quickly added, "We weren't expecting this to happen while we were still here."

"My apologies. We didn't want to risk the traitor having the chance to slip away," Bryel said.

Before Valinther could say anything else, Lahkaba asked, "What's going to happen to all of these other people? Surely they can't all be traitors."

"That's unlikely," Bryel agreed, looking at the Kowwoks being led out of the room. He had a small frown on his scaly face. "They will be interrogated. Those who we can prove were just in the wrong place at the wrong time will be released."

As Lahkaba watched impotently, the remaining Kowwok patrons were ushered out, all with a clear view of him and Valinther standing beside a Dotran officer.

Chapter Eighteen

"We've got two thirds of the crew onboard already," Arzesaeth said. "The rest are either on leave somewhere on Kol or coming up on the next few shuttles."

"Forget about anyone on leave. It will take too long to recall them. We'll make do with those who make it aboard on the next two shuttles," Saracasi said.

She was splitting her attention between listening to updated reports, such as Arzesaeth's report on the crew, and going over technical specs. She didn't like splitting her attention, but she couldn't afford to do one thing at a time right now. There would be time to catch up on anything that she missed while in hyperspace. Far too much time.

Average speed for a journey to Irod from Kol was seven days. A fast transport like the *Cutty Sark* could do it in a little over five. A packet ship could do it in three and a half. If the *Audacious* hyperdrive worked like it had been designed, they could be there in less than three.

But that was a big if. The ship's hyperdrive had been used once before, after they had stolen her from an Alliance depot near Ailleroc. That time, they had almost become stranded in the middle of nowhere. She and Chavatwor had repaired many of the problems with the ship, but neither one had felt comfortable declaring it 'fixed.'

Even if *Audacious* did work, it had already been more than a month since the location of Irod had been transmitted to the Alliance fleet fleeing Mirthod. Mirthod was far closer to both Sulas and Irod than Kol. The Alliance would have had plenty of time to launch an attack force from Sulas.

She cleared another few routine matters with Arzesaeth, and then he left to address his other duties. He had been left in command of the

Audacious for the last few months, keeping guard over Sulas. While she respected his abilities, he had only been a commercial pilot before the war. His only time in combat had been as her XO defending Kol. She needed someone with more experience leading this fight. The irony of that statement was not lost on her.

"Commodore," Jerik's voice said, interrupting her.

Saracasi turned from the tactical console and saw an eclectic group standing just inside the bridge. Jerik stood beside two armed marines, who had a shackled Terran between them. She felt a small touch of relief to see that Davidus Brieni looked no worse for his time in captivity.

Davidus had an eyebrow raised in amusement at Jerik's statement. A lot had happened since she had ordered him arrested. She had always regretted the necessity of that decision. Now she had a chance to remedy it somewhat.

She nodded in response to Jerik but directed her attention to one of the marines. "Deja, what's the report on Mr. Aerinstar?"

Deja'z'reth Adat'to shook his head, his antennae twitching grumpily. "No sign of him, Commodore. We searched the base and the shipyard and are beginning a sweep of the surrounding area."

"Continue the sweep, but don't push your marines too far. Odds are he's long gone by now," Saracasi said wearily. This disappearance seemed to confirm her suspicions. Kaars was likely the traitor, and he had run the moment he thought he would be discovered.

"You can release the cuffs," she added, gesturing to Davidus's shackles.

The other marine unlocked them and placed them on her belt. Deja'z'reth kept his rifle in a ready position, though. Once the cuffs came off, Davidus rubbed his wrists, even though there didn't appear to be any marks.

"Commander Brieni," Saracasi began, immediately feeling weird, "I believe the identity of the true spy has been discovered. I'm pleased to be able to release you and return you to duty."

Jerik's eyes grew wide in shock. He hadn't heard any of the news yet, so he would be playing catch-up during this conversation. She regretted that, but she could only do so many things at once.

"Evidence has come to light that the power surge aboard *Defiant Glory* while at Mirthod was the result of sabotage. Kaars Aerinstar is suspected and has now all but proven his guilt by disappearing. Even if it's not him, there was no way it was you.

"Unfortunately, in addition to the sabotage of the DeeGee, Kaars also managed to access her navigational records and transmit them to an Alliance fleet. It's assumed that the Alliance has the coordinates of Irod. As such, I'm preparing to take *Audacious* to the moon in expectation of an Alliance attack force. Commander Brieni, you will follow up with the remainder of the fleet as soon as it can be assembled."

"Commodore," Jerik said, his tone still sounding shocked, "are you sure we can be confident that Commander Brieni isn't also an Alliance spy? No offense, Commander."

"None taken. You're right. You can't be sure I'm not also a spy," Davidus said, his tone flat.

"No, I can't, but, then, I can't be certain of anyone—not really," Saracasi admitted. "That's where trust comes in. I never really believed you were a traitor. But we knew someone was. That, combined with General Dustlighter's warning, left me with little choice. Now, I have one again. And I'm choosing to trust you."

Davidus gave her another considering look. For a moment, she felt like a child again, sitting around while Maarkean hung out with his older friends from the navy. Davidus had always been older and more experienced. He had given her much of her instruction on how to be a naval officer. Now, because of a decision she had made, she held authority over him. And it didn't feel right.

But she wouldn't let it stop her from doing her duty. He and Maarkean had taught her that. Personal feelings had to be put aside by those in command.

"Thank you . . . Commodore," Davidus said, the word sounding strange coming from him.

"Major Needa can fill you in on what has occurred and what the status of the fleet is. We'll need backup on Irod as soon as possible, but let me stress this: unlike *Audacious*, this fleet cannot withstand an assault from a superior Alliance force. Come together, or don't come at all. Right now, the cutters are the only thing ready to fly, and they'll just be cannon fodder by themselves."

Davidus frowned but didn't say anything more. She got the impression he disapproved of the order, but he didn't say anything, which she felt grateful for. He was not someone she wanted to argue with in front of others.

"Commodore, I must protest," Jerik said. "This ship, as advanced as she may be, cannot take on an entire task group by herself. We can't even be sure the hyperdrive will function all the way to Irod. Wait for the rest of the fleet."

Even though she felt some irritation at needing to argue with Jerik, she felt a bit of relief that he was challenging her. Ever since their first encounter, where she had burned a hole in his leg with a plasma torch, he had been far too obsequious. Most of the time, though, she felt confident he had genuinely agreed with her, and it was good to know now that he was capable of voicing his concern if she was doing something stupid.

Unfortunately, this time she had no choice but to do something stupid. Not if she wanted to have any reasonable chance of protecting the people on Irod. "I appreciate your concern, Major. But I left the people of Irod defenseless. I relied too much on secrecy to protect them, and that's gone now."

Davidus's frown deepened, but he still said nothing. Jerik looked like he wanted to continue the debate, but she cut him off. "See to your ship, Major. We'll need the *Defiant Glory* ready to go as soon as possible. I've already tasked Chief Tadashio with a special assignment to check for possible viruses left by Kaars. Be sure to complete that before departing."

The possibility that *Defiant Glory* might be compromised did the trick in getting Jerik to stop. She didn't think they would find anything. Rigging a power surge and causing the comm to transmit an unauthorized message as a result was not the most nefarious of sabotage. But it was far easier to hide that than anything that might be affecting the ship's main systems.

"Commodore, may I have a word before I depart? I have a lot of catching up to do," Davidus asked.

Saracasi felt sure his "word" would be more along the lines of a berating. But she had locked him up for several months. She owed him the chance to speak his mind.

"Of course," Saracasi said. She turned to Jerik and Deja'z'reth. "Major, good luck. Master Sergeant, keep up the hunt, but also expand your search to look for other possible sabotage Kaars might have left behind."

The two men nodded and then departed the bridge in front of her and Davidus. She led him a short distance down the corridor off the bridge to the CO's office. Arzesaeth had done nothing to personalize it during his time aboard, easing some of her guilt for usurping command.

"All right, Dav. Let me have it," Saracasi said once the door had shut behind them. "I'm sorry for locking you up. And I know this is a crazy, foolhardy mission to be taking."

Davidus just shrugged. "I can't say I enjoyed being in a prison cell for the last few months. I was pretty mad at you at first, but I also had plenty of time to think about it. Given the circumstances, I expect I would have made the same decision."

Hearing that eased one strand of guilt that Saracasi had been forcing herself to ignore for a while. She didn't like the idea of imprisoning a man without a trial or evidence, but it had been necessary, and hearing Davidus agree with that did ease some of the guilt.

"And I don't know enough about the present situation with the fleet, the war, or this ship to say whether or not your plan is crazy, stupid, unnecessary, or none of the above," Davidus continued. "But I do have to be sure you know why you're doing it. Back there, you said, 'I left the people of Irod defenseless.' That sounds a lot like guilt making your decisions for you."

Saracasi considered that. She had been the one to order the cutters away from Irod and Cardine. Irod, especially, was defenseless because of that order. That was her fault, without a doubt. Did she feel guilty about that now that they were in danger?

Surprisingly, she felt confident that the answer was "no." This had been the kind of thing she had once worried about doing, back when she had tried to avoid getting more involved in the war, but the decision had been necessary, and she had known the possible consequences.

Looking back at Davidus, she shook her head. "No, I'm not doing this because I feel guilty. I removed the ships defending Irod for a reason. Now I'm merely responding to the consequences of that decision. It's my duty to try to protect the people on that moon."

Davidus considered her for a long moment and then nodded his head. "As long as you're sure." He let out a loud sigh and shook his head. "I have no idea how you ended up in command of this fleet. If someone had asked me if you could do it, I probably would have said 'no.' But the Alliance hasn't won yet, and that's not nothing."

"No, they haven't. And as long as I have something to say about it, they won't."

Chapter Nineteen

Zeric staggered into the army command building. The small room buzzed with activity and everyone seemed to be talking at once. People rushed around like they didn't know what to do. Others stood cradling weapons, as if they expected Alliance troops to come through the door at any moment.

The orbital bombardment had continued after the transport had blown up. Fortunately for everyone with him, they had been able to make it under Lost Hope's protective shield barrier before any fire found them. The existence of the shield itself had been an unexpected discovery for him.

The chaos in the command center annoyed Zeric more than anything he could remember being annoyed at. He had just witnessed the death of over a thousand people and was not in the mood to deal with it. People were already dead because someone hadn't been doing their job.

"Everyone shut the hell up!" Zeric shouted.

Unshaven, covered in mud, and breathing heavily from a long run, Zeric imagined he looked quite disconcerting. He decided to roll with that. He snarled at the group, "Who's in command here?"

A short Notha woman stepped forward. "Colonel Pendergra, sir. I was on watch."

"What's the situation?" Zeric asked, mellowing his tone just slightly.

"A task force of Alliance vessels appeared in orbit a few minutes ago. They were already firing their weapons by the time we detected them. After destroying two of the incoming transports, they shifted fire to one of military camps that are outside the shield perimeter. We've lost contact with the camp," Pendergra said.

"I assume the other camps are already moving under the shield," Zeric asked, coming forward to look at the holographic map of the area on the central table.

"They're moving, but it's a fair distance between us and some of the camps," Pendergra explained.

"Why aren't they all under the shield envelope?" Zeric asked.

"It's not a very big shield, sir. It was decided to use it to protect the main part of town and as much of the civilian population as possible."

Zeric nodded in response, studying the map. The land around Lost Hope tended mostly toward trees. The city itself had cleared much of that away, as had the actual camps. But between them was still mostly forest.

The majority of the camps were within a few kilometers of the protective shield bubble. Most of those troops would have made it underneath by now, Zeric thought, if their camp commanders were even halfway competent. One camp stuck out to him.

"Why is this camp so far away?" Zeric asked.

"They're mostly Camari. They wanted to be close to the water," Pendergra said.

A sinking feeling weighed on him as he studied the map. The lake they had set up near put the Camari camp over ten kilometers away from the safety of the shield. Camari had also been the vast majority of those killed aboard the two destroyed transports.

"Order the camp to disperse," Zeric said. "Tell them to spread out as far apart as they can. They won't make it back here before the Alliance can bombard them. A wide net will make it harder for them to get targeted."

Pendergra relayed the order, and then Zeric finally allowed himself to ask, "What happened to the other transport?"

"They were on their approach, but still in a higher orbit, when the Alliance appeared. They had enough time to alter course and head toward the curve of the planet. They were being pursued by an Alliance corvette when we lost contact with them."

Zeric wanted to curse but knew there wasn't anything he could do to help the transport. If she had a good captain, they might make it to hyperspace before getting caught. Might.

Before Zeric could start to think any more about their present situation, one of the watch standers shouted out, "Contact! Alliance drop ships on approach vector!"

Four icons appeared a moment later over the map, showing the approaching ships. The ships moved quickly toward the city. Zeric looked at Pendergra. "I don't suppose that shield came with some air defense weapons or anti-orbital batteries?"

She shook her head. "No, sir. That's all we've got."

"And no troops in the area," Zeric said. The drop ships were coming in on a shallow vector that would put them down outside the shield, furthest away from any of his troops. To make matters worse, that part of town was on the other side of a river from most of the troops. The closest bridge over the river lay outside the shield cover. To get there, his troops would need to cross the river, exposing themselves to orbital fire, or go the long way around.

"Start moving these units"—Zeric pointed to icons on the map—"down to this river crossing." Something about the area of the city struck him as familiar. As he stared at the map while his orders were relayed, it clicked. Ceta's home was in that district. His daughter would be there.

"Tell them I'll be joining the troops there," Zeric said, stepping away from the map.

"No."

The sudden refusal brought Zeric up short. It took him a second to realize that it had come from Lei-mey and not Pendergra. He had completely forgotten that the Ronid woman was with him. "What?" he said.

"Your place is here," Lei-mey said. "Not in the front lines."

"Listen, lady, my daughter and your sister are over there. I'm not sitting here when I can help them," Zeric growled.

"And those troops will get them out. You have a whole city to protect," Lei-mey said, her tone steady.

Zeric was tired of her always interfering with his actions—especially since she was almost always right—but he didn't care about that now. The rest of the city be damned—he had a daughter to protect.

He was about to tell Lei-mey to shove off when Gu'od spoke. "I'll go. I'll make sure they get out."

Zeric looked up at Gu'od. He'd made a promise to bring Gu'od home safe as well. Gamaly deserved to have her husband returned to her alive and well. But Gu'od was an adult, and this wouldn't be the first time he had gone into danger. If anyone could get Ciara out, it was him.

"Thank you, my friend," Zeric said, relieved. "I already owe you my life a dozen times over. I'll never be able to repay you."

Gu'od shook his head. "You would do the same for my child." With a quick slap on Zeric's back, Gu'od turned and ran out of the room.

Zeric still wanted to follow his friend. Not only to look after his daughter, but also because he could do more good out there than he could in here. He was a soldier, not a leader.

The next half hour passed slowly for Zeric. The holographic tactical map turned out to be mostly just a map. Techs would add details as reports came in, but it was far from real time. That left Zeric with even less to do on a minute-by-minute basis.

As time dragged on, he started to regret the loss of the rest of his alcohol stash aboard the transport. It would have made this waiting a lot easier.

In his spare moments, he took to staring at the display that showed the portion of the battle where Gu'od had gone. After a while, reports came in about several Alliance forces breaking through their lines. The attacks caused major disruptions to the rescue efforts, costing lives of many rescuers and civilians alike. Could Gu'od, Ceta, or Ciara be among those?

Zeric ordered Union troops positioned along the bridge over the river to begin fanning out from there into the Alliance-controlled parts of the city. They directed all the civilians back across and eventually managed to push the Alliance to a half kilometer from the edge of the shield. For a change, the Union forces actually had numerical superiority.

Gu'od was looking after Ceta and Ciara. Zeric had done what he could. He trusted his friend to do the rest. Now, he just had to do his part and protect the rest of the city. Gu'od had the easier job, he thought.

"One Alliance corvette," Arzesaeth said. "Could be worse."

"It will be," Saracasi replied.

They had come out of hyperspace over Zod. Due to the direction of their travel and the planet's orbit, they had been forced to either overshoot and make a second hyperspace jump back toward Irod or exit on the opposite side of the gas giant the moon orbited. She had elected for the long journey around the gas giant. They had already risked enough by even using the hyperdrive. Adding an extra jump would be asking for trouble.

Despite her concerns, the journey had gone smoothly. Making the trip from Kol to Irod in record time, they had arrived less than three days after departing. But even at that speed, they still hadn't beaten the Alliance here.

"One corvette on the wrong side of the moon from the colony means more ships," Saracasi said. "Helm, give me an estimated time to intercept the corvette and an estimated time to orbit the moon."

Saisee Traze, the ship's Camari helmsman, acknowledged and began the calculations. The corvette was in pursuit of a transport, most likely a Union vessel, though they had failed to respond to hails. She had a duty to protect that ship, but there was likely a need to get to the colony as fast as possible.

"Twenty minutes to orbit, six to intercept. Twenty-two minutes to orbit, departing from the estimated interception point," Saisee informed her.

Saracasi smiled. Only two extra minutes, plus however long the fight lasted. She could live with that delay. Aside from protecting the transport, she didn't like the idea of leaving a potential threat capable of causing problems for her later.

"Arz, all weapon batteries target the corvette. Fire for effect," Saracasi ordered. "Saisee, increase acceleration. They're lighter than us, so let's get our speed up now."

The time to intercept the corvette dropped for another minute at a rapid pace and then scaled down. Saisee's calculations had been good, she thought. He'd made an accurate guess on when the corvette would begin fleeing and on their acceleration. They came into effective weapons range at just about six minutes.

"Fire," Saracasi ordered.

Arzesaeth relayed the orders and firing patterns to the gun batteries. The corvette's shields quickly lit up from all the energy pouring into them. Blaster bolts flew across space back at them, but with less than a sixth of the heavy firepower, they did nothing to *Audacious*'s enhanced shields.

Under normal circumstances, a corvette was no match for a frigate. Frigates killed capital ships like corvettes, and corvettes killed fighters. The enhancements that she had helped make to Solyss's captured *Gallant* should have made that ship an equal to a frigate, but this one had nothing along those lines.

"We've disabled the weapon systems," Arzesaeth announced just a few minutes later. "Reading a few hull breaches. They still have engines and maneuvering."

"Continue firing," Saracasi ordered without hesitation. "We need the Alliance to have no idea what happened to their ships here. That means nothing hyperspace-capable survives."

Arzesaeth gave her a startled look but nodded. She didn't relish destroying disabled enemies any more than he did, but it was necessary. Irod's best defense had always been secrecy. If no one from the Alliance attack force returned, Admiral Sartori would think long and hard before sending another one.

"They're launching escape pods. Sensors mark them as standard style," Arzesaeth told her.

Letting out a sigh of relief, Saracasi said, "Let them go. Continue fire on the corvette."

Some escape pods carried hyperdrives. Getting off a doomed ship did little good if you were stuck light years away from a habitable planet. But that didn't happen often. There wasn't much use in fighting in deep space. So for most pods, the inclusion of a hyperdrive was an unnecessary additional cost.

It didn't take much longer to finish destroying the corvette. As soon as it was beyond any hope of repair, Saracasi ordered them to begin the orbit of the moon Irod. She had taken down one Alliance ship easily enough, but she still had no idea what she was up against.

During the transit, Saracasi nervously drummed her fingers on the console before her. She forced herself to sit down and keep her hands still. They could be facing the entire Alliance fleet, or it could be a single ship. Until they knew, there was no sense worrying. Or at least, appearing to worry about it.

"Multiple contacts," Arzesaeth announced as the sensor data appeared on the tactical display. "Five—no, six contacts. Looks like an assault cruiser, two frigates, and three troop transports. There are also two drop ships being deployed to the surface."

Saracasi looked at the range to their target. There was no way they could intercept the Alliance fleet before those drop ships made it to the surface. They would have plenty of time to land and deploy their troops. On the plus side, if they were deploying troops, it meant that they hadn't already wiped the colony out from orbit.

Saracasi said, "Target those troop transports. I want three barrages of torpedoes."

Arzesaeth leaned in close to her. "Captain, we only have six torpedoes."

"We're not going to win this with torpedoes, Lieutenant. Commence firing," Saracasi replied. "Program the torpedoes to sync their intercept speeds."

The Union hadn't been able to acquire much in the way of munitions. Torpedoes were deadly weapons that, unlike blaster bolts, could change course to pursue an enemy. They were great long-range engagement weapons. Unfortunately, they were also expensive and hard to come by. The ones she was using now had come from the frigate captured over Dantyne.

Two torpedoes launched from the ship's two forward launchers. They had several minutes of travel time to go to reach the troop transports. Saracasi waited, watching the clock. It took the automated reload systems more than two minutes to ready the next pair of torpedoes. But soon, they were following the first pair, and then the final set launched another two minutes after that.

As the torpedoes drew closer to their targets, *Audacious* also moved closer to the Alliance ships. Positioned in a geosynchronous orbit over Lost Hope, the ships were relatively stationary compared to *Audacious*. However, once they detected the incoming torpedoes, they quickly changed that.

"Looks like the troop transports are running, trying to get away from the torpedoes. And one of the frigates is moving to protect them," Arzesaeth said, a grin on his face. "One less ship to deal with."

"For the moment," Saracasi said.

She felt satisfaction at the successful ploy but forced it down. This battle wouldn't be won with tricks. It would soon come down to a slug fight between them and the three Alliance warships. Then she'd find out how good their shield really was.

"Helm, alter course three zero mark one seven. I want to make that cruiser choose between us and the colony," Saracasi ordered.

Assault cruisers carried a large array of weapons, but most of them were arranged along one plane. That allowed them to fire a devastating barrage down at a planet, but it also meant that their underside was far less of a threat. She doubted she would be able to engage that weaker side, but at least if she couldn't, the cruiser wouldn't be able to fire on the colony at the same time.

"Alliance fleet is firing torpedoes of their own," Arzesaeth pointed out.

"Now we get to see if the theory behind these shields holds up," Saracasi said to herself. Then she spoke to her crew. "Point defense batteries, begin firing when in range."

One of the reasons torpedoes were so devastating was that when they detonated, they threw out a shaped charge consisting of several dense waves of high-velocity shrapnel. This dealt a lot of kinetic energy—more than most shields could withstand. It was the equivalent of being hit by dozens of kinetic rounds in a small area. Normal mass driver weapons could devastate small ships but could be absorbed by the shields of bigger ships. But not at the concentration delivered by a torpedo at close range.

Two torpedoes came in at them. The frigate would not have enough time to fire a second batch before they were inside gun range. Point defense fire lanced out from *Audacious* and took out one of the torpedoes. At least they wouldn't have to see what would happen when hit by two torpedoes at once.

"All hands, brace for impact," Saracasi said over the ship-wide speaker.

A slight shudder in the floor proved to be the only immediate sign of impact. Saracasi had been expecting something more daunting. She looked to Arzesaeth for the damage report.

"The shields absorbed the first wave and regenerated before the second and third waves hit. Only minimal hull damage. No systems offline," Arzesaeth said with a smile. "Entering weapons range in three minutes."

Now Saracasi had to decide which target to hit first. Both the frigate and the cruiser outgunned *Audacious*. Greater shield capacity had come at the expense of weapons, giving them fewer than a standard frigate. She still had teeth—just not enough to split between two ships and still hope to penetrate their shields.

"All weapons, concentrate on the frigate," Saracasi decided. The cruiser was the bigger threat, but she could take out the frigate faster. The fewer things she had shooting at them, the better chance the shields had of holding up.

"Frigate Two is engaging our torpedoes," Arzesaeth said.

Saracasi said nothing in reply. Even launched several minutes apart, the torpedoes had adjusted their speed so that all six came at the transports together. That made it harder for the frigate to try to shoot them all. For once, luck was on her side. Had they not already taken out this fleet's corvette escort, the job would have been a lot easier for the Alliance.

"Incoming fire," Ops reported. "Shields holding."

"Helm, evasive maneuvers. Try to stay with the frigate but keep us a moving target for the cruiser," Saracasi ordered.

Saisee began shifting the ship's course and rotation at random intervals. At their current range, even miniscule shifts would be enough to throw off the aim of the blaster shots. The Camari pilot proved good at anticipating when attacks would come in, moving just as the shots were fired.

"Reading minimal damage on the frigate. We're not penetrating her shields. She's trying to maneuver to put us between herself and the cruiser," Arzesaeth pointed out.

"Exactly where we don't want to be," Saracasi said quietly. "Saisee, new course. Bring us in a tight loop around the cruiser. Keep us on the opposite side of her from the frigate. Keep us as close as necessary. Weapons, shift target to the cruiser."

Compared to the cruiser, *Audacious* was more maneuverable. If they could orbit the cruiser, *Audacious* could control their relative positions. That would only work for as long as the second frigate remained out of range, though, and it also made them an easier target for the cruiser.

"Damage to shields increasing," Arzesaeth said. "Regeneration keeping pace, but only barely. We're going to start taking some hull damage."

"Yes, but so is that cruiser. All batteries, focus on taking out their weapons," Saracasi said.

The dance around the cruiser continued for several minutes. One lucky barrage hit them hard enough to break through the shields, disabling one of the point defense weapons. But they succeeded in doing much worse to the cruiser, taking out half her main battery. If they weren't so vastly outgunned, Saracasi might have considered it a fair trade.

Chapter Twenty

Pacing around the small command center, Zeric continued to stare at the map of the city. Another Alliance drop ship had landed, deploying troops to another part of the town. Fortunately, that part of town was on the same side of the river as the others, allowing Zeric to keep his forces concentrated around protecting the bridges.

Shortly after issuing the orders to move troops to intercept the new threat, Zeric found himself staring at the map of the city. The command post he occupied also housed the shield generator station. Since it wasn't quite in the middle of the city, the shield bubble missed some areas. It was those unprotected areas that the Alliance now used to stage their assault.

But for the life of him, he couldn't figure out why.

Initially, it had taken him a long time to get troops over there, due to the limited bridge crossings. And the urban fighting provided the Alliance a lot of cover as they advanced. However, on the opposite side from where they were deployed, a wide open field stood—what had once been the city's equivalent of a starport. Areas of it had already been ruined by debris from destroyed transports and craters caused by the orbital bombardment, but drop ships could land there easily enough. Also, that would have placed them closer to the shield generator.

He thought about the battle from the other side. How would he assault the city? A pure orbital bombardment would be safest, but against a shielded target, that could take a while. Landing troops meant casualties. It would also mean a quicker end, especially if the shield generator could be knocked out in the fight. So why were the Alliance troops massed on the wrong side of the river?

Zeric let out a curse, this time out loud. Pendergra and the techs looked at him, surprised. He ignored them. "Call these units back. Expand the scout parties out. Have them fan out through the city to the edge of the shield. Lock this building down and put snipers on the roof."

"Sir?" Pendergra asked, confused by the sudden order.

"That attack across the river is a feint. The Alliance is coming for the shield generator. Probably a special ops team," Zeric explained.

Pendergra dispatched the orders, and Zeric listened as scout teams spread out from the command center. Regular reports came in. No signs of any Alliance activity were seen.

Zeric had just started to think he might have been mistaken when one of the teams stopped reporting in. When no response came from them on the comm, he felt sure he had been right. The last position they had reported from placed them only a few blocks away from the command center.

Looking at the map of the city in that area, he zeroed in on one of the buildings: the recently expanded hospital. Most of Lost Hope stood no more than two or three stories high. At five stories, the hospital towered above everything else.

"Dispatch two companies to the hospital," Zeric said. "From there, the Alliance Spec Ops guys will have a clear line of sight to the shield generator."

"You want to have a fire fight in a hospital?" Pendergra asked, aghast.

"It's either that or the Alliance wipes us out from orbit," Lei-mey interjected. "Isn't that right, General?"

Zeric glared at her but nodded. "Keeping the shield up is the most important priority. So far, most of their attacks have been against military targets, but that might change."

"Oh, it will," Lei-mey said, her tone grave. "This colony isn't on an Alliance world. Not even one in rebellion. As far as the laws of war go, we're just an enemy. They won't have the same moral objection to blasting us from orbit that they would when assaulting another world, like Enro or Dantyne."

Lei-mey's comment sent a chill down Zeric's spine. That probably also meant that the fight in the hospital would be more ugly than it had to be. Assuming the Alliance was even there. It was where he would be, anyway—go to the top floor, fire a missile, and then boom, done. Shield down.

He itched to race out of the building to join the troops surrounding the hospital, but unlike his desire to go save his daughter, this was purely out of impatience. Though close, the hospital was still far enough away that by the time he got there, the situation would be over, one way or the other.

While waiting, Zeric turned his attention to a commotion coming from the hall outside the command center. He briefly considered the possibility that the Alliance Spec Ops team had advanced further than expected and had infiltrated the building, but he was quickly reassured when the doors to the room were opened by a Union man.

Through the doors came Ceta Darshawn. She looked disheveled and frightened. Relief washed over Zeric as he saw the small girl in her arms. Ciara was crying but alive.

"Thank you, Gu'od," Zeric said to the empty air. His friend hadn't come with them, but then, that was Gu'od. He would have gotten Ciara out first but wouldn't have left until all the civilians were free.

Ceta ran into the room and over to Lei-mey. Zeric felt slightly dejected at that. But then, he hadn't exactly been very close to Ceta.

After giving them a moment, Zeric cautiously approached. He felt the desire to reach out and touch the little girl, to comfort her somehow. But if being in her mom's arms wasn't working, a strange man holding her certainly wouldn't help.

"I'm glad you're OK," he said to Ceta instead.

Casting tear-streaked eyes at him, she gave him a small smile. "Thank you, Zeric. I don't know if we would have made it across if it weren't for Gu'od." Fresh tears started to roll down her cheeks. "Gu'od. I'm so sorry, Zeric. He . . . he . . ."

A lead weight suddenly appeared in the pit of Zeric's stomach. Gu'od's absence here hadn't surprised him a moment before, but now it suddenly felt important. He grabbed Ceta's shoulder frantically. "He *what*?!" Zeric shouted.

Ceta said nothing, her panic returning at his jostling.

He backed off, struggling to keep himself from shouting again.

"Sir," a quiet voice said beside him. Zeric turned to see Kumus standing there. With all that had happened lately, he hadn't realized until now that he hadn't seen the boy in quite some time. Not since Gu'od had left, in fact.

As Kumus started to speak, Zeric felt himself clumsily falling down into a sitting position. "Sir, Master Sergeant Dos'redna died while escorting Ms. Darshawn away from the Alliance forces. He took out a team of soldiers cutting us off, but one of them got off a shot at him before he finished. It wasn't fatal, but it did slow him down. He made me take these two—"

A spark of hope surged in Zeric. "Then there's a chance he's still alive!"

Pain and regret crossed Kumus's face as he shook his head. "No, sir. As we ran ahead, another team of soldiers came up from behind us. Gu'od . . . he . . . turned to confront them, using one of the downed soldiers' rifles. They shot him, sir. He's dead."

The despair Zeric felt flashed with anger. "You left him behind!"

Kumus's face dropped and his shoulders sagged even further. The boy wasn't really even old enough to enlist, but he had served Zeric faithfully since Enro. Without orders, he, like Gu'od, had volunteered to go and try to protect Zeric's daughter. But none of that mattered to Zeric at that moment. Gu'od was dead. The one person he always knew he could count on to be there would never be there again.

"Now, wait a minute," Lei-mey said. "Kumus risked his life for your daughter. I'm sure he did what was necessary."

"What was necessary?" Zeric growled. "No, that's what I did. Because you told me to. I stayed here. It should be me dead out there! Not him!"

"If you were dead, what would happen to the rest of us?" Lei-mey argued. "You're the only one who saw the sneak attack coming. Without you, the shield would likely be down now."

"So what? My friend is dead. His child will grow up without a father." Zeric cursed. "And it won't matter anyway. This shield can't withstand a sustained bombardment. Even if we stop that team, it won't matter. We're still dead. It will just take longer."

Lei-mey looked like she was about to continue arguing, but Zeric had had enough. "Get out. I don't want to see you near here again."

When Lei-mey didn't immediately move, he shouted again, "Go! You and Kumus. Get out!"

Turning away from them, Zeric moved back to the tactical map. He had Alliance soldiers to kill.

"The second frigate is now closing," Arzesaeth said.

Saracasi had lost track of that frigate and the transports during the fight. She expanded the tactical display. For a moment, she was confused when she couldn't find the transports. Then she smiled. "Looks like our torpedoes got through," she said, giving herself a second to celebrate, and then moved on. "Helm, next loop, allow Frigate One to catch us and give a full burn toward them, keeping our engines angled away from the cruiser for as long as you can."

As the ship rotated around the cruiser, Saisee found an angle that put them pointing right at the first frigate but kept their engines away from the cruiser, safe from enemy fire. Then he launched the ship at the frigate. At the same time, all weapon batteries shifted their fire back to the frigate.

The sudden shift in movement caught the frigate off guard, and it took several seconds for them to shift their fire. By that time, *Audacious* was practically on top of them. Once they had moved past the frigate, relative to the cruiser, Saracasi ordered a complete stop compared to the frigate. For a precious few seconds, they had an easy line of attack on the frigate and the cruiser could not fire on them without risking hitting the frigate.

"We've disabled the shields!" Arzesaeth announced triumphantly.

"Continue firing. Knock out their weapons and engines," Saracasi ordered.

The exchange of fire had been to *Audacious*'s advantage, since her shields were able to keep up with just the one frigate's fire. But that advantage hadn't lasted long. Now the cruiser could fire on them, and the second frigate would be in range in a matter of minutes.

A sudden shudder went through the deck of the ship. Some of the weapons fire had penetrated through the shield before the barrier could be regenerated. For a moment, the vibration was severe enough Saracasi felt sure they had taken some damage. "Damage report," she ordered.

"We lost the second point defense battery," Arzesaeth answered.

They could live without that, Saracasi decided. They were too close for a torpedo engagement now, and cruisers didn't carry any fighters.

"Frigate One is disabled!" Ops shouted in triumph.

Saracasi breathed a sigh of relief, but it didn't last long. One frigate was out of the fight, but a fresh one was just about to enter the battle. They had damaged some of the cruiser's weaponry, but that still left them far outgunned. Only one barrage had penetrated *Audacious*'s shields, but it had been enough to take out some of her weapons. The longer the fight went on, the more that would occur.

"Saisee, reverse course. Bring us back to the disabled frigate and get us behind her," Saracasi ordered. "Arz, ready the tractor beams. Engineering, stand by for emergency engine thrust."

Arzesaeth relayed her orders to the tractor beam crews, giving her a concerned look. Tractor beams couldn't be used while shields were up, and they would be defenseless without the shields, but she didn't think they'd survive another extended exchange between two ships. She had to do something outside the box.

"Tractor beams ready." Arzesaeth's tone was flat. Quieter, he said, "You know we'll have to lower the shields to use them. We won't last long without those."

Saracasi gave him a nod but then ordered, "Helm, line us up with the cruiser. Activate tractor beams and then engage emergency thrust." She took a deep breath. "Saisee, ramming speed."

The unorthodox order made Saisee pause for a moment, his eye stalks fully extended in a look of shock. But, to his credit, the reaction only lasted a moment before he turned around and oriented the ship. The ship shuddered as all of her available propulsion systems kicked in at their maximum potential acceleration. With the additional mass of the other frigate attached via the tractor beam, the acceleration proved to be well under their normal.

Seeing the derelict form of their former frigate hurling toward them, the Alliance cruiser began going evasive. Unfortunately for them, the recent engagement had brought all three ships very close to one other. The cruiser slowly moved out of the way of the incoming frigate. Once the angle grew, they once again had a line of attack on *Audacious* and began firing.

Blaster fire started to impact the hull, but there was nothing Saracasi could do about that for the moment—not without abandoning her best hope for taking out the cruiser. "Saisee, rotate our thrust ninety degrees. Adjust tractor beam angles to keep them at the same position relative to us."

Rotating the ship, Saisee pointed the main engines toward the cruiser again. Their previous vector would have passed them directly beneath the cruiser, but with their momentum along that path still going, plus the thrust from the ninety-degree offset, they now began moving toward the cruiser at a sharp angle.

The sudden shift in approach occurred faster than the cruiser could compensate for. A collision was now inevitable, unless the cruiser did something drastic. As Saracasi watched, it did just that. The shields on the large ship dropped and a tractor beam of its own appeared. *Audacious*'s acceleration suddenly slowed dramatically, as they were now pushing against two ships and her engines were unable to move that much mass.

Saracasi smiled. "Disengage tractor beam! Saisee, get us a shot on the cruiser! Shields up!"

No longer tethered to the other ships, *Audacious* shot forward from a relative standstill. Only careful control by Saisee kept them from ramming the frigate. Now clear of the cover provided by the disabled frigate, both warships began laying into each other with blaster fire.

Several shots made it through to *Audacious*'s hull before her shields came up, but after only a handful of seconds, their protective barrier was fully in place. This close to the cruiser, the massive ship could hardly miss, and her wide array of guns pounded into the smaller one, puncturing the shields on a few occasions. However, the advantage was clearly to *Audacious*.

While the cruiser had a few clear seconds of time to bombard *Audacious*'s unshielded hull, *Audacious* had several minutes while the frigate was unable to raise her own shields, as her momentum toward a collision hadn't yet been fully halted, and then she had to contend with the usual delay in standard shield formation. The shield layers, forming gradually, were continually punched through by *Audacious*'s insistent barrage.

After several minutes of fire, Arzesaeth reported, "They've stopped firing. Engines and hyperdrive are offline."

Saracasi nodded and called out, "Damage report!"

The maneuver had taken out the Alliance's main ship but had also given them a number of clean shots to *Audacious*. And there was still another frigate out there.

"One gun battery down. Capacitor systems disabled. Damage to the reactor control systems," Arzesaeth summarized.

Other than hearing that they had become disabled, that news was the worst she could have gotten. Saracasi cursed to herself and then said, "Begin moving all nonessential personnel to escape pods. Change course to begin pursuit of the frigate, all batteries constant barrage. XO, you have the bridge."

"Aye, I have the bridge," Arzesaeth replied.

She turned away from the tactical display, trusting Arzesaeth to handle the details of the coming fight. Moving to the aft part of the bridge, she stood by the engineering monitoring station. A quick look told her that her fears were coming true.

The regenerative power system for the shields required some unconventional power transfer systems. The capacitor cells they had installed to prevent any reactor trouble from overloading and destroying key systems had been destroyed in the engagement. Matters were worse now that the reactor had also been damaged. In a matter of minutes, they would reach an unstoppable overload.

Working with the ship's engineering staff, Saracasi tried to reroute past damaged systems and even started jettisoning spare anti-matter pods. Their magnetic containment fields were incredibly resilient, but once the end came, they would fail. No sense in allowing more anti-matter/matter explosions than necessary.

When she had done all she thought possible for them to do, she ordered the engineering staff to get to the escape pods. She turned her attention back to the rest of the bridge. Arzesaeth had already dismissed most of the crew, leaving only him and Saisee manning weapons and helm controls.

"We've managed to disable the frigate's hyperdrive," Arzesaeth said. "But that's about it."

"That will have to do." Saracasi's shoulders slouched as she accepted her defeat. She caressed the tactical table and whispered, "Goodbye, old girl. You've served us well." Then she activated the ship-wide comm. "All hands abandon ship. All hands abandon ship."

Chapter Twenty-One

"What did you do?!" Valinther shouted as soon as Bryel dropped them off back at the apartment. He had turned to Zoeko, his fur standing on end and a wild look in his eyes. As he advanced on Zoeko, Lahkaba suddenly felt very sure the confrontation was about to turn physical. Fortunately, Lionell intervened and stopped Valinther before he could get too close.

"What are you talking about?" Zoeko exclaimed, her eyes narrowed.

"You know exactly what I'm talking about!" Valinther growled. "You betrayed us!"

"What?" Zoeko said, her tone showing evident confusion.

Lahkaba cleared his throat and then moved between the two. Lionell still held onto Valinther, but the Terran man was much older and frailer than the Kowwok. Valinther had spent many years working in a mine, and while machines did much of the heavy lifting, it had still been more physical work than Lionell had likely done in his entire life.

Glancing at Lionell, Lahkaba gestured his head toward the jamming device on the table behind him. Lionell glanced quickly at Valinther before easing his grasp. When Valinther didn't resume his advance on Zoeko, Lionell stepped back and picked up the jammer, turning it on.

Once the indicator light flashed that the device was working, Lahkaba said, "Our meeting with the Kowwok resistance operative was disrupted by a Dotran raid. They arrested our contact, along with everyone else in the club."

He watched Zoeko as he spoke, but her expression of shock appeared genuine. He continued, "All except us. What made that particularly surprising was that Bryel treated it like we were working with them. Apparently, the Dotran believe we took this meeting in order to identify members of the resistance."

"That's because you told them," Valinther spat. "You're the only one who could have done it."

"No, she's not," Lahkaba said as he turned to Lionell.

The Terran man's shoulders drooped and he looked down at the floor, unable to meet anyone's gaze. Lahkaba's accusation hung in the air for a long minute—Lionell made no effort to refute it.

"No, Lionell would never do this. He believes in Kowwok independence. Tell them you didn't do this," Valinther said, his voice becoming more pleading toward the end.

"I'm sorry, Val," Lionell finally said. "I do believe in Kowwok freedom, but not at the expense of Ailleroc's. That's where my responsibility lies. Working with the resistance is noble, but it would also likely end up causing a war with the Confederacy. We might not be able to beat the Alliance without their help. We certainly can't defeat both of them."

For a moment, Valinther stood there, staring at Lionell, a look of exasperation on his face. Lahkaba began shifting his position as subtly as possible so that he could be between the two, should Valinther decide to renew his earlier charge. Fortunately, the other Kowwok remained standing there.

"I owe you my life, and that's the only reason I'm giving you this chance to explain yourself. But it didn't have to go this way. We could have just told them 'no.' Why betray them? Why do it in secret?" Valinther asked.

"It was an opportunity to get a treaty out of the Dotran. I took it," Lionell said.

"A treaty?" Lahkaba asked, shocked.

Lionell nodded. "In exchange for helping to identify members of the resistance, along with other intelligence sharing and trade rights, the Confederacy has agreed to send a fleet to Kreogh to combat the Alliance. The matter of the shield technology was tabled for now."

Valinther looked like he was trying to decide what to say, but Lionell pressed on. "We got what we came here for. All it cost us was some trade concessions we were prepared to give anyway and turning over a few minor resistance members. If they're organized properly, they won't be able to reveal anything important. If not, then they would have failed eventually anyway."

Letting out a low growl, Valinther said, "A few minor resistance members? Everyone in that bar was arrested. I can guarantee most of them were innocent. I doubt any of them will see the light of day again. The resistance had a plan to take over the Dotran fleet that was going to be sent to us. They would have helped us with our Alliance problem before returning and reclaiming our homeworld. But now, the Confederacy is likely going to execute every Kowwok on that fleet as a potential traitor. You've likely caused the deaths of thousands of my people."

Lionell's face went white. "Surely the operative they captured won't reveal anything. Even if he does, he can't know all the names of the people involved."

"It won't matter who's involved!" Valinther shouted, and Lahkaba was forced to put a restraining hand on him. "The Dotran won't care who's involved. A Kowwok planned to mutiny, so therefore all other Kowwoks are guilty. They'll take every single Kowwok off that fleet. At best, they'll be sent to a work camp. At worst, they and their entire families will be killed. And it's your fault."

"It makes no difference," Zoeko said, interrupting Valinther's tirade. "The mutiny never would have succeeded. All involved would have ended up dying anyway."

Things were quickly spiraling out of control, Lahkaba saw. Valinther was nearing a state of uncontrolled rage at both Lionell and Zoeko. Zoeko's attempt to support Lionell's decision would only make the situation worse. As much as he might disagree with the whole ugly mess, it fell to him to resolve it.

"Enough!" Lahkaba bellowed, momentarily grabbing everyone's attention. "Why anyone did what they did, or what might have happened had things gone differently, makes no difference now."

Looking each of them in the eyes, Lahkaba said, "The Confederation needs to think we're united on this. It doesn't matter how we feel about it—what's done can't be changed. The Union will get the support it needs. We need to focus on that and only that. We can deal with the rest of it when the war's over."

Zoeko was the first to nod consent, but she was the one Lahkaba was the least worried about. Valinther and Lionell were at the heart of this matter. They had been friends, he thought. Would that be enough to get them through this, or would it just make the inevitable confrontation more terrible?

Finally, both men nodded, and Lionell reached down and deactivated the jammer. Watching him, Lahkaba couldn't decide if he hated the man or felt grateful. Lionell had done what Lahkaba had thought might be necessary, saving the Kowwok from facing that choice himself. But he didn't have to like it.

"The station is yours now," Solyss said, extending a hand to Kueth Kahl-Amar.

"Thank you, Captain. I mean that sincerely," Kueth responded, casting a glance sideways toward his wife as he spoke.

It had taken longer than Solyss would have preferred, but they were finally preparing to depart Okaral. Securing all the station's Alliance personnel and transporting them to the surface had proven to be a difficult task. Training the locals on the station's basic operations had turned out to be equally challenging.

He had briefly considered leaving a contingent of his crew on the station. Securing the Union a foothold in Trepon might be useful in the future. In the end, it had come down to a manpower issue. After injuries, he didn't have any crew to spare to leave behind, especially for an unknown period. Besides, everyone aboard had joined to free the Kreogh sector from Alliance rule. No one wanted to waste away on a lonely space station in Trepon.

Solyss released Kueth's hand and started to turn toward the airlock, but Kueth stopped him by saying, "What should we do when the Alliance returns?"

That was the one question he'd hoped the man wouldn't ask. It had been the other reason he had decided not to leave any crew behind. Grimly, he said, "That depends on how much force they bring. This station is fairly well defended. If you don't make the mistake of letting them board you, you should be able to hold off one frigate. And the one we fought won't be combat capable for some time."

He left unsaid what would happen if the Alliance, inevitably, sent more than a single ship. A sense of guilt rose in him, despite knowing that what happened next wouldn't be his responsibility. The people of Okaral had decided to follow Josserand and rise up against the Alliance all on their own, even if they hadn't done this until *Gallant* had showed up and taken out the orbiting warships.

Still, he felt as if he were abandoning them. One space station wouldn't be enough protection. "The station has a few hyperspace-capable transports. Why don't you use them to get your family off Okaral?"

Kueth looked at his wife, and she said, "Despite it all, we actually have a home here. It was a prison planet, yes, but it wasn't all bad. The only thing missing was Kueth, and we have him now."

"I'll tell you what," Solyss said, still feeling as if he should do something more, "I'll take the *Gallant* to the coordinates that we found in the station's computer. It's where they've been sending all the food shipments from Okaral. It looks to be in the middle of deep space, so it's likely just a transit jump point, but maybe we can learn something about what kind of forces you'll be up against, or do something to slow them down."

Mirel smiled and squeezed Kueth's arm as he said, "Thank you, Captain. You've already done more than enough for us. I can't begin to repay you."

Glancing around them, as if checking to see that they were the only three people in the airlock, Kueth added, "I will warn you, though: don't trust Josserand. I started working for him in order to free my family. I thought it was the only way. I got to know what kind of man he is. Don't turn your back."

Solyss said, "Thank you. I knew what kind of man he was when I started this mission. But, like you, I don't have any choice. Gamaly knows how to handle him, though. We'll be fine."

Kueth nodded in reply, and Solyss added, "It's different for you now, though."

Both Kueth and Mirel gave him a curious glance.

"You don't have to rely on Josserand anymore. He'll be gone from here for at least six months—possibly years—fighting the war. You could convince the rest of your people not to follow him anymore. Okaral could be truly free. You could even choose to join the Union, or form a similar one here in Trepon. Your future is open."

Deciding that was enough pep talk and good sentiment for now, Solyss shook Kueth's and Mirel's hands one more time and then stepped through the airlock. As the airlock cycled, he put the people of Okaral behind him. He had other things to deal with now.

When the door slid open, granting him access back aboard *Gallant*, Solyss let out a sigh. He had been hoping to put off dealing with at least one of those things for a while still, but when he saw Asheerah waiting for him, he knew he wouldn't be able to wait.

"You can't put this off any longer," she said unnecessarily.

Grumbling, Solyss said, "I know. I know."

As the pair of them started walking down the corridor, Asheerah continued, "I don't see why it's so hard. Isaxo engaged the enemy. This is war. He did what he's supposed to do. If you feel it's necessary, give him a slap on the wrist and be done with it."

"It's not that simple and you know it," Solyss said, irritated. He understood Isaxo's desire to fight the Alliance and could sympathize with his desire for vengeance for his lost brother, Owrik. But there was more to it. "Isaxo is a senior officer. He disobeyed a direct order from Tess to return to the ship and then a direct order from me. How would you handle one of your marines running off on his own and almost getting several people killed?" Solyss asked.

"If he succeeded, I'd reward him. If he failed, I'd shoot him." After a moment, Asheerah grunted and said through gritted teeth, "But you're right. That wouldn't be a very good way to run a military."

They made their way to the forward section of the ship, where the officers' quarters were. Solyss pressed the buzzer outside Isaxo's door. When the reply to enter came, he stepped into the tiny room with Asheerah.

Isaxo sat up from where he had been laying on his bed but remained there. The tiny room had little floor space for standing, and Solyss and Asheerah took up most of it. They stood there in silence for a moment, with Solyss unsure how to begin.

Breaking the silence first, Isaxo said, "I want to apologize for my action. I let my personal disagreement with Tess interfere with my judgment. I thought we could take out the frigate."

Solyss considered his friend's words. Isaxo and Tess had never gotten along, that he knew. He now thought it stemmed from Tess's belief that Isaxo wasn't fit for duty, being emotionally distraught over his brother. His actions during the battle appeared to corroborate her theory.

If the disagreement were more personal, as he had thought before, then the situation would be easier to deal with. Then Isaxo's decision to ignore Tess would have been unprofessional, but not a sign of instability. He just wished he could know which version was true.

Taking Solyss's silence as cause to say more, Isaxo continued, "We were doing well, too. It was only a lucky shot that disabled Ion Four.

Unlike the engagement that killed Masaque, where we were just sitting there, shooting away, as easy targets."

That comment filled Solyss with a fresh sense of guilt. It had been his order that had gotten the Ion pilot, Masaque, killed during the battle. The plan had worked, disabling the frigate's weapon systems and effectively ending the battle, but it had been a costly decision.

Pushing the guilt aside, Solyss said, "Regardless of your intentions, or the outcome, the fact remains that you disobeyed a direct order to return to the ship. I can't just let that slide. Discipline on this ship would suffer if a senior officer got away with that without punishment."

Isaxo nodded. "I can understand that, but if you let Tess have her way and court martial me, I won't be any use to the Union. And we need all the pilots we can get."

Frowning, Solyss silently agreed with Isaxo. They were fighting a war for their right to determine their own destiny. Isaxo had done the wrong thing, but for a good reason. And he was right—they did need good fighter pilots.

"How about, instead of court martial, accepting summary judgment by the captain?" Asheerah suggested.

"That would look like favoritism," Solyss said.

"Not if the punishment were harsh enough. Say, sixty days in the brig," Asheerah said.

"Sixty days!" Isaxo blurted. "That's a long time to sit in the brig."

"No longer than our journey in hyperspace back to Kreogh," Asheerah said, a coy smile on her face.

A smile crept onto Solyss's face as well. Sixty days of solitary confinement was a long punishment that would show the crew that disobeying orders carried consequences, but it would also keep Isaxo from missing any of the fighting.

"Very well," Solyss said, deciding. "Lieutenant Mahon, you're hereby sentenced to sixty days solitary confinement in the brig for failing to obey a recall order. Lieutenant Aru, please escort him to the brig."

"Aye, Captain," Asheerah said.

She led Isaxo out of the room, taking hold of his arm once they were in the main corridor and could be seen by the rest of the crew.

"Captain, we're approaching the coordinates," Lieutenant Tess said, breaking Solyss out of his daydream.

The ship had left Okaral three days before on her journey back toward the Kreogh sector. As he had promised, Solyss had ordered a slight detour: to the location the Alliance station's computer had suggested that the frigate *Tornado* had gone. The destination was more or less in the same direction they would need to travel home and wouldn't cost them much time on their return journey.

"Thank you, XO," Solyss said. He didn't expect to find anything except an empty system, but caution made him give two additional orders. "Sound general quarters. Raise shields as soon as we exit hyperspace."

The crew responded to his order in the quick, professional manner he had come to expect from them. In the drills conducted during the journey out to Trepon, they had already improved. Now, after seeing combat—many for the first time—their movements were fluid. They had a reason to be quick about getting the ship ready to fight.

By the time the helm announced they had reached their destination, all stations aboard the ship had reported ready for battle. The familiar nausea coursed through Solyss as the ship reverted to normal space. Around him, the crew carried out their tasks without additional orders from him.

After several minutes of intense scanning, Dar'su gave him the report he had been expecting. "No ships or stations on sensors, Captain. We appear to be inside an unremarkable nebula. In addition to the gas field, I'm detecting a faint ion trail that could indicate the use of a standard sub-light engine within the last few days."

"That would suggest that the *Tornado* did, indeed, come here," Solyss said before turning to Tess. "Have the navigational computers identified any likely candidates for destinations they could be headed to?"

Tess shook her head. "The computer has identified a half-dozen scouted systems that you could reach from here but couldn't reach from Okaral without a course change. Only two are inhabited. The others were charted but had nothing of value in them. One world is a Camari world, and the other just has a small research station."

"Hmm," Solyss said, thinking out loud. "It's possible that research station is just a cover. Or those unremarkable systems are false entries in the database."

"Or they could have journeyed to any number of uncharted systems," Tess added.

"Right," Solyss agreed. "Ops, can you extrapolate the destination of the ion trail?"

Dar'su nodded. "Aye. It heads away from this location on a course of one three mark two four eight. The trail gets lost among the rest of the nebula's gas beyond a quarter AU."

That seemed unusual, Solyss thought. When a ship stopped to make a course change, it was for only a few reasons. Either they didn't want anyone to know their final destination, which was common among smugglers, criminals, and military vessels, or they had to go around something.

Hyperspace existed in another realm than the standard space that they lived in, but it wasn't completely isolated. While you *could* fly right through a planet in hyperspace, sometimes you wouldn't come out the other side. The larger the object, the greater the odds were of the two realms interacting. Most hyperspace courses avoided passing through star systems for this reason.

But when you made a course correction to avoid a star system, it merely involved flying to a point that would give you a straight shot at your final destination. Moving around in real space would be unnecessary.

"Helm, follow that ion trail. I want to see where they went," Solyss ordered.

The ship began moving through the emptiness. Minutes dragged by, and the tension of the crew faded, replaced by boredom. Traveling through hyperspace was never very exciting, but at least you were moving toward home.

After twenty minutes of flight, Dar'su reported, "Sir, I'm still not detecting any ships or structures, but I'm getting some unusual readings along our present course."

Solyss cocked an eyebrow. "Unusual how?"

Dar'su turned in her seat and gave him an embarrassed look. "Unusual in that I have no idea what they mean. The computer identifies it as some kind of anomaly. I'm no astrophysicist and can't interpret the data. I've run a system diagnosis and it comes back clean."

"Is it safe to proceed?" Solyss asked.

"Unknown, sir. Some of the anomalous readings are energy spikes across the spectrum and gravitational fluctuations. Nothing jumps out as clearly dangerous, but, then, we don't really understand what's going on," Dar'su replied, her tone not reassuring him in the slightest.

For a moment, Solyss considered his options. They still had no idea what had happened to the Alliance frigate. With all the gas from the nebula and this unexplained anomaly, it was entirely possible the ion trail didn't actually belong to their missing frigate.

In the end, despite his curiosity, Solyss had to admit that the frigate was irrelevant to his primary mission. He needed to get Josserand back to Kreogh Sector and gain control of the *Black Market*. Anything else would just be a personal indulgence.

With a reluctant sigh, Solyss ordered, "Helm, resume our course back home."

Chapter Twenty-Two

Saracasi had never been bothered by tight spaces before. For more than a week, though, her world had consisted of a room just slightly bigger than her quarters on the *Cutty Sark*. And she had to share it with two other people.

While the escape pod could technically hold five people, she, Arzesaeth, and Saisee, who had been the last ones off the *Audacious*, were the only ones aboard. This gave them slightly more space than the rest of the crew would have, but they had also been the ones closest to the ship when it exploded. Between the damage done to the pod and the radiation resulting from the explosion, they had been unable to maneuver or communicate with anyone.

After the third day, she had given up on trying to make any repairs. Escape pods were designed to keep people alive, not operate like a fully functional starship. They lacked tools and spare parts, and accessing damaged systems without a space walk proved impossible. While they did have vacuum-rated environmental suits in the emergency supplies, there was no airlock. An EVA would mean venting a lot of the precious air supply into space. The situation had forced her to do nothing, which she wasn't used to.

When a shudder rang through the pod, Saracasi thought nothing of it at first. They had been colliding with pieces of debris from the battle periodically. Anything that didn't kill them wasn't worth worrying about. But when the vibrations continued after several moments, she woke up from her half-doze.

Sharing a glance with Arzesaeth and Saisee, she allowed herself to feel a small tingle of hope. A tractor beam was the only thing she knew of that would cause this level of constant low-level vibration. That meant someone had found them.

After several minutes, the vibration stopped. Its absence filled the pod with an eerie calm. It lasted long enough for her to start to think it had all been a dream. She was about to lay back down when she noticed something: sound.

Noises could be heard outside the pod, and Saracasi smiled. Noise meant atmosphere. She tried the external environmental sensor on the pod but got no reading in response. Like most external systems aboard, the sensors weren't working.

Saracasi forced herself to wait calmly for several more agonizing minutes. Finally, the pod's hatch opened from the outside, and a rush of light and fresh oxygen flooded in. Squeezing her way through the small opening, Saracasi stood fully erect for the first time in a week.

She found herself on the shuttle deck of an Alliance corvette that she quickly recognized as belonging to *Gallant*. A Camari woman in medical garb stood beside two crewmembers. The woman came forward and began looking Saracasi over with her medical scanner.

"Casi!" a shout came from behind the crew, and Saracasi saw Solyss Novastar making his way toward her.

"I'm glad to see you!" he said with a big grin.

"Not half as glad as I am to see you, Solyss," Saracasi said with a smile. "I see *Gallant* made it back from Trepon safely. Any word on the rest of my crew?"

"About 90% have been accounted for, now that we've found you three," Solyss answered. "We arrived in system yesterday and immediately joined the search-and-rescue operation with the rest of the fleet."

"What of Irod?" Saracasi asked. *Audacious* had succeeded in destroying most of the Alliance fleet attacking the planet, but one frigate had remained and ground troops had already landed.

"My information is limited," Solyss confessed. "But when we got here, we found the fleet conducting SAR operations and there was no indication of fighting planet-side."

That was good, she thought. Zeric must have been able to deal with whatever forces the Alliance had managed to get planet-side. Davidus had been as good as his word and brought the fleet, which presumably had taken out the remaining frigate. Assuming, of course, they hadn't managed to repair their hyperdrive beforehand and report what had happened.

"What can you tell me about the situation?" Saracasi asked. "And how soon can you get me over to *Defiant Glory* or down to see General Dustlighter?"

Before Solyss could answer, the Camari woman who had looked her over said, "Not until I've had a chance to give you a thorough scan and you've had time to rest."

"I've had nothing but time to rest," Saracasi replied irritably.

The Camari woman lowered her eyestalks and fixed her with an intense stare.

Solyss intervened before either of them could say anything else. "Perhaps Dr. When is right, Commodore. You've been exposed to a lot of radiation over the last few days. And our shuttle is out with the search teams. She's due to dock in two hours to refuel."

Saracasi frowned but nodded. "Very well. Run your tests."

With a satisfied nod, Dr. When led her, Arzesaeth, and Saisee from the hangar deck. Solyss walked with them down the narrow corridors. As they walked, he said, "This will also give you a chance to get to know our newest crewmember."

She gave him a curious look, but he just smiled. Instead of pressing him any more, Saracasi walked in silence the short distance to the *Gallant*'s small sickbay. Inside, she felt relieved to see a few members from the crew of *Audacious* resting comfortably. They looked injured but were alive.

In the sickbay's remaining bed, she caught sight of a familiar Liw'kel woman. In the woman's arms, held close to her breast, was a small, light-blue baby. Ignoring Dr. When's instructions, Saracasi went over to the pair. "Gamaly! Congratulations!" she said to her friend.

Looking up from the suckling baby, Gamaly gave her a faint smile. "Thank you, Casi. It's good to see you alive. I'd introduce you properly to Ga'mod, but he's a little distracted at the moment."

"I didn't realize you were already due," Saracasi said, wanting to look at the baby but not sure what was acceptable with Liw'kel mothers when it came to breastfeeding. Braz women felt no shame breastfeeding in front of others, but she knew many Terrans did. Most other species fed their young in very different ways.

"He came a little early. I had hoped to make it back before giving birth so that Gu'od could be there," Gamaly said, a sad look on her face.

"Well, he might have missed the birth, but he probably isn't far behind. I'm surprised he isn't aboard. Zeric is on Irod, and I expect Gu'od's with him," Saracasi said.

Gamaly frowned. "I've not been able to get in touch with either of them. Solyss says things are pretty chaotic down there and with us involved in rescue efforts, he hasn't been able to send me down in a shuttle. Not that Dr. When would let me leave sickbay."

"Well, don't worry. Once I'm allowed out of here, I'll get Gu'od on the first shuttle I can find," Saracasi said with a smile.

A non-subtle cough behind her made Saracasi turn around and see Dr. When waiting impatiently by a scanning device. "The sooner you let me get this over with, Commodore, the sooner you can get out of here."

Gamaly gave her a sympathetic smile, and Saracasi left her friend to tend to her baby. It was good that some happiness could still be found in all the ugliness of this war.

Around him, people talked. Zeric ignored them. He never liked meetings under normal circumstances. This one should have been better than most, even though politicians were the ones currently talking, because it was ostensibly a military briefing and planning session. He really should have been paying close attention. A short time before, he had been grateful for the meeting to start.

When Saracasi had arrived on the surface, she had immediately approached him with news that Gamaly had given birth to a healthy baby boy. Instead of inspiring elation, the reminder about the baby had almost sent him running from the room. He had been ducking Gamaly's attempts to talk to him since the *Gallant* had arrived in orbit. Fortunately, until now, he had managed to keep them away from the surface.

But all the missing crew were now accounted for, and Saracasi had asked about Gu'od. Hastily, Zeric had rushed her into the meeting, dodging the question. She still sat there, around the table from him, giving him curious glances. He wasn't ready to have to tell Gamaly about Gu'od's death, and he would have to as soon as Saracasi found out.

He tried focusing on the Cardine delegate speaking. "While the Camari Republic regrets they cannot send any ships or personnel, they did sell us a supply of weapons on credit. And they're raising the alert levels of their forces near the Alliance border. The appearance of Camari ships in the Monab system, which is jointly owned, will keep the Alliance on alert and tie up some of their fleet in defensive positions."

While the news was good, the Cardine delegate speaking reminded Zeric of the promise he had made to Marshall Teev. He'd promised to get his troops back to Cardine. Instead, over half of them had died—obliterated when their transports were destroyed. Rather than helping to win the war and then returning to Cardine to liberate their own homes, they had died in a useless and senseless way.

The thought of their deaths brought Zeric's mind back to Gu'od. Everything eventually did lately. His best friend, one of the only people in the universe who had ever truly cared about him, was dead. Dead because he'd gone to save Zeric's daughter. A daughter he'd never wanted. A daughter he now couldn't look at without thinking of Gu'od and blaming her for his death.

Guiltily, Zeric chided himself. None of that should be blamed on the girl. She was just a child whose home had been attacked. Gu'od was dead not because of her, but because of him. He hadn't gone to her rescue like he should have.

Ignoring looks from the other people in the room, Zeric pulled a flask out of his pocket and poured the contents into his empty mug. The local moonshine tasted terrible, and it was still early in the day, but he needed something to clear his head. All this boring talk just left him plenty of time to think about Gu'od. He had to bury those thoughts somehow.

The Camari from Cardine had sat back down while Zeric poured his drink, and Lahkaba had stood up. Zeric tried to make himself pay closer attention. He liked Lahkaba, and, unlike the other politicians, he didn't drone on pointlessly. Not as much, anyway.

"Negotiations with the Confederacy went well. They've agreed to dispatch a fleet to assist us against the Alliance," Lahkaba said, though the frown on his face appeared counter to the positive nature of his words. "Let me introduce Lieutenant Commander Bryel Prytoker, our liaison officer from the Confederate fleet. He'll brief you on their intentions."

A blue-scaled Dotran stood up. "Thank you, Delegate Lahkaba. General Dustlighter, Commodore Ocaitchi, it's an honor to be able to fight alongside you in the name of freedom."

Bryel nodded his head to Zeric and Saracasi. Zeric lifted his mug in response, suppressing a laugh. Now he would be fighting alongside his old enemy. How many Dotrans had he killed during the last war? He couldn't remember.

"Our fleet, under Grand Admiral Makvelli, intends to launch a surprise offensive against the Alliance stronghold on Ailleroc. He believes that hitting the Alliance at their strongest point before they've had time to prepare for the Confederate's involvement will allow him to take—liberate—the planet. That will cut off Admiral Sartori's main source of supplies and support," Bryel said.

"When and where will we need to rendezvous with his fleet?" Saracasi asked.

"You won't," Bryel said. "As per our agreement, Grand Admiral Makvelli has final command of all naval forces. He's instructed your fleet to maintain your minor harassment tactics."

"Minor harassment tactics?" Saracasi said, her tone defensive. "We've pushed the Alliance fleet from orbit of four worlds, defeating three separate task forces."

"My apologies," Bryel said. "I meant no disrespect. I merely meant to convey the admiral's wishes that you continue your present tactics of avoiding major engagements at Sulas or Ailleroc so as to keep the Alliance off balance and not expecting an attack."

Not waiting for a reply from Saracasi, Bryel turned to face Zeric. "However, General Dustlighter, Grand Admiral Makvelli wants you—would like to request—that your forces on Sulas increase their operational tempo so as to cause a distraction for the Alliance leading up to our assault. It would be good if their attention were focused on Sulas."

The request caught Zeric's full attention. He had only been half-listening before, ignoring most of the naval squabbles.

There were many things Zeric had neglected in his life. Most had come at a great cost to others, such as Gu'od. Sulas was one of those areas he had abandoned. But there was still time to correct that mistake. He could still see Sulas freed and those trapped troops allowed to return to their homes alive. He wouldn't neglect his responsibility there anymore. "I'll make sure Sulas is plenty distracting for the Alliance, Commander. I'll be returning there to oversee the operation personally," Zeric decided.

Everyone at the table turned to him, clearly surprised by his declaration. Lei-mey, of course, was the first to speak. "General, you're needed here to oversee the rest of the sector. It wouldn't be prudent for you to return to behind enemy lines."

"I'll be the one to decide where I'm needed," Zeric snapped, anger at the politician flaring up in him.

Lei-mey returned his dark look. Zeric waited a long moment for her to argue with him, but this was a military briefing, and she was just an advisor here.

He smiled when she said no more, but he decided to moderate his tone. "The guerilla campaign waged by General Kil'dare has gone on long enough. The Alliance should be lulled into a false sense of security by now. It's time for me to return and oversee the liberation of the planet."

And that way I don't need to face Gamaly. It would give the Alliance plenty of opportunity to kill him before she did.

After the military briefing ended, everyone tried to speak to Zeric. To avoid getting sucked into any one of a thousand different discussions—especially having to listen to Lei-mey try to stop him—Zeric bolted from the meeting room the instant he could. Now that he had made his decision about what to do, he needed to act on it quickly.

It took him a while, but he finally tracked down Fracsid and Sienn'lyn. He was fortunate that both were planet-side. Having to wait for Sienn'lyn to shuttle down would have taken hours.

"Fracsid, I need you to make *Cutty Sark* ready for my immediate departure. Sienn, I'm going to need you to fly me. You're the only one who's done an atmospheric insertion before," Zeric said once he had gathered them together.

"Sir," Fracsid said nervously, "I can't just send the ship to Sulas indefinitely. She's needed with the fleet."

"She's needed for this mission more, Major," Zeric growled, his tone uncharacteristically sharp. "Don't question me again."

"Zeric," Lahkaba said, appearing from nowhere, causing Zeric to jump.

Everyone turned to look at the Kowwok delegate, who said, "I take it you're not wasting any time going to Sulas?"

"Don't try to stop me, Lah," Zeric said forcefully. "I don't want to be lectured. Not even by you."

"I wasn't planning to," Lahkaba said, putting his hands up to show surrender. "I actually want to go with you."

Zeric gave him a cautious look. What game was he playing? He trusted Lahkaba, but he was still a politician. On the other hand, Lahkaba was from Sulas, so he had every reason to want to go back there. After a moment, Zeric nodded.

"All right, you can come, but you better be ready to go, because we're leaving now," Zeric said. He turned back to Fracsid. "All right, Major. Let's go."

With a shrug and a curious glance at Sienn'lyn, Fracsid led the group toward the city's landing field. Most of the wreckage from the destroyed troop transports had been cleared away, though the burned husk of the vessel hadn't been moved far. The sight of it as they approached the field reinforced Zeric's desire to get off this moon.

When they came within sight of the *Cutty Sark*, Zeric suddenly stopped and let out a curse. Ahead of them were Saracasi, Lei-mey, Kumus, and Gamaly, standing at the bottom of the ship's ramp. He had been so close to getting off Irod without having to confront either of them. To make matters worse, in Gamaly's arms was a bundle that looked distinctly like a baby.

He could just run. They were still several meters away. Gamaly wouldn't be able to catch him—not while carrying her baby. And Saracasi wasn't a good runner at all. He could run now, find another ship to commandeer, and get off Irod before they caught up to him.

But before he could do anything, Lahkaba waved and shouted, "Gamaly! Is that your baby there? I'm glad I'll get to see him before leaving. I'm sure Zeric is, as well."

The big white Kowwok drew everyone's attention to their group, and Zeric knew he'd lost his chance to run. Reluctantly, he finished walking the short distance to the ship. At the last second, he decided he had one final thing to try: pulling rank.

"Lieutenant I'fu, get aboard and start pre-launch. Major Relis, clear your crew off. Commodore Ocaitchi, I'm departing for Sulas immediately. I need you to move these people away from the ship," Zeric said, trying to sound authoritative.

He continued to move forward, increasing his speed. Saracasi immediately started to raise an objection, but he just ignored her. Ignoring his problems had worked before.

But before he made it fully up the ramp, the baby made a small cry, and then Gamaly asked, her voice quiet, "Zeric, where's Gu'od?"

The simple question, and the pleading tone that said she knew what he would say—didn't *want* to hear it, but had to—brought him up short. He didn't want to have to tell her. He wasn't sure he could really say those words out loud. But, in the end, she was his friend, too.

Stopping midway up the ramp, Zeric slumped his shoulders. Without looking back, he managed to say, "He's . . . he's dead."

He braced himself for what would come next. Either Gamaly would break down crying, which he knew he wouldn't be able to bear, or she would decide to take her revenge on him immediately. He preferred the second option.

Instead, he heard nothing for a long moment. Eventually, curiosity got the better of him, and he turned around. Tears were running down Gamaly's face, though she was remarkably composed. In her arms, she squeezed the bundled form of her baby tight across her chest.

"How did it happen?" she finally asked.

"He died in the battle against the Alliance forces invading Lost Hope. He died doing what I should have been doing. He died because of me," Zeric said, tears welling in his own eyes.

"Don't be an idiot," Lei-mey said, her usual brusque tone ruining the solemnity of the moment. "Gu'od died a hero. He died saving Zeric's daughter while Zeric oversaw the defense of the entire city. The *effective* defense of the city, which saved tens of thousands of lives, I might add."

Gamaly gave Zeric an astonished look, replacing her sad gaze for a moment. "Is that true? You have a daughter?"

Zeric nodded. "Apparently Ceta got pregnant when we, ah, reunited after the Olan prison break."

"And she's here? Gu'od saved her?" Gamaly asked.

"The Alliance forces were moving in through the section of the city where she and Ceta live. Gu'od went in my place to get them out. Gamaly, I'm so sorry. I never should have let him go. He died because of me," Zeric said, feeling his throat constrict as his own tone turned pleading.

To his surprise, Gamaly let out a sad laugh. "You're not wrong. But it's not your fault. Stopping Gu'od from saving your child would have taken more than an entire Alliance army. That's just who he is ... was."

Gamaly's words caught on the last word and fresh tears rolled down her cheeks. She closed her eyes for a moment before speaking again. "He never would have told you this, but I stopped being his sole Focus a long time ago. He had originally left his Ni'jar Conclave because he thought his mission in life was to protect me and redeem me from my life of crime. I straightened him out from those foolish notions early on. But he stayed because he loved me.

"Eventually, Gu'od expanded his Focus beyond just me. He decided that his role in the Balance was the preservation and betterment of life for his family. And he included you in that family. We joined this rebellion because he felt it was your calling, and he wanted to help you follow it.

"But he died doing what he felt he existed for: protecting your child so that you could protect others, including me and his child. I'm sad that he's gone, and part of me wants to beat you until you can't get up. But I know, in the end, he died because of who he was, and that's why I loved him."

Zeric felt tears running freely down his cheeks now. He realized he hadn't cried since learning of Gu'od's death. It felt good, despite the pain it brought. He didn't even care that he was surrounded by others. Looking around, he realized that many of them looked just as sad as he felt.

Gu'od had been important to a lot of people, he realized. Saracasi and Lahkaba had been with him since this whole rebellion had started. Sienn'lyn had become his student. Zeric had been about to use her to escape Irod and hadn't even considered telling her what had happened.

"I'm sorry. To all of you," Zeric said. "I'll stay here and not go to Sulas."

To his amazement, Gamaly gave him a harsh look. "Why would you stay here?"

Zeric blinked at her in response, but Lei-mey jumped in. "Because that's where he's needed."

Ignoring the Ronid delegate, Gamaly looked at Zeric. "Were you going to Sulas to avoid facing me or because it was the best strategy?"

He almost answered that it was just to hide from her, but he stopped himself. Going to Sulas *now* would have been the best way to avoid facing Gamaly, but that wasn't the only reason to go back. He still felt responsible for the troops he had left behind there. And what army the Union still had—that was not trapped on Sulas—had been decimated by the recent attack.

"Both," Zeric finally answered.

"I thought so. No, you should still go," Gamaly said, her tone decisive

Zeric blinked at her comment. That hadn't been what he had expected her to say.

In response to his expression, she added, "Gu'od would want you to keep fighting. That's the only way to ensure a safe future for his child. And yours."

Nodding slowly, Zeric said, "I'll make sure they both have a shot at that future." He turned to Sienn'lyn. "I'm sorry to you, too. I should have told you about Gu'od. I won't order you to come on this mission."

For a moment, Sienn'lyn stared at him, her face strained. He guessed that she was trying to maintain a look of emotional detachment, much like Gu'od would have, but her expression had none of confident wisdom Gu'od's always had.

Finally, she shook her head. "I'll do it for Master Dos'redna. He said you did many things well, but that taking responsibility wasn't one of them. But you appear to be trying to correct that, in your own twisted way."

Zeric stifled a frown. He didn't know Sienn'lyn very well, so he found it annoying for her to point out one of his faults like that. Gu'od could have gotten away with that, but he never would have said it quite so bluntly. He let Gamaly do that for him.

She continued, "And I've also seen you fly. I won't be responsible for the leader of our military being killed by crashing into a planet."

On second thought, Zeric thought, maybe she had learned more from Gu'od than he had thought. Either way, he was glad to have a pilot to get him to Sulas. He didn't much like the idea of dying by crashing into a planet.

He cast another glance at Gamaly. "When I come back, this war will be over. And I'll be there to help you with the baby. You won't have to do this alone."

A slight flush of emotion crossed Gamaly's face, and she gave him a small nod and then pulled the baby closer to her cheek.

Ignoring Lei-mey's protests, Zeric turned and headed up the *Cutty Sark*'s boarding ramp, calling behind him, "You're in charge now, Casi. Sorry. All right, Lah, if you're coming, get onboard."

Lahkaba started up the boarding ramp, but Lei-mey, apparently intent on stopping someone, grabbed his arm. "You're needed here as well."

The white furred Kowwok glared back at her. "The only thing I've done here is get us in bed with the Dotran. I think I've done enough *good* here."

"What do you hope to do on Sulas?" Lei-mey asked. "You were a soldier once, but you're a politician now. That's where your skills lay."

"Then I'll use those skills. I plan to negotiate the release of Maarkean and Lohcja," Lahkaba said, surprising Zeric.

He cast a glance at Saracasi. They had discussed several options for rescuing Maarkean before departing Sulas a few months ago. Each one ended with getting everyone involved captured or killed. "Lah," Zeric said, "I want to see them free as much as you do. But the Alliance is not just going to let them go."

"I don't expect they will," Lahkaba conceded. "But I can offer myself up in their place. A political leader is a more valuable hostage."

Zeric frowned. He didn't think he agreed with his friend's assessment. If Lahkaba tried to negotiate that way, they would just take him prisoner. He had to know that. Something about this plan didn't make any sense to him.

Before he could say anything more, Saracasi chimed in, a grim smile appearing on her face. "Lah, I think I might have a more valuable bargaining chip."

Chapter Twenty-Three

"Well, well. I do love a woman in uniform."

The smooth, self-confident sound of Josserand Renard's voice made Saracasi inadvertently cringe. Every other time she had met the crime boss, he had made some kind of lewd comment to her. It had always bothered Maarkean more than her, but with him absent, she felt the annoyance for the both of them.

"Good to see you again, Joss. Please have a seat," she forced herself to say politely.

Josserand strolled confidently into the ready room of *Defiant Glory*. Solyss Novastar, Asheerah Aru, and a marine guard followed him inside. All except the two marines took seats in the front row of briefing chairs. She remained standing beside the holoprojector with Davidus.

She had to forcibly remind herself that Josserand didn't have any power over her now. Before, she and her brother had been reliant on Josserand for work just to keep themselves fed, but now, he was at her mercy. She had the power to make the sniveling scoundrel just disappear, or leave him locked in the brig on any ship in the fleet.

Pushing aside those brief fantasies, she said, "Major Novastar tells me you've agreed to help us gain control of the *Black Market*. Let's talk about how you're going to make that happen."

"We have a preliminary agreement in place," Josserand said. "The final details need to be ironed out."

"We'll get to those. First tell me how you can gain control of the ship," Saracasi said, making her tone firm.

Josserand studied her for a moment. She suspected he was deciding how far he wanted to push his position this early in the negotiation. He must have decided that he would benefit from showing what he was worth first, because he said, "During my time aboard, I was able to implant several computer programs. These will allow me to access key portions of the ship. In addition, I have several contacts onboard to ensure a quick transition of power."

"We're going to need those codes," Saracasi said.

Josserand gave her a wide, slick smile. "Of course."

Saracasi frowned. Anytime Josserand agreed to anything, you had to ask yourself exactly how you were being screwed. Not wanting to play any of his games, she asked, "All right, what's the catch?"

"Oh, nothing important. I just have to be the one to enter them. They're tied to my biometric signature. So even if I were stupid enough to give you access, they wouldn't do you any good," Josserand said, a touch of glee in his voice.

Hiding her frustration, Saracasi forced a smile onto her face. "That's fine. You were going along with the assault team either way."

"An assault team won't be necessary," Josserand said. "My people can handle it. Just drop me off on Mirthod and tell me where you would like me to bring the ship."

"Joss, you seem to be misunderstanding the situation," Saracasi said, keeping her voice quiet. "You're going to take my team onboard, and you're going to help them seize control. Then you're going to stay out of their way until the end of this war. Then, if you've done all of that and haven't pissed me off, we'll hand the ship over to you.

"Now, if you decide you want to be obstinate, we're just going to find the nearest empty rock and dump you on it. Either you're going to help us just like I've described, or you're useless to us. The choice is yours."

Josserand gave her a look through narrowed eyes. When he didn't immediately respond with some form of sleazy comment, she knew he would agree. Putting the loathsome man out of her mind, she turned to Solyss. "Solyss, how did you want to handle the infiltration?"

"It's a big ship, but I think a small team will be best," Solyss said. "The Fox has a big security force, but it's mostly used to keep riffraff in line. Assuming the bypass codes work out, a small strike force should be able to take the bridge and engineering sections. At that point, we can signal the rest of the fleet to jump in and secure the rest of the ship."

Saracasi nodded. "The *Chimopori* is still undergoing repairs, but you can take any of the remaining gunships."

"Actually, the *Chimopori* will be perfect. Coming in with a damaged ship will better explain why we're fully loaded with marines. We fled to the safety of the *Black Market* after a failed attack on the Alliance. We do have the Fox's permission to use the ship as a repair base," Solyss said.

"Good idea. Let's make it more convincing. All of our gunships have been operating as a unit. We'll send the entire force in, loaded with marines. Unless the ships moved, they aren't far from Dantyne. You can say you were raiding the Alliance forces there but were caught by a task force and had to flee.

"I'm also sending Commander Brieni along with you. He's the only one here who's served aboard this class of ship and will have knowledge that could be useful, should Josserand's virus not live up to the hype," Saracasi said.

Solyss frowned, but before he could say anything, Davidus said, "The commodore has made it clear to me that this is your mission. I'm just along as an advisor."

"All right, then, let's get this started."

As Zeric strode into the Ba'aar sports complex, he wasn't sure if he felt glad to find the Rogues still here or not. Their presence in the complex meant they were still alive—and he didn't have to search the planet for them—but it also meant they hadn't made much progress in the fight against the Alliance.

The sentry at the entryway passed ahead word of his coming, and by the time Zeric reached the basement's main room, it had filled with soldiers. He felt pleased to recognize so many faces among them. There would have had to have been deaths among them in the months since his departure, he knew, but at least not everyone he knew had died.

In the center of the group, her eyestalks hovering in a neutral mid-extension position, stood Ymp. She hadn't been thrilled when he had announced his departure. He couldn't blame her, since he had left the responsibility for all the lives here on her shoulders. On the other hand, a neutral expression wasn't one of her disquieting glares, so he took that as a good sign.

After spending a few minutes smiling and shaking hands, Zeric managed to make his way to Ymp. Even though he felt glad at every familiar face, he was especially pleased she was still here, alive and well. He had grown attached to her, relying on and respecting her, but he could never let her know that.

"It's good to see you again . . . General," Ymp said with a pleased tone. "I see you've brought guests."

Beside Zeric were Lahkaba, Kumus, Sienn'lyn, and an Alliance prisoner, Hari Dolan, who had come in with him. Saracasi had offered the Alliance officer to Lahkaba to help with his negotiations. Zeric hadn't relished the idea of keeping track of a prisoner during their insertion, especially while trying to make his way here quietly, but Dolan had proved to be no trouble. And if it helped get Maarkean out, he could go along with it.

"Oh, you know me—the more the merrier," he said, then made his tone formal in order to settle the celebration some. "What's the situation, Major?

"All's quiet, General," Ymp replied. "Since your departure, we've run several raid and sabotage operations, resulting in damage or destruction to multiple Alliance vehicles and personnel. We've lost five troops to enemy fire. Currently, we're in a stand-down position per orders from Minister Kantor."

Zeric frowned. Only five deaths was a nice low number but also very surprising. Even with troops as good as the Rogues, deaths were bound to occur during war. Either the Alliance had been especially inept, or Ymp's definition of 'several' was low.

Out of the corner of his eye, Zeric saw his aide, Kumus, embracing his brother, Kelvine. The family reunion brought a slight smile to his face. Maybe the low number of operations, and resulting low number of deaths, was a good thing. It had allowed two brothers to reunite.

His feeling of cheer faded quickly as the sight reminded him that Gu'od and Gamaly would never have that reunion. Thousands of other families were in similar positions. As much as he might be glad the war hadn't destroyed the Stryker family, he hadn't come here to avoid fighting.

"Major, I'll need a full briefing on what has occurred planet-wide. And set up a meeting with the other division leaders. It's time we showed the Alliance the door," Zeric said, his tone grim but confident.

Ymp's eyestalks perked up, and she smiled that eerie Camari smile. "Sergeant Ocif, send a message to all unit commanders."

"Aye, ma'am. What shall I tell them?" Obod Ocif asked.

"Tell them, 'Zeric's back.'"

The full report Zeric had gotten from Ymp about what had occurred since he had left had been disappointing reading. He had expected Jairyd to mandate an increase in operational tempo along with reducing information-sharing, given that the other man's plan had been to wage a guerrilla war against the Alliance.

The troops had done that, but not to an extent Zeric thought useful. What the troops on Sulas had accomplished would amount to little more than a minor annoyance to the Alliance. In some ways, their actions hardly counted as more than petty vandalism.

When the conference call with all the division commanders started, Zeric had a pretty good idea of the cause. As the commanders came onto the screen, each made some comment of greeting to him. Most appeared pleased to see him. Jairyd and Kantor were the prime exceptions.

"General," Jairyd said, "I didn't expect to see you back here without our fleet coming with you."

"Our fleet's needed elsewhere at the moment," Zeric answered evasively. "I'm here to ensure that when they do come, Sulas offers a warm welcome and not blaster fire."

"We're making progress there," Jairyd said defensively. "Our insurgency has kept the Alliance on their toes."

"Right," Zeric said, trying to keep his reply non-accusatory. He didn't want to turn this meeting into a fight. "And now it's time to cash in on that disruption to end the occupation."

"Mr. Dustlighter," Kantor said, not using Zeric's rank, "Sulas has been doing very well defending itself. Your advice is appreciated but unnecessary. General Kil'dare has done a remarkable job running things in your absence."

Zeric said nothing in response. He found Lei-mey annoying, but she had given him some useful advice for how to deal with politicians. Instead of immediately following his instincts to tell Kantor to shut up and go to hell, he carefully considered his response. The man was, after all, doing what he thought best for his planet and his people. He should take that into consideration in deciding how to respond.

After taking that moment, he then decided to go with his instinct. "Thank you, Minister Kantor. Your recommendation has been noted.

Now, kindly get the hell off this comm channel. This is for military use only."

Kantor's face went red, and he started fuming. "The Union military is here at the request of the Sulas—"

The screen with Kantor shut off as Kumus dropped him from the conference. Zeric nodded appreciatively to his aide. The young man really knew how to help without being told.

"Now that that's out of the way," Zeric said, trying to sound light, "let's move on to important matters. The guerilla campaign has run its course. It's succeeded in keeping the main part of our forces intact and the Alliance from reasserting full control over Sulas."

Zeric felt that that characterization of the situation was an exaggeration, but he didn't want to pick a fight with Jairyd. Giving Kantor the brush-off might have some negative consequences later, but that was later. Getting into a pissing contest with Jairyd might undermine the entire operation.

"Now it's time to push them off the planet," Zeric went on. "First step, we need to improve our intel on Alliance deployment. We need to know how many troops we're facing and where they're deployed. We're going to begin a series of small raids, just like you've been doing for the last few months, but this time, a few of them are going to have more objectives than simple destruction.

"Once we ascertain where they're weakest, we'll hit them and hit them hard."

Several heads on the screens nodded in approval. Jairyd frowned but didn't argue. He did, however, raise the point that was Zeric's biggest concern. "What about the fleet in orbit? The main reason we've stuck to guerilla tactics is to avoid a retaliatory orbital bombardment. Once we come out in force, there's nothing stopping the fleet from doing that," Jairyd said.

"The fleet will have something more pressing than us to worry about," Lahkaba replied cryptically.

Zeric had completely forgotten that Lahkaba was here. After kicking Kantor off the line due to this being a military conference, he probably should have done the same to Lahkaba. But he didn't think of Lahkaba as a politician. He had asked him to come to Sulas in order to fight.

When the Kowwok had told him that he would be able to get the fleet away from Sulas for a short window, it had surprised Zeric. Lahkaba hadn't said how and had refused to explain further, though Zeric guessed it must have something to do with their Alliance prisoner, Dolan, and Lahkaba's plan to get Maarkean released. Zeric trusted the Kowwok, but he still found the whole suggestion sketchy.

"And either way, it won't matter," Zeric said. "The Alliance fleet won't fire on a civilian population center. We're enemies, and they've done a lot of terrible things, but Admiral Sartori isn't a butcher. We cannot underestimate her and the response she'll give, and the fleet will definitely pose a threat—but not from a blanket bombardment."

He hoped.

Katerina smiled. It amused her that the rebels thought so highly of her. While it wasn't her goal to win the hearts of the rebels, she couldn't help but feel flattered. She had always considered it a sign of a good military leader to be respected by one's enemies. Most commanders thought it was more important that their enemies feared them, but fear only went so far.

"This report from our asset is recent?" she asked, looking up from the transcript.

"Yes, ma'am." Brigadier Rendaliss, her intelligence chief, nodded. "We received it just hours ago. We can confirm that Zeric Dustlighter and Lahkaba have returned to Sulas."

The results from the intelligence report were disturbing. The guerrilla tactics the rebels had used on Sulas had been annoying but insignificant. While their intelligence unit had been unable to learn the location of the rebels' hiding place, they had been able to learn the times and locations of many of the attacks. To cover their ability to intercept the rebels' communications, she had been forced to allow most of the attacks to occur without response, but she had been able to avoid any serious harm befalling her troops.

Now the rebels were going to step up their assaults. While this would be good for her—the Alliance had the advantage in a straight confrontation—the note about her fleet being preoccupied worried her. It could just be bluster from Dustlighter, trying to reassure the troops, but she had learned never to underestimate her opponents.

An attack by the rebel fleet was possible. It had been several weeks since she had lost contact with the task force sent to the rebels' hidden capital of Irod. She had held off on sending any other ships for the time being. If the rebels had repelled her forces, the fleet should have reported back by now. If they had completely destroyed the task force, then they were more powerful than she had anticipated, and sending more ships would likely be a waste of resources.

"Let's not drag this conflict out any further," she decided. "Plant false intelligence where they intend to strike. Allow these raids to be carried out. Find us a weak spot for the rebels to attack. If they want to come out of hiding, let's give them the chance."

Rendaliss nodded. "I'll meet with IX Legion command and figure out a good location. We'll have details for you by this afternoon."

"Very good, Brigadier," Katerina said and returned his salute.

When Rendaliss left, Major Anderson, Dolan's replacement, came in with a thoughtful look on her face. Once they were alone, she said, "I've just received a report. It seems one of the rebels' congressional delegates, Lahkaba, has turned himself in to our forces. He's requested to speak to you."

Katerina leaned back in her chair. This was an unexpected turn of events. According to their intelligence, it was Lahkaba who had a plan to distract her fleet. Likely, turning himself in had something to do with that plan. But how?

"I assume he's been searched?" Katerina asked.

"Yes, ma'am. He had nothing on him but his clothes. Full medical scan as well. No subcutaneous implants," Anderson answered.

A bomb or assassination attempt had been an unlikely plan, she knew. While she knew the rebels were capable of such an attempt, it wouldn't gain them anything here. Her death would do nothing to move the fleet and would, in fact, increase the odds of a retaliatory bombardment against Zeric's forces.

She could throw Lahkaba into a brig cell just like Maarkean and Lohcja, but her curiosity was piqued. "Very well. Let's see what the delegate has to say," Katerina decided.

Chapter Twenty-Four

It felt good to be back aboard his old ship. Solyss liked *Gallant* and was proud of what she and her crew could do, but *Chimopori* had been his home for years.

Of course, crowded with Marines and all the various combat upgrades, she didn't feel quite the same. It was nice to have Kard back on the crew, though. His old Braz crew member had been commanding the ship in her role as a gunship for the last several months. It had matured him. Gone was the carefree boy with fantasies of grand adventures. In his place stood a much more somber man who had seen people die as a result of grand adventure.

As much as the old Kard had had a tendency to annoy him, Solyss felt a pang of sadness that he was gone. So many things had changed and so many people had died so far in this war. The crew and pilots aboard *Gallant*. General Numba, General Ocaitchi. Gu'od.

Shaking himself out of the dark place his mind was going, Solyss returned his attention to the approaching *Black Market*. The giant former warship hung in space before them. The hangar bay door stood invitingly open.

Over the comm system, he heard Htaretter's voice. "*Black Market*, this is *Bright Blade*, leading Union Gunship Squadron One. Requesting permission to dock and make repairs."

It had been decided for Htaretter to do all the talking with the ships. The Fox was a dealer in information, and odds were that he would know that Fracsid commanded the squadron from aboard *Cutty Sark*. With *Cutty Sark* gone with Zeric, and given their cover of escaping a losing battle, they had opted to pretend that the ship was part of the losses.

A tense few seconds went by before the reply came. "Permission granted, *Bright Blade*. Enter starboard docking bay."

Solyss let out a breath he hadn't realized he had been holding. Getting aboard the ship was the biggest obstacle. If they had been denied docking rights, the whole plan would have gone nowhere. It could still fail in a multitude of ways, but at least it could get started.

"All right, Sax. Take us in," Solyss said, clapping a hand on his Nothan pilot's shoulder. "I'm going to check on the marines."

Isaxo nodded in reply, and Solyss left the flight deck. He passed through the crew area before coming to the entrance to the cargo bay, which was filled to bursting with marines. Before he opened the door, Asheerah stepped out of her quarters.

She had her armor on, though she wasn't yet wearing her helmet. Her face wore that perpetual frown of grim determination and the silent threat not to mess with her. He had known her long enough to get to know the person underneath that tough shell, and, he admitted, he loved that woman.

But this was Asheerah in her armor, preparing to go on a mission. She had taken to the role of marine officer well, though she didn't like being subject to others' authority. Fortunately, she respected Zeric and Ymp, the officers above her. And, though he had never really understood why, him.

"Everything ready, Ash?" Solyss said, taking advantage of the moment of privacy to use her name. From here on out, it would be Lieutenant Aru and Major Novastar.

"You know it," she said, hefting her large rifle. He knew she had weaponry built into the armor but preferred to carry a gun in her hands.

"Let's keep everyone on stun. Most of the people on this ship are no more criminals than we are. No need to kill any of them unnecessarily. And we don't want to risk damaging our new ship," Solyss said, adding the last part to soothe her objection.

She still frowned but nodded. Solyss turned toward the door to the cargo bay, but an armored glove on his shoulder stopped him from hitting the release switch. Turning back around, he was startled to see Asheerah's face centimeters away.

Without a word, she leaned in closer and kissed him. He was too shocked to respond at first, but after a second, he let himself get into the kiss.

After a moment of eternity, Asheerah pulled away. She gave him one of her rare smiles. "If a Ni'jar master can get killed in this war, there's a chance even I could be brought down. Not to mention a wrinkled old man like you. I'm not waiting anymore for you to man up and get over your silly belief that captains shouldn't be involved with anyone." With that, she pulled her helmet over her head.

Still surprised by what had just happened, it took him a moment to reach over and secure the seals on it. Gone completely now was the beautiful woman, replaced by the terrifying visage of death. He wondered if the last minute had really happened. They had slept together on a few occasions, usually after a battle, but Asheerah had never kissed him on the mouth before, and he had never pursued her romantically.

Putting that aside, Solyss stepped back and triggered the door. Asheerah strode through and then shouted through her speaker, "All right, boys and girls. Remember to set your weapons to stun. We're going to play nice until they give us no choice. Keep things simple and clean. We don't need to take the entire ship, just reach our objective. Clear?"

"Yes, ma'am." The response from the other armored marines rang through the cargo bay.

Solyss stood back, away from the cargo ramp. The marines would precede him, and with luck, he wouldn't have to get involved in any of the fighting. He had killed before, so he knew he was capable of it, but he wanted to avoid it as much as possible.

A few minutes later, Kard appeared beside him, escorting Josserand Renard. The crime boss gave Solyss a sneer. "I believe it would be best if I had a weapon. To defend myself."

"Sorry," Solyss said, no hint of actual regret in his voice. "We're all out of weapons."

Josserand frowned. "This boy beside me has four guns. He could certainly spare one."

Solyss glanced at Kard, who had strapped on his usual assortment of pistols—two on his hips and two on his back underneath a black jacket. Not looking at Josserand, Solyss said, "Like I said, all our weapons are in use."

A shudder went through the deck of the ship, ending the conversation. They had been set down on the *Black Market*'s deck. It was almost show time.

Several tense moments stretched out into minutes. Isaxo would lower the ramp as soon as the other two gunships docked, and moving early would be a mistake. Even knowing that, Solyss felt eager to go.

When the boarding ramp finally lowered, it took him by surprise. Fortunately, the marines were more prepared. They stormed off the ship in twos. Immediately, he heard the sound of blaster fire as they started taking out automated defense systems in the hangar.

Even after all the marines had exited, Solyss and Kard remained where they were. If the reception the marines received proved tougher than anticipated, they would need to make a quick getaway. It would also be within the Fox's power to blow the air in the hangar. As neither of them had airtight armored suits, remaining on the ship would be safer until that danger had passed.

Finally, Asheerah signaled him that the coast was clear. Moving quickly, Solyss led Kard and Josserand across the hangar to the nearest door leading off the hangar. As he ran, he caught sight of the other two gunships. Fracsid was leading a group off the *Bright Blade.* He noticed that Fracsid wore a new duster that was surprisingly similar to the one Maarkean used to wear. He really hoped Fracsid had bought his and not pilfered Maarkean's from the *Cutty Sark*, though he wouldn't put it past him.

Leaving the other teams behind to their own objectives, Solyss followed Asheerah's squad into the corridors of the ship. They came across several people who were leisurely moving through the corridors, unaware of the events on the hangar. Not taking any chances, the marines dropped anyone they saw. That was one advantage of using stun—you could shoot first and ask questions later.

They moved several dozen meters down the corridor before coming up against a security barrier. A sealed bulkhead blocked the way forward, and a set of automated turrets deployed from the ceiling. The lead marine took a few blasts on his armor but managed to pull back around the corner before taking too much damage. Asheerah sent the marine back to the center of the group and brought another scout forward.

"Now it's your turn," Solyss said pointedly to Josserand.

With a slick smile, Josserand pushed past the marines. Before anyone could stop him, he walked around the corner toward the turrets. To Solyss's amazement, Josserand wasn't blasted.

Turning back to face them, Josserand smiled. "I told you, they're keyed to my biometric signature. They won't fire as long as I'm in their firing arc. So I suggest you stay close."

Solyss exchanged a look with Kard and then followed. Asheerah and another marine took flanking positions beside Josserand, who managed to walk as if he had an honor guard. Solyss doubted that Asheerah saw it that way, but at least Josserand was living up to his end of the bargain. The other teams would have a much tougher time.

When Josserand got close to the sealed door, it unlocked and receded into the wall. They walked through, and it sealed behind them, almost cutting off the rear-guard marines. Bunching closer together, they continued down the corridor.

They passed two more checkpoints before encountering any security forces. A team of four guards stood outside an elevator access. As soon as they spotted the marine scout coming around the corner, they started firing. Their shots missed and the scout returned fire.

The rest of the marines came around the corner, blasting away. Fortunately, these guards weren't equipped with similar armor and were taken down without much trouble. Josserand summoned the elevator and stepped aboard.

"Doesn't look like there's enough room for all of us onboard," Solyss said.

Asheerah said, "I don't think we should split up."

"We can go in two groups," Kard suggested.

"The lift is only working because of me. We don't have time to come back for anyone. As brilliant as my plan is, the crew of this ship will eventually find the virus and shut it down. We can't delay," Josserand said impatiently.

Solyss frowned. "As much as I hate to say it, he's right. Asheerah, leave a squad of five to guard our retreat."

He could almost hear the objection in Asheerah's head, but she didn't voice it. More than half of their marine squad remained outside the elevator as Solyss climbed aboard. The doors shut, and they accelerated through the ship.

They reached the deck with the ship's bridge, and the doors opened. The three remaining marines and Asheerah took position in front of the door, protecting Solyss and the other unarmored people. As soon as the doors opened, blaster fire started coming into the narrow opening.

The two lead marines ran off the lift, followed by Asheerah and the remaining marine. Solyss took up a position on the right side of the door. There was almost enough room to fully cover him. He raised his pistol and fired shots over the heads of the marines, trying to cause some confusion among their attackers.

This time, the forces they faced wore armor similar to the marines. Their stun blasts proved ineffective against the armor. It took several valuable seconds for everyone to switch their weapons to a lethal setting. It was the exact situation Asheerah had always warned him against when using stun.

Fortunately, their opponents didn't prove as effective at aiming. The blasts coming into the elevator failed to find him, Kard, or Josserand. One of the lead marines dropped from combined fire, but by the time he hit the ground, Asheerah and the other two had taken care of his attackers.

The remaining members of the ship's defense force backed down the corridor, disappearing behind a corner. As soon as they did, a turret deployed from the ceiling. Josserand stepped into the corridor, and the turret sat motionless.

With the way clear, Solyss raced forward to the fallen marine. "How is—"

Asheerah cut him off, her voice more a growl than words. "Dead. We need to keep moving, or we'll all end up the same way,"

Not waiting for him to reply, she led the way down the corridor with the two remaining marines. Blaster fire erupted as soon as they turned the corner. Solyss tried to catch up, but a shout from Kard held him back.

"Behind us!" the Braz yelled, and then he started firing with both blasters toward a door that had just opened.

Solyss dropped to his knee and raised his pistol. His aim was poor, but the new defender was close enough that it didn't matter. The figure coming out of the door dropped, and his pistol slid across the floor.

They had been fortunate that the man hadn't been armored. Solyss doubted that his or Kard's pistols had enough power to penetrate combat armor, though he couldn't be sure about Kard's. The man often bragged about how tricked-out his guns were.

"Let's move," Solyss said, pushing the group forward to catch up with the marines.

Cautiously coming around the corner, he found Asheerah and the marines standing over the bodies of the rest of the armored defenders.

A destroyed turret hung from the ceiling, sparks popping out of the severed power cable. Each of the marines bore burn marks on their armor, but all appeared to be in relatively good shape.

"What took you so long?" Asheerah asked.

"Reinforcements came from behind," Solyss said.

"Don't worry, I got him," Kard said with a self-satisfied grin.

Solyss sighed at Kard's enthusiasm. Some things never changed. "We need to keep moving and get to the bridge."

The marines started to move forward, one holding back to take rear-guard position. Before they got very far, the rear marine called, "Where's Josserand?"

Solyss looked back and saw that the crime boss was no longer with him. He ran back toward the corner they had come around. As soon as he stepped around the corner, blaster fire shot out at him. He managed to dive backward to safety.

"That blast came from the turret," he shouted.

Kard asked, "You think they found his virus and neutralized it?"

"I'll check," the marine said. He peeked his head around the corner, drawing fire from the turret. He pulled back a second later. "No body. He must have gone down a different corridor."

"I told you we should have just killed him," Asheerah said. "But it doesn't matter now. We're not far from the bridge."

Solyss thought for a moment and then shook his head. "Josserand wouldn't have left us now unless going to the bridge wouldn't help him take over the ship. There must be a more important objective nearby." Looking back at the corner with the defense turret, he said, "We need to follow him."

Chapter Twenty-Five

Lahkaba sat in the interrogation room for what must have been several hours. When he had turned himself into the Alliance, he had never expected first-class treatment, but he hadn't anticipated the casual brutality he'd gotten from the guards. His sides hurt, and sitting in one place, chained to a table, hadn't helped.

The waiting had given him plenty of time to question his sanity. He had made a snap decision to join Zeric on Sulas. At the time, he had only had a vague idea of what he intended to do once he got there. Even now, the plan was still vague, but every variation of it involved him sitting here, in Alliance custody.

Even though he had come this far—past the point of no return, as far as his personal safety went—he still debated whether or not he would go through with it. Saracasi's offer of Commodore Dolan for a prisoner exchange gave him only a little leverage, but then, getting Maarkean and Lohcja released had only been part of his reason for coming.

He had never supported an alliance with the Dotran, but he'd gone and secured their help anyway. It had cost the lives of an unknown number of Kowwoks. The Dotran had to pay for that atrocity. Revealing the existence and attack plans of their fleet to the Alliance would do that. He had no doubt in Admiral Sartori's ability to defeat a Dotran fleet if she knew about them in advance.

Unfortunately, doing so would mean betraying the Union. Saracasi had done amazing work with the fleet they had, but he knew that they would not survive a direct fight with the Alliance's main force. They needed the Dotran for that.

The door to the interrogation room opened suddenly, drawing Lahkaba back to the present. Through the opening, Admiral Sartori strode into the room. A marine guard came in behind her, but she waved him back.

Taking the seat across from him, she sat down. He was surprised by her appearance in person. He'd seen her on videos before, but those didn't do her justice. She looked much older in person, and far more tired, but there was an air about her that radiated authority and confidence.

"So you're the famous Lahkaba, champion of the downtrodden aliens of Sulas, delegate to the Kreogh sector congress, former Confederate soldier, traitor against the Alliance," Sartori said after looking him over, her tone overly grandiose.

Lahkaba said nothing in response. He could have argued about her characterization of him, but it was all true.

"Why, exactly, are you sitting in my holding cell?" Sartori asked. "We didn't capture you. I won't believe for a moment that you've changed your mind about the rebellion. What could be so important to your cause that you would allow yourself to be in our custody?"

Remembering the accusatory faces of the Kowwoks who had been arrested at the club on Dotra, Lahkaba said, "I've come here to negotiate with you for an end to hostilities."

Sartori raised an eyebrow. "I see. You're prepared to surrender and disband your insurgent government?"

"No, but we wish to make peace. A treaty between governments," Lahkaba said.

Shaking her head, Sartori said, "The Alliance doesn't negotiate with terrorists. Even terrorists calling themselves a government."

"Not even in its own best interest?" Lahkaba asked.

"Negotiating with terrorists is never in our best interest."

"What if I told you I could help you prevent a war with the Dotran Confederacy by making peace with us?" Lahkaba said, leaning forward as best as his restraints would allow.

Sartori frowned briefly and considered him for a moment. Finally, she said, "All right, I can save my intelligence officers some work and hear what you have to say."

It wasn't much, Lahkaba thought, but it was a start. "In exchange for the Alliance pulling out of the Kreogh sector and ending the conflict between us, I will reveal full details about a planned Dotran attack against the Alliance."

"A Dotran attack against the Alliance? How convenient," Sartori said. "How about, instead of surrendering to a bunch of rebels, I promise that you don't get the death penalty."

"Admiral, it should come as no surprise to you that I'm not at all concerned with what happens to me," Lahkaba said, summoning as much bravado as he could. He held Sartori's gaze for a moment. "However, I'm willing to negotiate. I have no wish to see the Confederacy win in a fight with the Alliance."

Sartori gave him a thoughtful look and then said, "No, I don't suppose you would. Despite what many in the Fleet might think, I don't believe you're actually a Confederate agent. But the fact remains, we don't negotiate with terrorists."

"What if I told you I'm not here on behalf of the Union, but on my own initiative?" Lahkaba said. "You do negotiate with informants."

"Only informants that provide valuable information. And you don't strike me as someone who would turn coat for a few credits," Sartori said suspiciously.

"I'm not," Lahkaba said, his tone more defensive than he had intended. "Release Maarkean Ocaitchi and Lohcja Cargon. Do that, and I'll provide you the details of the Dotran attack."

"Ocaitchi is far too valuable to release on spurious claims," Sartori said dismissively.

"Then, in addition to the information, I'll get Commodore Hari Dolan released from our custody," Lahkaba added.

For a moment, Sartori's face showed signs of shock, followed by what might have been relief. Then, a dangerous look took over. "I will not participate in a hostage negotiation," Sartori said, her voice low.

Taken aback, Lahkaba stammered, "I meant nothing like that. Commodore Dolan is a prisoner of war, as are many other Alliance officers. They're being treated according to the terms of the Treaty of Ailleroc. As I'm sure are all Union prisoners in Alliance custody."

Sartori frowned slightly with an expression Lahkaba couldn't decipher, though he didn't take it as a look of suspicion. He continued, "I only meant to offer him as part of the exchange for General Ocaitchi and Colonel Cargon."

After a long moment, Sartori seemed to recover herself, and she said, "You ask a lot for an informant."

Lahkaba thought he might be running out of options. He could just tell Sartori the information, but then he really would be a traitor. If he got something out of her that helped the Union, it wouldn't be a complete betrayal.

"But Cargon is fairly minor. I would be willing to release him in exchange for Commodore Dolan," Sartori said after a moment.

Restraining himself from agreeing immediately, Lahkaba paused, pretending to consider the offer. "Agreed. Once I have confirmation that he's safe, I'll share the details with you, as well as the location of Commodore Dolan."

Sartori stood up and left the room without another word.

Lahkaba took in a deep breath. He could still change his mind. Once Lohcja was free, he could refuse to say anything more to the Alliance. He would be their prisoner, but Lohcja would be free. That was still a net positive.

An eternity passed while Lahkaba continued to go back and forth about what he would do. When Sartori returned to the room, he still hadn't decided. But then, she might have changed her mind as well.

She placed a datapad on the table before him. It showed the familiar figure of Lohcja. As he watched, his Ronid friend was marched down the boarding ramp of a shuttle and left in an abandoned street.

"There, we're prepared to release your friend," Sartori said.

Lahkaba nodded. "Good. Give me a comm unit."

Sartori showed a suspicious look but handed him a comm.

Tuning it to the frequency he had arranged beforehand, he called Zeric. "I've reached an agreement with the Admiral. You can release the prisoner."

He could almost feel Zeric wanting to reply, but they had agreed he wouldn't give any response. Sartori likely already knew that Zeric was back on Sulas, but if she didn't, there was no reason to confirm it for her.

Lahkaba turned to Sartori. "Train your satellites to downtown Ciread, Blueth Park," he said.

She issued the order and Lahkaba watched as an image appeared. The park was an open field in the center of Ciread. At this time of day, the place was mostly empty. It took them only a few moments to identify the figure of Dolan standing there.

A look of profound relief crossed the admiral's face. "You're as good as your word, it seems," Sartori said. "Now, about this Dotran invasion?"

"As soon as the shuttle takes off again, I'll talk," Lahkaba said. He thought Sartori was someone he could take at her word, but you didn't get very far in politics if you assumed that too often.

She gave him a slight nod of what almost looked like begrudging respect and then keyed a button on the datapad. "Return to the ship."

The image on the screen switched to what must have been an external cam on the shuttle. It showed Lohcja still standing in the street, looking confused. Then a wave of dust brushed past him, and he started to shrink as the shuttle took off. At that, Lohcja must have decided to take his chances—he started running into the darkness.

Lahkaba let out a big sigh. Now was the time to decide. Had he sacrificed himself merely for the safety of his oldest friend, or to betray the Union's trust to avenge the lives of his native people?

"A Dotran fleet will be launching an attack against Ailleroc in fifteen days," Lahkaba began and then proceeded to lay out the composition of the strike force and every detail he could remember from Bryel's briefings.

Sartori listened to him explain everything, only asking a few clarifying questions. Once he was done, she sat there for several long minutes.

"Your rebels made a treaty with the Confederacy. And now you're betraying them. It wasn't for your friend's life, and it wasn't to end the war—you knew I would never accept that demand. So I ask, why are you doing this? And you better answer sincerely, or I might decide to send that shuttle back down to the surface to hunt down Mr. Cargon," Sartori said, her tone calm but serious.

Lahkaba took a deep breath and decided that since he had said this much, he might as well tell the whole story. "As part of our deal with the Confederacy, we became involved in helping them identify elements within a Kowwok resistance movement. This led to the deaths of several thousand Kowwok resistance fighters, which we hadn't anticipated happening. Now, the fleet that's headed to attack Ailleroc has been stripped of all Kowwok crew members. Allowing you to destroy it would exact retribution for that atrocity."

As he spoke, he found his voice growing colder and angrier. When he finished, Sartori merely nodded and then left the room without another word.

Following Josserand proved harder than Solyss had originally thought. Bypassing a security checkpoint without the aid of his virus meant taking out any turrets the hard way and then hacking through the security door. They didn't have enough high-yield explosive to punch through more than one door, as they were built specifically to withstand explosives.

Fortunately, Asheerah and her marines had trained for this. When Zeric had first organized her platoon, he had set them up as a space assault force, intended to perform missions exactly like this one. Their armor wouldn't hold up against sustained fire forever, but it lasted long enough to take the necessary shots at the automated turrets. Working in conjunction, one would draw fire while the other two dropped the turrets with combined fire.

Hacking through the security doors took far longer, but there were less of those. The biggest obstacle Solyss faced proved to be simply not knowing where Josserand was headed. At first, assuming he hadn't reboarded the elevator, there had only been one possible direction. From there, they avoided any turn that showed signs of being guarded by people—the one obstacle Josserand's program would not let him bypass. But that still left them choosing between several turns.

After fifteen minutes of not finding any sign of him, Solyss called a halt. Time was not on their side. Activating his comm gear, he said, "We're going to have to break radio silence."

He opened a link to Davidus, who was with the team moving toward the engine room. Without Josserand, they had to face the defensive emplacements, though they had more marines with them. Unfortunately, now that Josserand had gone rogue, getting to engineering would not help their efforts to take the ship. If the crew were halfway competent, they would lock out the computers. The plan had been for Josserand to override those lock-outs from the bridge and restore control.

"Commander," Solyss said, "our companion has gone rogue and slipped away. He's not headed for the bridge. Any idea of a location he might be headed that would be important?"

Solyss had originally been against Davidus coming on this mission. This plan had been Solyss's. Sending a superior officer along had seemed like an insult. Now, considering Davidus's knowledge of this class of ship, Solyss was glad to have him.

"The closest equally useful location would be auxiliary control, but that's two decks above you," Davidus replied, making Solyss want to curse. Moving between decks would take even more time.

Davidus continued, "However, this Fox has done a lot of retrofitting. It wouldn't be surprising if he'd set up his own personal auxiliary control center. The easiest place to do that would be on the same deck as the bridge. Aft of frame forty-seven on the starboard side. A lot of the network control links run through that section."

Solyss looked around for a sign. After a second, he spotted one—frame fifty-two—and knew where he was. They would need to back-track some but were at least already on the starboard side of the ship.

"Let's go," he said to Asheerah and the others.

Moving back the way they had come at least allowed them to go through areas devoid of defensive emplacements. They narrowly avoid-ed a firefight with another team of guards but reached frame forty-seven without incident. Solyss suspected that reinforcements would be headed toward them shortly.

Moving around the area, Asheerah spotted a pair of dead bodies. Neither was one their team had killed. Moving cautiously, they ap-proached the door next to the bodies.

The door, while locked, was not one of the heavy security barriers. Not wanting to wait for a hack through it, Solyss ordered Asheerah to place some of their explosives. Even though her helmet obscured her face, he could sense her smile.

Asheerah placed a stick of explosive, and then they all backed away a short distance. Solyss started to back around the corridor, expecting any explosive Asheerah placed to be dangerous to anyone within twen-ty meters, but she shook her head. Apparently, they needed whomever, or whatever, was on the other side of the door intact.

There was a small pop, and a puff of smoke appeared, and then the door slid open. As soon as it did, the marines moved, two pushing the door wide enough for people to get through and the last one running into the room, rifle ready. Solyss and Kard hung back until all the marines were inside and then followed.

The inside of the room surprised him. It was spacious. Clearly, sev-eral sections of the ship had been retrofitted to be one large area. Beau-tiful paintings and tapestries hung from the walls, representing art from many different worlds. A large fish tank took up one entire wall.

Not every part of the room was given over to opulent luxuries. One section of wall was full of control panels and holographic displays. A holo-communicator took up one corner.

In the chair of the communicator sat a wizened old Liw'kel with a light bluish skin. The color had faded with age compared to the brightness of Asheerah and other Liw'kel Solyss knew. The old man had his eyes locked onto the figure of Josserand, who stood before him, holding a rifle aimed at him.

"Josserand!" Solyss shouted. "Put the gun down."

Turning his head slightly, Josserand gave them one of his characteristic sleazy smiles. "I see you managed to catch up with me. Good for you. I was wondering what was taking so long."

"What was taking so long was that you ran off," Solyss growled. "Now put down the weapon. We're only using lethal force when necessary. This man is unarmed and unarmored."

"This man," Josserand sneered, "is the most powerful crime lord in the history of the galaxy. This is the mighty Fox. Don't imagine for a second that he's not dangerous." He turned back to face the Fox. "And I've beaten him. Once I kill him, I take over his ship and take over his empire."

The man identified as the Fox said nothing in reply.

Solyss cast a glance toward Asheerah. He gave her a small nod, and she returned it. He then holstered his pistol, gesturing to Kard to do the same. The marines followed suit, lowering their rifles.

"All right, Joss, you've beaten him, but we're not here to kill him. You heard Saracasi's order: the Fox is not to be killed, nor his people, unless necessary. Put the gun down, and let's unlock the systems so our teams can get control of the ship."

Josserand considered him for a second and then said, "Very well. We can access everything from here. This old shut-in never left this room." He started to lower the rifle but then shook his head. "No. Before we do that, he needs to die. No one throws me off this ship. Not anymore."

As Josserand started to re-aim his rifle at the Fox, Asheerah fired a blast from her own rifle, hitting Josserand with full-power bolts. His body fell to the ground at the Fox's feet.

"Asheerah!" Solyss shouted. "You were supposed to stun him."

"I couldn't risk that he was wearing stun-resistant clothing, and I only had enough time for one shot," she said, her tone making it sound like she was stating the obvious.

Solyss frowned but didn't say anything in response. He wanted to reprimand her. Not because he cared that Josserand was dead, but because they had needed the criminal to take over the ship, and because Solyss didn't like unnecessary killing.

But he thought back to the incident aboard the *Gallant* when they had taken the ship from the Alliance. There, he had killed the ship's

Alliance captain because he wore a stun-resistant uniform. Because Asheerah and the other marines had their weapons on stun, the captain had almost had time to get off a distress signal, which would have caused the mission to fail.

Now, doing the opposite had been the quick, necessary action that had saved the Fox's life, though it still might end the mission in failure. Without Josserand, gaining control of the ship's systems with the small strike force would be difficult, if not impossible. They would need more skilled code-breakers and technicians from the fleet. But they couldn't signal the fleet to jump in closer until they could guarantee control over the ship's weapons.

There was only one option available to him now. "Mr. Fox, I'm Major Solyss Novastar of the Union Navy."

"Oh, I know who you are, Major," the old Liw'kel said with a smile. "Your reputation extends from here to the Trepon sector. Liberator of worlds, hero of the people. I suppose you're here to 'liberate' my ship?"

Solyss frowned at the sarcastic comment but said, "Yes, sir, we are. In the interest of preserving the freedom of the people of this sector, we have need of your ship. You've made it clear that you're unwilling to negotiate with us. As distasteful as it is, we need this ship."

"I can applaud your resolve," the Fox said. "But I'm afraid I can't just let you have it."

Solyss sighed. He found he liked this old man. He had never liked the idea of taking the ship by force—people should join the cause of righteousness willingly. But that was an idealistic notion, not the real world.

"However," the Fox continued, a sly smile crossing his face, "I would be willing to let you borrow her. For the right price."

Chapter Twenty-Six

"Thoughts?" Katerina asked.

Across from her, Major Anderson looked contemplative. The wall monitor beside them still showed Lahkaba sitting in the interrogation cell. After finishing her discussion with the Kowwok rebel, Katerina had left to consider her options.

"It appears incredibly convenient that a Confederate fleet would be coming to attack Ailleroc right now. Especially after we just learned from our intelligence branch that the rebels are planning a major uprising on Sulas. Lahkaba said specifically in that meeting that he would remove our fleet from the equation," Anderson speculated, a hint of nervousness in her voice. "And now he's here, with talk about a sudden Dotran attack force requiring our departure from this planet."

Anderson continued, "However, the two don't have to be mutually exclusive. The attack could very well be real. From what I saw of Lahkaba, I definitely got a sense of genuine hatred for the Dotran and disgust at this alliance with them. He could be using us to get his revenge and to give the rebels a temporary advantage all at once."

Katerina nodded. She missed having Dolan to discuss these matters with and would have preferred waiting for him for this discussion, but it would take some time for the doctors to look him over and for the intelligence officers to debrief him. For now, she had to be content with Anderson. At least her new aide's thoughts matched her own.

She didn't relish being stuck between two equally untenable positions, even though it was a common problem to have in warfare and a familiar feeling. "If we take the fleet to Ailleroc, we can meet and crush the Dotran forces. If we stay here, if the fleet is real and the size

Lahkaba says, it will probably overwhelm our defenses there. But if we leave, the rebels have a chance to attack our ground forces without our ability to assist," Katerina said, thinking aloud.

"Unfortunately, I think we only really have one choice," Anderson said. "We have to meet the Confederate fleet. Their involvement in this conflict has been our biggest concern all along. Our ground forces should be adequate to counter the rebel assault, especially if our false intelligence proves successful. We can't allow Ailleroc to fall to an outside threat."

Despite the situation, a smile came to Katerina's lips. Dolan had been her right hand for several years, and she had come to rely on him. Fortunately, he hadn't been the only one paying attention among her staff. Anderson saw the situation clearly and had come to the same conclusion as she had.

"Very well, Major. Signal the fleet to prepare for departure. We won't take any chances. Send a packet ship to the MEF and have them redeploy to Ailleroc. Tell the ground bases to have their fighters take over blockade duty. If the rebel fleet shows up, the ground weapons should be able to hold them off," Katerina ordered.

To herself, she said, *assuming the Dotran aren't really coming here.* Then Sulas would fall to them easily. But she doubted this. If Lahkaba was playing them, then the Dotran fleet likely didn't even exist. If it did, and was planning to attack Sulas, it would be in the rebels' interest to have her fleet here, caught off guard by a surprise attack and potentially wiped out.

With luck, she would crush the Dotran fleet at the same time that her ground commanders crushed the rebels on Sulas.

As useful as the *Black Market* would be, Saracasi found herself not thrilled about making the ship part of the fleet. Even though she hadn't wanted to take the ship from the Fox by force, at least then it would have been no different than the *Gallant* or any other former Alliance ship they had captured. But that mission had failed, and the mighty warship still belonged to a criminal. That disturbed her some.

Union ships could be counted on to be loyal and fight to the end. Even with Davidus in command, she couldn't be sure the *Black Market* would follow all her commands as long as the Fox still had authority onboard.

What really disturbed her was the deal Solyss had made with the Fox. In exchange for the use of the ship to finish the war, he had agreed not only that it would be repaired and restored, but also that it would be upgraded with the *Audacious's* regenerative shield technology.

Having that power in the hands of a freelance criminal worried her, as it should have worried Solyss. On the up side, she knew that even with the upgrades, the *Black Market* wouldn't be nearly as powerful as *Audacious* had been. It just wasn't possible to retrofit a ship with the tech very well. Only a ship built from scratch could take full advantage of it. She doubted Solyss had known that when he had made the deal.

What was done was done, she thought. The fleet was now in hyperspace, about to arrive at Enro. It was time for her to focus her attention on the upcoming battle.

She had kept her flag aboard *Defiant Glory*. Not trusting the *Black Market*, she hadn't wanted to run the risk of being cut off from the fleet if the Fox decided to renege on the deal. Even with all the retrofitting and changes the Fox had done, the *Black Market* had a much better equipped CIC, but she liked the familiarity of the old mining ship.

The coming battle was going to be the greatest challenge they had faced yet, outside of the disastrous encounter over Sulas that had cost them most of the fleet. Without the *Black Market*, this mission would be suicide. With it, it still might be.

"Dropping out of hyperspace in one minute," Tadashio announced from Ops.

Saracasi stood up and stretched her shoulders. Realistically, she could run the entire battle while remaining sitting, but it felt wrong somehow to do so. So she stood before the tactical display, waiting tensely for them to exit hyperspace and learn what they would be facing.

From the front of the bridge, she shared a look with Jerik and gave him a nod. She still doubted she would have ever liked the former bounty hunter in a social setting but had developed a respect for his abilities as a pilot and commander. He was harsher and more dismissive of lower-ranked crew than she liked, but he got the job done.

The timer for hyperspace reversion hit zero, and she took a deep breath, letting the nausea of reversion wash over her. She watched the tactical display slowly come to life as the ship's sensors scanned the system. Jerik ordered an immediate launch of their fighters.

The *Black Market* did the same, launching the gunship squadron, all the remaining fighters they had retrieved from Kol, and those freelance pilots the Fox had convinced to fly for him. It was a far cry from the number of craft the ship was capable of launching, but it was more than they had had in any other battle.

Studying the tactical display, Saracasi frowned. "Chief Tadashio, confirm that sensor telemetry is being transmitted to the tactical display."

The Kowwok operations chief responded a moment later. "Confirmed—all data is being relayed. No enemy contacts are on sensors."

A bad feeling came to Saracasi. The last time they had sent in a scout ship, the Alliance's entire marine expeditionary force—a strong force—had been in orbit. While it was possible that the fleet had bunched together on the opposite side of Enro from them, it would be unusual.

"Wildcard Squadron, get a scan of Enro's dark side. All other ships, hold formation outside the planet's gravity well. Keep hyperdrives on active standby," Saracasi ordered over the fleet comm.

Assuming the Alliance wasn't laying out an elaborate trap for them, like had occurred over Sulas, where had the MEF gone? Data from scans of the surface of Enro were starting to come in, and Alliance ground forces still appeared to be in control of the planet. Some of the fleet might have landed and would be difficult to detect, but the MEF's command carrier and cruiser weren't designed to land on a planet's surface.

Several tense minutes went by while the squadron made a full burn to orbit the planet. One flight took up a position near the terminus so it could relay communications from the other ships and the fleet. Shortly after they lost sensor contact on the main flights, data came in.

"No sign of Alliance ships in orbit," the squadron leader reported.

Saracasi frowned. They had apparently found Enro completely unprotected by Alliance forces. That meant one of two things: either the Alliance was once again laying a trap for her fleet, or the MEF had gone somewhere else to cause trouble.

"Can you estimate how many of their forces are still on the surface?" Saracasi asked.

Tadashio responded, "I'm reading several dozen active shield barriers and signs of vehicle activity at each one. It's impossible to gauge specific troop numbers, but based on quantity of resources, it would equate to approximately eight to ten divisions."

From what she had been briefed on, an Alliance MEF consisted of four or five corps or about twenty divisions. She knew that some of the marine forces had been deployed to Sulas to bolster the forces there. If almost half were still on Enro, then wherever the fleet had gone, it hadn't taken many marines.

"All ships, move into a high orbital position over Perth. Target the Alliance military positions near the city," Saracasi ordered.

"Commodore," Davidus said to her after requesting a private channel, "that will put us inside the gravity well."

"I know, Dav," Saracasi said. "But if this is a trap, we can't sit here doing nothing waiting for them to spring it. We're going to start firing on those troops. Either there's no trap, in which case we can help the Enro defenders, or there is, and we'll still be in a high orbit."

"None of our ships are designed for planetary bombardment. It will take a while to penetrate their defensive shields," Davidus said.

Saracasi let out a small chuckle. "Well, either we're walking into an ambush, in which case it doesn't matter, or the fleet really is gone, in which case we have all the time we need."

Davidus didn't state the obvious: wherever the fleet had gone was where they should go as soon as possible. The Alliance could be staging another, stronger, attack on Irod or might have learned that the *Audacious* was no longer defending Kol. Unfortunately, they had no way of knowing, and flying around blindly wouldn't do them any good.

"We've achieved our orbital position," Ceno said from the helm.

"All ships, commence firing," Saracasi ordered.

Every ship in the fleet with powerful enough blaster cannons began firing them down toward the surface of Enro. She could imagine the fiery display as they all converged against the Alliance's protective shield over their troops. For anyone below the shield, it would be a beautiful cascade of colors and a terrifying visage of doom.

The bombardment continued for several minutes before Tadashio gave her a report. "Commodore, I've made contact with the Enro defense force. They're requesting our assistance against a priority target."

That was good, Saracasi thought. She had feared that the Enro troops had all been wiped out by now. They must have been putting up a hell of a fight to still have a command structure in place after months of fighting hardened Alliance marines and an orbital fleet with no outside support.

"What do they need, Chief?" Saracasi asked.

"They say they've been targeting supplies held at the main Alliance camp outside Perth. A supply convoy is en route with replacements, including fuel. If we can take out the convoy, they might not be able to keep their shield up for very long on the fuel they have," Tadashio relayed.

"Do they have a location on the convoy?" Saracasi asked.

Spotting something on a surface from orbit could be easy, if you had some idea where to look, but planets were big, and trying to find a few vehicles on a great swath of land could take significant time, even knowing where the convoy was headed.

"Yes, ma'am. Beginning a scan of the general region they've identified," Tadashio answered.

Saracasi's holographic map of Enro's surface changed, zooming out and away from the Perth base by several dozen kilometers to a small suburban area outside the main city. Several seconds went by as Tadashio used the sensors to scan all the objects, identifying houses and vehicles.

Mixed in among the homes was a collection of objects tagged red for hostile targets. Saracasi picked out a convoy of about two dozen Alliance trucks and SPCs. The SPCs would potentially be tough targets, since they were shielded and maneuverable. The trucks wouldn't be hard to destroy.

The vehicles were all currently stopped. Their proximity to a large collection of homes gave Saracasi pause. Her fleet's weapons fire could be fairly accurate, but not accurate enough to avoid endangering those homes.

"Chief," Saracasi asked, "ask the Enro forces if they know if there are still civilians in the homes where the Alliance convoy is parked."

A moment later, Tadashio came back. "They report that the homes should be clear. They ordered the neighborhood evacuated months ago."

Saracasi frowned. "Should be clear" wasn't definite. She switched her display back to the Alliance camp. Her data showed that the Alliance shield hadn't weakened significantly. Taking it down would take a fair amount of time via a traditional bombardment. Having the shield fail from lack of fuel would greatly speed up the process.

Making her decision, she transmitted the coordinates of the troop convoy to the fleet. "All ships, shift targets to this convoy. They're carrying critical supplies to the Alliance camp. Saturation bombardment."

A saturation bombardment would make it much harder for the vehicles to dodge incoming fire, since it would be everywhere. Many civilian homes would be destroyed this way, but that was an inevitable side effect of an orbital bombardment. Her job wasn't to protect property. It was to win the war.

As the bombardment began, Saracasi thought back to her first battle, here on Enro, right outside Perth. At the time, she had never killed anyone. She had operated the gun turret aboard *Cutty Sark,* and the very idea of shooting at and killing Alliance vehicles full of troops had made her feel sick. Now, almost a year and a half later, she was ordering an orbital bombardment against several dozen vehicles located in a civilian population center, and she felt no hesitation. Even knowing that there might be civilian deaths as a result didn't sway her decision. The odds were low, and stopping the Alliance's ability to fight would save more civilian lives than the handful who might have refused to leave their homes.

The bombardment continued for several minutes. A few of the SPCs made a break for safety, some managing to make it out of the primary fire zone. But the terrain was flat and they had nowhere to hide, so even those lucky few didn't last long.

Once all the Alliance vehicles were confirmed destroyed, Saracasi shifted the fleet's fire back to the main camp. Now they just had to wait out the Alliance's fuel supply. A sustained bombardment was a drain on ship power systems, but they should be able to keep it going longer than the Alliance.

While the bombardment continued, Saracasi redeployed the cutters to a wide orbit around Enro. She wanted a wider sensor net watching for an Alliance counter–attack, and the cutters were useless for planetary bombardment. She also pulled the gunships and *Gallant.*

"Major Relis," Saracasi said over the comm, "dispatch your gunships to Sulas, Cardine, Kol, Dantyne, and Irod. Have them do a quick check to see if our missing MEF is there and then get back here."

"Aye, Commodore," Fracsid replied. "What if the fleet isn't there?"

It was a twelve-day round trip from Irod to Enro, even with the speed of the gunships. A lot could happen in that timeframe. "If we need to bug out, we'll meet at emergency jump point beta. If we go anywhere important, we'll have the EDF let you know."

With everything taken care of that she could, Saracasi sat back down. She would just have to wait out the Alliance shield.

Chapter Twenty-Seven

It took more than a week to move enough troops close enough to Chuthor to begin the assault. During that time, Zeric quietly fretted that the Alliance would catch them. Moving thousands of troops covertly was not an easy task.

Fortunately, there hadn't been any sign of detection so far. The biggest risk that they still faced was that the Alliance had reinforced their base in the intervening time. All the intelligence they had gathered indicated that the base had been stripped to a bare minimum number of troops. They'd obtained reports showing the base commander had requested more troops on several occasions. It would be just their luck that his wish had been granted while Zeric moved people into place.

When the night of the planned attack came, none of Zeric's scouts had seen any sign of reinforcements arriving at the base. That, combined with the news that the Alliance fleet in orbit had indeed departed for parts unknown, gave him an uneasy feeling of hope. Maybe things would work out the way he planned for once.

At 0100, Zeric gave the signal and his troops began the attack. Using one of the oldest tactics in history, Zeric and a team of Rogues climbed aboard stolen Alliance trucks. Dressed in Alliance uniforms, they drove toward the base. Behind them, the main body of his attack force followed, firing wildly toward Zeric's trucks.

Once they came into sight of the base, Zeric directed Kumus to start transmitting a distress call. Behind them, his troops kept firing. Once they got within a hundred meters of the base, the rearmost truck exploded. That bit of theater had been Ymp's suggestion. Seeing the fireball behind him, Zeric agreed that it really did add to the realism—almost too much.

The driver of Zeric's truck accelerated as they turned onto the straightaway leading to the Alliance base. Confused shouting was still coming in over the comm, but Kumus yelled back in a convincingly hysterical manner. Almost at the last second, the guards at the gate opened it and cleared the way for Zeric's trucks to race into the base.

After Zeric's trucks rolled inside, a line of SPCs lifted off and headed back out the gate. He hoped Ymp wouldn't take the attack feint too seriously and would back off from them. She had some heavy weaponry to deal with SPCs, but until Zeric could do his job, her force would be vulnerable.

Turning back to the troops in the cargo area, Zeric said, "Everyone ready?"

He got several nods from grimly determined faces. Among them was Sienn'lyn. Once the fleet had departed, he had tried to convince her to leave Sulas with *Cutty Sark* and return to the Union fleet, but for some reason, she had refused.

Zeric checked his rifle and then gave the signal. The Rogues leapt from the truck and began running across the base. He followed them out as the team headed toward the base's shield generator control room. Around them, chaos erupted as troops spilled from the other three vehicles.

It didn't take long for the Alliance to realize their mistake. Troops manning the wall defenses rotated them inward and started blasting the ground around Zeric's troops. Screams of pain sounded out and bodies dropped all around him. He pushed himself harder, moving to the front of his squad's line.

Despite being in the middle of a war, it had now been months since Zeric had been in a firefight. Even when the Alliance had attacked Irod, he hadn't picked up a gun or had blaster fire come anywhere near him. He suddenly felt more alive than he had since he had left Sulas.

With a surge of adrenaline, Zeric pushed himself even faster, lifting his rifle to make wild shots toward any group of Alliance soldiers he saw. He doubted he'd hit anything, but even wild fire might prevent them from hitting him. Tearing through the open space, he was the first to reach the shield generator building.

A handful of others made it to the building's wall and pressed themselves close against it. Before the entire team had made it, a repeating blaster emplacement above them activated and started blasting away at the rest of the squad. Four marines dropped within seconds. The rest scattered, one or two more making it to the wall and below the gun's firing angle, the rest backtracking toward the next closest building. Three more from the squad were gunned down before everyone made it to some kind of safety.

Inwardly, Zeric fumed. His plan of a surprise attack had been based on being able to get inside the Alliance base and reach critical points before defensive emplacements could be fully manned. He had already lost seven from his squad of twenty, and they still had to get inside.

Forcing himself to put the dead marines out of his mind, Zeric pushed forward. While the defensive gun above them could not target them here, the Alliance troops guarding the installation knew where they were. He had to get to them before they got to him.

Hugging the wall of the building, Zeric's squad ran around to the nearest corner. Just around the bend, they found an emergency door. It was the type that had no outside handle or means of opening the door, intended merely as a way out in case of fire or other disaster, but anything that could let people out could let them in.

Placing explosives around the edges of the door frame, Zeric backed the squad around the corner. Once they were clear, he triggered the explosives. A loud thunder sounded, and he could feel the shockwave vibrate along the exterior of the building. Counting to three after the explosion, Zeric gestured his squad forward.

They ran back around the corner and into the cloud of debris and dust that now filled the air. Rushing into the cloud, they ran through the former doorway and into the building. Blaster fire greeted them, but the dust served to obscure them from Alliance fire. By the time Zeric made it through, his marines had cleared the first room.

Not wasting time checking every room or leaving a rear guard to protect their flank, Zeric ran forward. They had nowhere near enough forces to hold the base. His team's job was to get in, cause chaos, and shut down the shield and defensive guns. Once that happened, Ymp's forces could safely advance and take the base. But that required speed, not caution.

They exchanged sporadic fire with a few Alliance soldiers in the building but didn't stop to ensure they got them. Their speed proved advantageous, as by the time Zeric reached the main control room, the defenders were still setting up their position. Tossing grenades ahead of them, his squad paused only long enough for the grenades to detonate before advancing on the soldiers.

They had moved in too close for rifles, so the final confrontation with the control room guards turned into a melee. Zeric swung his rifle like a club to bash one soldier and then raised it a second later to block a rifle being swung at his head. Holding the two rifles locked together, he shoved the soldier back, then let go of his rifle, unbalancing the soldier. In that brief second, he drew a combat knife from his belt and slashed it forward.

The knife penetrated the soldier's chest armor, a light mesh energy-absorbing cover. The man's eyes bulged as he collapsed, and Zeric felt sick. He hated it when combat got this close and personal.

Beside him, the rest of his squad had engaged the soldiers. It had been in situations like this that Gu'od had shone. He caught sight of Sienn'lyn dropping several soldiers for every one the others did. Her movements weren't as fluid and graceful as Gu'od's, but she still knew her stuff.

The melee lasted only a handful of seconds, even though it felt longer. Two of Zeric's squad were severely injured, but everyone had some kind of cut or bruise. He would have to see to the wounds later. Taking a quick survey of the downed Alliance troops, he spotted an officer and used his key card to open the door to the control room.

The technicians manning the stations inside didn't put up a fight. They weren't armed, but Zeric ordered them stunned anyway. No sense leaving potential threats right in the room with him.

After helping the injured marines inside, Zeric sealed the room and disabled the locking mechanism. It wouldn't be hard for the Alliance to bypass the lock or blow up the door, but it would slow them down a little. Every advantage they could get would help.

"What's the situation?" Zeric asked as the marines took over the techs' stations.

"Disengaging shields now," Sergeant Obod Ocif, the squad's leader, said. "Tam, how's the wounded?"

Tamarynn Farr, the squad's medic, looked up from a marine with a stomach wound she was tending. "Not too bad, considering. But this one needs to stay off his feet."

"You heard the doc, Private. Don't move," Zeric said with a pointed look. Marines didn't like being told to remain seated. He then clicked on his comm. "Sigfa, how's your team?"

"Intact, for the most part. We've reached the main battery. Two guns are clear of Alliance troops. The rest are being defended," Sigfa Neith said, his voice strained. "We're as clear as we're going to get in the near term."

"Hold tight, help's on the way," Zeric said and then switched his comm frequency. "Major, begin your assault."

"Aye, we're coming in," Ymp said, an excited lilt to her voice.

Zeric took a seat at one of the terminals and started bringing up security footage. He watched as the main body of the Rogues ran across the open field toward the Alliance base. With the shield disengaged, no barrier stood between them.

When he had started calling the marine force he put together "the Rogues," they had mostly consisted of former mercenaries and criminals. As recruiting efforts on each planet had picked up, those original roguish figures had been joined by upstanding citizens, but the name had stuck. Now, after fighting on Sulas for months, the name encompassed more than just the battalion of marines who had come to Sulas. But they were still doing what they had been assembled for—fighting an impossible fight in unconventional ways.

With some of the main guns taken out by Sigfa's team, the attacking force received less counter-fire than they normally would have. The understaffed base further helped. Still, this base, even understaffed, had far more defenders and defensive emplacements than the isolated gun batteries they had taken when first arriving on Sulas. The advance was not without casualties.

Nervously, Zeric watched through the cameras as marines and soldiers dropped. He wanted to get out there and help, but his team had to stay and secure the shield control room. If they lost it, and the Alliance got the shield back up before all the Rogues were inside, they would be cut off from reinforcements.

The first wave reached the security wall around the base. Zeric lost track of them on the camera, but a wave of dust and smoke appeared, suggesting they had breached the wall. More and more Rogues appeared, rushing toward the base.

"We've got incoming," Obod said, drawing Zeric's attention back to the control room.

He looked up and saw a team of Alliance soldiers moving down the hallway toward them. Zeric pointed out defensive positions for the few marines he had with him and then took a place behind one of the control panels. He hoped the fight didn't do much damage to the control systems—if they won this fight, it would be good to have control over the shield.

The camera footage vanished as the soldiers destroyed it. *Any time now*, Zeric thought. Tense seconds went by, filling him with aggravation. He hated the waiting before a fight more than pretty much anything else. At some point in the very near future, he would have to fight for his life. He didn't want to die, but he wanted to wait for it even less.

"Ah, screw it." Zeric stood up from his position. "Grenades ready," he said, drawing his last one. He gestured for the marines nearest the door to pull it open.

As it slid back, he and the others lobbed their grenades, then the marine slammed the door shut again. Several muffled explosions could be heard through the door.

Zeric gave a count of three and then the marines pulled the door open again. Zeric charged out, firing his rifle before him, not bothering to aim. After he was clear of the door, he dropped into a crouch on the left side, allowing the others to follow him. Now that he wasn't moving, he gave himself a second to scan the scene.

Two Alliance soldiers lay dead right outside the door with explosives at their feet. Zeric fervently hoped they hadn't yet armed the explosives—otherwise, he wouldn't get to put up much of a fight. Beyond them, crouching near the dead bodies of the room's original guards, was another squad of Alliance soldiers.

Taking careful aim now, Zeric slowed his breathing and slipped into his killing trance. He let go of conscious thought and let his training take over. Moving quickly from soldier to soldier, he aimed his rifle and fired off three quick shots. He tuned out the other members of his squad and the blaster fire coming back at him.

Seconds or years later, after scanning the area and finding no more targets, Zeric felt the adrenaline receding. He took a second to check himself for injuries. His left shoulder had been hit by a grazing shot, but the arm was still usable. He could worry about it later.

Others in the squad would not be so lucky. Obod had been killed and another marine was severely injured. That left him with four able-bodied marines and three injured ones. Plus Kumus, he remembered. The boy had remained in the control room, firing his rifle from inside it, just as Zeric had told him to do.

"Corporal," Zeric said, cursing himself for not being able to remember the Kowwok female's name, "let's get Sergeant Ocif and the injured back inside."

The corporal nodded and then bent down to drag Obod's corpse inside. It was, in some ways, an unnecessary waste of effort, but Zeric didn't like the idea of leaving the man, even dead, to lie beside their enemy. The marine had been with him on several raids and was a good soldier. He deserved better than that.

Once everyone was again inside the relative safety of the control room, Zeric ordered the door almost sealed and placed one of the uninjured marines to stand guard, looking out of the narrow opening. He then moved among the injured, checking on their condition.

Two had relatively minor injuries, slightly worse than Zeric's own graze, affecting their ability to walk or shoot. However, the third marine had a severe gut wound and was slowly bleeding out. He had been injured in the original fight for the control room but hadn't obeyed his orders to stay back in the last fight, exacerbating his wound.

Zeric helped the medic, Tamarynn Farr, bandage him up again, but he could tell by the expression on her face that things didn't look good. Once they finished, he pulled her aside. "How is he, Doc?"

"Not good, General," Tamarynn said. "He needs emergency surgery."

Zeric frowned. They couldn't make a surgery happen anytime soon. "Do what you can from here. This will all be over, one way or the other, soon."

Positioning himself near the door, Zeric settled down to wait. When the Alliance squad had cut off his camera, they had cut his feed to everything. The only thing this room had control over now was the shield generator itself, but that was all they needed.

Tense minutes turned into an agonizing quarter hour. Zeric resisted the urge to call for a status report from Ymp or Sigfa. They were busy, and there was nothing he could do by calling them other than distract them.

After almost an hour, the marine at the door let out a muted alarm. "Movement!"

Zeric moved into a crouch from the relaxed position he had been in. The others all raised their weapons, taking careful aim at the door. Holding his rifle to his shoulder, he prepared for the next round of combat.

"General Dustlighter?" a familiar voice called out.

Zeric felt his shoulders slouch as relief washed over him at the sound of Sigfa's voice. "In here, Lieutenant. We're clear."

The marine at the door slid it open, revealing Sigfa Neith and a squad of marines carefully stepping down the hallway over the dead bodies of Alliance soldiers. Sigfa gave them a grim smile. "The base is 90% secure, sir. There's still some holdouts in the barracks, but they're contained. All our forces are inside the perimeter."

"Excellent," Zeric said and turned to Kumus. "Reactivate the shield. Alliance reinforcements can't be far behind."

Sigfa shook his head. "No, sir, they aren't. They already have us surrounded."

Zeric looked up in surprise. There was no way the Alliance could have redeployed troops here that quickly. The nearest base was at least thirty minutes away by air, and there would have been delays in issuing orders and gearing up. They should have had at least another hour before having to face reinforcements.

"There's more, sir," Sigfa said. "The base's main orbital guns have been disabled."

"Disabled?" Zeric said, thinking. "That means they thought we might take the base. And they would only think that if they knew we were coming. This was a trap."

Sigfa nodded. "Looks that way, sir."

Zeric shrugged and then said with a smile, "Well, the joke's about to be on them."

Chapter Twenty-Eight

Waiting was the universal constant in all military operations, Katerina mused. The enlistees and NCOs always blamed their officers for the long periods of inactivity. The officers blamed their senior officers. And now that she was the senior officer, she blamed the enemy. No matter the cause, there was always a lot of waiting.

She sat in her office off the main operations room she had at her disposal. All around the fleet, crewmembers were at their stations, prepared for combat that would not begin for some time yet. One advantage of being the senior fleet commander, rather than a ship captain or task force commander, was that she could hide in her office, as she had nothing to do right before a battle.

According to their intelligence, the Dotran fleet should have just arrived. Katerina had positioned her fleet twenty light minutes away from Ailleroc—far enough away to avoid detection, even by a cautious Dotran commander, but close enough that the Dotran would not have enough time to do any significant damage to the planet.

She was assuming, of course, that Lahkaba hadn't lied to her, which she doubted, although there was still the chance that the Dotran had lied to Lahkaba or had changed their plans. Either way, while redeploying her forces here had left several openings for the rebels to exploit, that was a small matter compared to potentially letting the Dotran seize control of an Alliance world. The rebels, at least, were originally Alliance citizens.

Her last thought triggered an idea. Activating the comm, she said, "Major, have Maarkean Ocaitchi brought to my operations room."

There was only a second of confused hesitation from Anderson before she said, "Aye, Admiral."

Bringing an enemy combatant, even a prisoner, into a command center during an operation was unorthodox, but the process of breaking the rebel leader was going slowly, and this coming battle gave her a chance to try a new tactic.

When the signal finally arrived from Ailleroc announcing the arrival of a Dotran fleet, Katerina let out a sigh. She hadn't been duped after all—though she thought she would have preferred being a dupe. Now she had to go fight a major battle that would costs hundreds—or, more likely, thousands—of lives.

Moving from her office into the operations room, a miniaturized CIC, Katerina surveyed her staff. They were all competent officers and crew, but this would only be the second battle most of them had ever seen—actually, the first real battle, as the pounding she had given the rebels over Sulas hardly counted as a battle.

She felt a moment of comfort at the sight of Dolan standing in the operations room, coordinating things once again. After the techs had cleared him to return to duty, the first thing he had done was to hand her his resignation, citing the loss of his ship and task force as a court-martial–worthy offense. While he would have to face that court martial eventually, it could wait. She needed him here now.

Katerina looked over the initial report that came in from Ailleroc. The Dotran fleet was smaller than the numbers Lahkaba had given her. Either the Dotran hadn't sent as many ships as promised, or the rest were still to be deployed. She waited another five minutes to see if any new data came in before issuing orders.

"All ships, this is the fleet commander. Jump to preassigned positions. Begin Operation Coldmountain," Katerina said over the fleet-wide comm.

Together, the ships of her fleet activated their hyperdrives and jumped the relatively short distance to Ailleroc. She had deployed them in a wide net formation around the concentrated Dotran fleet, like she had against the rebel fleet at Sulas. The net pinned the Dotran between her and the defensive batteries of the planet.

The trip to Ailleroc took only a fraction of a second. Her main display began to light up with enemy contacts as data from the fleet filtered in. It had been a long time since she had faced a Dotran fleet in a battle, and the last time had also been here, over Ailleroc.

Even though she now enjoyed the element of surprise, she didn't have a clear advantage. Even with all the ships from the MEF, her fleet was outnumbered compared to the Dotran. Her crew had also been on station for more than a year without relief, while the Dotran had left home only a few months ago. At best, she could call their positions even.

For the moment, Katerina left the task of beginning the engagement to her taskforce commanders. She had overall authority over the battle, but there was no need to interfere. Waves of fighter craft launched from both fleets and accelerated toward each other.

The capital ships began firing, though this was another area where the Dotran had an advantage. Any shots her fleet fired that missed would continue on until they hit something or the energy dissipated. In the vastness of space, this meant nothing, but with Ailleroc providing the backdrop for the battle, many shots would hit the planet. However, the atmosphere would dissipate all the weaker blaster bolts, and most of Ailleroc had advanced protective shields around the major population centers. The odds of any missed shot hitting an unshielded town were remote, but still there.

"Admiral," Dolan said beside her, "we've got new enemy contacts."

Dolan brought up the new contacts on the tactical display, and what she saw caused Katerina to smile in appreciation. The Dotran commander had left a rear guard force just in case he ran into an ambush. Clearly, she was not fighting an incompetent.

"Task Group 42, reorient and engage new enemy targets," Katerina ordered.

Now things were going to get interesting.

Maarkean hadn't seen another living person for several days now. The Alliance guards had taken Lohcja away without explanation and had never brought him back. Maarkean suspected that it was a trick to make him worry. After the treatment they had received when they were first captured, he supposed it was possible that something terrible had happened to Lohcja. But he doubted it, based on his read of Admiral Sartori.

Even though he wasn't really worried about Lohcja's health, being alone and isolated still had a profound effect on him. He hadn't realized how much having Lohcja there had helped him hold onto his sanity. The simple act of having another person to talk to had kept his mind in check. Having another person there to remind him why the Alliance was the enemy had also helped.

When the guards came for him, he expected to be taken to another interrogation session. He walked with them through the ship's corridors, but their destination turned out to be an operations room. The room buzzed with activity, and displays showed tactical data. It appeared that a battle was in progress.

Made to stand in a corner of the room, away from everyone else, Maarkean watched as Admiral Sartori directed a battle against someone. He had a brief hope that it was against the Union, but then he changed his mind. That would mean his sister would be out there.

During a lull in activity, Admiral Sartori turned to look at him. "Come over here, Major. Take a look at the battle."

Curious, Maarkean walked over to the tactical table. He got a better look at the holographic display. What he saw shocked him.

The sensor data indicated that the ships the Alliance fought were Confederate warships. He identified the nearby planet as Ailleroc. Why were the Dotran attacking the Alliance?

As if in answer to his question, Sartori said, "Your rebel friends have allied themselves with the Dotran. We're at war with the Confederacy."

Shaking his head, Maarkean said, "No, they would never do that. We rejected the idea of working with the Dotran months ago."

"It seems they've changed their minds," Sartori said. "Once again, the entire known galaxy will become embroiled in a war for control over this sector of space."

Maarkean felt his heart sink. He had never wanted war with the Alliance, but on Enro, he had felt there was no choice. He had fought to ensure democracy and freedom for the people of the Kreogh sector. Never had he imagined it would result in another war with the Dotran.

Suspecting—hoping—that he was being manipulated, he asked, "How do you know the Union sided with the Dotran, and this isn't just the Confederacy being aggressive on their own?"

Sartori sighed. "I wish that were the case, but we have confirmed evidence."

She activated one of the smaller monitors and brought up the image of a prison cell. Maarkean recognized the white furred figure of Lahkaba sitting in the cell. *When was he captured?* he wondered.

"Former delegate Lahkaba came to us a few days ago and turned himself in. He had decided he could no longer support the rebels after they joined the Confederacy. He made a deal to reveal their attack plans in exchange for your former cellmate's freedom," Sartori explained.

The sight of the Confederate fleet had been a shock, but this news left Maarkean speechless. Lahkaba had betrayed the Union? He had been one of the founding delegates. It had been his convictions that had helped bring Maarkean over to the rebels' side.

Had that all been a mistake? Had he started a war with the Alliance for nothing? Lost in his own thoughts and self-doubt, he allowed himself to be moved back to his cell without another word.

Things weren't going as well as Katerina would have liked. The Dotran commander had proved far more cautious and determined than the ones she had last faced. She had been unable to extricate her fleet from two Dotran divisions. Likewise, she had been unable to push the battle closer to Ailleroc, leaving the ground defenses mostly useless.

"We've just lost the *Melbourne*," Dolan said, his tone showing uncharacteristic signs of emotion.

That was the third ship in the fleet to be destroyed or completely disabled. Every ship had taken damage to some degree. While they had done just as much damage to the Dotran fleet, in the long run, being outnumbered meant that equal damage would be a win for the Dotran.

"All ships, emergency jump to standby coordinates alpha," Katerina said, deciding on a new tactic. "All fighters, emergency burn to Ailleroc. No retrieval."

Dolan gave the smallest hint of a frown but said nothing as he relayed her orders. No one wanted to retreat. In fact, no one would have thought the great Admiral Sartori would ever consider it, she mused to herself. But she wouldn't let the legend keep her from doing what was necessary.

The capital ships started engaging their hyperdrives as soon as they had a clear line of departure, while the fleet's fighter craft engaged their engines, headed back to Ailleroc. They were small and fast enough to get past the Dotran capital ships pinning the fleet in. It would likely cost the lives of several fighter pilots, especially all those adrift from ejecting, but most would make it through. Trying to retrieve them to the carriers would cost more lives in delays.

A nauseous feeling passed over Katerina as her ship jumped. It lasted only a few seconds, as the rendezvous point was a short distance outside the Roc system. The jump point was merely a way of keeping the Dotran ships from ascertaining their final destination.

Several minutes went by while the rest of the fleet appeared at the jump coordinates. After a quarter of an hour, not all the ships had appeared, and Katerina was forced to assume that they were losses. Fortunately, they only amounted to a gunship and an escort carrier. She hated losing any ship, but those were the weakest in the fleet.

"All ships transmit damage reports and shield status to the flagship," she ordered.

As the data filtered in, she watched the indicators for the fleet's shields. The time away from the fight allowed the crews to make emergency repairs and the shield generators to power up. Not for the first time, she wished for the regenerative shield technology the rebels had stolen and somehow gotten to work.

She ignored incoming communication requests from the task force and task group commanders. They wanted to know her plan, but until she knew whether it was feasible, she didn't want to share it. If the fleet's condition had deteriorated below combat-capable, she wouldn't send them back in to die.

Finally satisfied that repairs had restored enough ships to fighting condition, she ordered, "All ships, I'm transmitting jump coordinates. Rig ships for silent running. We'll be operating under radio silence."

At her order, the fleet once again jumped to hyperspace. They emerged seconds later back in the Roc system, in a very close orbit of Ailleroc. With all the ships from the fleet running silent, no active scans were performed, and the tactical display remained blank.

"Major Anderson, link us with the Ailleroc orbital satellite system," Katerina ordered.

Soon, limited data began appearing on the tactical display. The defense satellites weren't as accurate as a ship's sensor suite, but they did provide full coverage of the space around Ailleroc. As she suspected, the Dotran fleet had remained in an orbit that placed them over the planet's biggest ocean—their weakest defense points, where defense batteries were scattered wider than was ideal due to the limited availability of land to build them on.

This ocean currently lay on the other side of Ailleroc from Katerina's fleet. Hopefully, with their limited energy emissions, any scout ships the Dotran fleet had observing this side of the planet wouldn't have detected her fleet's appearance. The Dotran should be unaware of her return to the fight.

Activating the fleet's comm, she sent a low-power signal to the near-by ships. "Transmitting deployment orders. Maintain radio silence and keep energy emissions low except for shields. Begin powering up to full strength. Link with satellite network for target data."

The ships of the fleet began moving again, breaking out in task-force formations. They spread out around Ailleroc in all directions. She had timed it so all ships would cross the terminus of the planet and gain line of sight on the Dotran fleet at the same time.

The slow orbits necessary to achieve the maneuver added another long period of waiting. This time, she didn't mind. Every minute spent slowly orbiting meant another minute crews had to repair their ships. While the Dotran were undoubtedly doing the same, they were still engaged with the planetary batteries.

As they passed over Ailleroc, the ship's passive sensors started picking up signs of the Dotran fleet. Weapon energy signatures and engine emissions reached them. Combining this data with the satellite network, her ships would now be able to make targeting solutions.

With a grim smile, Katerina transmitted another order: "All ships, commence firing."

Chapter Twenty-Nine

Punching through the Alliance troops' shield, even with their limited fuel supply, had taken longer than Saracasi would have liked. They had finally succeeded and laid waste to the previously protected troops and equipment. A small part of her felt bad about the slaughter, but it was overruled by the knowledge that the Alliance had done the same thing to the Enroian defenders when the MEF had arrived.

Fracsid's gunships had started to return from their recon missions, and the news gave her both hope and apprehension. There had been no sign of the Alliance forces over Sulas, Kol, or Cardine. In fact, there hadn't been *any* Alliance forces over Sulas. Where before the planet had been under a massive blockade, now there was nothing.

Had the Sulas force and MEF combined forces somewhere? Either one was more powerful than the Union's entire navy. Together, they would be unstoppable. Perhaps Admiral Sartori had decided that small, equal-strength task forces protecting every world in the sector was giving Saracasi's fleet the advantage. If that were the case, it meant Saracasi would have more freedom to move about but would have to avoid battle.

The other possibility worried her. If the Alliance had somehow gotten word of the approaching Confederate fleet, Sartori could be setting up an ambush for them. She had discussed this possibility with Bryel, but he had dismissed it as impossible.

Even if it were true, and Saracasi had proof of it, there was little she could do about it. The Confederate fleet would be making its first appearance in the sector in the attack on Ailleroc. The only way to warn them would be show up in the system—potentially alerting the Alliance if they were unaware, or getting her fleet destroyed if there was an ambush.

Her comm device buzzed, and Saracasi reached for it from where she lay on her bed. "Yes?"

"Commodore, the *Durandall II* has returned," the officer of the deck, OOD, told her.

Ar'cher's ship had been sent to Irod—the furthest away—and was the last gunship to return. Now Saracasi would know, at the very least, where the Alliance wasn't. "Patch me through to Captain Ar'cher."

A moment later, Eri'dos's gravelly voice came over the speaker. "Yeah? What is it?" Eri'dos Ar'cher had been with the Union before there was a Union, yet he still made no effort to conform to military protocol. Saracasi ignored it.

"Captain, what's the word from Irod?"

"The word's nothing. System's clear, as far as we could tell," Eri'dos said.

Responding to him in kind, Saracasi shut the comm channel without another word and called the OOD back. "Wake Captains Brieni, Needa, Relis, and Novastar. Set up a conference for ten minutes. Then signal all ship captains we'll be meeting in half an hour."

Saracasi climbed out of bed and hopped into the shower. The conference would be done via computer link, but she hated working while feeling dirty. It was close enough to when she normally got up, and since she had already been awake for the last hour, she had no plan to return to bed. After the quick shower, she pulled on a fresh uniform and took a seat at the room's desk right at ten minutes.

She connected to the conference and found her four senior commanders waiting for her. Solyss, like always, had an immaculately pressed and clean uniform, not looking at all like he had been woken in the middle of the night. By contrast, Fracsid was still rubbing his eyes and hadn't dressed for the day, though fortunately his pajamas were decent.

"Gentlemen, our last recon ship has returned. As of a few days ago, no Alliance ships have been spotted at any world in the sector. We only didn't get eyes on Ailleroc, due to their distance from here, nor Dantyne or Mirthod, due to our lack of gunships. I find it unlikely they've gone to either of those worlds. That leads me to two possibilities. One, the Alliance has combined their forces at Ailleroc, either to meet the incoming Confederate fleet or by sheer coincidence. Or, two, they're planning a massive assault somewhere and were either in transit or waiting in deep space during our recon visits," Saracasi said, laying out her thoughts.

Davidus nodded in approval of her assessment. "The most likely explanation is that the Alliance gained intel on the Dotran fleet. They undoubtedly have a strong spy network in the Confederacy, and we can't rule out that there are still spies among us."

The fact that he made that point, potentially implicating himself, was particularly poignant, but Saracasi had already made the decision to trust him completely. "I agree. That means we have two choices: rush to Ailleroc and try to help the Confederate fleet, or take advantage of some undefended worlds."

"What about that report we got about the Dotran showing up on Kol and attacking our shipyard?" Fracsid asked.

Saracasi frowned. She hadn't liked the sound of that report. The Dotran turning on them would be an insurmountable problem. But it had just been a rumor received from some transport crews, and she couldn't make decisions based on rumors.

"If it's true, then it means the Dotran have already engaged the Alliance and survived. If it's not, which I tend to believe, then it's just a rumor. Transport crews are prone to exaggeration.

"Mirthod and Dantyne have been clear of Alliance ships since we chased them away a few months ago. I ruled them out as locations for the Alliance fleet, given their relative strategic unimportance. But this may be our best chance to liberate Sulas," Saracasi concluded.

On the screen, Solyss frowned. "Isn't General Dustlighter leading an effort to do just that right now?"

Saracasi nodded. "He is. We may be able to help him."

"What about the planetary defense guns?" Fracsid asked. "If the general hasn't recaptured any of the batteries, they'll tear us to shreds. The fleet has grown a lot since the last battle there, but we still don't have any cruisers. Our only heavy ship is the *Black Market,* and she's not at peak fighting shape."

"He's right," Davidus said. "A battle carrier would normally be able to withstand an attack from defense batteries for a reasonable amount of time—at least long enough to provide some support to ground forces—but I wouldn't want to try it for very long in our condition."

Saracasi frowned. Gaining control of the *Black Market* was supposed to have opened up those kinds of options to her, but due to the lack of dry-dock maintenance after years in deep space and all the modifications the Fox had made, the ship was almost more of a liability. She still had lots of guns, at least.

"I still think Sulas is the best option," Sarcasi said. "Even our threat might be able to help General Dustlighter. According to the timeline Commander Prytoker gave us, the Confederate fleet has already reached Ailleroc. If the Alliance set a trap for them, it's already been sprung.

"We've already deployed what few troops we have to help the Enroians. As we've discovered, our orbital bombardment ability is lacking in effectiveness. And if the Alliance fleet survives the confrontation with the Dotran, which, given Admiral Sartori's reputation, we all have to accept as a very real possibility, we can't face the combined fleet, making us useless as a defensive force. So we're going to Sulas, unless anyone has another suggestion or objection," Saracasi said.

When no one said anything, she briefly hoped they weren't holding anything back. She really did want to know if this plan was idiotic—or even more idiotic than she already knew it was. In the end, though, the decision fell to her.

"How's the shield holding?" Zeric asked, unable to keep his nervousness from his voice.

"Well, we're not dead yet. So, pretty good," Ymp said, her tone sarcastic.

Zeric frowned and gave her a dark look. "Very funny. You know what I meant."

"We've drained fuel from everything on the base we could find. The Alliance didn't leave us much," Ymp said.

Outside the shield bubble around their captured base, the Alliance had rows of artillery and tanks arrayed, firing blaster shots into the protective field. They had been doing this for several days already. Zeric felt very fortunate that Lahkaba had succeeded in getting the orbiting fleet away. Had the more powerful guns aboard the cruiser and carriers been in use, this siege would have ended long ago.

"Well, at least the Alliance didn't really expect us to take the base," Zeric said. "Otherwise, they would have brought in heavier artillery or wouldn't have left the shield functional at all—like they did with those defense guns."

After securing the base, Zeric's forces had discovered that the guns used to defend Sulas from orbital attack had been disabled. They were working on repairing them, but they hadn't been able to find the necessary parts. The Alliance had done this as insurance, in case their trap failed.

Although the shield functioned, most of the base's deuterium fuel supply had been removed, leaving them little power to operate it. What they had would last for a while in maintenance mode, but while being bombarded, the shield drained more power.

He wasn't confident they would even outlast the shield. A massive array of Alliance troops had been assembled outside the base. They had arrived too quickly to have come from other parts of Sulas but hadn't been deployed in advance. However the Alliance had known about his attack against this base, they hadn't known the exact details. Otherwise, he doubted they'd have ever gotten inside the base in the first place.

"So, how long until Armageddon?" Zeric asked.

"Just under a day," Ymp said grumpily.

"Still no luck breaking the jamming?"

Ymp shook her eyestalks back and forth in imitation of a Terran shaking their head "no." "No luck. It's a pretty tight field."

"So, no way to tell our friends to pick up the timetable," Zeric said with a sigh. "Well, we succeeded in getting the Alliance's attention focused on us. So, in that sense, the plan has been a rousing success."

"You never planned to live through it, anyway," Ymp said bluntly.

Pretending she had just made a joke, Zeric said nervously, "I don't expect to survive any of my plans. They're *my* plans, after all."

An awkward silence hung in the air for a long moment. Ymp said nothing in reply, and Zeric knew she hadn't bought it. He said nothing more, though. If she wanted to continue this line of questioning, she would have to do so all on her own.

"I notice you haven't been drinking," Ymp said.

"We're in the middle of a siege. Plus, there's no booze," Zeric replied.

"The base commander's office had a full liquor cabinet," Ymp said. "Ever since you had to take command of this military, I haven't seen you without a drink of some type in your hand, but then you insist on leading this very dangerous mission—something a general should never do—and you stop drinking. I can only conclude you're prepared to die."

Zeric frowned. "Have I really been drinking that much?"

Ymp just stared back at him.

"All right, maybe I have. But I didn't stop because I'm ready to die. I don't want to die. I actually feel more alive than I have in a while. I'm not cut out to lead from behind a desk, if I'm even cut out to lead at all.

"If friends die beside me on the battlefield, it sucks, but at least I know I was right there beside them. When friends die because I ordered them to do something while I sat safely behind the lines, I can't stand it. So I won't do it anymore. Maybe that makes me a terrible general, but you know, I always said I'd be a terrible general."

Ymp said nothing for a while. She was never one to hold back a rebuke for his behavior, so he wondered how bad her comment would be. Finally, she said, "Actually, I think it makes you a great leader. Though you're right, it does make you a terrible general."

Zeric chuckled and then more grimly said, "Well, doesn't really matter anymore. In the next few hours, unless we can hold out longer, I'll become a very dead general, whether I want to or not."

After Katerina's fleet had returned to Ailleroc, refreshed and moving in for a sneak attack, repelling the Dotran assault had happened quickly. Fortunately, she had lost no more ships and had destroyed several Dotran ones before they had fled. She had expected the enemy fleet to return soon after, but it had been more than a week without a sign of them.

Unfortunately, while she had defeated the Dotran, the battle had been costly. Six ships had been completely destroyed and several more were in need of repairs that would take months, all while a rebel fleet was still out there somewhere.

Her biggest problem was what to do next. Was the Confederacy ramping up for a full-out war or had this attack been an isolated incident? She had received intel that the Camari Republic was making noise near the Alliance's border. That had delayed reinforcements being sent already. If the Confederacy did the same, she would be stuck with the ships she currently had.

The rebels were weak but not impotent. Every time she had engaged them with small forces, they had come out ahead. She was determined not to make that mistake again, and that meant deciding where to focus her remaining ships.

Taking the fleet to Irod and wiping out the rebel leadership would be an effective blow. However, the task force sent to Irod had somehow been completely wiped out. That left her with no information on the strength of the rebel defenses on their capital world.

Mirthod and Dantyne were too small to be worth focusing on. Enro had already been pacified by the MEF. That left Sulas, Kol, and Cardine.

So far, Cardine had stayed out of the main fighting. The local garrison commander reported tough resistance but still remained confident he could hold out and repulse the rebels. Bringing the fleet there might flip the balance.

On the other hand, taking out the rebel shipyard on Kol would be a good strategic move. Her last report still had the FX-21 guarding the planet. She felt confident her combined force would be more than a match for even that ship, but would it be worth the cost? If the rest of the planet's defenses had been upgraded or the rest of the rebel fleet arrived, that one ship might be enough to flip the fight the rebels' way.

In the end, it all came down to Sulas. That world had been the spark for the rebellion, and it still held most of their army. She had been forced to leave the planet unprotected for a period, but it was time to go back. As long as she kept control of Sulas and Ailleroc, the rebels would eventually fail.

"Commodore," Katerina said after calling her aide into her office, "have task force and squadron commanders identify which ships are not combat ready. Those vessels will remain at the shipyards here and continue repairs. The rest of the fleet will be departing tomorrow morning at 0700."

Dolan nodded. "Aye, Admiral. Some reports have already come in. Would you like to see them now?"

Katerina shook her head. "No, wait until we get them all and then assemble a complete fleet-readiness report for me. I need to know how much force we'll be able to bring against the rebels."

Dismissing Dolan, Katerina decided that now was the time for another meeting with her prisoners. Unlike before, she had ensured that Maarkean had had no contact with Lahkaba. She suspected that his former cellmate had helped strengthen his resolve. That had been part of the reason she had agreed to Lahkaba's request to let him go. She could have just moved him to another cell, but the Ronid had had no useful information. His release had been well worth the intel on the Dotran attack.

First, she went to speak with Lahkaba. Sitting in his cell, he looked up at her when she entered. He looked impatient and nervous but said, "I take it from the sounds of battle a few days ago that you found the Dotran?"

She nodded. "We did. They put up a tough fight, but their fleet is no more."

There was no harm in exaggerating the casualties to the enemy. Keeping her reputation as an undefeated opponent would only help in the continuing fight with the rebels. She continued, "Now, since your word has been proven good, I'm willing to reopen negotiations for the release of General Ocaitchi."

Lahkaba looked shocked for a moment, or so she thought—it was hard to tell with all that fur. He said after a second, "Very good. We have many other prisoners we'd be willing to exchange, including several ship commanders."

Katerina shook her head. "A major general is a very valuable prisoner. Especially when he's also the head of your military. You will release all prisoners captured over Irod."

Lahkaba frowned at her demand.

She knew it was a horribly unbalanced suggestion, but whether or not he considered it would tell her how valuable Maarkean was to the rebels, and if she got more of her troops released as a consequence, it would be a major victory.

For a long moment, the Kowwok said nothing. He finally shook his head. "I can agree to releasing the officers."

Katerina had to force herself not to smile or chuckle. He was, indeed, a shrewd negotiator. Releasing all the officers appeared to be a magnanimous concession on his part. However, the enlisted personnel and NCOs were far more valuable, especially with Katerina's manpower shortage.

But it would do, she decided. "Agreed."

"I'll need to be released so that I can make arrangements with my people," Lahkaba said.

"Very well. Once we return to Sulas, you will be released and given clearance to depart the planet," Katerina said. "We'll do the exchange in deep space using transport ships."

After Lahkaba consented, Katerina left and went to one of the ship's other brigs. Now, she had to see if her plan would work. In one move, she might end the war.

In contrast to Lahkaba, Maarkean sat in his cell with a look of defeat. His shoulders were slumped, and it took him several minutes to notice her presence. When he finally looked up, his violet eyes looked through her, unfocused. He said nothing.

"I thought you would like to know that we managed to drive the Dotran off, though just barely," Katerina said, twisting her story far too close to the truth for her liking.

He nodded slowly, and she continued, "But I have no doubt they'll be back. I need to end this pointless fighting among our own people so that we're ready to face them again. Are you willing to help me?"

She had tried to lace just a hint of pleading into her voice—a tone she was not used to using—because she knew he needed to feel a sense of urgency to help. That would be critical.

"How can I help?" Maarkean asked.

"You're the leader of those fighting. You can convince them to stand down. Together, let's end the bloodshed and then work together to defend all our homes from the Dotran," Katerina said.

"What about the Union?" Maarkean asked.

"The Union betrayed you and the people of this sector to the Dotran. They're the real traitors. People like you, who stood up and fought for justice, are still loyal Alliance citizens at heart. Convince them of this truth, and we can put aside the past. Their actions will be forgiven, and we can begin to repair the damage done, both from the fighting and by the Alliance governors who abused their power and started this mess," Katerina said, throwing Maarkean a few concessions.

He sat there for several minutes, and she thought he had drifted off. Then a sense of energy suddenly returned to him as he said, "So, if I convince the Union to end the fighting, you'll address our grievances?"

Katerina shook her head slightly. "Not the Union, but the loyal Alliance citizens. Those who still ally themselves with this Union must be brought to justice, but I suspect that's a small segment of corrupt leaders. Convince the people to stand down, and let's face the Dotran threat together, as Alliance citizens should."

Maarkean considered this for another long moment. He no longer looked dejected and defeated but appeared to have been filled with a new energy. Finally, he said, "OK. Let's end this war."

Chapter Thirty

When the fleet exited hyperspace, Saracasi felt like her heart skipped a beat. Her worst nightmare had come true. Even though their recon mission a week ago had identified Sulas as clear of Alliance defenders, arrayed before them, blocking her access to the planet, was the combined might of the Alliance fleet.

As sensor telemetry continued to pour in, however, she felt indecision. The Alliance had far fewer ships than she had originally estimated. That meant one of three things: the rest of the fleet was waiting as a trap for her, the other ships were elsewhere in the sector, or the Dotran fleet had engaged them and dealt a serious blow.

While the Alliance still had more ships and more firepower than the Union, they had never been closer in strength than they were right now. She now had three captured Alliance frigates, and while only one of those was technically in fighting shape, at this range, Alliance sensors wouldn't be able to tell that. Had she been able to get the cruiser up and running, it would have looked like a formidable force.

"Commodore?" Jerik whispered beside her, reminding Saracasi that everyone was waiting for her orders.

She nodded and then activated the fleet comm. "All ships, prepare for combat. Launch only alert fighters, stand by on full wings. Hold our current position relative to the Alliance fleet."

That would give her more time to decide. They were far enough away from Sulas that the gravity well would not prevent entry into hyperspace. Assuming that the Alliance didn't advance and that an assault force didn't appear out of hyperspace to pin her in, she had time to consider options.

"Chief," Saracasi said to Tadashio at Ops, "what can you tell me about the situation on Sulas?"

Tadashio answered through her earpiece, "There are active shields up around many cities and bases. The one in Chuthor is currently being bombarded by ground vehicles. A heavy jamming field is in effect over that area."

"Any way to tell whether our people are the ones shooting the shield or the ones inside?" she asked.

"No, ma'am. The ground forces are not being fired upon by the orbiting Alliance ships, however, and they do have shields of their own in place," Tadashio answered.

"Thank you, Chief. Let me know if anything changes planet-side," Saracasi said and then switched her comm channel over to a direct link to the *Black Market*. "Fleet Actual requesting to speak to *Black Market* Actual."

After a second, she heard, "*Black Market* Actual, go ahead, Commodore."

"Dav, there's a jamming field over an area on the surface currently in the midst of a battle. You think the comm array on that carrier is powerful enough to punch through?" she asked.

"Possibly," Davidus replied. "We can probably get a message through, but we won't be able to get a reply back unless they have an equally powerful array, which I doubt."

"OK, give it a try," Saracasi said. "Tell them we're here, and ask for any info on General Dustlighter's status."

Davidus agreed, and Saracasi sat back to wait. If Zeric had control of even a single ground defense battery, the tide could be turned against the Alliance. Shields were up all over the planet. All signs suggested that that had occurred before her fleet had even arrived. Whatever was going on down below, it was major.

"Size and strength of the enemy force?" Katerina asked.

"Nineteen ships," Dolan replied. "Five armed transports, eight cutters, one escort carrier, one corvette, three frigates, and one battle carrier. They're deploying fighters now."

Katerina frowned. *Where did the rebels get a battle carrier?* she wondered. Maybe the rumors about this *Black Market* were true. Regardless of where it came from, its presence would be problematic.

She faced a difficult choice. Under normal circumstances, she would engage the rebel fleet without question, but she had left many ships at Ailleroc for repairs and the rebels had a stronger-than-expected force, so she was not guaranteed overwhelming force.

Withdrawing the fleet from their present orbit above the ground battle would force the rebels within range of ground batteries if they engaged her, but it would also give the rebels a free line of attack against her ground forces. That would be unacceptable.

"Launch all fighters," Katerina ordered. "Tell ground bases to deploy their space-capable units to join us here."

Studying the map, Katerina considered her battle plan. The rebels were stronger than she had anticipated. Defeating them would be costly, but it could be done. Her main goal had to be protecting her forces on the ground until they retook the base.

"Spread the fleet out in a wide dome above the Chuthor base," Katerina began. "Place our heavy ships on the furthest exterior, over the gap between where the Chuthor guns and other ground batteries converge. Arrange our fighters and corvettes in the center of the dome. We need to keep any fighters from getting to the surface. Signal our ground-based fighters to converge on Chuthor."

Dolan nodded. "Aye, Admiral. You think the rebels will fall for it?"

Katerina smiled. "I don't think they'll have a choice."

"Attention, General Dustlighter. This is Commander Brieni aboard the Union warship, *Black Market*. Our fleet has arrived in orbit of Sulas and has encountered a sizable Alliance fleet. Commodore Ocaitchi has requested a status update from your forces and details of how we can assist."

Zeric listened to the message a second time, having not believed it the first time. When the Alliance fleet had appeared in orbit, he had thought all hope was lost. Their shield was already weakening, and if the fleet joined the bombardment, it wouldn't last long. If Saracasi and her ships were a threat to them, though, that might give him some time.

"Ymp, any luck breaking through this jamming to get a reply out?" Zeric asked, already knowing the response.

Ymp waved her eyestalks in a negative gesture. "There's no way. The array just isn't powerful enough. They know exactly what strength and what frequency of ranges we're vulnerable to."

"Of course—it's their base," Zeric said, trying to add a sly grin to his words but failing. He paced the small control room for a few seconds. They had repaired some of the base's guns and started firing on the closest Alliance forces, but the artillery pieces were out of range of their current weapons. None of that would help him contact Saracasi. "How's work on the planetary defense battery?" Zeric asked.

"One set of guns is now functional, but unlike the local defense guns, they aren't independently powered. They draw power from the main reactor, just like the shield," Ymp said. "If we fire the guns, we'll lose shield containment sooner."

Zeric thought for a moment and then asked, "If we reduce the size of the shield's coverage, can we account for that difference? Fire the gun and still maintain a strong shield?"

Ymp shrugged her eyestalks and turned to the man working the control board. After a moment's thought, he said, "It's possible. Though that would give the Alliance an opening."

"Can you keep it small enough that they can't get anything big inside?" Zeric asked enthusiastically.

He nodded. "People and some vehicles, but not the big artillery cannons."

Zeric smiled. "All right, Major, prepare your forces to defend the base."

Ymp gave him a determined nod and left the room.

Zeric moved to stand behind the gun battery controls. "OK, Sergeant, let's tell Commodore Ocaitchi where we are."

The sudden barrage of fire from the surface of Sulas took Solyss by surprise. When the barrage impacted the shields of an Alliance corvette, it turned into a very pleasant surprise.

He heard Saracasi's voice over the fleet-wide comm. "Launch all fighters. I say again, launch all fighters. All ships, maintain position over the Chuthor planetary battery—we have friendlies in control of those guns. We're moving in to assist. Gunships, *Gallant,* and fighter squadrons, clear a path through the Alliance fleet for the bombers. Bomber squadrons, designate targets among the Alliance forces laying siege to the base."

"Helm, engage engines. Take us to the vanguard of the fleet," Solyss started ordering. "Sax, launch your fighters—we'll provide cover."

Gallant began advancing toward Sulas. Sporadic fire started passing through the empty space between them, but at this distance, hits were few and far between. That wouldn't last much longer.

Solyss held *Gallant*'s fire while they advanced. No Alliance ship in this sector had yet gotten a look at her upgrades, so from their perspective, she was still just a regular corvette.

"Sir," Lieutenant Tess said quietly.

He looked at his XO, who had a pointed expression on her face, but she said no more.

Behind him, Asheerah chuckled. "You were drumming your fingers on the controls, old man. It was getting distracting."

Looking down at his hands, Solyss realized what he had been doing. He hadn't even noticed. This coming battle wouldn't be like anything he had ever experienced. He must be more nervous than he thought.

He nodded an apology to Tess and frowned at Asheerah. Her marines were positioned around the ship in case they were boarded. Since that was a very remote possibility, she had taken a position standing behind him on the bridge. He wasn't sure why.

"Helm," Solyss said after turning his focus back to the battle, "alter course and bring us within range of targets designated CR-1 and CR-2."

Two Alliance corvettes had positioned themselves directly between the wave of Union fighters and the planet. They would provide a blistering swath of fire to the craft. Behind them lay the bulk of the Alliance fighter groups. After the devastating barrage from the corvettes, their fighters would then have to engage the Alliance fighters, and it might very well turn into a bloodbath.

As they moved closer, the two corvettes ignored him, firing their weapons toward the fighters behind *Gallant*. Corvettes weren't designed to fight other corvettes. Still holding his fire, Solyss smiled at the irony.

When they reached the optimal firing range, he said, his voice as confident as he could manage, "All batteries, fire."

Heavy blaster bolts started lancing out from *Gallant* at the two corvettes. From their position between the two Alliance ships, Solyss was able to bring two heavy batteries against each ship, while each only could manage one against him. In balance, it was equal fire, but the attacks that lanced back at *Gallant* hit separate shield facings—a significant advantage in keeping them up.

As *Gallant* engaged the corvettes, the fighters behind her accelerated and moved past the fighting capital ships. The two corvettes still lashed out at them but were limited in how they could direct their weapons without giving *Gallant* an opening. Far more fighters got through than were destroyed or forced back.

The battle had a long way to go, but Solyss smiled. A Novastar had already won them a small victory.

"They've dropped the jamming!" one of the marines shouted to Zeric.

"Try to open a line to General Kil'dare!" Zeric said eagerly. It had been far too long since he had heard anything from the outside world.

Several tense moments went by while the marine tried to establish contact. At any moment, the Alliance might reestablish the jamming, or they might be overrun. Every second spent waiting could be a second too long.

Finally, the marine said, "I have him, sir!"

Zeric grabbed a headset and said eagerly, "Jairyd, what's the word?"

"The word is good," Jairyd said excitedly. "The uprisings have begun in every city on the planet. Our troops have taken two gun batteries and every other one that's in a city is being contested. Drawing all the Alliance's attention to you worked like a charm."

"Do any of the guns we control have line of sight on the Alliance fleet in orbit?" Zeric asked.

"Unfortunately not. The nearest city is Ciread, but that's under heavy fighting. We're inside the base there, at least," Jairyd said.

"OK," Zeric said, thinking. "Your focus is control of those guns—or, at the very least, denying them to the Alliance. Our fleet's in orbit now, so we have to keep the Alliance from turning them on our people."

"We'll do our best. How is your force holding up?" Jairyd asked.

Zeric glanced at the bank of security monitors. Alliance forces had already started advancing along the unshielded ground. "Things are about to get a whole lot more interesting."

Chapter Thirty-One

"A hole is opening in the Alliance line," Jerik remarked.

Studying the tactical display, Saracasi frowned. The gunships and *Gallant* had succeeded in breaking through a line of Alliance corvettes. The main bulk of her fighters were now pushing toward the planet. With Zeric in control of at least some of Chuthor's planetary defense guns, Sartori had held back the bulk of the Alliance force. Yet something still didn't feel right.

"All ships, advance. Hold orbital position over Chuthor. All fighters, pull back and reform with the fleet," Saracasi ordered, seeing no reason to justify delaying the advance.

"Commodore?" Jerik asked. "The general could use support from those fighters."

"He'll get them," Saracasi said. "We're too spread out right now. We need to get the main fleet closer to support the fighters."

Almost as if they were trying to prove her point, within minutes of her fleet accelerating, the Alliance ships began to change position. The gunships and frigates accelerated ahead of the slower carriers. They would be within weapons range of her gunships and *Gallant* several minutes before her main force could rejoin them.

"All ships, launch torpedoes at closing Alliance frigates," Saracasi ordered.

The fleet only had a handful of the powerful weapons, and she would have preferred to save them for use against the Alliance battle carriers. But if she held back now, she would likely lose *Gallant* and Fracsid's gunships. Impatiently, Saracasi watched helplessly as the ships closed, out of ways she could help.

The sounds of battle echoed in through the hallway. Zeric itched to go out there and help keep the Alliance from retaking the base. But he now had communications back, so he had to oversee the larger operation. Ymp could handle things here, if anyone could.

He had shifted his position from the base's shield control room to the main command center. Some consoles had been damaged in the effort to seize the room, but enough were still functioning to give him some tactical awareness, though he had to rely on relayed reports instead of a linked computer network. It limited his information but made it feel more like a battle and less like a game.

"Alliance fighters are converging overhead," the marine at the sensor station reported. "It looks like they've cut us off from getting fighter support from the fleet."

"Probably," Zeric said matter-of-factly. "But that works out well for everyone else. Get me General Kil'dare."

"Jairyd," Zeric said when the man appeared on the screen. "It's time to launch the fighters."

"So soon?" Jairyd asked.

Zeric nodded. "The Alliance is focused on the battle above. I'm sure you've noticed the lack of Alliance fighters strafing you?"

"Actually, I hadn't," Jairyd said. "Though now that you mention it, I would expect more of them."

"Those are just the atmospheric craft. The main forces are here, ready to meet the fleet's wings. You're in a good position to gain control of the air."

Jairyd smiled. "Then let's light 'em up."

Zeric waited, fidgeting the entire time, as orders were relayed. After an eternity, reports started to come in. After the first battle above Sulas, all the fighters that hadn't been destroyed had landed at the captured gun batteries. During the hasty evacuation from those vulnerable positions, Zeric had managed to get most of the craft into hiding, waiting for the right time.

Pacing around the cramped room, Zeric found himself continuing to look toward the door. The sounds of the battle outside had gotten louder. Was Ymp losing? Had Alliance troops breached the walls?

He then noticed the absence of sound. The loud reverberations from their heavy blaster cannon had stopped. The battle outside hadn't gotten louder—it had just stopped being drowned out.

"Why has the gun stopped firing?" Zeric asked.

"We don't have any good targets," Kumus replied after sending a message to the gun control room. "The Alliance warships are either out of our firing arc or too close to our own ships to get a clear shot."

Zeric considered his options. He could keep the gun powered up and wait for a good shot, or shut it down and restore power to the shield. Preserving the shield would delay the Alliance retaking the base, but he would be unable to help the fleet.

"Tell them to power down," Zeric reluctantly ordered. "Restore full power to the shield."

Saracasi would be on her own.

"Hard to port!" Solyss bellowed. "Begin axial rotation."

The space around *Gallant* filled with blaster fire from two frigates, which, he had to admit, was the good news. Torpedoes fired from the main fleet had damaged or scattered several of the Alliance warships. The rest had gone after the gunships, leaving him to deal with just two—two more than they could handle without fighter support.

"We just lost number two engine!" Lenanhy, his chief engineer, reported.

Solyss cursed out loud. Their main advantage against the frigate came in the form of faster acceleration and maneuverability—in some ways, it was more important than shields—but engine damage would negate that advantage.

"Tess," Solyss ordered his XO, "hold fire. I'm going to bring us around close to F3. Prepare for a full barrage when we're at optimal position."

She nodded and Solyss turned back to the helm. "Helm, prepare to reverse course. Stand by for maximum burn. Continue rotation."

Watching the tactical display, Solyss ignored the new damage reports coming in. He had to time this maneuver perfectly. Even then, he didn't know how well it would work.

He'd done amazing things, like his ancestor had during the Kravic Occupation. Novastars had defied the odds and fought bravely. But he knew the inevitable outcome. His ancestor had fought the Kravic—something few had tried. He had also died doing so.

"Helm, now!" Solyss ordered.

Gallant rotated around to point back toward the pursuing frigates. Her remaining engines fired against her direction of movement, slowing her velocity. They were close enough to Sulas that the planet's gravity field, which had been trying to pull them down to her surface, started to succeed.

Dropping like a rock, *Gallant* began falling to a position relatively below the frigates'. Still accelerating, the frigates attempted to match the maneuver but didn't have enough time. As they rotated, Tess took the opening.

Firing all of their weapons in sequence, they blasted the ventral aft portion of one of the frigates. While not unprotected, the frigate had weakened her shield in this area to further protect her bow dorsal shields, which had been the only area *Gallant* had been able to attack before. As the frigates drifted above her, trying to correct their mistake, *Gallant* unloaded volley after volley.

"We've disabled three batteries of weapons and two engines!" Dar'su reported from Ops. "F3 is breaking off."

Solyss smiled. One enemy down. Glancing at the neglected damage reports, he saw what it had cost. Flashes of red priority reports filled the screen. Multiple hull breeches had occurred, and they had also lost one of their heavy blasters. Their shields had depleted to almost nothing.

"The other frigate is coming back in," Dar'su warned.

Standing up straighter, Solyss prepared to meet his end like a Novastar.

Chapter Thirty-Two

Not long after Maarkean heard an alert klaxon's sound, a pair of marines came and hauled him out of the brig. Admiral Sartori's fleet had apparently run into trouble before he could be released. He just wondered if it was from more Dotran or the Union.

Escorted to Sartori's command center, Maarkean saw the room as busy as the last time he had been here. The tactical displays were filled with icons and data. People talked into headsets, some almost shouting, and aides rushed in and out of the room.

At the center of it all, Admiral Sartori stood, her body relaxed and her eyes focused on one of the tactical displays. Maarkean strained to see the displays. He could discern the enemy formation making a dive maneuver through the Alliance fleet as it approached Sulas, but he could not tell who the enemy was.

After several minutes, Sartori turned to him. "Ah, Major. We may need to move up the timeline on your cease-fire plans. The rebels have attacked Sulas with their full force."

The marines allowed Maarkean to move closer to the tactical display. With the greater detail, he started to recognize ship symbols and formations. Beyond the orbiting fleet, a conflict on the surface appeared to be raging as well.

From what he could see, the situation looked bad for the Union fleet. Outnumbered and outgunned, they were now surrounded by the Alliance fleet in an attempt to reach Sulas. It looked like Zeric's ground forces had control of a few defense batteries, but many of the Alliance troops hadn't yet been committed to the fight, as they were caught in transit between different locations. Once those troops joined the battle, Union forces would be facing tougher odds.

"How can I help, Admiral?" Maarkean asked, genuine concern in his voice.

Sartori frowned at him. "Order your forces to stand down. Tell them that all those stand down now will be pardoned. Explain the threat of the Confederacy and the need for unity now."

Maarkean listened to Sartori's pledge. He felt that it was an extremely generous proposition from a military commander putting down a rebellion. It would allow the Kreogh sector time to prepare for any coming Dotran hostilities. And it would ensure that his sister made it through the conflict alive.

But, he admitted to himself, it didn't solve anything. Standing down in exchange for a pardon was admitting that the fight had been a mistake. The Union might have been foolish for siding with the Dotran, but he didn't know the details of that arrangement. And it at least suggested that the Dotran recognized the Union as a sovereign power—something Sartori's proposal didn't.

"No," Maarkean finally said, his voice weak. He spoke again, adding more resolve to his voice. "No."

"What?" Katerina asked, her tone disbelieving. It had been a long time since anyone had told her "no."

"My people will not stand down in exchange for a pardon. We will, however, stand down as the first step to a negotiated peace," Maarkean said.

She looked at her prisoner with incredulity. It had taken a while, but she had felt sure she had succeeded in winning his loyalty back to the Alliance. How had she been wrong? "And why would we accept that?" Katerina asked. "Your forces are going to be crushed. I'd prefer to end this war without more loss of life, but your forces cannot win. You've seen the sensor data. You know I'm not exaggerating."

Maarkean nodded and then smiled. "Admiral, we don't have to win this battle. All we have to do is continue to bleed your forces and wait for the Dotran to do the rest.

"You're right, your forces probably will win this battle," Maarkean continued. "But you've already been decimated by the Dotran. And you won't win this fight without significant losses. You'll win, but at what cost? Once before, you destroyed us, but we came back for more. We'll do so again. The people on Sulas have risen up in mass for this fight. The Union doesn't have enough forces to be waging battles in every city on the planet. I suspect you know that. You will have to treat the planet like a conquered world.

"And then, with your fleet decimated and your ground forces suppressing worlds in rebellion, the Dotran will come back. This time, they won't do so as the ally of the Union, but on their own initiative. They will take control of this sector, and in time, they will have a strong chance of crushing the Alliance.

"So, Admiral, whether we win this battle or not, you'll lose." Maarkean fixed his eyes on her as he spoke. She saw steely resolve there for the first time. He genuinely believed what he said.

Was he wrong? As she studied the man, the scars and bruises on his face suddenly came into sharp focus. He had gotten those at the hands of Alliance officers—officers who had sworn to uphold the principles of the Alliance, but who hadn't.

She turned her gaze away and to her trusted aide. Dolan stood beside her, tall and strong. He had been a prisoner of the rebels for several months, yet no sign of it could be seen on his face. He had returned unblemished and in good health. The rebels had treated their prisoners according to the laws of war, and the Alliance hadn't.

A long period of silence hung in the air of the operations center. All the staff members had stopped talking during Maarkean's speech. Their eyes were focused on her. *Do they want me to stand down or order them to keep fighting?* she wondered. Probably both, she realized. No one had wanted this war, but they would keep fighting as long as she asked them to.

Eventually, Katerina made her decision. She reached down and activated a speaker on the comm. "All Alliance forces, this is Fleet Admiral Sartori. You're ordered to cease fire and stand down." She then gestured for Maarkean to speak.

A tremble went through him as he stepped up to the microphone. "All Union forces, this is Major General Maarkean Ocaitchi. Cease fire and stand down. Negotiations are underway with Admiral Sartori for a permanent end of hostilities."

The battle was not going like any of Saracasi's previous battles. The Alliance fleet completely outmatched hers. Two of the cutters had already been completely destroyed—one from a spontaneous barrage from a planetary battery that had, fortunately, not repeated itself. *Gallant* was adrift, half their fighters had already been destroyed, and several gunships were adrift and presumed destroyed. As much concern as she had for Fracsid and Solyss, she couldn't allow herself to think about them now.

Her two newly captured frigates, hastily repaired over Irod, were of little help. They just had a few weapon systems active and could really only be used as cannon fodder for some of the more vulnerable ships. Much to her chagrin, the only thing that was keeping her force from being overwhelmed was the presence of the *Black Market*.

She had an odd feeling that this battle would end up much like the last battle over Sulas: with her fleet's complete destruction. But she kept that thought to herself. The battle wasn't over yet.

"*Hurricane*, shift targets to Carrier One," Saracasi ordered. "Jerik, move us to join them."

The two ships began to move into a closer formation with the *Black Market*, adding their fire together against one of the Alliance's battle carriers. All around them, other Alliance ships moved to counter them, continuing to bombard all of her ships with waves of blaster fire. Suddenly, the fire started to lessen.

A voice then sounded over a broad-spectrum transmission. "All Union forces, this is Major General Maarkean Ocaitchi. Cease fire and stand down. Negotiations are underway with Admiral Sartori for a permanent end of hostilities."

Saracasi couldn't believe her ears when she heard her brother's voice. It had been months since she had heard anything from him. Now, suddenly, there he was, speaking and apparently alive and well.

She had all but given up hope of ever seeing him again. Guilt stabbed at her for that, but she knew that hope hadn't been an option. Until this very moment, she had had no idea where he was being held or even if he was alive.

But as much as the thought of her brother being alive filled her with joy, his call for them to stop fighting angered her. Maarkean had never wanted to fight the Alliance. Now, after months in custody, right when they were on the cusp of victory, he was calling for them to surrender. She might lose most, or all, of her fleet in this fight, but the Alliance would as well. That would allow Zeric to retake Sulas and free the sector.

As much as she wanted to trust her brother, she couldn't—not now.

"Tell all ships to stand by. Get me General Dustlighter," Saracasi ordered.

Zeric heard Maarkean's voice and felt a great sense of relief. His friend was alive. And he was ordering an end to the fighting.

"Signal all forces to hold tight. Take no further aggressive action. Only fire if fired upon," Zeric ordered.

He looked up at the security monitor and watched as the wave of Alliance forces currently rushing the base's walls halted and then turned back. Sporadic fire continued between the two sides for several more moments but then stopped.

Can it be over? Zeric wondered. *Really over?* With just some words from two people aboard a ship, could the fighting be stopped?

As if in answer to his question, a wave of communication requests started coming in for him. He accepted the ones from Saracasi and Jairyd, putting the pair onto a conference call.

"General, you aren't planning to accept this trick, are you?" Jairyd demanded.

"Yes, actually, I am. That's General Ocaitchi you heard. He says the Alliance is prepared to negotiate," Zeric said crossly.

Jairyd looked down as if trying to decide what to do but then said, "Zeric, I didn't want to do this because it would be bad for morale, but I have some information you'll need to hear." He gestured off camera, and suddenly Lohcja appeared.

Surprised to see the Ronid—he had assumed he was still a prisoner, like Maarkean—Zeric smiled. "Lohcja! Glad to see you free."

"Zeric, Casi," Lohcja said, his tone dejected.

"Colonel, tell them what you told me," Jairyd said forcefully.

Lohcja's antennae drooped and he sighed. "While I was still a prisoner, the Alliance did a number on Maarkean. When I left, he was pretty close to breaking. I did what I could to help him keep up his resolve, but with me gone, I fear they may have broken him. I'm not sure we can trust anything he's saying."

Zeric's heart dropped. Maarkean as a traitor? Granted, the Alliance had branded him with that title a long time ago, but Zeric had never thought that it fit. Maarkean had always been loyal to his friends. His commitment to the Union had been what had brought Zeric fully into the fold.

"He may be right," Saracasi said, a pained look on her face. "Maarkean was never comfortable fighting the Alliance. I was afraid time in Alliance captivity might do this to him. As much as I love my brother, we may not be able to trust him. Admiral Sartori is devious. This may be a trap. If our forces stand down now, they'll become easy pickings."

Jairyd continued to press. "We have momentum right now. Stopping now will cost us everything we've gained."

Turning to the marine at the communication controls, Zeric said, "Get me a link to the Alliance command ship. Tell them I want to speak to General Ocaitchi."

A moment later, Maarkean appeared on the screen. His friend showed signs of numerous wounds still in the process of healing. It had been months since his capture. They couldn't be from that. Could he have been tortured into doing this?

"Maark, you're looking . . . well," Zeric said uncomfortably.

"I've been worse," Maarkean replied with a small smile.

"Look, I'll just come right out with it," Zeric said. "There's some concern that you may not be fully in control of yourself. That maybe we shouldn't listen to this stand-down order."

Maarkean nodded solemnly. "I can understand that. I've been a captive for months now. Who knows what the Alliance could have done to me? I won't pretend they didn't mess with my head. But this stand-down is legitimate—Admiral Sartori really has agreed to a cease-fire. She understands that even if she wins here, she will face the Confederacy again, and she can't afford to fight a war on two fronts with a decimated military. She's giving up the war against us, Zeric."

That all made sense, but it could also just be a ruse that Sartori had told him to use. Despite talking to Maarkean, Zeric wasn't sure he could dismiss Lohcja's warning. "Maark, your own sister has some doubts."

Surprisingly, Maarkean smiled at that. "I'm sure she does. I never was the most gung-ho rebel. You're just going to have to make a call here, Zeric."

Zeric thought it through. Tempting as it was to just end the war, Jairyd had a point. With the two navies fighting it out, their ground forces had succeeded in gaining ground in most of the cities. If the fighting continued, they would soon win control of Sulas back, even if the fleet lost in orbit. It hurt to hear that Maarkean might have been broken, but Lohcja had been with him in the Alliance prison, so he would know, and Maarkean's own sister thought it was possible. It would be irresponsible to ignore that.

But then, Zeric thought, he'd never been very responsible.

Switching the comm channel back to the others, Zeric said forcefully, "We're standing down. That's Maarkean Ocaitchi up there telling us to stop fighting. He started this war. If he says it's over, then it's damn well over."

Jairyd looked like he was about to argue more, but Saracasi appeared bolstered. She spoke to someone off-screen for a moment. In the meantime, Zeric stared Jairyd down, not giving him the chance to say anything.

When Saracasi returned, she said, "I've ordered our forces to stand down. The Alliance ships are doing the same."

"Then it's over?" Lohcja asked, his tone hopeful.

"It's over," Zeric said and then grinned. "And it looks like we won."

Epilogue

A hot, sand-filled wind blew over Saracasi. Had it been coming from in front of her, instead of behind her, she might have used it as an excuse to turn around. Unfortunately, the planet didn't oblige her.

Before her lay a dozen fresh gravestones. They all bore names she recognized. She had worked in the shipyard for several months and had gotten to know many of the workers and marines here. She was only interested in one name, though.

Positioned on the edge of the row, she found Asirzi Z'ren's. Tightness filled her chest as she read the name, and fresh tears came to her eyes. It had been a month since the Dotran had raided the shipyard to steal the technical data on the regenerative shield before heading back to Confederate space. Many workers had been killed, including Asirzi. This was Saracasi's first time here, and seeing the grave finally brought home the reality of the situation.

She would never again see Asirzi. Before, when she had just thought that their relationship was over, she had felt hurt and sad, but that had been of her own doing, and anything she could do, she could potentially repair. She was an engineer—that's what she did.

But there was no repairing this. Asirzi was gone, killed as an afterthought to the war. She had believed in the fight against the Alliance, even if she had never wanted to participate, but she hadn't died in that fight.

"I'm sorry we never got to see where things would go," Saracasi said, speaking to the grave. "If I hadn't rushed off to fight, maybe you wouldn't be here, or I might be there beside you. I'll never know, I guess."

After that, she stood there in silence for several minutes, only a few tears escaping her eyes.

This wasn't the first loss she had experienced. Her parents and sister-in-law had all died when she was still a teen. If she could get past that, she knew she could get past this.

But, while that had been tragic, and she still missed her family, it had been different. The tragedy of the loss of Asirzi wasn't just the loss of a loved one. Though she did love the woman, she now also grieved for the loss of a choice in her future.

When the war ended, she would have had a choice between leaving the navy and pursuing a life with Asirzi or remaining to help the Union grow as a nation. Now she didn't feel she had a choice. The universe had chosen. It had taken Asirzi to balance the scales for all the lives Saracasi had taken.

She knew she could still resign and go back to work strictly as an engineer. What would be the point, though? She liked the navy. There was nothing left for her in the civilian world.

With one final look at the grave, Saracasi turned and started back toward the shipyard.

Katerina Sartori surveyed the people gathered around her. People of every species, all dressed in some form of fancy attire, mingled in the room. All the Alliance officers, like her, wore their dress uniforms. The dark green uniforms stood out amongst the crowd, especially next to the white jackets the Union officers had adopted for their dress uniform.

It had only been three months since she had given the order for the Alliance forces to stand down. The draw-down of her forces had gone surprisingly quickly. All the marines had already been retrieved aboard the ships of the MEF. Gathering the army troops would take longer and prove to be a more complicated mess. Many of the soldiers were natives of these planets or had lived here so long as to be indistinguishable. She felt sure a fair number would elect not to return to the Alliance with her fleet.

Dolan appeared beside her, carrying two glasses of a local alcoholic beverage. He handed one to her, and she took a sip. The bubbles of gas in the liquid reminded her of champagne, but the flavor was far too sweet.

After a moment of silence, Dolan remarked, "It occurs to me, Admiral, that the entirety of the Union command structure is present in this room. We could easily take them out with one stroke."

Katerina nodded. "Technically, yes, but it's too late for that. They aren't rebels anymore. You said it yourself, this is the Union."

"I'm sure there are those back at command who would disagree with that assessment," Dolan said quietly.

"Undoubtedly," Katerina agreed. "Which is why we're signing this peace treaty now, before they have a chance to comment. They gave me the authority to address this conflict. So I have."

Neither spoke for several minutes. The flood of people moved around her, most avoiding her. Even though she had lost this war in the eyes of many, she still had a fearsome reputation. Now, though, she suspected that many of the Alliance officers avoided her out of fear of the consequences of that association once they returned home.

"You did see the report I sent about the incident at Kol?" Dolan asked, his voice hinting at something.

"I did," Katerina replied, waiting for him to ask the question.

"The Dotran attacked the Union's shipyard. They likely have the FX-21 regenerative shield specs and have turned against their former ally. You ended this fight to prevent a war with the Dotran, but it looks like they had already pulled out of their treaty. Did we surrender prematurely?" Dolan said, his tone hesitant.

Katerina took a long breath. She had known he had wanted to ask that question for a while. It wouldn't be the last time she had to answer it, and his polite tone would probably be the nicest way it was ever asked.

"We didn't surrender," she said forcefully. "We ended a fight that should never have happened. The Dotran involvement is completely irrelevant to that.

"But, to answer your actual question, look over there," she said, gesturing to the blue-scaled Dotran wearing a Confederate officer's uniform. "Despite the incident at Kol, whatever really happened, the Union and the Confederacy are still pretending to be friends, at least in front of us. Had we not ended the war, that friendship might not have lasted, but it would have been even worse for us. Then we would be fighting a second war against them. Now, their fleet left in disgrace and that means they'll abide by this treaty. Now was the only time to end the fighting."

Dolan seemed satisfied with her answer, as he said no more. She doubted he had really been concerned, as he was smart enough to have seen the situation as she described. But his question would be one discussed by many—first by the politicians and her senior commanders, then by the people of the Alliance. Eventually, it would be left to the historians to decide whether she had done the right thing. They would have the advantage of hindsight.

Lahkaba felt uncomfortable with the conversation going on around him. The subject matter came far too close to an issue he hoped no one would talk about, but that was an unrealistic hope, he knew.

"They attacked us!" Valinther said, his voice almost too loud for the party setting. "They shouldn't be included in this treaty!"

"Ending hostilities with the Confederacy was the only reason the Alliance agreed to end them with us," Lionell said, clearly exasperated. "If we force those two to sign a separate peace, they'll keep fighting and we'll be caught in the middle. This was the entire point of our alliance with the Dotran. At least Lahkaba seems to understand that."

Lahkaba cringed at that. He did agree with Lionell's assessment, logically. Which was why he hadn't told anyone of his involvement with the defeat of the Dotran fleet by Admiral Sartori. Aside from it being treasonous, if anyone found out, it would be bad for the Union.

"We have to put this incident aside," Faide said, joining the conversation. "None of us have to like it. I was personally affected by the tragedy on Kol with the loss of a good friend. But it was a misunderstanding."

Lahkaba didn't agree with Faide's assessment of what had happened on Kol. The Dotran had sent a raiding party down to the shipyard, not a diplomatic envoy as they claimed. Dotrans didn't ask for things.

Not wanting to be part of this conversation anymore, lest it turn to the Dotrans' defeat over Ailleroc, Lahkaba turned away from Faide and Valinther. Beside him, he saw Zeric standing with a glass in his hand. Uncharacteristically, the glass was full.

"Looking forward to finally being able to take that uniform off?" Lahkaba asked.

At first, Zeric said nothing. Not until Lahkaba said the Terran man's name did Zeric look up from the stare he was giving the floor. He blinked a few times before saying, "What?"

"I asked if you were looking forward to being able to get out of uniform. Now that the war's over, you can resign if you wish," Lahkaba said, wondering how many drinks Zeric had had so far. Though, the man could hold his liquor, so that might not be it at all.

"I, uh, probably won't," Zeric said, still unfocused. "I have a kid to take care of now. I could use a steady paycheck. By the way, how much does a general make?"

Lahkaba shrugged. "No idea. That wasn't something we discussed all that much. We still need to get a permanent government set up. That will be our greatest challenge yet."

Zeric looked at him, confusion evident on his face. "I thought we had a government. What have you been doing for the last year?"

A smile came to Lahkaba's lips. "Congress was just a temporary meeting of representatives from each planet. We need to form something with greater accountability to the people of each world. What that will look like . . . that will be an interesting fight."

"This is one of those metaphorical political fights, right? You don't need me to go kill Lei-mey, do you? Because I can . . ." Zeric said, though his tone didn't make it clear how much he was joking.

"Yes, one of those," Lahkaba said, feeling relieved that he had stepped away from the other conversation. "Are you looking forward to seeing your daughter again?" He had asked the question hesitantly but was surprised by the look that crossed his friend's face.

"Yes, actually. I didn't think I would be. I don't know how I'll be as a father, or if I actually want to be one. But it doesn't look like I have a lot of choice in the matter. At least she won't be shooting at me. For a few years, at least."

Before Zeric could say any more, their conversation was interrupted by Bryel walking up to them. The blue Dotran moved through the party with ease, since everyone unsubtly stepped away from him as he walked. Despite his hatred for Dotran, Lahkaba couldn't help but feel sorry for the man. The incident at Kol hadn't been his fault—he had just been the one forced to try to defend his people's brutality.

"Delegate Lahkaba, might I have a moment of your time?" Bryel asked deferentially.

Surprised by the request, Lahkaba merely nodded and allowed himself to be led away from Zeric. The Terran went back to staring at his drink, still not taking a sip.

They walked to a corner of the room. Unsure what the Dotran wanted, Lahkaba waited, saying nothing. After an uncomfortably long moment, Bryel said, "I wanted to apologize again for the misunderstanding that occurred between our two peoples. I regret the loss of life."

"Thank you. But we've decided to put the matter behind us," Lahkaba forced himself to say diplomatically.

"I would find it hard to do the same thing in your place," Bryel said. "But since this will probably be the last time we meet, I wanted to make sure you knew that not all of us Dotran agreed with the decision to strike against you."

Nodding, Lahkaba said, "I believe that. But why will this be the last time we meet? I assumed you would remain as our ambassador with your people for now."

Bryel shook his head. "A formal ambassador will be dispatched, I'm sure. But for now, I'm being recalled. There will be an investigation into how the Alliance managed to learn of our attack on Ailleroc."

Lahkaba felt his heartbeat increase and his fur stand on end. He tried to force himself to calm down as he asked, "You don't think Admiral Sartori was just prepared for it?"

"No, the timing was too perfect. They knew we were coming and when. The blame will probably fall on me," Bryel said.

"Why?" Lahkaba asked.

"Because I was not supposed to reveal the timing of our assault to your military. Even if the leak didn't come from my action, I'll be held accountable," Bryel said.

"You weren't supposed to tell us that? Then why did you?" Lahkaba asked, confused.

"I thought you would find it useful," Bryel said, putting a slight emphasis on the word "you."

A sudden realization came over Lahkaba. Bryel knew what he had done. Hesitantly, he asked, "How do you think the leak occurred?"

"An Alliance spy, no doubt," Bryel said. "It was only a short time after the Alliance learned the location of Irod and attacked the planet. It's conceivable they left intelligence assets behind. Or another spy in your midst. Kaars Aerinstar probably wasn't the only one. I don't think my people will blame you."

There was the slight emphasis again, Lahkaba thought. Or was his guilt playing tricks on his hearing? "Commander, I—"

Bryel cut him off. "This defeat was a major blow to the ruling class. And it came without Kowwok loss of life or rebel insurgence. It will take them a while for them to recover, and it will make their position of power less secure. It will be interesting to see if our people follow your example—Kowwoks and Dotran working together, regardless of class or species."

"That would be a nice future to live in," Lahkaba said, realizing what Bryel was trying to tell him. "I intend to do whatever I, and the Union, can to help make that a reality."

An eerie smile crossed Bryel's toothy face. "Then perhaps we'll get to work together again in the future, after all."

When Solyss received the summons from the Fox, it intrigued him. He hadn't spoken to the old Liw'kel since negotiating the use of the *Black Market*. Why he would suddenly ask to see him, in the middle of the peace ceremony, he had no idea. But he wanted to find out.

The Fox, whose real name he still didn't know, had been invited to attend the festivities, since they were being held on his ship, after all. But he had declined, undoubtedly in part to keep his identity secret. Solyss found him in the man's private command center.

"Commander Novastar, I'm glad you could join me," the old man said with a toothy smile.

Solyss straightened a little at his new title. Promoting him had been one of the last things Saracasi had done before stepping down as the fleet's commander and handing control back to Maarkean. Even though securing the *Black Market* hadn't proven to be the decisive blow against the Alliance he had hoped, its presence had helped bring about the end of the war. It would go down as another victory for the Novastars.

"It's no problem, sir," Solyss said, not really sure how to address the Fox.

"No, I imagine Delegate Darshawn had lost your interest after the tenth minute of her speech," the Fox said.

"Not at all," Solyss lied. "She's very captivating."

"Usually. But she seems to be floundering tonight. Winning will do that to someone such as her. She doesn't know who to oppose at the moment."

Solyss just nodded. He really hadn't been that bored with Lei-mey's speech. Though, when he saw the hologram beside the Fox, which showed Lei-mey still speaking, he did feel glad he had left. "What can I do for you?" he asked, his curiosity getting the best of him.

The Fox turned a steely gaze on him. "It's me who can do something for you."

His interest piqued, Solyss said nothing, waiting for the Fox to continue.

"You did good work on Okaral, freeing the people from the Alliance. And then almost gaining control of my ship. You're a very resourceful man. I like working with resourceful people. I would like to offer you a job."

Solyss smiled but shook his head immediately. "I'm flattered, sir. But I already have a job. The Union is going to need experienced people to build up the fleet. The war may be over, but now we have to protect ourselves."

The Fox slowly stood up from his chair. Taking slow, wobbly steps, he moved over to a computer terminal. Solyss watched the man as he walked, feeling the strain must be difficult. Maybe he didn't leave this room for more reasons than just privacy. Or maybe he was being played again. Nothing could be assumed with a man as secretive as this.

When he reached the terminal, the Fox brought up a sensor scan result. Various graphs and numbers appeared. Some of the information Solyss understood—gas concentrations, velocity indications, radiation levels—but most of it he didn't.

"Do you recognize this?" the Fox asked.

Solyss shook his head. "No. Looks like the results of some sensor scan. But most of it means nothing to me."

The Fox smiled. "But, Commander, this scan was taken by your ship. This was the scan of deep space where you lost track of the Alliance frigate in Trepon."

Shifting his gaze from the computer to the old man, Solyss wasn't sure why he felt surprised that the Fox had managed to get sensor logs from the *Gallant.* Information was the man's main commodity, and he had been with the Union fleet for months now. Anyway, pressing that issue would be pointless.

"OK, so what am I looking at?" Solyss asked.

"I don't know either," the Fox admitted, surprising Solyss. "Access to academics, even for me, has been a little limited in recent months. But, whatever it is, the Alliance has devoted a large force to guarding it."

Solyss cast a sharp look at the Liw'kel, who changed the data. He focused in on a smaller segment of the result and enhanced it. When it came into focus, Solyss started to recognize power signature and metallic readings. The readings were intermittent and weak, which is why

Dar'su had failed to notice them. But they definitely indicated a large number of warships inside the anomaly area.

"The Alliance had an entire fleet sitting there. We would have been easy prey. With that interference, they could have taken *Gallant* and we never would have stood a chance," Solyss said as shock washed over him.

"Assuming they saw you. Which, with that many ships being there for who knows how long, we have to assume they did," the Fox said. "The question remains, why didn't they?"

Solyss pondered that for a few moments. He hadn't seen the ships on his scans, so it was possible they hadn't spotted him. But if they had, what reason would they have had for ignoring him? To avoid detection? Because whatever they were doing required remaining there?

Before he could answer, the Fox continued, "We'll never know until we investigate. That's what I want to hire you to do. Find out what they're guarding. Or defending against."

The way the Fox said the last phrase made Solyss sure he knew more than he was saying. "I do want to know. But I won't do it for you. The Union needs me. We'll follow up on this."

The Fox smiled. "Very well. But when you give up on convincing the Union to care about anything outside of the Kreogh sector, consider my offer. It remains open." He deactivated the display and started to walk back to his chair.

The door to the room slid open, suggesting to Solyss that it was time to leave. With one final look at the blank display, he headed toward the door. He would find out what was going on in Trepon, he decided—one way or another.

When the door on the transport opened, a wave of sound washed over Zeric. A crowd of people stood on the landing pad, cheering. At first, he thought they were cheering for him, which confused him, but then he realized that they were cheering for all the Union soldiers on the transport behind him who had made their homes on Irod and were returning home.

The crowd continued the cheers as Zeric and the other soldiers walked down the boarding ramp. He couldn't help but smile at the enthusiasm and gratitude emanating from the crowd. Once they were clear of the ship's blast zone, people swarmed over him and the others, shaking hands and offering hugs and sometimes more.

Slipping through the crowd as quickly as he was able, Zeric avoided getting swamped. A few very attractive women had tried to get his attention, but he managed to divert their attentions to the soldiers behind him. He already had three women on his mind.

Once he reached the edge of the crowd, moving became easier. Walking past the cars lined up outside the spaceport's gates, he opted to walk. He would have to get to know this city if he were going to live here.

The stroll through town took him past a few burned buildings, but for the most part, very few signs of the Alliance assault remained. The locals had done a remarkable job of cleaning and repairing things. It felt good to see a thriving stream of happy people for a change.

Approaching the house, Zeric hiked the pack up on his shoulders. He reached up to knock, but the door opened before he could. Ceta stood there, holding a small child. It took him a moment to realize that this small child was his daughter.

It had been over seven months since he had last seen her. That made her over a year old now and not a little baby anymore. It dawned on him that she could probably walk now and likely speak at least some words. And he had missed all of those earlier stages. He stood there dumbfounded for a moment.

Ceta took pity on him and smiled. She looked at the little girl. "Ciara, this is your father."

As Maarkean stretched for the first time in a long time, he didn't feel any relief of his tension. He hadn't been tortured, he hadn't ordered anyone into battle, no one he loved was in immediate danger, and the war was over—but he didn't feel better.

Giving up on the stretches, he attempted to move into a meditation.

Most people would say that the Union had won the war. The members of Congress were certainly acting as if they had. They treated him like a hero. By all rights, he should be ecstatic. Regardless of anything else, they had succeeded in freeing the Kreogh sector from Alliance control.

But at what cost? Tens of thousands were dead. The Alliance had granted them independence but had hardly been beaten. Many of their leaders called for the war to be resumed and the Kreogh sector retaken. Only the Union's alliance with the Dotran Confederacy held them off—an alliance that was tenuous at best.

What really ate at his mind were the more personal costs. He felt bad thinking it. After all, thousands of people had given their lives, while he survived. His sister and most of his friends had survived, too. But not all of them.

Gu'od had paid the ultimate price. His friend and mentor had died protecting others, including his best friend's daughter. It had been a hero's death. But it was still death.

Gamaly wouldn't be the same, he knew. She acted fine, putting on a brave face. But he had lost a spouse himself, and he knew what it did to you. And he hadn't been with Erysis for but a brief time. Gamaly and Gu'od had been together for over a decade. In truth, the bond between them had been something he could only dream of having with someone.

Even those who had survived wouldn't make it through the war un-scathed. Saracasi was alive. She had made it through the war. But, in a way, he thought maybe she hadn't. The woman she had been was gone, replaced by someone else.

He couldn't exactly claim to be the same person, either. Decorated Alliance officer, loyal citizen—those things were gone. He was a hero to the Union, to be sure, but it had come at the cost of what he had once held dear. He knew that what he had done had been the right thing, but it had still come hard.

And as petty as it was, he felt the loss of *Cutty Sark,* too. She had been his home for years. Flying her had been what had kept him sane after his parents' and wife's death. She had allowed him to keep Saracasi out of Alliance custody on Braz and to break her out of Olan on Sulas.

She had fought in every major engagement of the war, except the final one. That one she had sat out in a small docking port. When the docking port had been hit during the battle, it had collapsed.

Giving up on meditation, Maarkean picked himself up. As he opened the door to his small room, he found Saracasi standing there, her hand raised as if to knock. She looked startled, and he smiled.

She had changed, and he wasn't sure if it was for the better, but she was still his little sister. Small moments like this reminded him of that. Ignoring her protest, he reached out and took her into a hug.

"Keep doing that, and I'll begin to wonder if you've been replaced by a Kowwok," Saracasi said when he released her.

"Lahkaba and Chavatwor have converted me to their ways. Resis-tance is futile," Maarkean joked.

"Then you'll have no problem coming with me. You've been summoned by our Kowwok overlords," Saracasi said.

Maarkean nodded and followed Saracasi out of the building into the Kol sun. The shipyard buzzed with the same level of activity it had always had. The workers were still going overtime, trying to repair the damage from the last battle to all the fleet's ships.

They reached the main building and found Chavatwor standing before the sealed hangar, fidgeting. He smiled at Maarkean and Saracasi, pulling both of them in turn into one of his powerful hugs. "She's all ready, General. Good as new," Chavatwor said with a wide smile.

Maarkean cast the Kowwok shipwright a curious glance and then turned to Saracasi. She had an impish grin on her face that he recognized. She thought she was being clever.

Saracasi nodded to Chavatwor and then said to Maarkean, "Since you turned down any offers of a position within the new government, I thought maybe you might be looking for a new home."

As if on cue, the main doors to the hangar began to open. They revealed the interior of the hangar. Sitting inside, as shiny and bright as she had been the day she had rolled off the assembly floor, was *Cutty Sark*.

Maarkean felt his mouth open in shock. He turned to Saracasi. "I thought she was destroyed in the battle."

"That's because you underestimate my engineering skills," Saracasi said. "Or rather, Chavatwor's."

The Kowwok shipwright grinned, looking embarrassed, and Saracasi added, "All the marine equipment and bunks have been removed, as well as most of the heavy guns. She's just a regular old transport again."

"As it would happen," Chavatwor interjected, "I'm in the market for a freelance transport ship to carry some specialty parts for the shipyard. Since you'll be needing a job, you're welcome to apply."

Maarkean felt a wide smile come to his face. Even after everything that had happened, maybe some things could go back to normal.

Acknowledgements

Many thanks are owed for helping bringing this series to fruition.

First, Grey Gecko Press for making it a reality.

My editor, Hilary, for making it the best story it could be.

All my beta readers who helped weed out the good
bits from the bad: my Dad, Everett and Erik.

And to all my readers whose kind words expressing
their enjoyment have made it all worth it.

ABOUT THE AUTHOR

As a child, Wayne Basta was introduced to science fiction at a young age by his father. Mainstream hits like Star Trek and Star Wars were followed by old Tom Swift novels and then classics like Asimov and Clarke. Growing up on Florida's space coast only served to fuel his imagination and love of space, science and adventure.

Wayne currently lives in Houston with his wife, son and dog. He remains a fan of geek culture, board games, video games, fantasy, science fiction and all around silliness.

CONNECT WITH WAYNE

Email:	wayne@waynebasta.com
Web:	www.waynebasta.com
Twitter:	@WayneBasta
Facebook:	http://www.facebook.com/WayneBastaAuthor

Grey Gecko Press

Thank you for purchasing this book from Grey Gecko Press, an independent publishing company that focuses on new and emerging authors, bringing readers the best in fiction and non-fiction at reasonable prices in all formats.

With books in nearly every genre of fiction and non-fiction, there's something for everyone, and you can be sure that buying books from us leads directly to the support of independent authors like Wayne Basta. Grey Gecko pays our authors some of the highest royalty rates in the business and strives to produce only high-quality books.

Visit our website to purchase our titles, pre-order upcoming books at a discount, sign up for our free monthly newsletter, and find out about two great ways to get free books, the Slushpile Reader Program and the Advance Reader Program.

And don't forget: all our print editions come with the ebook free!

Authors First!

www.greygeckopress.com

store.greygeckopress.com